**DON'T MISS THESE EXCITING
TIME PASSAGES ROMANCES
NOW AVAILABLE FROM JOVE!**

My Lady in Time by Angie Ray
Nick of Time by Casey Claybourne
Crystal Memories by Ginny Aiken
Waiting for Yesterday by Jenny Lykins
Remember Love by Susan Plunkett
A Dance Through Time by Lynn Kurland
This Time Together by Susan Leslie Liepitz
Lost Yesterday by Jenny Lykins
Silver Tomorrows by Susan Plunkett
Echoes of Tomorrow by Jenny Lykins

MYSTIC MEMORIES

Susan Leslie Liepitz

JOVE BOOKS, NEW YORK

TIME PASSAGES is a trademark of Berkley Publishing Corporation.

MYSTIC MEMORIES

A Jove Book / published by arrangement with
the author

PRINTING HISTORY
Jove edition / April 1998

The Penguin Putnam Inc. World Wide Web site address is
http://www.penguinputnam.com

ISBN: 0-515-12262-9

A JOVE BOOK®
Jove Books are published by The Berkley Publishing Group,
a member of Penguin Putnam Inc.,
200 Madison Avenue, New York, New York 10016.
JOVE and the "J" design are trademarks
belonging to Jove Publications, Inc.

PRINTED IN THE UNITED STATES OF AMERICA

10 9 8 7 6 5 4 3 2 1

To my daughter

Adrienne Phillips

and

my son

Wes Phillips

... for tolerating all the crazy field trips, eclectic family vacations (Remember the Excelsior Hotel in NYC?), and dubious dinners ("Will she or won't she cook tonight?"). I can only hope that this eccentric mother of yours has inspired you to seek your own creative paths through life. As corny as it still may sound, I have to say it ...

Follow Your Hearts

and

Dare to Dream.

I love you,
Mom

Special thank-you to:

Amy J. Fetzer, Colleen Fliedner, and Linda MacLaughlin—for the brainstorming sessions

Mindy Neff, Charlotte Maclay, and Marlene Suson—for the critiques

Captain Ian McIntyre and crew of the *Hawaiian Chieftain*—for your dedication to nautical history, which made a significant contribution to the realism of this story

Gail Fortune—my editor—for unbridled enthusiasm, as well as invaluable expertise. I don't know what I'd do without you.

We must come down from our heights, and leave our straight paths for the byways and low places of life, if we would learn truths by strong contrasts; and in hovels, in forecastles, and among our own outcasts in foreign lands, see what has been wrought among our fellow-creatures by accident, hardship, or vice.

—RICHARD HENRY DANA
Two Years Before the Mast

Prologue

"TAKE WHATEVER CAN be hauled by cargo wagon to my shipyard. I want it there at midnight Monday. No earlier—you understand?"

"Aye, sir."

"Do you swear on God's good name that no one else knows of this?" His lantern cast a flickering shadow across the deserted beach, illuminating the bow of the shipwrecked brig.

"Not a one, sir. She blowed up here last night during the storm. Full sails and all, sir. Thar weren't a soul aboard. Gone, all of them. The ship is cursed, she is. I heard old salts spinnin' yarns about her for years—mysterious deaths and vanishings of shipmates. But never the whole crew before, sir."

"Enough! Do you think I haven't heard the rumors as well? Why in the devil's name do you think I want your work kept secret? I intend to use her piece by piece to repair other damaged vessels. Now that the blockade has been lifted, the demand for materials to build new ships has exceeded beyond my grasp. I cannot compete with the half-dozen other builders on the Mystic who have the means to meet the costs. Salvaging her is the answer to my prayers."

"Prayers, sir?"

"Indeed—I have needed a turn-of-the-luck for some time now. It appears to have happened."

"What if the curse she carried goes with these boards and timbers to the other ships? What then?"

"Nonsense. It is all nothing but superstition, my boy. I don't believe a bit of it. Mark my words—as long as no one knows that she's been used for repair, those fanciful rumors will stop. Not one of the ships to leave my dock will be haunted by the history of this ill-fated brig."

"No one will learn the truth from me, sir."

"Keep it that way and you will not need to be looking over your shoulder the rest of your life."

"Aye, sir."

"Monday, then. Midnight."

"Aye, sir. Have a safe ride back to Mystic, sir."

"I intend to." Extinguishing the lantern light, he turned to leave, then paused. "On the off chance anyone should happen by while you are working on her, it might be wise to destroy any evidence of her name."

"Consider it done, sir."

Chapter 1

"I NEED YOUR help. My ten-year-old son is missing."

Cara Edwards studied the father of the young boy, her heart going out to Victor Charles in his desperate situation. He looked like a man on the brink of collapse, his emotions held only by a fine thread of control.

She already knew of the bizarre disappearance, as did anyone with a radio or television living anywhere on the continent during the past three months.

Fourth grader Andrew Charles of Huntington Beach had been with his class during an educational overnight experience aboard a nineteenth-century sailing ship, the *Mystic*. The following morning he was reported missing. No one, not even his fellow classmates, saw or heard anything unusual during the night. Nor had his body been washed ashore.

"I agreed to meet with you, Mr. Charles, but only to explain that I—" Her stomach tightened into a painful knot that she tried to ignore. It was extremely difficult to keep her objectivity in cases that were so gut-wrenching, such as this lost child. "I don't think I'm the person to solve this case. My brother never should have given you my phone number."

"You are a private investigator, right?"

"Yes, but—"

"And you are also psychic, right?"

She held up her palm to stop his interrogation. "I'm afraid you may have the wrong impression about me, sir. My brother has a tendency to misrepresent my . . . talents in that area. I don't deny I have a seemingly unique ability to be led in the right direction by a sixth sense. But I prefer not to advertise myself as a—"

"Psychic detective?"

She winced. "Is that how Frank put it?"

The man nodded with a bittersweet smile. She couldn't blame him for grasping at the last bit of hope Frank had thrown at him. If only Mr. Charles knew it was nothing more than a cruel joke by her older brother—a maneuver to get even with Cara. Frank had tried to humiliate her at their parents' anniversary party over the weekend, taunting her to offer her unique services to find the missing boy. She had sidestepped his barbs and he'd ended up looking like the fool. Now he'd paid her back by putting her in this awkward situation with Mr. Charles.

"Please don't turn me down." His blue eyes beseeched her. He reached inside his silk suit coat and withdrew a checkbook and pen. "Name your price."

She gently touched the sleeve of his jacket. "It isn't about the money. I simply don't believe I can do any more than the rest of your people have been doing for the last several weeks. I've seen the news reports. I know you've had at least one well-known psychic on this hunt."

"She didn't come up with any useful information."

"Nothing at all?"

He shook his head.

"Then what makes you think I can do any better?"

"Your brother said—"

"Frank had no business making claims that he himself doesn't believe. You see, Mr. Charles, my brother—in fact, my entire family—has never been able to conceptualize this phenomenon. Even I don't quite understand how or why I was born with an acute intuitive sense of knowing things, seeing things through my mind's eye. Once in a while it works in my favor to help a client. But I don't guarantee success.''

"All I ask is for you to give it a chance.''

Cara shook her head, turning away from the man to escape the desperation and anguish in his eyes. From press coverage, she knew he was in his mid-forties, but he looked ten years younger and closer to her own age of thirty-four. He had the boyish-blond good looks of a surfer who had made it big in the boardroom. He was also married to an equally attractive woman who looked more like his sister than his spouse. The small, tight-knit family lived in Huntington Harbour with a moderate-size yacht tied to their private dock. Cara had caught a glimpse of the elegant waterfront home on the evening news. She had also seen the security force protecting the property from the reporters and cameramen camped outside on the doorstep—as well as anchored in the canal.

She glanced nervously toward the closed gate, expecting any one of those media maniacs to leap over the fence of the historic Rancho Los Cerritos, where she'd arranged this private meeting during the early-morning hours. Mr. Charles had managed to elude the news-hungry field reporters, but for how long?

As the two of them stood between their cars in the enclosed compound, Cara heard a sorrowful mourning dove. It seemed to echo the sentiments of the distraught father with a sad poignancy that tugged at her conscience.

Walking a few steps away, she ran her fingers through her close-cropped curls and released a sigh of frustration, her back to the man. "The last thing I want is to have my face flashed into every household in America, identifying me as a psychic investigator. I can forget about working undercover if I become known as 'that California Quack on TV.' '' She hooked quotes in the air. "Without anonymity, I may as well kiss my business good-bye.''

Mr. Charles came over and paused at her side, following her gaze toward the single gray bird perched high in the winter-bare branches of a sycamore. She noticed he'd put

away the checkbook and pen. His hands were stuffed into
the pocket of his slacks. Earlier his face had been in
shadow, but now, caught in the morning sunlight, it showed
the ravages of this three-month nightmare.

"Do you have children, Ms. Edwards?"

"No."

"A husband?"

"I'm surprised you didn't do a thorough background
check on me, if you don't mind my saying so."

"I don't. And I did."

"Then you already know the answers to these questions.
Make your point."

"Your husband died six years ago on a hike in the moun-
tains. You weren't with him. It was reported as an accident.
But somehow you managed to dig up the truth and bring
his murderer to trial . . ."

Cara tensed, feeling her fingernails dig into the palms of
her clenched hands as her mind flashed images of those
horrendous days following Mark's death. After seeing his
killer brought to justice, she had been commended by one
of the detectives, who had called her a "natural" at investigative work. Abandoning her well-planned future that had
included Mark, she'd considered the police academy but
chose to go it alone as a private investigator. Hiking and
kayaking with Mark had given her not only physical endurance but also a sense of self-reliance, self-determination.
She had also learned that an ordinary woman didn't attract
attention. People didn't suspect a woman to be a down and
dirty detective. They believed what they saw, whether she
portrayed a homeless bag lady or an overzealous real estate
agent. She was good at her line of work. Damn good. And
proud of it. She liked to think Mark would've been proud
of her too.

". . . And with the exception of your brother," Mr.
Charles solemnly concluded, "your family is somewhat
embarrassed by your unusual abilities."

" 'Somewhat embarrassed'? My mother is mortified; my
father, barely tolerant. And my kid sister wishes I would

just act normal. What does normal look like anyway? I've never met a normal human being."

"In your line of work, I don't suppose you would."

"Not just in my line of work. Scratch the surface of anyone you know and you'll find secrets and neuroses no matter how well they are hidden."

"Yours being . . . ?" He lifted one brow, pinning her with a knowing gaze, then answered his own question. "You're not comfortable in your own skin. Your special talent is a gift but also a curse. You went after your husband's murderer out of misplaced guilt because you didn't sense the danger before he was killed."

Cara felt her anger leap from the depths of a secret hell that had been sealed shut for nearly four years. "Is that your opinion or did you hire someone to dig it out of my shrink's private files?"

"In my business, I make a point of knowing who I'm dealing with. This is no different. My source tells me you keep a low profile but have an exceptional track record."

Flattery didn't take the sting out of his violation of her privacy. "You should have put your 'source' to better use—such as finding your son."

"Already done. He was the first man on it, Ms. Edwards. The news reports didn't exaggerate when they said Andrew vanished without a trace. Everyone on that ship on December twenty-second has passed every conceivable interrogation, including lie detector tests."

Cara watched as he walked to the trunk of his Mercedes sedan, opened it, and pulled out a baseball cap. He came back with it in his hands, worrying the bill.

"If you won't take the case, will you at least see if you can pick up something from his Anaheim Angels hat?"

"Did he wear it much?"

"Sometimes."

She'd have preferred a ring or watch, something solid that wasn't washed frequently and that the boy wore most of the time. But she was willing to give it a try. She reached for the cap and held it for several moments in silence.

"Do you recall the last time you saw him wearing this?"

she asked, unable to pick up anything but a feeling of contentedness. If nothing else, she sensed that Andrew Charles was a happy kid.

"I can't really remember. I've been rather distracted with my work the last several months . . ." His words trailed off with a tone of regret.

"I'm sorry, Mr. Charles. I wish I could help you." Her stomach clenched as she handed back the cap. She flinched.

"Are you ill?" The man leaned toward her as if she might need assistance.

"No, not really. Just a little reaction to something."

"I should have known you had a good reason to turn me down. I understand if you aren't feeling well."

"I only wish my brother would have consulted me before he called you. It could've saved us both a trip out here."

"I'm grateful for his desire to help."

She held out her hand. "Good-bye, Mr. Charles. I hope you find Andrew soon."

As the man accepted her handshake, Cara experienced a flash of images in her mind's eye. Unlike the posed head shot of Andrew released to the media, these were snippets of the young boy through his father's eyes. Looking down on him, she saw his youthful face turned up in adoration.

No—I don't need this! I don't want to see him! Don't show me his face! Cara yanked her hand away, holding it protectively against her as if she'd been burned by a hot flame.

"Ms. Edwards? What's wrong?"

"I—" She cleared her throat, struggling to make her voice sound calmer than she felt. Why did she have to see the boy through his father's eyes? It was so much easier to turn down the case when the victim was only a black and white photo in a press release. Now . . . those youthful blue eyes would forever haunt her. "I saw your son."

"Where?!"

She shook her head. "It's not what you think. I didn't see him lying in a ditch. I saw your memories of him."

The man's shoulders sagged. "I guess I should be relieved you didn't see him dead."

"I'm sorry—" She cut off her words, realizing how much she seemed to repeat her apology. The knot in her stomach was tighter than ever. "You know, Mr. Charles, it's usually just plain old everyday investigative procedures that solve the case, not a paranormal camera lens in my head."

"I understand." He reached into his jacket again and brought out a small business card. "If you change your mind when you're feeling better, please call me. Anytime. Day or night."

Cara took the card, holding it in both hands as he drove away. She turned and walked into the restored adobe building where her Aunt Gaby worked in the visitors information office. Her great-aunt had unlocked the gates to allow Cara and Mr. Charles the clandestine visit. Eighty-three-year-old Gabriella Salazar was a docent of the rancho during a retirement filled with activity. The small, white-haired woman was a sharp-minded historian with the strength and agility of most fifty-year-olds.

Aunt Gaby looked up from a pile of research books, pushing her glasses up from the end of her nose. "You look like you could use a sip of this. Here . . ."

Cara blindly accepted her aunt's personal cup of Yerba Santa. The holy herb was blended with mint and chamomile flowers to create a distinctively sweet flavor that soothed the senses before it even reached her upset stomach. Holding the stoneware mug in one hand and the silver-gray business card in the other, she propped one hip over the corner of the massive desk.

"I turned him down," she said, then grimaced at the sharp twinge in her abdomen. She sucked in a short breath and held it, waiting for the spasm to subside. Her own body badgered her as if, on a deep-down level, it knew the right answer and would not let up on her until she made the proper decision. But she had *made* the proper decision. Hadn't she?

"Perhaps you should have accepted."

"I don't need the notoriety."

"You will handle it with the utmost grace."

"You make it sound like I'm going to change my mind and take the case. I'm not."

"You will if you want to get rid of that bellyache."

"It's just a little indigestion."

Her aunt softly clicked her tongue in admonition. "This is your Aunt Gaby you're talking to, Cara—not your mother or father. When will you learn that I understand how these things work? Listen to your body. It's trying to tell you that something isn't right."

"Yeah, well, the only thing not quite right was last night's green peppers in my stir-fry."

Cara hated to admit that her aunt might be right . . . again. Gabriella Salazar had guided Cara through her childhood experiences when her parents had refused to believe the peculiar psychic revelations. Aunt Gaby had encouraged Cara to open up to her inexplicable insight, telling her stories of their ancestors who had similar abilities. Those same ancestors were part of a secret history no one else would acknowledge among the living descendants in her family— no one, that is, except Gabriella, Cara, and Cara's kid sister. Her own father was raised to believe in his singularly Latin heritage, which had been traced to the Spanish settlers of early California. Although her mother was half Italian, she also claimed that the other half of her bloodline was Hispanic. This was partially true. Only Aunt Gaby would talk of the Indians who became known by their mission names—Gabrielino and Luiseño. Only Aunt Gaby believed that the powers of the native people had been passed on through the generations who had denounced their blood ties to avoid persecution.

Her aunt flattened her palms on a scattered array of papers, levered herself to her feet, and leaned forward. "Cara, you must pay attention to what your soul already knows. You won't have a minute's peace until you do what you know is right."

Of all the women in her family, Cara resembled their matriarch, Gabriella, the most—in strong opinions as well as physical appearance. Both had light copper skin, a round face, and wide-set dark eyes. Both possessed the thick hair that held its own soft curls, though her aunt's had long since lost the deep brown-black color. In her youth, the woman had been as much in love with the physical challenges of outdoor life as Cara was. They were kindred spirits, the two of them. So it was no surprise that Aunt Gaby could dig right to the heart of the present situation.

"I realize how cold I must sound," said Cara. "I do care about the boy's safe return. I just don't think I can help."

"What if you can?"

"His father's had the best-of-the-best working for him for three months." Cara set the mug on the coaster beside her aunt's splayed fingers. With a shake of her head, she thought of the culprit who'd given her name to Mr. Charles. "What I would do to get my hands on Frank right now. My brother is a thirty-eight-year-old adolescent. It's his fault I'm in this mess."

"*In* it, are you?" Aunt Gaby's white brows arrowed upward, her eyes bright with amusement. "Why, only a moment ago you had washed your hands of it all."

"I'm not actually *in* this mess," she backpedaled, wishing her quick-witted aunt wasn't quite so fast at picking up a mere slip of the tongue. "It was just a figure of speech. I *was* in a mess. I've told Mr. Charles I'm out now."

Her abdomen knotted again. Cara tried to hide her discomfort.

"How is the pain?"

With a sigh of resignation, she grumbled, "Worse."

"See?"

"See what? I just need an antacid." Glancing around for her purse, she realized she'd left it in her car.

"Deny it all you want. Sooner or later you'll come around. That little boy is lost somewhere. And you won't be able to live with yourself if you don't do what you can to find him. Even if you come up empty-handed, you'll be no worse off than all the others who have tried and failed. But I guarantee you won't be hunting antacids anymore."

Absentmindedly, Cara fiddled with the business card in her hand, turning it over and over with the dexterity in her fingers she'd learned playing poker in college. She contemplated her aunt's advice. Maybe it wouldn't be so difficult to take a look around the ship. Maybe she could deal with the media attention. Maybe she wasn't giving enough credit to her own investigative abilities.

Aunt Gaby moved around the corner of the desk and slipped her arm around Cara's shoulders. "Stop being afraid of your psychic powers."

"I'm not afraid."

"Yes, you are." Gabriella spoke gently yet firmly. "You are also ashamed of them."

Cara tensed under the truth of her aunt's statements. Her own heated response surprised her. "Yes, I *am* embarrassed to admit I am different than most people. I'm afraid to be singled out by the reporters and labeled a weirdo, a freak. I don't know if I can ever truly let go of this fear."

"Then don't. Instead, you must allow yourself to feel the fear, experience it, embrace it . . . then do what you must do anyway. Let yourself be who you are."

The quiet words seemed to echo in the room, bouncing off the adobe walls as if blasted from a bugle. Cara couldn't deny the plainspoken reality. Acknowledging the challenge in her aunt's words, she looked down at the business card in her hand.

"Would you mind if I made a call?"

Grinning, Aunt Gaby gestured toward the desk phone with a wide sweep of her arm. "Be my guest."

With permission from the corporation that owned the *Mystic*, Mr. Charles arranged to take Cara aboard later that same morning. The hour-long drive south on the freeway took her onto Interstate 5 and past the exits for Laguna Beach and San Juan Capistrano before she finally turned off for the quieter Pacific Coast Highway. Within minutes she found Dana Point Harbor Drive and followed it north a short distance until it ended in a small parking lot at the base of steep bluffs near the Orange County Marine Institute. She cut the engine and hopped out of her eight-year-old Camry, activating the alarm with a remote on her key chain. The car chirped as she made her way through the full parking lot that served the congested marina.

Approaching the institute, Cara looked at the ship anchored several yards out in the water. The *Mystic* was smaller than she'd expected—about ninety to a hundred feet in length. As a meticulously restored nineteenth-century square-rigger, it looked as if it had been plucked from the pages of a history book. The dark wooden hulk was a sharp contrast to the sleek lines and bright colors of the contemporary pleasure boats moored in the east basin of the marina beyond the brig. It was hard to imagine that such a small ship plied the waters off California, let alone sailed the great distance around the tip of South America to New England. Though her school lessons were a bit foggy, she did remember the assigned reading of *Two Years Before the Mast*, recounting the experience of the author from whom the coastal community had taken its name.

"Ms. Edwards?"

She turned to see Victor Charles emerge from the front door of the building with a casually dressed gentleman at his side. He approached and introduced the other man. "This is Samuel Schermerhorn, director of the institute. He'll be taking us onto the ship."

The director offered a welcoming handshake. "I'm only too happy to cooperate with the corporate owner and the Charleses, Ms. Edwards."

She shook his hand. "Please call me Cara."

"We would like to see this unfortunate incident resolved for everyone's peace of mind. I understand you're psychic."

Cara gave Mr. Charles a furtive glance of annoyance. "I assumed we had an agreement about divulging that information."

"To the press," Victor corrected pointedly. "Samuel isn't any more eager than you to have the newspapers exploit this ship as haunted. Such PR may have boosted the popularity of the *Queen Mary*, but it certainly wouldn't be an asset in this case."

Schermerhorn led them toward the dock. "Our primary focus is overnight visits for elementary students, usually in the nine- and ten-year-old age group. The idea of ghosts may be appealing at an amusement park or a historical building. But here we need the kids' attention on the reenactment of history and interaction with each other in problem-solving situations. Their imaginations are vivid enough without frightening horror stories to distract them. The word from parents has confirmed the opinion. Only recently have we been able to reopen the program, after the authorities ruled that our safety procedures were not at fault.''

The three of them climbed down into a small powerboat, motored the short distance to the *Mystic*, and climbed the ladder to board her. Cara managed far easier in her jeans and running shoes than Victor did in his business clothes.

The deck was neat and orderly, with coils of thick ropes at the base of tall masts. The gray sky above was scored with lines and angles of rigging and cross timbers, the names of which Cara had forgotten from her school studies. The scents of the salty breeze and the old wood sparked her imagination with the danger and excitement of a more primitive era. An element of darkness and fear crept into her thoughts. She paid close attention to the sensation, seeking its source, waiting for something more to come to her. The feeling became like a black veil, obscuring shadowy thoughts and images that seemed to lie just beyond her mental grasp.

A gull flew past with a raucous "Scree—," effectively interrupting her concentration.

Turning to the director, Cara said slowly, "How old is this boat?"

"The actual *brig*," he corrected, "has been refurbished a number of times—the latest of which was in Connecticut at Mystic Seaport, hence her name. There probably isn't a single board on her that is original. I have the history of her in my files. It's spotty, at best."

"I'd like a copy when we're finished here."

The visit proved unproductive, which was as much a disappointment to the two men as it was to Cara. She didn't need special perception to read the expression on their faces. It was her own attitude of frustration that surprised her. Hadn't she expected to fail when she'd first met with Mr. Charles? Hadn't she told him she couldn't do it? Then why did it bother her so much that she'd been right?

A revelation came to her with such crystal clarity it startled her. She knew the answer to why she was bothered about being right . . .

Because her gut told her she'd been wrong.

Chapter 2

CARA KNEW WITH a deep-down conviction that she was going to be the one to find Andrew. What's more, her stomach didn't hurt any longer. She could already imagine Aunt Gaby's reaction to that news. But just because she'd taken a 180-degree turn, she found the job no easier than her predecessors had. She went back to the ship two more times without Mr. Charles. On each visit, she sensed the same darkness and fear, particularly in one small cabin below deck. Digging further into the history of the ship didn't supply any information that hadn't already been documented in the papers from Schermerhorn's files.

The *Mystic* had been built smaller than most ships of the early 1800s—small and speedy for the smuggling trade. When she'd read of its illicit past, she'd felt a quiver of dread run down her spine. While there was no proof that innocent souls had died on board, she had sensed an ominous dark cloud hanging over the ship, as if it were shrouded in such secrets. Yet she was fairly certain Andrew was not one of the departed spirits. The brig had also gone through a number of owners, resulting in several different names. ''*Mystic*'' had appeared more than once during the last two centuries. In the 1830s it had been a merchant ship sailing between Boston and California, carrying dry goods to the West Coast and returning with cattle hides.

And yet nothing, absolutely nothing, shed any light on

the disappearance of Andrew Charles on December 22, 1997. There was one thing left that she hadn't tried—putting herself on the ship under the same circumstances as the young ten-year-old would have experienced.

"I want to go on the *Mystic*," Cara told Schermerhorn on Friday afternoon.

He checked his watch. "There's still a few hours before our school group arrives."

"I don't need another look around. I want to be on that ship tonight to stand watch at the same time Andrew did."

"I told you I was only too happy to cooperate, but I'm afraid this may be going a bit too far, don't you think?"

"I *think* it may be just the right atmosphere I need to help me finally pick up something."

"Ms. Edwards—Cara . . ." The patronizing tone didn't surprise her, even though he hadn't shown such open disapproval during previous meetings. She'd sensed that he had been masking his true opinion of her credibility. "Our own people are in full costume and trained to act their parts during the experience. Since you are quite obviously not one of the schoolteachers or parent chaperons, how would we explain your presence on board? You can't go unnoticed dressed in your jeans and sneakers. And we can't very well tell them you are a private investigator."

Cara folded her arms across her chest. "Train me."

"But that's—"

"—*Not* impossible. I'm a quick study with a sharp memory for details. I have the athletic ability to climb the ropes—literally." She dropped her hands to the edge of his desk and leaned forward. "I want on that ship. If I have to work my butt to the bone learning how to climb that rigging, I'll do it."

"I can't possibly authorize it."

"Then put me in touch with the person who can."

The director stared at her, then a slow smile of respect crept into the corners of his mouth. He reached for his office phone. "Let me see what I can do."

Several minutes later, Cara received the answer she'd

been counting on—one week of intensive one-on-one lessons, starting at seven on Monday morning. By next Friday, she would be ready to work the overnight "voyage."

On her way home that evening, she stopped at a local bookstore and bought a paperback of Richard Henry Dana's *Two Years Before the Mast*. She intended to study it over the weekend, memorizing every detail of a sailor's life in the early nineteenth century.

Bo's'n, halyard, yardarm, fo'c'sle, gaff, mizzenmast . . .

The maritime words and their meanings swam through Cara's head as she approached the enthusiastic young sixth graders on the dock the following Friday afternoon. Her muscles were still sore from the relentless week-long workout of hauling heavy ropes, climbing rigging, and rowing the longboat. Still, the daily training had been a piece of cake compared to some of the wilderness treks she'd taken with Mark.

Dressed in white duck trousers, red-checked shirt, and short blue jacket, she listened to the captain address his "men" and felt confident that she would be a convincing crew member. To begin the adventure, she manned an oar in one of the longboats to take the kids out to the brig.

Boarding the *Mystic* from the longboat, she blended in with the activities aboard ship, following orders from the curmudgeonly British captain as if he were actually in command on the high seas. The children formed a line hustling their gear down the companionway and into the forecastle in the bow, where the lowly sailors lived. When the first mate referred to it as a "fo'c'sle," the common sailor's term, one boy snickered, then whispered to another with a lewd wink. Cara had nearly forgotten how the prepubescent male mind could find a sexual connotation to just about any word in the English language. She stifled a grin and raised an eyebrow to let them know she had their number. One flashed a beguiling smile, while the other blushed and turned back to his work. Shifting the leather strap of her sports bag on her shoulder, she shook her head, picked up the rolled sleeping bag at her feet and moved on, wondering if Andrew was anything like the mischievous little charmer or his red-faced friend.

Cara had requested the small cabin adjacent to the captain's quarters. After stowing her things, she paused in the tiny cubicle, feeling the same uneasiness as before. She stood in the narrow space between the wall and the berth, which took up the length of the second mate's room. If there was anything to sense regarding Andrew's whereabouts, it wasn't coming through. Not yet anyway.

But the uneasiness persisted. Allowing herself to feel the aura of fear, she lightly rubbed her upper arms as if a chill breeze had crept across her skin, even though the musty air was close and warm compared with the cool ocean temperatures topside.

The fear she felt was not her own. There was no threat to her own safety. This she knew without question. She also knew she was on the threshold of a breakthrough. Something was different in this cabin. Something unsettling. Off balance. From somewhere in her mind came a solid conviction that she was definitely on the right track.

At twilight, a one-dish supper of beef stew was served to all except the captain and the adult chaperons, who had been invited to be his guests. Cara had declined, choosing instead to walk around the ship in hopes that her solitude would help her make a psychic connection with Andrew. And yet she had a moment of regret when the captain's dinner of roast chicken was ceremoniously paraded past the line of hungry sixth graders, reenacting the vast differences between the paltry crew and their superior officers. Cara watched the young faces turn sour at the sight of their own meal of cubed carrots, potatoes, and mystery meat in a pale-gray gravy. She felt the same way as she held out her tin plate.

After dinner, the children and their parent chaperons gathered in the between decks for a few of the captain's yarns, told by the light of a single lantern. As Cara headed for her cabin to catch a few hours of sleep before taking her turn on the night watch, she overheard two of the mothers whispering to each another.

"It gives me the creeps," said one, "to think of the poor kid who disappeared. I bet I don't close my eyes all night."

"Why did you volunteer to chaperon?"

"I couldn't let my daughter come alone."

"She's *not* alone. She's with her whole class."

"So was that Charles boy." The fretful mother caught sight of Cara. "Do *you* know what really happened to that child?"

As part of this living history experience on the nineteenth-century brig, every person on board—male and female—was regarded as an able-bodied seaman. Staying in character as a crew member, Cara addressed the woman accordingly: "What child might that be, sir?"

"Andrew Charles," offered the second one. "His disappearance was in all the papers."

Cara affected a swarthy tone. "There warn't no papers on me last ship, sir. I just made port b'fore signin' on the *Mystic*. Can't say I heard nary one word about a . . . boy, y'say?"

She stayed her course, playing it to the end. Those were the rules in her training class. The instructor had been adamant. No matter how much a visiting class might tease or pressure the actors to slip out of character, they were expected to maintain the illusion of the adventure at all times.

The first woman didn't seem to grasp the concept, however, and patiently explained in detail about the disappearance of Andrew. "I have my own theory that the gravitational alignment of the planets on the winter solstice might have something to do with all this."

The other mother spoke up with a skeptical laugh. "You may as well say that kid vanished on a spaceship. Or, better yet, blame it on those offshore earthquake tests! The subterranean explosions might have knocked him overboard."

Cara was more than a little amused and intrigued by the direction of the conversation.

"There might be some truth to those possibilities," said

the first mother. "What if the explosions disturbed the electromagnetic field—"

"Excuse me, sir," interrupted Cara with a waning smile. "I was about to turn in. I 'ave second watch, y'know."

"Oh—yes, of course," stammered the mothers, apologizing for keeping her too long.

Moments later, Cara pulled out a small penlight she'd hidden in a deep pocket. After hanging it from the same hook as her gear bag, she shucked the wool jacket and boots issued to her as part of her costume. Cara's watch would be the same as Andrew's had been, starting at midnight, or eight bells. Instead of the regular four-hour watches described in Dana's book, the *Mystic* observed "anchor watch" of two-hour shifts.

The short, narrow bunk seemed barely large enough for Cara's five-foot-six height, let alone a man of larger size. She wondered if sailors in the 1800s had been smaller in stature than today's standards or just more adaptable to tiny spaces. She shifted to her side, then yanked the top of the sleeping bag over her, leaving it unzipped.

Listening to the gentle creaks and moans of the floating antique, she contemplated the conversation between the two women. Centuries of superstition surrounded the change of seasons in many cultures. What if the winter solstice *had* played a role in the disappearance of Andrew? Stranger things had been known to happen.

Like private investigators who used psychic senses to solve cases.

Cara couldn't turn her back on any possibilities, no matter how far-fetched. Could the approaching spring equinox next week be a factor? If so, tonight might be a waste of time and she would need to return on the twenty-first.

Then again, there were fault tests to consider. She had read about them. Some people were afraid the underground explosions would trigger an actual seismic tremor, perhaps even a full-scale earthquake. So far, not so much as a geological hiccup had occurred, at least not anything that registered on the Richter scale. But what if the electromagnetic field *had* been disrupted? Cara wasn't a scientist, but she had long ago learned to open all mental doorways to let in any ideas, giving them equal importance. Nothing was ever discarded. Not until the case was closed.

The quiet knock came through the dark recesses of her sleep.

"Eight bells, sir," said a young male voice in a loud whisper, despite the order of total silence when rousing the next watch.

Instantly awake and alert, Cara quietly answered, "Aye, aye, mate." She knew from training that the new crew had ten minutes to relieve the sailor on the previous watch.

After switching on the flashlight that dangled overhead, Cara slipped her legs out of the sleeping bag and dropped them over the wooden lip of the berth. Sitting hunched over, she plowed her fingers through her hair, then took down her gear bag and pulled out a knit watch cap and a pair of leather gloves. As a thin-blooded native of Southern California, she didn't like the slightest drop in temperature. To her, March was one of the coldest months of the year. Especially on the water. And especially in the dead of night.

Turning to stow her bag, she was startled by a sudden image out of the corner of her eye. She swiveled to her left and pointed the halogen beam at the dark wood panel.

Nothing was there.

The skin on her arms prickled. Without a doubt, she had seen something a moment earlier. But it had been too fleeting to even register in her brain. Maybe she wasn't as awake and alert as she'd thought.

She stared at the blank wall. It was old and worn, scarred and scratched. Stretching toward it, she traced a long gash in the wood with her fingertip. White-hot heat radiated up her hand.

Anger.

Fear.

Terror.

She yanked her hand away from the marred wood, severing the painful sensation of the heat as well as the wrenching emotions. An adrenaline rush of anticipation quickened her heart rate. She closed her eyes, drew a deep breath, and let the air slowly leave her lungs. With each deliberate exhale, she emptied her mind of all thought, all preconceived ideas, all speculation about Andrew's disappearance. When she opened her eyes again, she felt a strange sense of weightlessness, as though her body was floating.

Staring at the bulkhead, she let her gaze drift slightly out of focus. A glimmer of light blossomed into shapes and shadows and images. The outline of a figure appeared, too small to be a grown man. He was dressed in dark, baggy clothing, and a misshapen oversized floppy hat covered his head. The momentary vision vanished. Gone. Winked out in the time it took to blink.

Damn it.

She heard only the creaking of the ship as it gently rocked with the roll of low waves in the sheltered harbor. Disappointed with the brief, inexplicable image of a faceless boy, Cara sighed in resignation and dropped to her feet. As she reached down for her shoes on the floor, the cabin tilted, pitching her off balance. She reached out to brace her fall, grasping the berth rail with one hand while flinging the other toward the bulkhead.

Her fingers disappeared through the solid wood panel.

She yanked her hand back and stared at her fingers, then at the panel. First the vision. Now this? And where had that rogue wave come from? The ship was anchored inside a protected marina.

Another wave tossed her violently toward the bulkhead. Her hand shot out in front of her and again disappeared into the wood. Only her grip on the berth kept the rest of her body from falling into the unknown.

Instinctively, she knew to remain calm and let her mind listen for the still, small voice inside her head—the voice of wisdom and insight. It guided her to close her eyes to her physical surroundings. She mentally pictured her upper arm, then let her gaze travel to her elbow, through the wood to her wrist, hand, fingertips, and beyond.

Her view of the other side was of the captain's quarters,

which she recognized from her previous visits to the *Mystic*. And yet the decor was clearly different. Gone was the sparse elegance of museum-quality restoration. Instead, a cluttered disarray of papers and clothing was scattered about the floor and over furniture. The dining table set for two was littered with platters of uneaten food. An unmade bunk was strewn with yellowed sheets and gray blankets.

It was another dimension. Another time.

For the first time since boarding the brig, Cara sensed Andrew's presence. She knew he was over there, somewhere. She was sure of it. But if she were to follow her gut instinct to go after him, she might not find her way back.

Slowly withdrawing her arm back into the second mate's cabin, Cara reluctantly opened her eyes.

You've got to go, her conscience prodded. *You've got to do this.*

Fear rose up inside her. It was one thing to climb over a security fence or face a couple of guard dogs while in pursuit of information on a case. She knew how to deal with those circumstances—and quite successfully, she admitted proudly to herself. But she had never, *ever* taken a leap of faith that came anywhere close to this one.

Maybe she needed to rethink the solstice theory. Maybe she needed to come back next week on the spring equinox. Yeah, that was it. Waiting a few days would give her time to pack a bag of necessities for whatever she might confront in the past. A gun came to mind, though she had a definite aversion to firearms.

A feeling of urgency pressed heavily on her. If she postponed her decision to go through the mysterious portal, she might find it closed next time. Now might be her only chance.

Battling her own instinct for self-preservation, Cara glared at the scarred wood panel, deceptively solid in its appearance. Suddenly, a muddied image of the rumpled child returned. He was lying on his side, bound and gagged. Two men stood over him, exchanging a leather pouch. One of them hauled the boy to his feet. Cara tried to see the face beneath the brim of the hat, but the boy was quickly shoved toward a door.

As the picture vanished, Cara could not be sure it had been a vision of Andrew. Yet she suspected the child had been bought and paid for. But why?

A sinister chill rippled down her spine. Even if the child was not Andrew, she'd been shown this vision for a reason. Perhaps the two boys were together. Or perhaps this child could lead her to Andrew.

Go, Cara!

But what if—

Go! Now! Before it's too late!

Cara crammed her feet into the shoes and shoved her arms into the sleeves of the jacket. Snatching the flashlight and bag off the hook, she stepped toward the bulkhead. Then stopped. She glanced down at her toes, inching one forward until the tip of the leather shoe almost touched the wood panel. Her heart hammered in her chest.

Praying she wasn't about to make the biggest mistake of her life, Cara forced herself to walk through the invisible portal.

MARCH, 1833
CALIFORNIA COAST, OFF SAN PEDRO

The flogging was merciless.

Despite his anger at the unwarranted punishment, Blake Masters held no authority to intervene. He was merely a guest aboard the *Mystic*. It was not his ship. These were not his men. He could do nothing but watch as the burly sailor was stripped to the waist, seized up, and whipped until he cried out for divine intervention. Captain Johnson clearly savored inflicting pain with each strike of the thick rope clenched in his hand, much as he had savored his dinner only a short while ago.

The meal had been interrupted by the first mate, a rat-faced, scrawny fellow who had reported an incident in the hold. Johnson had excused himself to deal with the situa-

tion. Blake should have taken his leave then and returned
to his own ship, the *Valiant*. But he had accepted the invitation to dine with the captain, and they were barely midway through the meal. Or rather, *he* was. The portly
Johnson had all but inhaled his first platter with great noise
and had begun a second when news of the scuffle had been
delivered. Shortly thereafter, Blake had been summoned to
the quarterdeck to witness the punishment, though for what
infraction he didn't know. Nor did he care to learn. Whip-
ping a man within an inch of his life was abhorrent to him.
Even though flogging was accepted punishment on most
vessels, he'd vowed not to use such brutality on any ship
he captained. No one challenged his leniency, however. Not
if they knew of his own stripes of degradation, emblazoned
across his back.

The rodent of a second officer called out the number of
the final lash, drawing Blake's attention back to the scene
before him. As the blond sailor hung limp and unconscious,
the captain ranted and raved like a damn lunatic, challenging any of the seven remaining sailors to cross him as their
crew mate had done. The cowering men hung their heads,
unable to look into the wild eyes of their captain. Johnson
laughed with a high-pitched cackle that sounded more like
a deranged crone than a man, if one could even call him a
man.

Sickened by the entire vile performance, Blake could not
bring himself to return to the captain's table. Determined
to depart at once, he saw the ominous signs of an approaching squall. The blood-chilling drama on deck had kept him
from noticing the darkening night sky or the shifting wind.

Blake glanced across the water toward the *Valiant*. She
was gone. During the commotion, she must have slipped
anchor and made for open sea to ride out the storm. He
trusted his men. They would save his ship, of that he had
no doubt.

"Captain Johnson, sir." Blake spoke in a polite yet loud
voice to capture the raving man's attention. The sorry excuse for an officer fell silent, clearly startled that anyone
would dare usurp his authority while he castigated his crew.

When he realized that the impudence came from his guest, his contorted face relaxed into a deceptive smile. Had Blake not witnessed the preceding episode, he would not have known what sort of odious monster captained this merchant ship.

"Ah—yes, Captain Masters." Johnson swept his hand in a grand gesture toward his quarters. "I believe our dinner still awaits us."

Couldn't the fool see that the wind had grown stronger? Couldn't he fathom the severity of the storm bearing down upon them? Blake resisted the urge to bark orders to the men standing together in the middle of the ship's deck, awaiting commands from their deranged captain.

"I believe our dinner will have to wait, sir," said Blake, his patience strained to the limit. "Might I suggest that necessary precautions be taken for the weather?"

The full import of the innocuous statement seemed to register in the officer's mind. He suddenly blinked as if coming out of a trance, glanced about at the starless sky and the turbulent seas, then turned upon the line of seven men.

"You!" Johnson bellowed at one sailor he had singled out from among the rest.

The young fellow stared at the accusing fingertip as if it were a sword point at his throat. "Me, sir?"

"*You* should have informed me of the southeaster. What sort of sailor are you?"

"But, sir—"

"Don't argue with me," barked the captain, closing the short distance between them. The young man's eyes widened with fright. "It will be on *your* head if we lose a man tonight. We'll be lucky if we come out alive."

Blake saw the lad's lower lip tremble. Good God, he barely looked old enough to shave, let alone stand up for himself against the captain.

"It warn't my fault, sir. I dinna know—"

Backhanding the sailor's cheek, Johnson shouted, "Shut up, you bastard."

The cracking sound could have been a jawbone snapping,

but it would have been hard to say with absolute certainty. For it was the lad's cry of pain that pealed loudest through the blustering wind.

Blake could not reach the captain in time to stop the brutalizing of another member of the small crew. A larger vessel would have carried enough ablebodied seamen to sustain the loss of two. As it stood now, there were barely enough left to make sail.

"Captain Johnson." Blake placed his hand on the man's arm before he could hit the young sailor again. "I urge you to give orders before we lose all your men. We will be hard-pressed to get under way with only the six you have left, sir."

"I have a full crew on board this brig. And the entire lot of them will do the work or they will all be flogged."

The man was beyond reasoning with. As the wind whipped at their clothing and the first raindrops began to fall, the young sailor clutched his jaw, sucking back sobs of pain and fear. The flogged sailor still hung unconscious from the shrouds, unaware and incapable of following any orders from the captain of the *Mystic*.

Staring at the seaman's bloodied back, Blake shucked his coat and tossed it to the cook. "Stow this for me. And get me an oilcloth." He then turned to Johnson. "I am taking that sailor below. When I come back, I will be his replacement. You shall have your full crew, *sir*."

"I forbid it! You are an officer. You are my guest."

"I am a sailor first, Captain. And right now you need my hands and my skills a hell of a lot more than you need one more goddamn officer on this brig."

He did not back down from his challenge, certain that Johnson would not refuse the renowned skills of Captain Blake Masters. A first-rate seaman, Blake was also well known as one of the youngest captains on the high seas. At thirty, he had more years of experience than most officers his age. For this reason, Blake was all too aware of the current breach of etiquette between fellow officers. This was not his command. Yet he could not stand idly by and watch the brig go down with all hands. Lives were at stake, including his own.

Johnson snapped to, commanding the ship as he should have done earlier. Precious time had been wasted. The crew hastily set to work.

Blake carried the beaten sailor to his berth. Sadly, there was no time to tend his open wounds. He could only leave the moaning man and return to the deck.

Moments later, he spied someone slipping out of the captain's quarters with a dark bundle held tight to his chest. The sailor glanced about. Amid the escalating wind and rain, amid the shouted orders and echoed responses, amid the chaos on deck and aloft, it appeared that one of the spartan crew was taking advantage of the confusion to commit thievery against the captain. Though that bastard deserved the loss of a few coins, Blake was infuriated that one man would risk the ship and his fellow mates at such a dangerous time as this.

Blake glanced up at the poop deck. Johnson had his back to them, the nefarious flogging rope in his hand. Blake advanced on the thief, hoping to hell he could divert trouble before the captain spied the criminal in his midst and again doled out retribution with the rope.

As he crossed the deck, he wondered how it was that he had not seen this sailor earlier. Nothing about the man looked at all familiar. Where had he been when the crew had been gathered for the flogging? There were so few hands on board that it was impossible for the captain or other officers not to notice his absence. Unless he was a stowaway. Unless he was . . .

The thief looked up as Blake closed the distance between them. He halted in midstride.

   . . . *a woman?*

Chapter 3

BLAKE THOUGHT HE must be mistaken as he looked into dark eyes that peered out beneath a rain-drenched fringe of hair and a knit cap. Surely the face could not belong to a young man. It was too pretty by anyone's standards. And yet the idea of a female on a ship, masquerading as a sailor, was even more preposterous. The fleeting moment of speculation vanished when the captain called out, "You there!"

The stranger glanced over his shoulder at Johnson, then slowly turned around while surreptitiously sliding the satchel behind his back.

"What have you there, boy?" demanded Johnson.

"It is mine, sir," Blake answered, taking one long stride and confiscating the leather bag. The thief looked up at him in surprise. Those hauntingly beautiful eyes mesmerized him. He felt his body respond with an unexpected flash-fire in his loins that startled him beyond comprehension. He had only a heartbeat of time to regain his composure. Dragging his gaze away from the exotic feminine eyes staring up at him, he looked at the captain once more. "I mislaid it earlier. He was bringing it to your cabin for me."

Blake hoped to heaven the rain obscured the old man's vision so he would not catch the lie. The rough seas pitched and rocked the brig, slamming the thief into Blake's chest. In spite of the layers of masculine attire, there was no question in his mind any longer that this sailor was a woman.

"Go to the fo'c'sle!" Blake shouted over the noise of the storm. He would tell the captain he'd sent the boy down to take care of the injured seaman. Later, he would allow himself time to wonder what brought a lady aboard dressed as one of the crew.

The woman mutely nodded and darted directly toward the hatch, managing the slippery tilting deck with the experience of an old salt. She certainly knew her way about the ship, by the looks of it. But her hasty escape was quickly thwarted by the first mate, who shouted orders for all hands to lay aloft. She paused, peering through the sheets of rain at Blake, with question in her eyes. Her hesitation cost her.

"*All* hands aloft!" The captain repeated the first mate's order, marching across the distance to the woman at the hatchway. It became clear to Blake that Johnson could not see that the sailor was neither a man nor one of the regular crew. The rest of the men were too busy at their duties to pay any attention one way or the other. Yet the captain— arrogant fool that he was—could not see what was quite obvious to Blake.

"I ordered you aloft, boy!"

The thief nodded, keeping his head down.

Wise of her, thought Blake as he approached the two on the wave-washed deck. If she were to look up and Johnson saw that slender neck and delicate chin, he was sure to realize she was not one of his own sailors.

She darted toward the rigging without acknowledging the order, which further riled the captain.

"I expect an answer from you!"

Though she paused, she kept her back to him. Blake closed in, not knowing what he would say. But he could not let anyone, least of all a woman, fall victim again to the madman's anger.

"Turn around and look at me when I speak!" bellowed Johnson, struggling to stay upright despite the erratic motion of the unsteady ship. Waves broke over the railing and rolled across the deck. The disguised woman began to turn around, but her response was not quick enough to suit the captain.

When the man jerked his hand back, Blake saw the flogging rope lifted high. Throwing his body between the officer and the thief, he took the full impact across his chest. Despite the searing pain, he grabbed the thick rope with both hands and yanked it out of the grasp of the startled captain.

Horror in his eyes, Johnson threw his arms across his face as if expecting Blake to turn the rope on him. For one brief moment, Blake was all too tempted to give in to the fury that raged within him. Before he could rein in his own urge to extract revenge for the innocent victims, a woman's scream startled him.

He spun halfway around as a towering wall of water crashed down on them. Knocked off his feet, he slid across the slick wood deck, slamming into unseen objects, gulping for air and swallowing seawater. Amid the cries and chaos, he heard a man holler . . .

"She's headed for the cliffs!"

Cara slowly emerged from a fitful sleep to the soothing sound of gentle surf rolling across rocks and pebbles. The terrifying nightmare was behind her now. She was no longer surrounded by an ocean of black water, numbing her body with its freezing temperature. As she drew her mind from the depths of the dream, she felt cold, yet safe. The water was gone. Only the sound of the sea remained.

Rolling onto her back, she opened her eyes to bright, glaring sunlight. She blinked once, twice, then shielded her eyes with both hands. In her groggy state of confusion, she realized she was not in her cabin on board the *Mystic*, but lying on a beach. A cool, salt-tinged breeze ruffled over her cheek. A shiver of cold rippled through her body.

She propped herself up on her elbows and looked around. Bodies were strewn about the stretch of sand, half in the water, half out. Only one man moaned. Were the rest dead?

The nightmare had been real.

Dropping back onto the damp sand, she let out a groan

of disbelief, struggling against a frightening sense of disorientation. Pressing the heel of her palms to her eyes, she felt the slight burn in them from sand and salt water. She tried to ignore the chill breeze as her mind raced through surreal memories of the previous night.

After she had stepped through the invisible portal into the captain's quarters, the ship had pitched and swayed in heavy seas. From the shouted orders topside, she had assumed all hands were on deck, but she couldn't go unnoticed for very long on the small brig, in spite of her authentic costume.

If she had been caught in the captain's quarters, she would have been in worse trouble. She'd had no choice but to sneak out during all the commotion, make her way to the hold, and seek a hiding place until it was safe to emerge. But her plan had gone haywire as soon as she'd reached the storm-battered deck.

Everything had happened so fast. It was all a blur of motion in her head now. The wind. The rain. The shouts. The commands. A man grabbed her bag, claiming it as his own. He wasn't one of the crew, she was certain—not by the way he addressed the captain. There had been no time to think. Less time to react. The wall of water took them by surprise. White foam. The roar of rushing bubbles in her ears.

Cara slid her palms from her eyes and gazed out at the deceptively calm ocean, recalling her struggle to stay afloat. She had swum until every muscle in her arms and legs burned with the pain of exhaustion. Her body rode the crest of mountainous waves only to plunge into deep troughs the next instant. Swamped by the salt water again and again, she had continuously fought her way to the surface, numbed by terror, driven on by her stubborn will to live. Somehow, some way, she had succeeded.

Now what do I do? she wondered uneasily, pushing herself into a sitting position. Her gaze traveled over her damp period clothing to the clumsy shoes on her feet. Another shiver shook her, as much from fear as from cold. Rubbing her arms with her hands to stimulate warmth, she shoved the heel of her foot into the moist sand, digging a furrow as she anxiously contemplated her fate. She had not been on the brig more than a couple of minutes when she'd found herself up to her neck in trouble, then tossed into the sea.

She wrapped her arms around her upraised knees and dropped her head forward, allowing the heat of the early-morning sun to seep into her spine. Mentally beseeching divine guidance, she murmured, "Where do I go from here?"

"You will be coming with me."

Her head popped up at the sound of the gruff masculine order. She had expected an inner prompting, a gut feeling that would guide her toward her next step. She *hadn't* expected the baritone message of the man kneeling next to her.

It was the man from the ship—her ally against the captain.

"You!" As she pushed herself halfway to her feet, her vision blurred, then nausea hit. She had swallowed too much saltwater. A firm hand on her upper arm gently lowered her to the beach.

Sitting on the sand, she stared at him, trying to bring his face into focus. Thick black hair framed his tanned skin, bringing back the memory of the moment when she had first seen him on the ship. He had spotted her coming out of the captain's quarters, yet he had not betrayed her. Instead, he had lied for her, protecting her from the commanding officer. This man with the firm set to his jaw had stepped in the way, taking the full blow of the flogging rope that had been meant for her.

Why?

Cara saw something disturbingly intimate in his deep-blue eyes. Unnerved, she looked away. Then she realized her jacket was missing. She didn't remember losing it, but she'd probably discarded it to keep its weight from pulling her under. The damp, red-checked shirt clung to her curves, revealing the outline of her small breasts. Her gaze snapped back to his.

"Yes, I know," he said, acknowledging her gender.

A split second of panic swept over her, urging her to take off at a dead run, to get as far away from him as she could. But her exhaustion would make escape across the sand impossible.

While her wary gaze lingered on him, he gently draped a damp peacoat over her shoulders. She didn't question whether it was his. She didn't care. At least it warmed her from the bone-chilling breeze on her damp skin.

"I knew you were a woman when I saw you on the ship."

"But the captain—"

"—was an imbecile and a fool. If he had an empty bucket for a brain he would have more sense than he displayed last night. And perhaps he would still be alive—though I have to admit the seas are safer today due to his demise."

"The captain's dead?"

"Yes, and all but two of the crew. The *Mystic* lies aground by the cliffs to the north." He tilted his head toward the rocky bluffs, a good half mile away.

Panic tightened her chest like a vise. She asked in an unsteady voice, "Is the ship salvageable?"

"Not without timber and tools."

How would she find her way back to the future if the time portal had been destroyed? "I need to see it for myself."

"No, the rocks are too slippery. Considering the harrowing ordeal you have been through, I doubt you are steady enough to keep your footing." The blue of his eyes deepened, and his narrowed gaze allowed no argument. "My offer still stands—"

"Your 'offer' sounded more like an *order*."

"Be that as it may, you are invited to come with me. My men will be coming ashore soon to look for me."

"Your men? Who are you? How do I know you're not a pirate of some sort?"

"I am Captain Blake Masters of the *Valiant*, a merchant-man that has been two years on the coast gathering cattle hides from the owners of the rancheros. We will soon be on our way back to Boston with a full hold. But, alas, no pillaged loot from innocent victims, I assure you. And you would be . . . ?''

''Cara Edwards.''

''Pleased to make your acquaintance,'' he responded with a single nod. ''As I was saying—I was a guest on the *Mystic* when circumstances altered the events of the evening.''

Cara could see that he'd planned to say something else but changed his mind. For a moment she sensed his intense anger and disgust, as though his feelings were her own. She knew, too, that his hatred was directed at the captain. ''I take it you weren't on friendly terms.''

''Captain Johnson and I met only yesterday when he made anchor here off San Pedro.''

Cara glanced around. ''*This* is San Pedro?''

''Yes.''

Her surroundings looked nothing like the same area in 1998. In her own time, a long and rocky breakwater protected the enormous twin harbors of Los Angeles and Long Beach, where oil tankers and cargo ships passed one another every day. Now she looked upon a barren stretch of land with little vegetation and no trees.

She had been on the *Mystic* in the twentieth century. And she had come through to the same ship in an earlier time and at a different location. What year was it? She couldn't ask without raising unwanted curiosity in Captain Masters. It was bad enough that she couldn't explain how she, a woman, had ended up on a merchant sailing ship.

''How is it that you came to be on the *Mystic*?'' asked Masters, startling her with the very thought that had been running through her mind. Was it merely a coincidence? Or had he unknowingly picked up on her thoughts? If so, she would need to guard her silent speculations carefully.

Avoiding his gaze, she cautiously answered, ''I secretly boarded the ship in Santa Barbara. I'm looking for a little boy. I thought he might be aboard the *Mystic*. I didn't expect to sail with her. I just—''

"Is he yours?"

"Mine?" Cara quickly calculated the benefit of claiming Andrew to be her own son. It would make it easier to explain her search—far easier than the reality of being a private investigator from the future. "Yes, of course he's mine. Why else would I go to such dangerous extremes?"

"Why, indeed," he answered with more of a statement than a question in his voice, while looking at her with sympathetic eyes.

She tried her hardest to make a show of motherly worry for the missing boy.

"Perhaps I may be of some assistance in your search. As soon as I take care of the present state of affairs here, I will be setting sail for San Diego. You may find some answers there."

"Do you know something about Andrew?" Cara searched his face, hoping for a sign of encouragement. With his tanned olive complexion and fine lines at the corners of his eyes, Masters had the rugged good looks of a strong, healthy athlete.

"I couldn't say I know the name—Andrew, you say?" When she nodded, he went on, "I recall a few young lads lolling about the hide houses while their ships were in port. He would undoubtedly have brown eyes and hair like yours, I assume."

"Light-blue eyes. Blond hair." Seeing his dark brows angle upward in mild surprise, she hastened to add, "He looks like his father who is—*was* very blond. White-blond, actually. And pale. Yes, Andrew is the spitting image of my Swedish husband. That is, my *deceased* husband, who passed away two years ago."

She couldn't resist including one tiny little tidbit of truth. After all, she needed to keep some element of truth in her story or she'd end up tripping over the lies later.

Her deception seemed to be working. He offered his apologies for her loss. "And now to lose a child as well—," he said gently with a sad shake of his head, "—must be more than you can bear. I only hope . . . Have you considered that—"

"Andrew is *alive*."

"You sound so sure. Ah, but then you are his mother. You would never give up hope. And that's a good thing."

"This isn't just about a mother's hope," she explained, meeting his gaze with open honesty. "I can sense it. I *know* he's not dead."

He stared at her for a long moment, appearing to weigh her words, as if he somehow understood her intuition. Which was ridiculous, she told herself. Few understood, and fewer still accepted.

"Very well, then." He rose to his feet as two longboats appeared in the distance. "It's settled. I will take you to San Diego to look for him. For now, however, stay here and rest while I check again on the other two survivors."

Cara watched him walk away with long, purposeful strides. Like her, his clothing was still wet and the cloth of his shirt clung to his broad shoulders and the tapered line of his back. In another time and place, she could easily find herself attracted to a gentleman of his caliber. And his attractive physique. But she couldn't let her guard down. She had to find Andrew and get back to her own time.

As she tried to draw her wayward thoughts away from the captain, she saw him kneel over a body several hundred feet away and gently roll it over. The arm flopped lifelessly to the sand. Masters shook his head, crossed himself reverently, and moved on to another motionless sailor on the beach.

A chill descended upon her, unlike the physical cold of the ocean breeze on her wet clothes. A sense of fear rippled down her neck to the base of her tailbone. She couldn't see the spirits of the departed sailors, but she perceived a cumulative presence in the air around her—a feeling of confusion and terror. The dead men were unable to comprehend their state of physical non-existence. Violent or tragic deaths were known to have kept some poor souls from completing their journey to the other side. And what could have been more violent than that deadly storm?

She looked over her shoulder to be certain she was

alone—as alone as a person could be with the hovering entities of lost souls.

"There's no reason to be afraid," she whispered aloud, knowing that Masters was too far away to hear her talking to the dead. Though she did not know the men, she could not help the swell of sadness in their plight. Tears filled her eyes. A sob caught in her throat. "Look for the light. You're going to be fine. Just head toward the light. It's time for you to go."

She continued to talk to the wind, sensing that each spirit was listening to her. Some went easily. Others took a bit longer. Eventually the air around her felt clearer, as if the weight of fear had been lifted. She had no way of proving any of it. Yet she sensed it in a way that was as normal to her as breathing. Scientifically, there was nothing to convince a person who didn't have this psychic awareness. But there was also nothing that could convince her differently of her own unique perceptions about life and death.

By the time the two boats from the *Valiant* reached the breaking surf along the beach, Blake had performed the unhappy duty of inspecting all the bodies that had washed ashore after the southeaster. Of the two crewmen still alive, only one was able to move about to identify his dead shipmates. The other was barely alive but looked as if he would survive.

When the familiar bark of a dog caught Blake's attention, he shaded his eyes against the reflective glare of the sun on the water. On the first of the two longboats, his large black mutt stood with its front paws braced on the bow, barking excitedly. The canine leaped out, splashing into a receding wave, then bounded toward Blake as four of his crew hauled the boats by the gunwales onto the sand.

Meeting the rescue party halfway, Blake knelt on one knee to give Bud a moment of praise and attention before he stood to greet the men.

"Good to see you, Cap'n," said his first mate, Mr. Bellows, with a mile-wide grin, followed by a similar hearty greeting by seaman McGinty.

"Aloha, Capnee!" added Lopaka, a dark-skinned Sandwich Islander. *"Aloha nui!"*

To the white merchantmen, Lopaka and others from the Pacific Islands were individually called Kanaka, a variation of their own word for "man." Addressed as a group, they were Kānaka. And they held the unusual and envious position of working for themselves, hiring out to hide-trading ships along the coast without being tied to a contract like a regular sailor.

Blake grinned at the enthusiastic young man. "Yes, Lopaka, a big hello to you, too."

Then he turned to Keoni Pahinui, who was the ship's cook and, on occasion, the doctor as well, owning an impressive collection of knives that served both purposes. He was also a cherished friend of many years. There was not another man alive for whom Blake would lay down his own life.

"Aloha, Kaikua'ana," Hello, big brother, Blake greeted him.

The large, smiling Kanaka shook his head, then grabbed Blake in a gruff hug and slapped him heartily on the back. Highly improper behavior, but Keoni was not one to follow protocol. Ever.

"You scare da hell outta me, *Kaikaina*," he scolded, referring to Blake as his little brother. "Thought maybe you *make*."

"If you thought I was dead, you'd have carved up ol' Bud by now and had him for dinner."

" *'A'ole*, not this Kanaka. Others eat dog. Not me. Bud, he my family, too." Keoni lifted his head, distracted by something behind Blake. Following his friend's curious gaze, Blake saw the short-haired woman in men's clothing coming down the beach toward the men. "What is this?"

Blake almost smiled at the ease with which Keoni could drop his Islander dialect for the educated demeanor taught at the missionary school on Oahu. "A *wahine*, my friend. Or have you forgotten what a woman looks like after all these weeks?"

All four of the *Valiant* crew stared in silence as Mrs.

Edwards approached. He couldn't blame them. He, too, felt a strange dumbness at the sight of her, despite her unconventional clothing and cropped dark hair. She was truly unlike any female he had ever seen. An exotic mixture of heritage, none of which he could determine.

It was Bud who broke the spell. His tail wagged slowly back and forth as he walked cautiously up to her, his head lowered.

Without fear or hesitation, she dropped to her knees and looked into the dog's eyes. "Hi, there, fella." She glanced at Blake, then back at the dog. "What's his name?"

"Bud."

The dog twisted his head around at the sound of his name, his tongue lolling out the side of his huge mouth as the woman scratched him behind his ear. Wishing he were the recipient of similar affection, Blake felt a lopsided grin quirk his mouth but quickly stifled it.

He cleared his throat and turned to his first mate. "Mrs. Edwards could use a blanket and some food. I assume you brought supplies with you."

"Aye, aye, sir." Mr. Bellows turned to McGinty and Lopaka. "You heard the captain, men. Bring the lady those blankets and the basket of food."

As the two trotted off down the beach to the longboats, the widow walked up, with the dog at her side. Blake introduced her to the first mate, then the cook, who raised the back of her hand to his lips like a gentleman suitor. The blush that stole over her cheeks did not sit well with Blake, who was all too aware of the easy way his adopted brother charmed the woman. Keoni was a fine-looking Kanaka, a few years older than Blake. He was also a man from a culture that enjoyed the pursuit of physical pleasure between the genders without the guilt and restrictions of civilized countries.

Blake felt a nudge beneath his hand and looked down to see Bud gazing up at him. At least someone had noticed he was still around. He stroked the top of his dog's massive head, then spoke to Mr. Bellows. "Did the *Valiant* fare well?"

"Beautifully, sir." The first mate gestured toward the cliffs. "Would that be the *Mystic*, then?"

"Aye, it is. We will need to check for any survivors aboard her."

"McGinty and I will take care of it, sir."

"Good. I'll have Lopaka help me. Keoni—" Blake turned to his friend. "There is an injured sailor in need of your attention."

Mrs. Edwards spoke up. "Please, may I ask a favor of the men going to the *Mystic*, Captain Masters? Could they look for my leather backpack?"

"Your leather what?"

"Back—um . . . baggage. Bag, that is. My leather bag. I had it with me on the ship."

"I doubt they will find it aboard the *Mystic*, but I will have them look for it."

By midafternoon, the bodies had been buried in the clay soil on a low hill overlooking the sea. Blake and Lopaka were walking back from their unpleasant duty when the search party of two returned to give their report of the shipwrecked *Mystic*.

"Sir, she was washed clean of most everything that wasn't nailed down," answered Mr. Bellows. "She's busted up real good. The tide's taken quite a toll through the hole in her starboard quarter. Here's the captain's papers, though."

Blake had already learned from a conversation with Captain Johnson that the *Mystic* had arrived from Boston only four months earlier with dry goods to trade with the cattle owners on the ranchos. Unlike the *Valiant*, which was nearing the end of its two years on the California coast, the small brig had a long way to go to fill its hold with hides before it could return to the East.

"Thank you, Mr. Bellows. Did you find the leather bag?"

"No, sir. Sorry, sir."

He noticed the way the sailors eyed the widow Edwards,

sitting at a small fire Keoni had built to warm her and the
two other survivors.

"That will be all," he stated firmly, dismissing the men
to make ready for the return trip to the ship. They had
finished their work here in San Pedro on the previous evening, so no hides would be collected today. Had it not been
for the storm, they would already have been halfway to San
Diego by now.

He clutched the scrolled papers in his left hand, lightly
tapping them against his thigh. Turning toward the drift-
wood fire, he approached Mrs. Edwards, who sat with her
back to him, still huddled in the woolen blanket. Her head
hung forward between her shoulders with the posture of
someone who was exhausted.

In the bright afternoon sun, he saw the color of her short
hair was not black, as he had assumed during the storm,
but actually a rich, deep brown. So were her eyes, he recalled. She appeared to be close to his own age of thirty,
perhaps a bit younger, but no woman of his acquaintance
had ever looked quite so physically strong and as able as
any young sailor. Yet she certainly did not possess any
other masculine qualities.

He felt a resurgence of his own wanton desire for her.

Chapter 4

BLAKE QUELLED HIS lascivious thoughts and addressed Mrs. Edwards. "May I speak with you privately, ma'am?"

The widow woman brought her bowed head up suddenly, as if startled. "Wha—? Where—?"

She craned her neck around, squinting up at him through sleepy eyes that made him think of waking up next to her in the early morning. What insanity to think such things! He dismissed the wild notion and held out his palm to help her to her feet.

"I would like to talk to you for a moment."

Taking his hand, she struggled to stand but faltered, her knees buckling. Instinctively, his arms went around her, pulling her up against him. Despite the layers of garments covering her feminine curves, she elicited an instant response in the lower regions of his own body. He was attracted to her, of that there was no doubt.

"I'm so sorry. My right foot went to sleep." With her palms resting on his chest, she looked up with an apologetic shrug.

A man could lose himself in the dark depths of her velvet-brown eyes. A weaker man than himself, he thought, determined to keep a level head while around her.

"It should be okay in a minute."

"It is better to walk it off." He shifted her to his side,

supporting her weight with his left arm bracketed around her waist. When she hobbled unsteadily, he tightened his grip, damning the blood warming in his veins. This was not a wench who was teasing his body with her caresses.

Little by little, she straightened her spine and her step grew surer. "I think I can go it alone now."

Must you? Surprised and relieved that he had not asked the question aloud, he lowered his hand to his side. "Yes, of course. How is that?"

"Fine, thank you." She gathered the wool blanket around her shoulders, pinning it together at her chest with one fist. "You said you wanted to talk? Your men didn't find my bag, did they?"

"No, but that is not why I asked to speak to you. It is a matter of your company aboard the *Valiant*." He felt obligated to see to her safety, perhaps now more than ever. Even his own men could not be trusted. Could *he*? In the twenty-four months they had been away from their home port, the only females available to the sailors were Indian women whose husbands brought them down to the beaches and shared in their profits.

His long pause drew a soft "Ahem" from the widow, reminding him he was not alone with his thoughts.

Realizing she had been patiently waiting for him to continue, he grew uncomfortable in the awareness that this strange woman had caused all kinds of addled thinking in the brief time he had known her. What effect would she have on him as more time passed?

"I must warn you," he began again, "your presence on board may be awkward, at best. Some sailors believe it is bad luck to have a female on their ship. When they learn you were a stowaway on the *Mystic*, they may blame you for its disastrous end."

"Do *you* believe such nonsense?" she asked, locking his eyes in her straightforward gaze.

"I believe," he said gruffly, "there is no such thing as bad luck where a lady is concerned. However, my opinion hardly changes the fact that it would be better if you did not show yourself on deck during the voyage."

"Do you mean I must hide in the hull?"

"No." He smiled faintly at the idea of locking her away as if in a dungeon. "You will be given suitable accommodations, comfortable for the short duration of two days and nights."

"Before I am confined to my quarters, would it be asking too much if I could interview—that is, *talk* to—the two crewmen of the *Mystic*?"

"Regarding your son, I assume."

"Yes."

"I will talk to them."

"I'd rather do it myself, if you don't mind."

"I do mind, Mrs. Edwards. Those men would not trust you enough to speak one word to you. It would be best if you leave the questions to me."

"It looks like I'm expected to leave *everything* to you," she muttered.

"Precisely. I'm glad you see my point."

"The only thing I see is that I'm pretty much at your mercy."

"Or the mercy of this beautiful but brutal foreign wasteland." He gestured with a sweep of his arm at the desolate scenery. "The nearest civilized town—if it could be called civilized—is Pueblo de los Angeles, which is thirty miles distant. You may take your chances here, madam, or come with me and follow my orders. Which do you choose?"

The woman narrowed her eyes as she gazed eastward from the hill on which they stood. The gentle sea breeze lifted the short layers of her dark hair, combing it in a manner that tempted him to raise his hand and touch it, touch her.

Finally, after a long and silent pause, she spoke directly to him, challenging him with a defiant gaze. "I want to be with you when you talk to those men about Andrew." He opened his mouth to argue, but she held up her palm. "I won't speak. I will only listen. I promise."

"On your honor?"

"Cross my heart and hope to—" She stopped. "Never mind."

"You have changed your mind?"

"No," she quickly answered. "I swear I'll keep my mouth shut. How soon can you speak to them?"

"We must do so now. They're not coming with us."

"Why not? There's nothing here for them. You said so yourself. Isn't San Diego a better place for them to find work?"

"They have decided to remain behind and take their chances that the owner of the *Mystic* will have sent another ship, though I doubt it."

"Then tell them to come with us. There's no food or medical help here to keep them alive, especially for the one who needs at least a couple more weeks of care and attention."

"Aside from leaving behind a fair amount of food, I am afraid it is out of my hands."

"But you're the captain."

"Of the *Valiant*, my dear. Not the *Mystic*. They have no allegiance to me."

"So? Those men might die if they stay here."

"They would rather take the risk."

"Over what? Sailing with you?" After a momentary pause, she continued with an amazingly accurate appraisal of the situation at hand. "It's me, isn't it?"

He reluctantly nodded. "So it appears."

"But that doesn't make any sense."

"Be that as it may, they've made their decision. Now, as for you, do you still wish to listen when I question them?"

"Yes, of course."

"No talking?"

"No talking."

When asked about a blond boy they might have seen three months earlier, the sailors described a mischievous little liar with wild stories and a mean streak. He had somehow slipped aboard ship in San Diego. Found in the captain's quarters, the boy had been accused of thievery, though he'd had no coin on him. The captain had beaten the lad. Not surprisingly, the boy had fled the next day.

The story jogged Blake's memory. He recalled the latter weeks in December, when the *Valiant* had been anchored off the beach of San Diego to deliver a cargo of cattle hides to the hide houses on shore. He had witnessed the return of a young cabin boy to the *Mystic*. Captain Johnson had offered a ten-dollar reward for the lad, half the price of an ablebodied sailor who deserts his ship. Blake had seen enough of these runaways to harden his heart to their plight. Still, he'd felt sympathy for the scrappy young blond boy. But he'd forced it out of his mind. He could not save every frightened green hand who had yet to double the Horn. Time and work toughened the stronger ones and turned the weaker ones away from any notion of further adventures at sea. Such was the way of a nautical life, and he had no authority to intervene.

Blake listened as Mrs. Edwards learned that the boy, quite likely her own son, had endured unspeakable punishment from the captain. He stepped closer to her when the tears trailed down her cheeks. But she bravely insisted on hearing everything. The boy had managed a successful escape with the help of two shipmates. They had hidden him on one of the boats when they rowed ashore at San Juan Capistrano for hides. The mission priest had agreed to take the boy in.

When the sailors finished their despondent tale, Mrs. Edwards turned to Blake. "I need to go to Capistrano."

"San Juan," he corrected. Although he would agree to make an unscheduled stop, he had no intentions of leaving her there alone and on her own.

On board the *Valiant*, Blake escorted the widow to his cabin at the stern of the ship. Followed closely by his dog, he was certain his guest would find the spacious captain's quarters to be more than suitable accommodations. Mullioned windows allowed an abundance of natural light and a picturesque view of seascape from port to starboard.

Blake opened the door to his private sanctuary and

stepped back to allow Mrs. Edwards to enter first, then ordered Bud to stay outside. The dog gave him a doleful look and dropped to the wood planks with a bone-jarring thump.

After closing the door, Blake retrieved a set of clean trousers and shirt for himself and his guest. "You will have to make do with my own wardrobe, though I imagine you will be swimming in my clothes."

Now that she was his guest aboard the *Valiant*, it was too late for him to be feeling uneasy with his decision. Yet something was amiss. He could feel it in his bones. Despite the softness in her eyes, he wondered whether he could trust her. The mysterious woman had claimed to be at his mercy.

Perhaps she had misled him.

Perhaps it was best to keep an eye on her. A close eye.

Cara stared for a long moment at the clothing he held out to her. His masculine hands gripped the material with a tension that permeated the close space between them. Her gaze moved from his long fingers to the back of his hand, from the wide cuff of his sleeve to the collar of his soiled shirt. Dark whiskers shadowed his neck and lower face. His unkempt appearance gave him an aura of an uncivilized pirate rather than a respectable sea captain. In his deep-aquamarine eyes, she saw distrust.

Could she blame him?

He had a right to be suspicious of her, even though he could not possibly know about her second sight or her life in the future. It was enough that she was a woman on a ship of superstitious sailors.

The floor of the cabin tilted beneath her, gently rolling with a low wave. She shifted her weight to balance herself, unaccustomed to the constant movement, unaccustomed to anything about this time or place.

Confusing thoughts and speculation muddled her mind. She mentally shook off the discomfort and accepted the clothing from the captain. "Thank you . . . for everything."

He acknowledged her appreciation with a silent nod. "Now if you will allow me a moment to gather a few personal articles to take with me—"

"I don't expect you to give up your room."

"Cabin," corrected Blake. "And I do not mind doing so for a few nights."

"I can sleep somewhere else. It's no problem. Really! Surely there's another cabin for me to use."

"Not one that is nearly as comfortable as this one."

"A bunk is all I need."

She glanced around the clean cabin paneled in rich, dark teak with a row of small windows at eye level wrapping around the back wall. In the center of the floor stood a polished table and four captain's chairs. Beneath the multi-pane windows, a wide berth beckoned her with thick bedding to cushion her sore, aching muscles. Though tempted to curl up under the blankets, she forced herself to say, "There is nothing here I can't live without."

"Privacy, perhaps? A lady should not be expected to do without certain necessities."

"I don't need—"

"Mrs. Edwards," argued the captain in a firm, low voice. "You are going to stay here in my cabin. There is no bathtub, I'm sorry to say. But I will have my steward bring a basin of fresh water and soap. He can wash out your clothes as well, if you would like."

"That won't be necessary." Her nautical costume had been made in a modern era with who-knew-what subtle differences that might rouse the suspicion of someone laundering it.

He moved past her to a bureau built into the wall and opened a drawer. With his back to her, he continued, "I will have some food sent down to you in an hour, unless you prefer it sooner."

"You won't be joining me at your own table?" she asked, recalling the parade of platters that had been marched to the captain's quarters aboard the *Mystic* of the distant future.

"I will take my meal elsewhere."

"Where?"

"It is not your concern."

"But it *is* my concern. My presence on the *Valiant* is

causing you to give up your bed and table, not to mention worrying your crew over a female on this ship.'' She paused, staring at the back of his head as he bent over his task. His black hair was cut in short layers that grew longer at the nape of his neck, curling over the fold of his collar. The style suited him, though he would probably look good with hair of any length.

Little things about him gained her notice in ways far beyond her professional observation. Sure, he was attractive. But she had met plenty of physically appealing men in her line of business without falling for one of them. It didn't have to be any different with this sea captain. She could maintain her objective distance. And he, she was certain, could be counted on to behave in the manner of a gentleman.

An officer AND a gentleman. Cara smiled to herself, knowing in her own unique way that this man had more honor in his little pinky finger than his 1990s male counterpart.

''We could share the cabin,'' she offered.

Captain Masters straightened with a slowness that accentuated every muscle movement beneath his soiled white shirt and dark pants. He turned to her.

''Share, you say?''

She nodded. ''I trust you.''

A glint of mischief twinkled in his eyes. ''Do you now? And suppose you misjudge me, ma'am?''

''I haven't. I am rarely wrong about people, Captain. You are a man of your word. And if you give me your word that you will respect my virtue, I will consider myself perfectly safe with you in this cabin.''

''It would not be proper, Mrs. Edwards. You know as well as I.''

She sighed in resignation. The man was more than an officer and a gentleman. He was a Puritan. Or pushing for sainthood.

His piercing gaze unsettled her. Looking for any excuse to turn away from those disturbing eyes, she stepped to the dining table and dropped the clean clothing onto the polished wood surface. The book she'd studied for her role as a sailor had not included information regarding the proper etiquette for a woman on her own in the nineteenth century. As it was, she had certainly crossed the line with her fictitious excuse about stowing away on the *Mystic*. And wearing men's pants had to be nothing less than scandalous.

Fingering the cloth beneath her hands, Cara murmured, "I have certainly made a mess of things."

"Desperate measures would be expected of any mother searching for her child. However, it is unfortunate you did not have a man to send, rather than putting yourself in such grave danger. This is no place for a woman."

"Where I come from, women are not as sheltered as they are here."

"And where would that be?"

Cara mentally kicked herself for the casual remark. She had to be more careful to watch her words. Oh, how hard it was to weave a web of lies without being caught in the stickiness of it all. Sometimes her job required playing a game of deceit and secrecy. Now here she was trapped by her own secrets.

"Actually . . . I am from everywhere and nowhere in particular." She fidgeted with a button on the folded shirt. "My parents were missionaries. I grew up all over the world."

"Is that how you met Mr. Edwards?"

"Yes, we spent some time in Switzerland, where his family became quite friendly with my parents."

"I understood you to say he was Swedish."

Swedish? Or Swiss? Already she was tripping over her own lies! This wasn't like her at all.

"Y-yes . . . Lars was *from* Sweden." Covering her eyes as if overcome by sudden sadness, she allowed her voice to waver just enough to sound tired and brokenhearted. "I'm sorry, Captain. Lars was my whole life. I loved him deeply. At times I can't contain my grief."

"I should not have mentioned him."

"No, it's all right. I must learn to cope with my loss."

She sniffed as if holding back a tear. "We were traveling to the Orient when he became sick in San Francisco. Our ship had to sail without us. We had every intention of finding passage on a later vessel, but Lars grew worse. He passed away only six short months ago, God rest his soul."

Her final few words tumbled out on choking sobs. Phony sobs. And crocodile tears. It was one of the best performances she had ever given on the job. So convincing, in fact, that the captain gently touched her shoulder. Caught up in the little scene, she instinctively turned into his arms to be comforted by him.

"I'm so sorry, Mrs. Edwards." His baritone voice rumbled through her with a tenderness that touched her heart, pressing guilt down upon her.

This had been a mistake, she realized too late.

She didn't dare look up into his face, afraid to witness the sincere compassion in his eyes. His honest sympathy would certainly unravel the fine fabric of her deceitful drama. Instead, she worked hard to make her sorrow as believable as possible.

"It has been difficult."

"I can only imagine. And now your son, too."

"Andrew," she said in a hushed whisper. The boy's name brought back the real drama of her situation. "I must find him. I can't go home without Andrew."

If I can go home at all!

The unbidden thought sent a shiver of dread down her spine. With the *Mystic* wrecked upon the cliffs, she wondered once more how she could possibly find her way back to the future when she finally located Andrew.

Masters took her chin in his hand and lifted her head. Through her tears, she reluctantly looked up at him.

"I wish . . ." He paused, studying her. "I wish I could promise we will find your boy. But you should know the odds are not good."

"I don't want to hear about the odds, Captain. I have come too far to give up now."

Much too far.

She allowed her lower lip to tremble slightly. Another

tear fell. As he brushed it away with his thumb, she felt the pad of skin against her cheek. The gesture was meant to be innocently consoling, yet she sensed an undercurrent of something entirely different flowing through his touch. Something deeper. Something hidden beneath layers of his memory, so that not even he was aware of its existence.

A flash of a familiar vision blinded her for a moment. She gasped at the startling image.

"What's wrong?" He leaned back and looked down at her.

Cara wanted to dismiss the sudden realization as a figment of her imagination.

It couldn't be.

Not him.

He can't be the boy I saw in the rumpled clothes.

The picture in her mind had come and gone so quickly. Could she really be certain it was the same image she had seen the previous night on the other ship . . . before she had stepped back in time?

She wanted to take his hand, to close her eyes again, to look into the darkness of his soul and see if she could find that battered little boy again. But how could she explain it to Captain Masters? How would he react if she told him of a past she could discern like a fortune-telling gypsy?

"It's nothing." Dropping her eyes from his gaze, she stepped away from him and wrapped her arms around her waist. "Perhaps you were right. Perhaps you should leave."

"As you wish."

She listened to the solid footfall of his boots as he departed. When she was certain he had left, the air seemed easier to breathe. She inhaled deeply, filling her lungs until her rib cage could expand no more. As she slowly released the breath in a long and quiet exhale, she felt her body relax, the tension drain from her tired and sore muscles. With each cleansing breath, she became more and more aware of the masculine essence of the captain, even though he was no longer physically present. His living quarters held his scent, wrapping around her with the warmth of a

soft down comforter. The smell of damp salt air mingled
with wood polish, shaving soap, and musk cologne. A faint
odor of tobacco told her the captain enjoyed an occasional
smoke—or entertained visitors who did.

She looked around the cabin, wondering about the man
who occupied this place. This was his domain. She sensed
the power, the independence.

And a hidden past.

Cara recalled the startling recurrence of the horrible vision. When she had earlier tried to zero in on Andrew, had
she stumbled across the tragic childhood of this man instead?

She glanced over at the bureau where Masters had been
riffling through the drawer. If she could find a personal
item, preferably a piece of jewelry, perhaps she could find
some clues to her clairvoyant vision. Invasion of privacy
was not exactly her favorite thing to do. In her line of
business, she often had to breach the private lives of innocent people to find out the truth. There was always justifiable cause, though—a trail of a criminal or a missing
person. But was snooping among the belongings of Captain
Masters justifiable?

Not really.

However, looking for necessary information about her
case would certainly be an acceptable reason to explore.
For starters, she wanted to know what year it was. Unable
to ask anyone without drawing more suspicion to herself,
she had hoped to have an opportunity like this one. If her
search for a calendar or a captain's log brought her into
contact with some of his personal items, so much the better.

Walking toward the ship's galley with his dog at his heels,
Blake was certain the widow had lied to him about her
husband. On the beach she had said the man had died two
years ago. In his cabin, she had claimed to have lost her
dear Lars only six short months ago. And it also seemed
the Swede might have been Swiss, if not for her adroit
explanation that he had chosen not to challenge. What else

was she hiding from him? Perhaps she was not a grieving wife at all.

Blake entered the warm galley as his cook leaned over the oven door and took out a sizable portion of roasted beef and vegetables. Bud crept forward, eager for a handout, only to be shooed away by Keoni, who then slipped the mutt a large bone from the counter.

"Now get out from under my feet, you old beggar," he scolded, sending the dog out of the galley to enjoy his treat.

The aroma of the hot meal wafted under Blake's nose, prompting a loud rumble from his empty stomach. Keoni gave him a sideways glance.

"You, too? Here, take this." The brawny Kanaka tossed a small red apple to Blake, who snatched it out of the air. "You look like hell, *Kaikaina.*"

"I appreciate the food, not your opinion." He bit into the fruit, one of a supply bought from a mission along their coastal run for hides. "Considering what I've been through since last night, I'm entitled to look like hell, *and* I deserve a little sympathy."

Keoni laughed off the request for pity. "Not you, oh-great-one. The gods not only save your life, they bring you a woman, too. I say you are entitled to nothing but envy."

The mocking respect went unchallenged by Blake. He took another bite, chewed for a moment, then swallowed. "The gods did *not* bring me that woman. She is a widow searching for her son. Though I suspect you already knew. Your galley is a brew-pot of gossip that rivals an old biddies' quilting bee."

The friendly gibe broadened Keoni's grin, which soon faded into a serious expression. "Are you going to help her find the boy?"

"She can't very well go it alone. A woman? Unescorted? She wouldn't last a day."

"It appears that way." The cook went back to his chore in the small work space, his dark brows beetled.

"What bothers you, my friend?"

"Nothing . . ."

"You have always spoken your mind to me, Keoni.

Don't tell me you're going to let your superstitions get the better of you.''

"It is more than that." He placed the roast on a large wooden platter with cooked potatoes and carrots, adding a loaf of crusted bread.

Blake realized there was enough food to feed more than the widow Edwards, and he remembered he had not informed Keoni that the woman would dine alone. How had the thought slipped his mind as he'd stood and watched the entire preparation? He was not one to forget such simple matters. But then, he was also not one to allow errant thoughts of beautiful widows to interfere with his duties. Yet he could not seem to shake her from his mind.

"I should have told you that I have given my quarters over to our guest. Give her only the amount of food she may need, leave the rest here.''

"What about you and the mates?'' Both of them knew neither he nor Mr. Bellows and the second mate would take their meals with the crew in the forecastle.

"A table in the between decks will be suitable.''

Keoni shook his head. "Not for you.''

"What do you mean, not for me? I am the captain here.''

"And you will dine at the captain's table.'' The cook picked up the heavily laden platter as the ship's steward arrived on silent feet, instinctively on time. Jimmy was a red-haired, freckle-faced Irish lad of sixteen, eager to please and efficient as hell. The young man held out his hands to take the food from Keoni, but the cook shook his head. "This time *I* will do the honors.''

The steward glanced at Blake for direction. "Sir?''

"Humor him, James. He has more knives than we do.''

"Aye, aye, Captain,'' he answered, glancing nervously at the array of sharpened blades on the wood counter before exiting the galley.

The arrogant Kanaka appeared pleased with himself as he carried the food out the door. Passing Blake, he murmured, "You no come with me, you no eat. She can't kick you out of your very own cabin.''

"She didn't kick me out. I offered.''

"You think so?"

"I know so!"

"That's a *haole* woman for you. They have you dancing on the end of a string before you know which end is up. Don't dance to her tune, *Kaikaina*."

"I am not dancing," insisted Blake, following the aroma of the food.

Sometimes he wondered if it was worth having such a deep friendship that was so damnably unconventional by ship's standards. Despite his respected authority over the rest of his men, he could not change his obstinate Island brother.

Keoni continued to tease in his broken dialect. "Maybe you not dancing . . . yet. But maybe you tapping your toes to da music. Think so?"

"I'm not tapping my toes and there is no *music*."

The Kanaka knocked on the cabin door, then winked at Blake. "It is an ancient chant, *aikane*. As old as the earth itself."

Chapter 5

THE DOOR OPENED without so much as a single question of who might be standing outside. It could have been anyone, Blake silently fumed. Mrs. Edwards needed to be more careful, even in the relative safety of his own ship. A woman could never be too cautious.

He nodded in greeting, "Mrs. Edwards."

"Captain Masters . . ." acknowledged the widow, stepping aside to allow the two men to enter.

In the lantern light, he saw she had changed into the clean clothing, though it had been necessary to roll up the cuffs of both the trousers and the shirt. She was also barefoot, and quite comfortable to be so, it seemed. For a lady who had gone through the battering of ship and sea, she appeared to be holding up quite well, much better than he would have guessed. What kind of life had she led that could produce such a strong female—in body as well as mind?

Once again he found himself doubting her story of her past. She did not seem to fit the typical mold of a docile and domesticated wife, not that he thought all women could claim those attributes.

Keoni stepped around Blake, who had not found the momentum to move from the doorway. "Dancing fool," murmured the cook under his breath for the benefit of his captain.

"Thank you . . . Kay-oh-nee, isn't it?" The woman shaped her lips around each syllable of the name, drawing Blake's attention to her mouth. A sudden desire to kiss her swept through his head, cascading downward to the lower reaches of his body. He stifled the inappropriate sensations that churned like a whirlpool in the pit of his belly.

Grinning, Keoni answered her question. "Yes, ma'am. You said it perfectly. You must have a natural ear for language."

"Only Spanish and French," admitted the woman with too much warmth in her eyes for the Kanaka to suit Blake. His friend set the platter on the bed, then prepared the captain's table with a clean linen cloth and candles before placing the food in the center. "I *have* visited the islands, though, so I'm familiar with the pronunciation of your words."

Startled to hear this latest bit of information about the mysterious widow, Blake was about to speak up when Keoni offered, "I will teach you my native tongue, if you are interested."

"That's very nice of you," she responded as the cook lit the candles. "I wouldn't mind a few lessons while I'm here."

"Keoni, you have hungry sailors topside," reminded Blake, interrupting the courtship before he could be asked to perform vows between them as captain of the ship. When it came to women, Keoni charmed, wooed, and bedded more members of the fairer sex than any sailor on the Seven Seas. Not that Blake was envious of his Island brother. That is, not until now.

"Aye, aye, Captain." His friend turned back to Mrs. Edwards. "Let me know when you want that lesson."

"I will, Keoni. And thank you again."

"My pleasure, ma'am."

"I *said* that will be all." Blake cocked one brow in a silent reprimand. And yet he was certain he saw a smirk on the cook's face when the man turned to leave.

As the door closed, he stepped to a chair and pulled it

out for his guest. She looked at him quizzically. "Are you joining me after all?"

"With your permission."

"You already had it."

"Very well, then . . ." He gestured for her to sit down. She glanced from the seat to him, then back again. "It won't bite."

"I know." As if unaccustomed to this common courtesy, she silently lowered herself onto the chair, then folded her hands in her lap like a schoolgirl waiting for her lessons. He, on the other hand, had thoughts no schoolmaster should be considering. Her short dark hair drew his attention to the delicate nape of her neck. His hands tightened around the finials of the chair, resisting the urge to touch her, to run his finger down the slender column of her neck. He imagined leaning down and pressing his lips to her skin, tasting her, teasing her.

But he would not want to stop there, he knew. To think otherwise was to be a fool. The fantasy of her in his arms— and bed—was far too tempting. He was deceiving himself with these fantasies.

Pulling himself away from her, he went to the cupboard where he kept a few bottles of good wine and stronger spirits.

"May I offer you a glass of wine?" he asked.

"What? Oh . . . yes, wine would be nice."

Fending off his inner demons, he swallowed once to loosen the tightness in his throat. Surely it was the effect of the salt water he had swallowed. Yes, that must be the cause. And his fevered blood was also from exposure to the elements. He was fighting off a slight case of the cold. Nothing more.

"Will Keoni bring some plates and forks?" she asked as he filled two glasses. "Or do we eat with our fingers?"

"We are not barbarians." Reluctant to risk the slightest touch of warmth from her fingers, he chose not to hand her the drink but placed it on the table in front of her. "And no, Keoni is not bringing anything. My personal service is already stored here."

He went to another cupboard to retrieve plates.

Cara slowly sipped the wine, studying the captain over the rim of the glass. When she was snooping around the cabin earlier, she'd seen the dishes but couldn't let on that she knew about them. She had learned little else about Blake Masters during her search. Writing papers had shown the most recent date to be March 12, 1833, which would have been two days earlier—*if* this time here in the past correlated with her time in the future.

Other handwritten pages in his voyage journal hadn't revealed anything out of the ordinary. There were only notes about the weather, ports of call, and other bits and pieces of nautical jargon that didn't always make sense to her. Among his personal effects, she hadn't found any jewelry to use as a means to connect with his life. Even the clothing that she wore against her skin held his scent but not any other clues to his past. His shaving articles were missing, as was a brush or comb. No doubt he'd taken those with him when he moved to other quarters.

Was it so odd for a man to have nothing personal in his own cabin? He was a sailor, a vagabond. If he had no other home but this ship, he should have some kind of mementos he'd collected during his travels.

After he sat down, she waited until he took his first bite of food before picking up her fork and knife. The gentle roll of the ship tilted the wine to one side of the glasses, then the other. The candle flames seemed to follow the same motion. While shadows flickered across the paneled walls, the wooden ship creaked in slow rhythm with the subtle back-and-forth movement. The clicks of their cutlery on the china sounded like a lethargic tap-tapping of a telegraph key.

Trying to ignore the uncomfortable wall of silence between them, Cara savored the taste of the beef, then carrots, then potatoes, meticulously chewing each mouthful. Aside from the dried meat and biscuit given to her on the beach, she hadn't eaten since her dinner meal aboard the *Mystic* of 1998. While she expected to be hungry, she didn't expect the enhanced flavor of the food. Her taste buds were in heaven. Was it her hunger that made the difference? Or was it the food itself, grown in a different century in the purest process of nature? Whatever the reason, she couldn't remember eating anything quite so delicious as the simple fare of meat and potatoes.

Too bad she couldn't take the secret back to the future. She could make a killing in the restaurant business. That's if she were interested in moneymaking schemes, which she wasn't.

Right now, she had to find Andrew and get back. She cleared her mind of the wild idea of restaurants and financial deals surrounding the delectable food available in the early nineteenth century.

"Where are you from, Captain?" The question escaped her lips before she even realized she'd been contemplating it. He paused, his fork halfway to his mouth.

"Everywhere and nowhere," he answered, repeating her own earlier reply.

"Touché."

One eyebrow lifted inquisitively. "Pardon me?"

"You're making fun of me."

"I merely turned the tables, did I not? Seems fair enough to me."

She considered his comment, wondering what he would say if she *were* to tell him she had been born and raised in the very same area where they'd been washed up on the beach. Trying to think of yet another creative fabrication about her background, she relied upon memories of the eastern seaboard from a summer spent there with her Aunt Gaby.

"I was born in Philadelphia in 1799," she stated flatly, then took another drink of wine. A long one. She needed to calm her nerves, certain she was not playing this deceptive game as convincingly as she had done on past assignments. When she had learned the present year, she had calculated backward to find her own birth year in case it was necessary. Now she was glad she had. Any woman willing to reveal her age—and it was an advanced age for this time period—might be considered an honest woman.

She could only hope Captain Masters would see it that way. "And you, sir?"

Instead of answering her question, he shook his head in disbelief. "You cannot possibly be thirty-four years old. *I* am thirty, and you do not appear to be four years older than I. On the contrary, you look at least four years younger. Never mind your youthful agility, anyone can see at first glance your teeth are proof enough."

She choked. "Thank you . . . I think." As the alcohol swirled warmly through her body, she thought back to her adolescent years of orthodontia and the daily brushing with whitening toothpaste, all in the effort to attain a dazzling smile that didn't fit into this world. "Healthy teeth are a family blessing, sir. I *am* thirty-four."

"Impossible."

"It's your turn to tell me where you were born."

"I have no memory of it."

"You're not getting off so easily."

"I don't know my birthplace. And that is the truth."

Though his voice remained calm and unemotional, he cut his meat with a vengeance, slashing it into small pieces with his knife. Cara leaned back against her chair, her fingers still curled around the stemware.

"You *are* telling the truth."

He nodded, keeping his eyes on his plate, forking food into his mouth. In silence, she watched him eat for another moment or two before he became aware of her eyes on him. He tipped his head, gesturing toward her food. "Eat," he grunted with a full mouth.

Continuing with her own meal, she told herself his past was none of her business. She should drop the subject, especially since it appeared the captain was not comfortable with the discussion. She chewed the meat and swallowed, looking for a benign topic of conversation to alleviate the tension in the air, even though a gnawing in her gut pressed her to continue the difficult line of questioning. She tried to ignore it.

They were back to where they had started, eating in silence. Despite her earlier response to the delicious food, she seemed to have lost her appetite. She pushed the carrots around on her plate, picking at them now and then. Occasionally she cut a bite of meat. The gravy had congealed on top of the potatoes, making them far from appealing. But without a convenient fast-food drive-through, there was no guarantee when or if she'd get another full meal such as this one. So she forced herself to finish the food on her plate.

Inwardly, Cara sighed, knowing how much she had fouled up this first meal with the captain, intentionally or not. If she didn't make amends, he might take back his offer to stop in San Juan Capistrano.

"I'm sorry we got off to the wrong start," she offered.

He glanced up, his face unchanged. "I, too, am sorry."

Since he didn't elaborate, she speculated that he was sorry for more than his surly behavior. He was probably also regretting bringing her on board.

He was a contradiction of himself. Sometimes keeping his distance. Sometimes opening to her. But she suspected it was his curiosity that attracted him to her. After all, she was an oddity in this time period. And, as a lone woman in a world of high-testosterone males, she was undoubtedly sparking his interest on a physical level as well. She wasn't exactly immune to him either.

Still, she'd seen his pain, his unease over not knowing his origins. She wanted to help him, and she could. Her gift could allow it. And therein lay another problem—if she wasn't accepted in the Anything-Goes-1990s, she'd likely be burned as a witch in 1833.

However reluctant she was to antagonize him again, her stomach gave her the same internal nudge she'd gotten at the rancho with Andrew's father. That experience had taught her not to ignore the pain in her gut when it prodded her to do something she didn't want to do. It would only get worse until she followed the inner guidance.

"Captain, I could help you if you'd only let me—" *Read your mind*, she'd almost said. "Maybe if you talked about your past, the parts of your childhood that you *do* remember—"

"I *said* I have no memory of my early childhood. Leave it be."

"But it obviously bothers you."

"Hell, yes! I have no idea who my parents are. Or where they might be. Whether they are dead or alive. Do you know what it is like to have no knowledge whatsoever of yourself?"

"Were you hurt in a fall? Head injuries can cause amnesia."

"Blast it, woman!" He slammed his utensils onto the table, upsetting his glass of wine. A wash of red stain spread across the linen cloth, but he ignored it. "My life is none of your concern."

Cara reached across with her napkin and attempted to blot the spill, but he waved her off. She settled back into her seat, letting the napkin drop to her lap while she watched him clean up the mess.

As the ship rolled on another wave, the cabin tilted farther than before. The serving platter slid into her plate, which knocked the stem of her glass. As it toppled, she grabbed to save it. A fraction of a second too late. Instead of spilling onto the table, the red wine sloshed over the lip of the glass, arced through the air, and splattered across the surprised face of the captain.

He let loose a string of curses and mopped his face with his napkin. Then he stopped abruptly, as if remembering his manners in the presence of a woman. The glare in his blue eyes leveled on her.

She bit her lip. "I am so sorry. I tried to stop it, but I wasn't fast enough." Even though she wanted to chuckle at the absurd comedy of errors, she knew the wisest thing to do at the moment would be to respect his seriousness of the situation. After all, he was her host.

Cara didn't need extrasensory perception to know the man was livid. From the way his narrowed, accusing gaze pinned her, he obviously suspected the wine had been deliberately thrown in his face.

She held up her palm in testimony. "I swear I did not do it on purpose, Captain . . . sir." His angry stare remained unchanged. ''Honest! The boat tipped and—''

He pushed his chair back and stood, then raked his stained napkin down the front of his jacket in an attempt to clean it. The effort didn't do much good. The wine had soaked into the navy-blue wool. Turning away from the table, he shed the coat and tossed it on the bed. Standing in profile, he acted as if she weren't there and stripped off his damp shirt as well.

Growing up on sunny Southern California beaches should have made her a little more blasé about the tantalizing view of muscled biceps and pecs, not to mention the flat, tight abs on Blake Masters.

But the sudden thud of her pulse and the erotic images that flashed in her mind were anything *but* blasé.

Lord, he had an incredible body. Coming to her senses, she reined in her unexpected reaction.

His upper right arm was tattooed with a wide band of geometric shapes. Wrapping around his thick biceps, the symbols looked like something from the South Sea islands. She watched him step to the bureau, presenting his back to her.

Covering her mouth, she held back a gasp at the faded scars between his shoulder blades. The crisscross of pale lines was a shade lighter than his deeply tanned skin. Neither reddened nor puckered, the scars didn't appear to be recently acquired. Still, the thought of him enduring physical torture, however long ago, sent a shiver down her spine. Unable to look at the ugly marks without wincing, she dropped her gaze to the tattoos of black triangles and other marks that circled his waist.

Cara wondered what kind of man could be beaten so severely as to leave scars, then willingly tolerate the pain of having his skin pierced and dyed with native symbols.

Her curious thoughts evaporated as Masters lingered in front of the open drawer. From her earlier look around, Cara realized he was staring into an empty space. Apparently he had forgotten that he'd lent her his last shirt. Just as with the dishes, she couldn't say anything without revealing that she'd peeked into his private things.

"I need a shirt," he growled more to himself than to her.

"That you do." *Before I go crazy.* She imagined she could shock this 1830s man with her 1990s boldness.

He glanced around sharply. "Hasn't anyone ever told you it is not polite to stare?"

She masked her embarrassment, mimicking him with a bit of his own medicine. "Hasn't anyone ever told *you* it is not polite to strip off your shirt in front of a lady?"

"A lady? Yes. A woman masquerading as a man? No." He came over to the table with his stained shirt clenched in one hand.

Naked from the waist up, he looked like a leading actor in a classic pirate movie. Even better. Her heart did a quick-step thump-thump at the delectable sight of his sun-darkened body. Tempted to reach out and touch the dusting of dark hair on his bronze chest, she kept her hands in her lap. Out of his view, her fingers twisted the napkin into a tight knot.

"So . . ." Although she hated to admit it, his words stung. "If I am not a lady—in *your* eyes, that is—then what exactly do you think I am?"

His glower deepened. "I have not yet decided."

"I am not—" Her mind scrambled to find the proper euphemism rather than a blunt term that would sound vulgar coming from a woman. "I do not prostitute myself, sir, if that is what you are thinking."

She combed her fingers through her short hair, feeling the stickiness from the salt water. Lord, she probably looked like a punk rocker who'd spent an hour in the mosh pit.

"I may look odd," she admitted, "but given my strenuous circumstances, I hardly think impersonating a man in order to find my son should disqualify me as a lady."

The captain draped his shirt over his arm to free his hands so he could applaud. "Brava, madam."

She wasn't quite sure if he was praising her guts or her performance or both. It was difficult to listen to her intuition, thanks to the major distraction of his bare chest.

"My clothes should be dry enough by now." She rose

and went to the corner of the cabin where her shirt and trousers hung. "If you'll give me a few minutes of privacy, I can return your own shirt."

"That won't be necessary. I will borrow one from Keoni."

She looked back and her gaze zeroed in on his flat stomach. Averting her eyes was a struggle, but somehow she managed. "Would you mind doing it now? Getting the shirt that is."

"There is one slight problem, however . . ." One corner of his mouth lifted in a mischievously crooked smile. He held his arms out to the side as if she might not have noticed he was practically undressed. Fat chance! "If I leave my cabin in my present state, I might give the wrong impression to my crew regarding our private dinner engagement."

For one brief, crazy moment, she considered letting him walk out of there. She didn't care what his men thought of her. Let them spin yarns down in the fo'c'sle till dawn. Glancing at the disastrous mess of dishes and spilled wine on the table, she could easily guess the tales of torrid sex between the handsome captain and the widow woman. Her vivid imagination created an erotic picture in her mind, bringing a hot flush to her cheeks.

"Turn around," she commanded, reaching for the top button at her throat. When his gaze fell to her shaking fingers, she repeated, "I said 'turn around' . . . *sir*. My things are still damp, but I'll wrap myself in a blanket until you come back."

He gave her a lazy nod. And a slow smile. She waited, but he made no move to do as she asked. There was an invitation in the depths of his deep-blue eyes. Oh, how she wanted to accept.

Here she was in a time that wasn't her own, lusting after a man who lived—no, *lives*—nearly two hundred years before she was born. In a remote part of her mind, she wondered whether she could've suffered a bump on her head and dreamed up this ruggedly dashing stranger.

But she wasn't dreaming. She knew all of this was happening to her. Pretending it wasn't real would not make it go away. She'd learned that difficult lesson in childhood when her oddity had made her the butt of jokes and taunting remarks. While she hadn't been able to do anything to change the painful rejection, she'd eventually understood the controlling fear of the unknown. Living with her mystical gifts had taught her to accept unexplainable situations that would drive a normal person to insanity. Granted, this time-travel experience was the biggest leap she'd taken yet.

Despite her attraction to the captain, she could not risk her mission to find Andrew by falling for this man, no matter how much he made her heart pound and her knees go weak.

Don't ask of me what I can't give, Blake.

As if he'd heard her plea, he pivoted and strode to the table. Keeping his back to her, he began to clean up the mess. As he set the dishes to one side, she kept her eyes on him and unbuttoned the shirt, wondering if he would turn back around at any moment, wondering if he would prove to be a gentleman or a cad. A wild side of her that she hadn't known existed opted for the cad.

When he removed the tablecloth, she felt naughty anticipation tingle in the depths of her body. She found herself wishing, hoping he would turn around to see her slide the shirt off her shoulders.

Watching him replace the plates, she felt the cool air in the room swirl around her bare breasts and imagined the feather touch of his fingertips on her heated flesh. The seconds ticked by as he reached for the candlesticks, the last thing to put back in its proper place.

A battle raged within her. She was crazy to want a man as much as she wanted Blake right now. It was insane to jeopardize her reputation, however much he questioned her virtue. Only a whore in this day and age would have sex with a stranger. And only a fool in her own time. No, she couldn't give in to this carnal lust. And that's all it was. Not love. Not caring. Just physical craving. By God, it'd been way too long . . .

Cara quickly grabbed for the blanket, then realized to her

embarrassment that it was still on the bed. She clutched the shirt to her chest to cover herself. "Don't move. I forgot to get the blanket."

"I'll get it for you."

"No!"

He ignored her command and retrieved one of the gray woolen blankets, then held it high so it blocked his view. She slowly walked up to him and presented her bare back. His arms encircled her as the blanket came around her shoulders with a gentleness that touched her soul. His warm breath caressed the side of her neck, making her long to rest her head against him, to let him hold her in this sheltered cocoon. The moment seemed to last forever, but it was over in a single beat of her heart.

When he turned her to face him, she clutched the blanket together with one hand. With her other, she gave him the shirt.

Wordlessly, he slipped into the garment, his eyes never leaving her face. "I wish I could trust you, but I don't," he confessed, his voice taking on a sadness. "There is no one—save Keoni, perhaps—who is beyond my suspicion."

"Even me."

"Yes, especially you." His gaze traveled over her features as if trying to figure out a perplexing puzzle. "I have a feeling you are not the person you say you are."

Tamping down her own fear of being revealed, Cara reached out and touched his forearm. She had meant to console him, to find words to lessen the pain of his lost memory.

But the dark vision arose like an evil curtain. Looming. Frightening. Making her dizzy and nauseous. She couldn't show alarm. Not this time.

Keeping her tone as steady and normal as possible, she admitted, "I'd like to help you remember, if you'll let me."

"What can you possibly do?"

"Usually talking about it can trigger suppressed memories." She laced together half-truths with her little knowledge of the subject. A white lie was still better than telling

him she was going to read his past through her touch and
telepathically send it back to him.

"Suppressed memories? You have a strange vocabu-
lary."

"I picked up odd sayings in the foreign countries where
my parents were missionaries."

Easing her hand into his, she gave him a slight smile of
encouragement. "Close your eyes and try to think of a
pleasant memory in the distant past. Concentrate on the
picture and tell me what you see."

He balked, looking at her as if she were mad. "I will
not close my eyes. Nor will I indulge your curiosity."

As he stared defiantly at her, Cara felt the heat of his
palm against hers. A tingling sensation climbed up her arm
like a vibration of electricity. It wasn't what she had expected. There was a primal feeling about it. Predatory. His
desire for her swirled through her mind. Her eyelids shut
out the candlelit room as she experienced his struggle to
suppress his heated longing to claim her.

His thoughts became her thoughts. His racing heartbeat
matched its rhythm with hers. Their shaky breath synchro-
nized together as one sound. Like a moth drawn into a
dangerous flame, she could not stop her own response to
the carnal enticement.

Without a seductive word or touch, she was drawn toward him, closer and closer, until she felt her body lean
into his. He released her hand and slid his arms around her.
His mouth found hers, tentatively brushing their lips. Uncertainty quickly vanished into a deep and demanding kiss.

In her mind's eye, she saw the image of him making
love to her. Wanting desperately for it to be real, she felt
the escalating passion of their union of body and mind. On
the brink of losing all control, she knew if he were to take
her now, she would give him anything he asked and more.

His firm hands gripped her bottom, pulling her into him,
pressing his arousal against her. Cara dropped the blanket
to the floor. Emotions spiraling out of control, she ripped
at his shirt, pushing it upward until her bare breasts touched
his flesh. His moan of pleasure hummed through her veins.

Slowly she moved backward, each step bringing them closer to the bed. He kissed her eyelids, her jaw, the curve of her neck, his ragged breath echoing in her ear.

Gone was all the earlier rationale against the very thing they were about to do. Nothing else mattered right now. At this moment she didn't want to think of yesterday or tomorrow.

She didn't want to admit that they were both caught in the gripping spell of erotic telepathy.

As the back of her knees bumped the edge of the bed, she reached for the buckle of his belt. The front of his shirt slid down, hampering her mission. She frantically undid the shirt buttons, then shoved the material aside.

Her eagerness fanned the fire between them. His mouth came down harder on her own. His fingers squeezed her buttocks with both pain and pleasure.

She reached once more for his belt, slipping it through the buckle with a slap of leather.

He reacted to the sound as if it were the sharp report of a pistol shot.

She felt him go rigid, *saw* his emotion in the dark swirl of his mind. Her eyes sprang open—too late to stop what had already been set in motion.

He shoved her backward onto the bed and dropped onto her with a force that knocked the wind from her lungs. Pinning her wrists over her head with one hand, he yanked at her belt with a force that nearly ripped the leather in half.

Startled and frightened, she looked up into his eyes. They weren't seeing her. They were black as midnight. Angry. Vengeful.

"Blake, don't—" Squirming beneath him, she pulled her hands free and pushed against his shoulders.

The images bombarded her, rolling in wave after sickening wave.

In her mind she suddenly saw a squalid, candlelit room. Looking down from above, she could see the dark-haired boy. Blake. No more than ten or twelve. Dressed only in short trousers, nothing more. His back flogged and bloodied. Crawling away. Glancing back with terror in his eyes.

Out of the shadows came a cloaked demon. The boy scrambled to escape, only to be dragged backward, his hands clawing at the floor.

No! Oh, dear God, No! Cara squeezed her eyes shut, trying to block the vision of the boy being stripped of his clothing. But she couldn't stop it. She saw it all. Sobs of pain erupted from her throat.

"BLAKE . . . !" cried Cara, reaching through the black fog of his hideously grotesque memory. Instead of fighting him, she wrapped her arms around him, held him tight against her.

"Don't do it, Blake," she whispered between choking tears. "Don't hurt me the way you were hurt."

Chapter 6

THE BRUTAL VIOLENCE ended as abruptly as it began. Blake's tense body collapsed onto her. He breathed in great gulps of air, his chest pressing down upon her breasts.

Cara held him until she felt his heartbeat slow to normal. He silently shoved himself off her and got up from the bed, turning away in shame and humiliation. "I can never apologize enough for what I have done."

"I'm unhurt. And you stopped before—"

"There's no excuse for my behavior. I don't know what came over me."

"You were reliving your past, taking out all the hurt and anger and revenge."

Caught up in his own private hell—the hell she'd witnessed—he wasn't hearing her. "How can you ever forgive me?"

"It wasn't me you were trying to hurt, Blake. I saw it in your eyes. You didn't know it was me."

He gave her a bewildered look. "You're talking nonsense."

"You don't remember it, do you?" she asked him as he buttoned his shirt, tucked it into his trousers, and fastened his belt. "You were abused as a child, Blake."

"Those are ludicrous speculations." He spoke barely loud enough for her to hear. "I told you I remember nothing."

"Even now?"

"Even now."

Since they were no longer touching, she couldn't be certain if he was telling the truth or lying to cover his shame.

"I will return with this shirt as soon as I borrow another from Keoni." As he started toward the portal, he said over his shoulder, "Lock the door when I leave."

Surprised by his lack of trust in his crew, she tried to make light of his warning. "And when you return, what will be your special signal so I know it's you?"

"Two short knocks, a pause, then a third."

"I was only joking."

"And I am not."

An icy finger of dread traced a wicked line down her spine. "In that case, hurry back."

"I will."

She started toward the portal to lock it as he had asked, picking up the blanket on her way. As she wrapped herself in it again, the door popped open, startling her. It was only Blake, much to her relief.

"Inside, Bud," he ordered softly. Without so much as asking her if she wanted the protection of his huge black dog, he let Bud enter the cabin, glancing at her with an odd expression of apology, pain, and confusion.

And suspicion.

Then he closed the door a second time. His voice came back from the other side of the wooden planks. "Lock it anyway."

Doing as he asked, she shoved the iron bolt with the base of her palm, then looked down at her bodyguard sitting at her feet.

"So you're supposed to protect me, huh, boy?"

Bud's tail slowly wagged back and forth, sweeping the polished floor. From the size and shape of his large head, he appeared to be a Labrador retriever, but she wasn't sure the breed had been introduced in America yet. The captain might easily have picked up a puppy in his travels, though. It was a beautiful dog with soulful dark-brown eyes. He had an intelligent face, too. She had a special affinity for

four-legged creatures, most of whom possessed more unconditional love and compassion than many of the two-
legged variety.

As the dog seemed to smile at her, she spoke to him with
a playfulness she didn't quite feel. "I suppose your master
taught you how to look sweet and innocent. I bet you aren't
interested in me at all at this moment. You're just hoping
you'll get some leftovers."

His tail thump-thumped, sounding a little like the way
her heart pounded when Blake . . . Captain Masters, that is.
Aw, hell, who was she kidding? Considering the way things
had nearly gotten out of hand a few minutes earlier, she
may as well be on a first-name basis with the man.

"Okay, Bud, I'll feed you." With the blanket wrapped
around her, she plopped down at her seat and offered him
a small bit of beef from her plate. Despite the dog's eagerness, he gingerly took the tidbit from her fingers.
"Somebody taught you some manners."

The dog gazed up at her expectantly. She scratched him
behind his ear with one hand as she offered more food with
the other. He had a calming effect on her.

Unlike his master.

The way things were going, she wondered if she would
be able to hold off her own lust for the two days it would
take to get to San Diego. As it was, she had hardly made
it past dinner.

Her gaze flitted to Blake's stained jacket lying at the head
of the disheveled bed. What had happened there played out
fresh in her mind. What had *almost* happened sent a shudder through her tired body. It wasn't fear or horror she felt,
but a deep sadness for the captain who had very nearly
raped her when she had been so willing to give him the
tenderness and compassion he really wanted, really needed.

Was this how he treated every woman he bedded? No,
she couldn't believe it. This Jekyll-and-Hyde behavior was
not the real Blake Masters. From the shock and confusion
on his face, she knew he had been as surprised as she. Her
questions about the past, her insistence on conjuring up a
memory had triggered the darkness in him.

Now that she had pushed him to open that door, would he begin to remember more? Would he have another lapse into violence, more overpowering than this time?

Exhausted tears stung the back of her eyes. She felt completely overwhelmed by her situation—caught in a world that wasn't her own, uncertain if she would find Andrew, not knowing if she could get home. And now, of all times, her dormant hormones were sounding a bugle call.

The dog nudged her hand with his nose. Looking down at Bud, she sighed heavily. "If you're here to protect me from the crew, who's to protect me from the captain?"

Or the captain from me?

Several minutes passed before two knocks at the door of the captain's cabin drew Cara's attention away from the dog. Bud got up and trotted to the door, then looked back at her.

"He said three," she reminded the Labrador as the third rap echoed through the small room. "See?"

Bud seemed to understand perfectly, turning back to stare intently at the door while she went over to unlock it. With the blanket wrapped around her, she needed to be extra careful to keep out of sight of any of the crew who might be able to see into the cabin. Staying behind the door, she opened it wide for Blake to enter.

"That was quick, Captain—Keoni?"

The cook chuckled. "Captain Keoni, hmmm? Sounds good. Maybe I give up da cookin', eh? Put on da blue jacket and maybe I get a ship of my own."

Her head popped around the edge of the door to look behind the cook. "Where's Captain Masters?"

"Not here."

"I realize that," she said, slightly exasperated with his all-too-obvious remark. He held up the shirt. She eyed it dubiously from the relative safety of the backside of the door. "Why didn't he return it himself?"

"Maybe not good idea. Think so?"

His pidgin English irritated her, especially since she had heard him speak so eloquently earlier. She reached out and took the shirt from him. "Tell your *haole*-captain that this *wahine* thanks him for the hospitality."

Her comeback quip brought out a huge belly laugh in the Kanaka. "*Haole? Wahine?* Good, Mrs. Edwards. Very good."

"I'm glad you approve. Now if you'll excuse me . . ." She began to close the door, but he stopped her. "Is there something else? A message from the captain, perhaps?"

Despite his warm smile, Keoni seemed to lose a bit of the humor in his dark eyes. "Captain Masters conveyed his apologies and wished you a good evening."

"I see." She *did* understand his avoiding her, but knowing this didn't stop the part of her that felt the sting of his rejection. Something had happened between them that was more than physical, more than lust. She had reached through the darkness and touched the depths of his soul, if only for a brief instant. It frightened him. And her.

"Mrs. Edwards? If you don't mind, I need to collect the dishes."

"Of course." Brought back from her thoughts of Blake, she noticed Keoni had dropped the heavy accent of the islands. "Just give me a minute."

After putting on the shirt, Cara let Keoni inside the cabin to collect the plates, waiting at the open doorway. Bud followed him to the table, obviously hoping for more meat to be thrown his way.

The cook shook his finger at the dog. "*E hele aku 'oe i kahi 'ē!*"

Bud tucked his tail and slunk over to her. She leaned down to console the animal. "What did you say to him?"

"I told him he will be on this platter tomorrow night."

"You didn't!" She blanched, then looked up at him as she covered the dog's ears. "Tonight's dinner? That wasn't . . . ?"

"'*Īlio*? Dog-meat?" The Kanaka gave her an impish grin.

"*Īlio* good eating."

"Keoni!" Her stomach churned up more than acid indigestion at the possibility that she had eaten one of man's best friends. "Tell me you're lying. Please!"

"Aww—," he scoffed playfully. "You know how to ruin good joke, lady."

Cara straightened and walked over to the Hawaiian. He was a good six inches taller than Blake, so she had to tip her head back to look up at him. "Don't do that to me again, Keoni."

The grin remained on his face. "You one tough *wahine*, eh?"

"When it's necessary."

"Not necessary with me."

"Oh, I think it's *mandatory* with you."

His laughter nearly caused him to drop the dishes in his hands. Chuckling to himself, he set the stacked dishes back down on the table. "Sit. We talk. Get to know each other betta, eh?"

Initially suspicious of his underlying meaning, she gazed into his open face and realized that Keoni was more than a big, handsome Hawaiian with a charming smile and an extra-large dose of self-confidence. Despite the glint of flirtation in his black eyes, she did not feel threatened that he would behave inappropriately toward her. Beyond the taunt and tease, he was respectful of her. Of *all* women, she sensed.

She stepped back and gestured with a flip of her hand for him to sit down. But she was too restless to take a seat. Instead, she walked over to one of the tiny windows and looked out upon the darkened sea. The sun had gone down, but she hadn't noticed when.

"What time is it, Keoni?"

"Six bells, ma'am. That would be seven o'clock to you." His voice came to her in a softer, gentler tone. She glanced back, noticing he hadn't opted for a chair either. Instead he had perched one hip on the edge of the table, his arms folded across his barrel chest. The sleeves of his shirt were rolled up, revealing a glimpse of bluish marks on his skin.

She shifted about to face him. "Is that a tattoo like the captain's?"

He nodded. "It is."

"You two go back a ways together, don't you?"

"We do."

"I thought you said you wanted to talk. Now all I can get out of you are a couple words."

"I want to get to know you. You get to know me. I didn't say I would help you get to know my *kaikaina*."

"Why do you call him that? What does it mean?"

" 'Little brother.' "

"He's not, is he?"

"A Kanaka? Would that make a difference to you?"

"Of course not. And if you knew me, you'd know I don't judge people by their race or color."

His big shoulders lifted in a shrug. "Tell me more about you, then. I want to know the mysterious widow who washed up on shore."

"Why? So you can report back to Blake—uh, Captain Masters?"

Her slip did not go unnoticed. The Kanaka grinned. "So I can *protect* Blake, Mrs. Edwards."

"From me?"

"Yes."

She felt a guilty flush because that had been her recent thought, too. "I'm not here to hurt him. He brought me on board to help me find Andrew."

"So he told me." His eyes were steady. Direct. "Your son is missing."

"Yes."

"And when we find him, you will leave."

"I . . . um, of course. Yes, I plan to return home with Andrew." She eyed him from across the cabin, wondering what he was really thinking. Keoni had a strong mind. It was as if an impenetrable wall was shielding his thoughts from her. Whether he was practiced at this sort of blocking technique or he came by it naturally Cara couldn't be sure. But she was sure he was not someone she could easily read.

"Okay, you win." She threw up her hands in defeat. "I'm a notorious pirate, La Grande Femme, who heads a band of cutthroat men from the dregs of the earth. Now that my secret is out, you can take me back to my secret island and I'll split all my plundered riches with you. There, how's that for a colorful history?''

"Good bedtime story." Smiling, he pushed away from the table, picked up the dishes, and walked toward the door. "I will be back later to see if you need anything else before I turn in for the night.''

"I hope you keep your promises better than your captain does.''

"Mo'betta." He winked. With a short whistle for the dog to follow, he stepped out of the cabin.

"When you come back later, will you leave Bud with me for the night?''

"I'll post him outside your door.''

"Actually, I'd rather have him inside the cabin with me''— Keeping a straight face, she looked at Keoni—"just so I won't worry about him ending up on the breakfast menu.''

Laughing at her gibe, he closed the door behind him, then tapped lightly and reminded her to lock it.

"I know, I know,'' muttered Cara, doing as she was instructed. After securing the bolt, she slowly turned and leaned back against the wooden door.

The ship creaked and groaned around her as she tipped her head back, closing her eyes. Her mind relived the turmoil of the last twenty-four hours. Flashes of memory assailed her. Feelings of fear, terror, sadness.

Nothing in her life had prepared her for this experience. Despite her acceptance of psychic phenomena, she had never believed she would ever travel through time except perhaps in her dreams. And in her own fantasy world, she'd never considered the feeling of isolation from all that is known and familiar.

An undercurrent of despair rose like incoming tidewaters, threatening her strong grip on the hope she carried with her—hope of finding Andrew, hope of taking him back to his family.

Pressing her palms to her closed lids to push back the

melancholy speculation of an uncertain future, she vowed to herself, ''I can't give up hope.''

Not now.

Not ever.

Under a canopy of high clouds the following morning, Blake stood on the quarterdeck at dawn, watching several humpback whales half a mile or so off the leeward side of the ship, following the southward course of the *Valiant*. Not even the graceful gray giants could lift his spirits. He'd been in a foul mood all night, unable to sleep in the cramped and unfamiliar berth of the first mate, who'd been bumped to the second mate's cabin.

They had made good time to San Juan, and were about to anchor a good distance from the rocky shore. Mr. Bellows handled the crew with speed and efficiency, carrying out orders with little need for the captain of the ship to be disturbed.

Walking toward the bow, Blake kept a watchful eye on the weather. Even under the best of conditions, landing here had always proved difficult. The stiff offshore breeze churned froth from the choppy waves, promising a challenging time in the longboat for the oarsmen.

It was still the middle of the season for southeasters, which would put them in danger if another storm surprised them, as had been the case in San Pedro.

He scanned the overcast skies, questioning his agreement to take Mrs. Edwards to the mission.

There was much that he questioned about his actions concerning the mysterious widow, especially his gross loss of control in his cabin. All night long he had called himself every form of despicable, lowly creature on this earth and beyond.

To make matters worse, she'd *forgiven* him. Not a single venomous word of reproach had come from her. By God, she had even made up excuses for his abominable behavior! Wild, irrational excuses that made no sense to him. No sense whatsoever.

For the life of him, he could not figure out why she

didn't hate him outright. Any other woman would have screamed at him, hit him, thrown half a dozen dishes at him. But not her. No, she had held him to her breast, soothing the dark beast within him—the beast he did not understand.

Thankfully, he had come to his senses before—

"Captain?"

At the sound of her voice behind him, he spun about and found her not three feet away, with Bud sitting obediently at her side. She was wearing her own clothing—shoes, trousers that fit, and the dingy shirt with loose sleeves that rippled in the chill wind. Despite her unfeminine dress, her dark beauty struck him silent for a brief moment.

He wanted this woman.

The intensity of his desire ripped through him like a whaler's harpoon, piercing his chest, his heart, his lungs—defying all reason. He wanted her as he had wanted no other woman. In that instant, he did not care a whit about her past, her questionable stories, or anything else.

Keoni had teased him about dancing to her tune. Hell, he would waltz on air if that was what it took to have her in his bed.

Suddenly, the memory of his brutality surfaced like a monster from the deep. After what he had done, he did not deserve her.

Self-loathing filled him. The muscles in his jaw tightened as he battled back the demon in his mind. He addressed her with a shortness of temper that was not meant to be directed toward her. "What are you doing on deck?"

"I needed fresh air."

If his curt greeting offended her, she did not show it in the least. Instead, she turned her face to the wind, closed her eyes, and drew in a deep breath as though she were smelling a sweet bouquet of roses.

Sighing contentedly, she opened her eyes and looked out across the water. "I absolutely love the ocean," she said without taking her gaze from the seascape. "Oh, look . . . whales! I've never seen so many in my life!"

His heart swelled in his chest. Watching her, he marveled

at her rejuvenation. She was hale and hearty despite her brush with death—and his own violence. He found himself in awe of her strength.

Out of the corner of his eye, he noticed the crew had slowed their work, darting furtive glances toward their passenger. The fact that she was a woman was no secret, even if she did dress in the clothing of one of their own kind. They were a moral lot of ablebodied seamen who would not likely overstep their bounds with Mrs. Edwards. But Blake could not be completely certain.

As captain of the *Valiant*, he was known for his fairminded treatment of his crew, though not for any degree of warmth or sentimentality. He was respected and admired. The Kānaka were the only ones to almost entirely ignore his rank as chief officer on the vessel, often trying to joke with him.

But they all knew the consequences of crossing the line with him. Torture was out of the question. However, insubordination meant being left at a foreign port to find passage home on another merchant ship, possibly with a captain as sadistic as Johnson, of the fateful *Mystic*.

Blake barked, ''Mr. Bellows, see to it McGinty and his mates keep their eyes on the sails.''

''Aye, aye, sir!'' The mate turned back to the crew, shouting reprimands for their sluggishness. The dawdlers scrambled to the task, knowing the first mate would have them on double duty soon enough if they failed to meet his standards.

Still agitated with his men, Blake turned back to Mrs. Edwards. ''I told you to stay below.''

''Aren't we going to Capistrano?''

''After breakfast,'' he answered brusquely, unaccustomed to having his orders ignored. He wanted her out of sight as much as possible.

''Will you join me?''

''No . . . thank you.'' He lowered his voice so it would not carry beyond the two of them. ''And you know why.''

She stepped closer. ''I'm not afraid of you, Blake.''

He stood his ground. ''You should be.''

The stiff breeze ruffled her short hair. She wrapped her arms around herself to ward off the cold. Her luminous dark eyes gazed up at him. "You are a good man."

"You don't know me."

"Yes, I do. More than you realize." His steward passed within earshot, causing her to pause. She smiled warmly at Jimmy. Blake glared at him. The young fellow hurried by, but not before stumbling over his own feet, then righting himself.

"See what you cause?"

"I only smiled, for crying out loud."

"Yes. My point exactly."

"What point? I can't be pleasant with another human being?"

"You are a distraction, madam." *To them and to me.* He gestured with his hand for her to proceed ahead of him. "Allow me to escort you back to my—to *your* cabin."

"I know the way."

Obviously fuming, she marched off with his dog at her heels, leaving him standing in the wake of her anger. Good. He would much rather deal with her in a full pique. He deserved her ire, not her soft-spoken sympathy. He felt mean-spirited, though, for ruining her innocent, glorious excitement over seeing the whales.

"Damn it all to hell," he muttered as he strode the short distance to the railing, half tempted to pitch himself overboard. Swept up in a maelstrom of feelings surrounding the mysterious woman, he didn't know from one minute to the next which would pop to the forefront of his mind. Whether it was his desire for her or his hatred of himself, he was at the mercy of the moment. If others were to know the confusion in his head, they would wonder if he was going mad.

Perhaps he was.

With an angry shake of his head, he called out to his steward, "Jimmy, have the cook put some food together for my immediate departure."

"Aye, aye, sir," answered the boy, dashing off toward the galley.

"Mr. Bellows, ready the boats!"

The first mate responded in voice and action.

Restless to get started, Blake made his way down to his cabin and pounded on the door. Receiving no response, he knocked again. Still no answer.

Where is she? A small amount of concern accompanied his curiosity. He had seen her come down here only moments earlier. Or had he? When she'd walked away, he had stepped to the railing. Perhaps she had disobeyed his order. Again. Where would she have gone?

The galley, of course, he thought to himself, recalling the camaraderie between her and Keoni. Jealousy pricked at his worrisome thoughts regarding her safety. If she was biding her time with his friend, there would be hell to pay.

He pounded harder this time. "Mrs. Edwards!"

"That's not the signal," she said petulantly from the other side. "Two knocks, then a pause, and a third."

"I was only testing you," he lied, having forgotten his own instructions from the night before. In spite of his dark mood, he could not help but grin at her refusal to answer the door. It also seemed his own foolish jealousy had been unfounded.

He heard her unbolt the door, then saw her face as she opened it. "What do you want?"

"I've changed my mind . . . we're leaving. Now."

"What about breakfast?"

"Considering the ride will be rough, anything you eat now would have a difficult time staying down. It would be best to take something along and eat it when we land."

"Salt beef and biscuits?"

"If so, we can manage to survive long enough to have a decent meal at the mission. It's only a mile from shore. I promise you won't starve."

She arched her brow. "Like your promise last night?"

"No." His sharp retort further provoked her sassy tongue.

"I'm not trying to be difficult, Captain."

"Trying or not, you have certainly succeeded."

"I haven't *done* anything!"

"Mrs. Edwards . . ." Blake reined in his temper once

more. "Can we possibly carry on a rational conversation without sparring with one another for the duration of our time together?"

In lengthy silence, he endured her studied gaze upon him, resisting the impulse to shift his stance like a recalcitrant student under the scrutiny of a disciplining schoolmistress.

Finally she spoke, her voice softened considerably. "It seems I can do nothing right in your eyes, Captain Masters. My mere existence appears to be an aggravation to you. I am sorry you have been forced into a position of responsibility for my safety. If I could somehow change our circumstances, I would. So for now"—she looked heavenward in divine supplication—"I *will* try extra hard to stay out of your way, to do as I'm told, and to not talk unless spoken to . . ."

Blake interrupted her as she was taking a breath to continue. "Let's just start with those three, Mrs. Edwards, shall we?"

Her mouth snapped shut.

"Very good. Are you ready to leave now?"

She nodded, already complying with her promise not to talk. He stifled the urge to smile. Confound her anyway. It was impossible to stay angry with the woman.

And yet at some deep level of knowing, he suspected it would be better if he could.

Chapter 7

CARA BRAVED THE harrowing trip to shore in the longboat, wishing she could man one of the oars so she would feel a little more in control of her situation. A few years earlier, white-water rafting with Mark had taught her how to handle even the most dangerous level-four rivers. While today's experience didn't measure up to the same degree of danger, it was a challenge to the Sandwich Islanders, who were pulling them toward land against a nasty headwind and waves breaking over the bow.

No words were spoken except orders given by Blake, who sat next to her in the stern. Though he had chosen the four Kānaka for their incomparable skill as oarsmen, he had forewarned her of the rough sea conditions they would encounter. She had been willing to take the risk. Now she understood his concern.

Jostled by another wave, she tightened her grip on the gunwale and the seat as salt water sprayed her face. She swiped her hand across her eyes, thankful she hadn't eaten breakfast. Even her empty stomach felt queasy. Beside her, Blake kept his balance better than she did.

Not much better, she realized, aware of every bump of their shoulders, every brush of their thighs. In spite of the animosity between them, her body reacted to his closeness like a sensitive car alarm that beeped, whooped, and buzzed at the slightest disturbance.

The ominous cliffs grew closer, larger, and more fore-boding, taking her mind off Blake, if only temporarily. She cast her gaze up and down the rocky coastline, wondering where they would find a place to put to shore. It looked inaccessible.

She looked at the stoic captain. His jaw was set. His eyes squinted into the wind. He glanced her way, barely ac-knowledging her silent concern before returning his atten-tion to steering the boat. With his gaze focused on one point ahead, he obviously knew the course to his destination.

Trying to see what he was seeing, she stifled the urge to ask questions, remembering her promise to say as little as possible and stay out of his way.

Soon she realized they were headed into a small cove. The oarsmen rowed the boat toward a narrow strip of sand in the shadow of the thirty-foot cliffs. She craned her neck to see the dizzying height nearly straight overhead. Birds of all different sizes flew in and out of nests in the crevices. Soaring on widespread wings, they were outlined against the gray ceiling of high clouds. The high-pitched screeches of the gulls and the calls of the other birds were all but drowned out by the echoes of crashing waves.

Feeling a little light-headed, she dropped her gaze to the shore ahead of them. A couple of deep breaths revitalized her. Maybe it was just a case of low blood sugar. Once her feet were on terra firma again, she might feel like eating some of the food Blake had brought along.

Upon landing, she followed his lead and lightly vaulted out of the boat, grateful to have her equilibrium fully re-stored. When he turned to find her directly behind him, he started.

She grinned smugly, and a frown creased his forehead as he noticed his Kānaka crewmen gaping at her. When one said something in his foreign tongue, they all laughed approvingly.

Okay, so her leap to the beach wasn't exactly ladylike. She wasn't here to play a helpless female in petticoats and crinoline who needed to be hoisted off the boat by a couple of strong men. She had to get it across to them that she was as agile and capable of handling herself in this harsh environment as they were.

"Lopaka!" Blake raised his voice over the loud surf. "We'll be back here by late afternoon. Be waiting for us."

"Aye, aye, Cap'nee."

Cara grabbed Blake's sleeve, breaking her short-lived vow to keep her distance. "Why aren't they staying here?"

With disdain in his eyes, he looked down at her hand until she dropped it to her side.

"They are needed on the *Valiant*."

Lopaka waved, then spoke to his dark-skinned brothers in their native language. Chattering among themselves, the four men launched the longboat back out to sea. Clearly, their serious mood had lifted. Probably because she was no longer on board.

"Why did you send them back?"

Answering loudly to be heard over the crashing surf, he watched the Kānaka pulling their oars in unison through the choppy waves. "There's always a risk of the wind changing direction suddenly and sending us another south-easter. We still have another month to six weeks to go of this season. Until then, we cannot be too careful. It's best if my ship has a full crew aboard."

Cara glanced at the gloomy skies. "I guess I should consider myself lucky to be on land."

"If we were in San Diego or Monterey, I would agree. But I never should have risked the *Valiant* or my crew by stopping here today. This particular stretch of the California coast is one of the most treacherous right now."

A twinge of guilt plucked at her conscience. "Then why did you offer?"

"A poor decision made in haste. It was a promise I should not have tried to keep."

Considering her earlier remarks about his unkept promise to her the previous night, she wondered if he had put their lives at stake because she'd goaded him.

"Then we'd better get going so we can get back to your ship before nightfall," she responded, unwilling to be associated with a second shipwreck in the superstitious sailors' minds. Her stomach complained, prompting her to ask about breakfast.

"The rising tide will soon cover most of this beach. We need to climb first, then eat."

She looked up and down the thin ribbon of pebbly beach. "Which direction?"

He swung the leather bag over his shoulder, then pointed south. "There is a circuitous path that leads to the top."

"Good." Relief crept over her. "I was afraid you were going to say we had to scale the face of this cliff."

"At times it may feel that way to you."

"Don't worry about me, Captain. I'm capable of keeping up with you."

"I'm sure you are." His deep voice almost roared over the sound of the sea pounding the rocks. Water spouted from a natural funnel hole in one of the nearby boulders, sending an impressive geyser into the air. "The tide is coming in. We had better move."

A few yards down the beach, the obscure trail ascended the steep bluffs like the path of a surefooted mountain goat. More than a few times, Cara thought they had lost sight of the route, which seemed barely as wide as one man's shoe. They crab-walked over several slippery faces of huge granite slabs, searching patiently for tiny outcroppings to use as toeholds and fingerholds. Cara observed Blake's progress, making sure to remember the places where his boot lost its footing on a loose section of boulder so she could avoid the same misstep when she reached that spot on her climb.

Despite the overcast skies, she was soon damp with perspiration from her exertion. Her throat felt dry and cottony. Their position on the bluffs kept them sheltered from the cold winds coming off the mainland, which was a minor blessing.

When the rocks weren't giving them trouble, they were hindered by brier and prickly pear. For a while she managed to get past them, then one thorn finally snagged her pants. Yanking her leg away proved futile. Her effort only caused more scratches from the sharp barbs. Leaning down to pull the cotton duck out of the claws of the bushes, she felt a thorn stab the back of her hand.

"Ow—! Dammit!" She shot up and sucked on her knuckle, trying to alleviate the stinging pain. The sudden movement caused a swirling head rush, momentarily blacking out her eyesight. Breathing heavily from the hard climb, she tried to hold perfectly still and wait for the dizzy sensation to pass. A moment later she was fine.

"Do you need help, Mrs. Edwards?" called Blake from his position several feet ahead. His formality agitated her as much as having to admit she needed his assistance.

"Yes!" she reluctantly shouted up to him, then sucked on her sore scratch again. Man, it hurt like the devil.

He ordered, "Stay there."

"As if I have a choice," she muttered into her hand.

Almost immediately, he lost his balance, flinging their bag of breakfast high into the air. Nearly breaking his neck in his sudden slide down the hill, he landed in front of her, while the bag ended up a few feet away. It was all Cara could do to maintain her own balance and not fall headfirst into the brier patch. Curses flew like a swarm of angry bees.

Panting and sweating, he got up and dusted himself off with a few aggressive swats at his stained jacket and pants. The action didn't do much good. The rain-dampened soil stuck to the knees of his britches and smudged the wine stain on his jacket.

"Hold still," she said calmly, her voice quieter now that they were high above the thunderous sound of the surf. He paused, looking at her. She reached out and gently drew her fingertips across his cheekbone. His thick, dark eyelashes fluttered as he jerked back from her. He might as well have shouted, "Don't touch!"

She held up her hand to show him the mud on her fingers.

He glanced down at it, then at her. No words were exchanged. He understood her intent and appeared appropriately sheepish for his skittish reaction.

"We'd get through this a lot easier if you weren't so jumpy and standoffish," she said cautiously.

"I shall keep that in mind."

His gaze dropped to her snagged clothing. Kneeling down, he slowly and carefully plucked a number of thorns from the cloth. Lifting the cuff of her pants to inspect her calf, his fingertips grazed her skin, sending a spiral of warmth up into her body.

Good Lord, why did she have to react to him as if everything was a sexual advance? She was a modern woman of the 1990s, yet she practically swooned from a brush of his knuckles against her ankle.

"You have some deep scratches," he said with a gentleness she hadn't expected. "We'll have to wait until we reach the mission before we can treat them. Do you think you can last that long?"

He gazed up at her with worry in his ocean-blue eyes. Even though she'd had several moments to rest, her breathing was as shallow now as it had been during their strenuous climb.

"I won't faint from the pain, if that's what you mean." She wanted to sound flippant. She wanted him to think she was still irritated with his earlier behavior. She wanted to keep her armor in place, protecting herself from the attraction between them.

But Blake seemed to see through it all—the glib remark, the dissipated irritation, the weak resolve to shield her emotions.

He stood up. "I believe you can do anything you set your mind to."

"I usually do."

His hands wrapped around her upper arms, gently kneading the muscles. "You are strong for a woman. Stronger than I had imagined."

"I . . . uh, I *like* to exercise," she answered lamely, not quite certain how to explain that a private investigator couldn't be an out-of-shape couch potato and still climb over a chain-link fence or outrun a Doberman guard dog. "I'm not exactly the type to sit and knit sweaters. I enjoy strenuous activity. Keeps me healthy. And in shape. Strong, that is. Just lucky that way, I guess."

"Rather like your teeth?"

"My teeth?" Suddenly remembering their conversation about white teeth running in her family, she quickly agreed, "Yes, I come from a *very* healthy family."

He cocked one eyebrow skeptically.

She knew he didn't believe her. Growing uncomfortable with his intent gaze, she moved out of his embrace. "I've been injured before," she explained, reassuring him. "Worse than this, actually. It's only a scratch. I'll live."

"Very well, then. Shall we continue? It is not much further to the top."

In a matter of a few minutes they stood on the crest of the cliffs, their backs to the Pacific. A mile or so across the flat, arid landscape, Cara recognized the first familiar sight since her leap backward in time.

The famous Mission San Juan Capistrano.

Alone on the land, not yet crowded by a twentieth-century city, the solitary mission was a poignant reminder of her bittersweet visits to the historical landmark as a little girl. Every year, Aunt Gabriella had taken Cara to celebrate the return of the swallows on St. Joseph's Day. During the long drive, her great-aunt told stories of the Spaniards, one of whom had become her own forefather. She'd also described the plight of their Indian ancestors who were pressed into the service of the church.

In those conversations with her aunt, Cara had learned her family's secret—her Indian heritage, her silent link to the proud natives of this dry and desolate land. Now she felt drawn toward the small huts surrounding the white mission building. These people were a part of her own ancestry, some of them with the same blood in their veins as her own.

A lump formed in her throat. Realizing that she would soon be walking among them, she fervently wished her Aunt Gaby could be with her now, not only to share in this deeply spiritual experience but also to share her wisdom of the supernatural world.

If only you were here to guide me, Aunt Gaby. I could really use your help.

Estoy aquí, mi Cara.

The sound of her aunt's voice in her mind startled Cara. But she had distinctly heard the Spanish words for "I am here, my Cara."

"Aunt Gaby?"

"Mrs. Edwards?" The captain's voice sounded like a distant echo. Yet he must have been standing beside her because she felt his hands lightly grasp her shoulders to support her. "You are white as a ghost."

"Wh-what?" She raised her fingers to her forehead, then realized her hand was shaking.

"You called out to your aunt. Are you feeling light-headed?"

Her knees weakened. "I-I guess I am."

His grip tightened just as her legs gave out under her. In a peculiar slow motion, she felt her entire body melting into a dark liquid oblivion.

From a far corner of her awareness, she heard a hoarse whisper of stunned desperation, "Dear-God-in-Heaven . . ."

Blake? Her mind called his name, but her voice was silent.

"Cara? *Cara!*"

Help me, Blake.

The mile to the mission seemed like a thousand as Blake rushed with Cara in his arms. His long strides quickly sapped the remaining strength from his muscles, already strained from their climb up the cliff. Ignoring the searing pain in his thighs, he picked up his pace. Her limbs bounced lifelessly.

Time and again he took his eyes off the ground ahead of him and glanced down into her ashen face, wondering if she was alive or dead. He didn't dare stop to find out.

What could have caused this? She had been fine only moments before her collapse. Was it merely exhaustion? Then he recalled her encounter with the briers.

It's only a scratch, she had said.

I'll live, she had said.

Her sassy sarcasm taunted him now as he berated himself for not taking notice of the thorny shrubs. Perhaps they were a poisonous variety. Or perhaps they were not the cause at all.

What if she had disturbed a rattlesnake under the dry bushes? What if the rustle of the branches had masked the sound of the rattles? What if she had mistaken the slash of venomous fangs for the painful scratch of a thorn?

"No—!" shouted Blake, breaking into a run, driving his fears from his mind. He fought off the demons as he fought for every breath, sucking air into his burning lungs.

In the distance, an Indian woman standing outside a crude hut turned at the sound of his cry. Startled by his approach, she dashed toward the mission doors. By the time he reached the steps, the Catholic priest had appeared with two Indian men.

"*Buenos días, capitán,*" greeted the gray-cloaked *padre,* eyeing Cara with suspicion.

"*¡Socorro, por favor!*" Blake said, asking for help with the few words he knew in the Spanish language.

"*¿Es contagioso?*" Contagious disease was an understandable fear for the Reverend Father, who was unwilling to lose more workers.

"No," answered Blake. "No con-ta-hee-OH-so. Her leg"—he nodded toward her dangling legs—"has many cuts. Maybe a snakebite."

His English reply was met with skepticism. His mind grappled for a rough translation. "*La pierna. Mas corta-dura.*"

The slender priest acquiesced. "*Adelante.*" Come in, he said, then spoke to his helpers, saying something about the "boy."

When the two men advanced with their arms outstretched to take Cara, Blake shook his head, refusing to relinquish her. With a curt nod, he gestured for them to lead the way so he could follow.

Within a few minutes, he lowered Cara to a shabby pallet in the corner of a squalid adobe-walled room with a high, small window. In the dim light, he couldn't determine her skin color, but he knew it could not have improved from the last time he'd checked.

Hovering nearby, the priest asked him what had happened to the child.

"Señora," corrected Blake, watching her, wishing for the smallest flutter of her dark eyelashes. The sound of the padre's shock did not surprise him.

He gently brushed his hand across her forehead. She was cold and clammy. Lowering his ear to her breast, he listened for her heartbeat. For a brief moment of panic, he could not hear anything but the rush of his own blood in his ears. Then came the faintest thump and a shallow breath that lifted her chest.

"She's alive!" Relief slammed into his gut, pushing him into action. He turned to the padre, searching his mind for the right foreign words. Somehow he managed to convey the need for soap and water to wash her cuts.

"Sí, señor," said the priest after listening to the choppy request, then motioned to the men to accompany him. As they were about to leave, Blake realized his sack was gone.

Returning his attention to Cara, Blake attempted to roll up her loose pant leg. The cotton material was resistant to his gentle tug. With greater care, he slowly peeled the cloth away from the dried blood. Gradually, he exposed more and more of her slender calf, covered with dirt-filled, blackened scratches, some of which had begun to bleed again.

Wishing for that basin of water to hurry up so he could cleanse the wounds, he did his best to examine her skin for any sign of punctures from a set of fangs. His eyes squinted in the poor light.

Behind him, the flicker of candlelight illuminated the tiny cubicle. He glanced over his shoulder. A small white-haired woman with wide, dark eyes and coppery skin smiled warmly at him. In one hand she held a metal candleholder with a stout tallow candle on it. With her other hand she motioned to someone behind her. Two other elderly Indian women shuffled into the room, their eyes downcast. One carried a basin of water, with towels draped over her arm.

The other carried a steaming cooking pot, which filled the air with an unfamiliar aroma.

Blake reached out for the water basin. *"Muchas gracias."*

But the first woman waved him off, still smiling at him as if she knew something he did not. *"Fuera, por favor."*

"I'm not leaving her."

Though she appeared to understand his defiance, her smile did not falter. Instead, she spoke to her silent friends, who set their pots and pans and cloths on the earthen floor near the bed and quit the room.

Again, he reached for the water, but she approached his side, placing her hand firmly on his shoulder. In Spanish, she gently admonished him. "You are no good here. Go, now. You wash. You eat. I care for her."

"No, I am responsible for her." As ridiculous as his claim sounded when spoken aloud, he *did* feel accountable for her well-being. His gaze was drawn back to Cara. He took her limp hand in his and stroked the back of her knuckles with the pad of his thumb.

"You must leave her with me," insisted the old woman in a firm but tender voice. "She is one of us."

His head jerked up. "What did you say?"

Surely he had misinterpreted her words. Mrs. Cara Edwards could not possibly be a Luiseño, the tribe of Indians that lived here at Mission San Juan Capistrano.

"She is one of us," repeated the woman, setting the candle on a rickety little table next to the bed. She cupped her hand over his and Cara's. Warmth radiated from her gnarled fingers as she curled them around his. Gently separating him from Cara, she lifted his hand and held it for a long moment.

Had he been right about the lies all along? Was the mysterious widow woman from the mission? Perhaps she had been sent away as a young girl to be educated, just as Keoni had been schooled in proper grammar and etiquette by missionaries.

Missionaries! Or course! Cara had spoken of her parents' travels around the world. Perhaps she had been born here but was adopted by a couple. Perhaps her lies about the deceased husband had been part of a plan to return here. But why? For what reason? He wondered if the story about a missing child was a falsehood as well?

Blake knew he was grasping for answers to questions too numerous to count. And this old Indian woman was not the one who could answer them. Only Cara could.

He knelt next to the dark-haired woman who had entered his life only a short time ago. Unable to keep from touching her one more time, he reached out and traced the line of her jaw with his fingertip.

Without taking his eyes off Cara, he spoke in halting Spanish to the old woman, attempting to explain about the briers and a possible rattlesnake. He prayed it wasn't a snakebite. Something inside him held on to a ray of hope that it had not been anything that would prove fatal.

The persistent woman cleared her throat with impatience.

"I won't go far," he promised Cara, then felt a pang of guilt over his broken vow from the night before.

A sad smile crept into the corners of his mouth.

"I *will* come back this time, Mrs. Edwards."

Blake rose to his feet, his strength all but drained from every muscle in his body. The white-haired Indian woman looked up at him with eyes that reminded him of Cara's. The similarity haunted him.

"You go rest, young man." She patted his arm affectionately, adding something about caring for his *esposa*, his spouse, his wife.

He opened his mouth to correct her mistaken assumption, then closed it and slowly nodded. *"Gracias, señora."*

"De nada," she said softly, then turned toward the bed.

As Blake was leaving the room, the old woman called out quietly, *"Señor?"*

He peered around the door. *"Sí?"*

Raising her eyebrows in question, she pointed to Cara's belly. *"¿Está ella embarazada?"*

"No comprendo."

"¿Un bebé?"

A baby!?

"No!" he answered adamantly. "No *niño!*"

The woman looked at him skeptically.

"Don't be so sure," she warned in Spanish, believing Blake and Cara to be husband and wife sharing the same bed. "Your wife may be with child. Maybe that is why she fainted. Too tired."

Blake felt his stomach drop to his toes. He had only been thinking of himself, knowing the impossibility of Cara being pregnant with his own child. It never occurred to him that she might already be carrying another man's child.

Numbed by an odd sort of disappointment, he nodded, forming the foreign words with the absence of emotion. "Yes, I suppose it is possible."

"Of course it is possible!" With a chuckle and a shake of her head, the old woman lightly scolded, "You men . . . you act so surprised when a baby comes. Ha! As if you don't know how it could have happened."

"I don't," he muttered in English as he closed the door.

Chapter 8

CARA SLOWLY AWAKENED to the cool touch of a damp cloth across her brow. Lingering at the end of a pleasant dream that was fading away, she murmured contentedly. Her eyelids too heavy to lift, she lolled her head to one side. The cloth skimmed down her temple to her neck and shoulder.

Her *bare* shoulder.

A hazy awareness of her state of undress tugged her mind away from the comfortable twilight at the edge of sleep. A sense of safeness permeated her thoughts, assuring her there was no cause for alarm.

The sound of a woman humming a familiar lullaby made her smile.

"Ah, *bien*," said the woman in Spanish, Cara's second language. "You wake up now, I see."

Cara blinked, trying to see the woman sitting by the bed in the shadowy room. Her body quivered with a sudden chill. Soft candlelight flickered across the facial features that she recognized as her eighty-three-year-old great-aunt.

It can't be.

She squinted her eyes, focusing hard on the round face and dark eyes. "I-I must be dreaming," she said in Spanish. Her voice was weak and raspy.

"Perhaps you are." Wiping the damp cloth across Cara's hot cheek, the woman gave a soft smile like a mother to a child. "Lie still now. I have some warm broth for you to sip."

"Where am I? Where's Blake?"

"You were brought here to the mission by the captain."

Cara could not stop staring at the woman sitting before her. "Who are you?"

Her eyes held a serene gaze. "I am Gabriella."

"Not my aunt," protested Cara, though the resemblance was uncanny. Nearly two hundred years separated the lives of the two old women. It was impossible. Or was it? "You *can't* be my aunt."

Strangely, the woman didn't answer but bent to one side and retrieved a small, deep wooden bowl, cupping it in both hands.

"Quiet, now," soothed Gabriella, bringing the soup stock to Cara's mouth. "Sip this."

Cara lifted her head, tried to drink the liquid, but found her position was too awkward.

"I can't," she sighed, dropping back to the mattress. Then she felt a hand slip beneath her shoulders and lift her. Gabriella had a surprising amount of strength despite her age and small stature.

Just like Aunt Gaby.

Would it really be so incredible that the essence of one spirit existed at different times in history? Was it any less believable than one person defying the space-time continuum and traveling to another era? If she hadn't done it herself, she might have argued the theory. At this point, nothing would come as a complete surprise, including her favorite aunt popping up in her time of need.

When Cara propped herself up on her elbows, the blanket slid down, exposing her breasts. Self-conscious, she grasped the edge of the scratchy blanket and covered herself, holding it while she drank a small amount of the thin soup. The warm, aromatic liquid soothed her dry throat.

Settling back onto the bed, she inquired in Spanish, "Where are my clothes?"

"I have sent them to be washed. You won't need them quite yet. Tomorrow, maybe."

"No, that's too late. The ship is sailing tonight. I need to be there when they come to get us."

Cara had a sudden thought that the captain might have already left without her. "Do you know what happened to the man who brought me?"

"Captain Masters has not abandoned you," Gabriella answered as if Cara had spoken her concern aloud. "He is a good man. But he has closed himself off from his heart far too long to know how to love. Within two weeks, you will receive a proposal of marriage."

"From Blake?"

Shaking her head solemnly, the woman added, "But you will have no choice but to accept, *mi Cara.*"

The familiar endearment startled her. "It *is* you, Aunt Gaby."

"Quiet now. You finish eating. Get your strength back." Gabriella offered more of the thin herb-laced soup.

Reluctantly Cara complied, even though she wanted to talk with Gabriella . . . or Aunt Gaby? Little by little, she consumed the entire bowlful. Toward the last of it, she felt her muscles turn to mush again.

Trying to keep her eyelids from closing, she asked, "What was in that broth?"

"Something for your chills and fever, *mi Cara.*"

Her vision blurred. The shadowy walls swirled around her. From somewhere came the soft and gentle voice of her aunt Gabriella,

Estoy aquí, mi Cara.

Her eyelids drooped. She snapped them open. "I want to tell you—"

"Hush now. Sleep."

"So much has happened . . ."

"I know everything about the storm and shipwreck, my child."

"You do? But how—" She cut off her sentence, realizing the absurdity of asking her clairvoyant aunt the how's and why's of psychic phenomenon. The mickey soup must have been the cause of this major brain-fade.

"How do I know these things? I am here with you, aren't

I?'' said Aunt Gaby, as if the rhetorical question explained everything.

But it didn't. Was she *really* here?

"You have been through so much, but you have so much more ahead of you. Don't give up now, Cara.''

"I'm not!'' Her adamant denial forced a cough from her lungs, weakening her further. After enduring hours of exposure in the icy water, she shouldn't have been surprised that her body had called it quits. "This flu or cold or whatever I've got, it's only temporary.''

"You have brought this on yourself. You needed the rest. And you needed my help.''

"I called upon you?'' Her memory was a blur.

"Yes, in your own way. Tomorrow you will be back on your feet.''

"Good, because I need to see Andrew. Is he here, Aunt Gaby?''

"No.''

Disappointed, Cara started to lift her hand to her eyes, but her arm would not respond. Her entire body was shutting down, unable to stay awake any longer. She fought against it, willing herself to find out the truth.

"*Was* he the boy the sailors rescued from the *Mystic* and brought here for his safety?''

"Yes, but he was taken away by men from another ship.''

"What?'' Cara struggled to hear the words fading in and out. "Kidnapped?''

"Yes . . . gone . . . you *will* find him . . . sleep now.''

"Don't go. Not yet.''

"I am here, my Cara.''

In the waning light of late day, Blake sent his men back to the *Valiant* with orders to come again the following afternoon. Returning from the beach with the leather satchel that he'd dropped, he passed the rustic huts, shooing off a couple of mongrels that sniffed at the food bag in his hand.

He entered the mission grounds and walked unescorted toward the chamber where Cara lay sleeping. He had been turned away twice by the old Indian medicine woman. Each time she told him his wife needed rest.

His wife . . .

A strange feeling of affection welled in his chest. How was it that Cara Edwards, a woman whom he had not known two days ago, could cause such a stir inside him? Never once had he thought of taking a wife. Mistress, yes. He'd had a few. Fortunately, none of them wanted a seafaring husband any more than he'd wanted to be tied to a lady living half a world away. Nor had he wanted to sire children who would grow up without their father's presence. He knew that loneliness in a boy's life. He would not subject his own son to the same sadness he had suffered.

Reaching the door of Cara's temporary room, he raised his hand and quietly knocked. The old woman came out, closing the door behind her. She looked up at him with kindness in her eyes.

"Ella está cansada."

"Yes, I know she is tired," he answered in English, frustrated with the difficulty in communicating. He had learned nothing about her condition during the entire day he had paced back and forth outside her door. Wanting to know if he could go in now, he asked, *"¿Se puede entrar ahora?"*

Shaking her head, the woman mentioned *escalofríos* and *fiebre*. Chills and fever were terms he knew. But surely the scratches could not have struck her down so quickly. And he'd found no evidence of a snakebite. Perhaps Cara *was* infected with a contagious disease. If so, he had already been exposed to it, so there was no reason for him to be kept out of her room any longer.

Refusing to be turned away again, he insisted upon seeing her. *"Yo quiero verla."*

She answered reluctantly, *"Sí, capitán,"* then told him she would go to eat while he visited with his wife. She offered to bring him a plate of food. He considered the contents of his bag, then nodded appreciatively.

"Gracias, señora."

As the woman left, Blake entered the sparsely furnished room. The east-facing window offered barely a hint of light in the lateness of the day. On the table, the candle had burned down to a short stub, which cast an eerie glow across the sagging rope bed.

Shaking off the macabre feeling of entering a tomb, he quietly approached the bedside and sat down in the chair. The blanket had been tucked under her chin. Her hair had been smoothed away from her forehead. Her lips looked cracked and sore.

Blake leaned forward. Bracing his elbows on his knees, he folded his hands under his chin.

Watching her.

Waiting.

She stirred. He dropped his hand to the edge of the bed, expecting her to open her eyes.

Hoping.

Wishing.

A slight frown creased her forehead. She gave a soft moan, then fell quiet again.

His shoulders sagged and he returned to his previous position, elbows on knees, chin on folded hands, eyes on her.

Even in sleep, she possessed a mystique like no other woman he'd known. Now here she was with an inexplicable illness that had him keeping a bedside vigil as if they were truly bound together for life.

He had fallen under her spell, and he didn't know how or why. One minute he wanted to shake her senseless and demand God's honest truth about who she was. The next minute he wanted to seduce her thoroughly, hear her cry out his name, and let the truth be damned.

She angered him. She enticed him. She frightened him.

But he had never felt so alive in all his life.

He dropped his face into his hands. "Dear God-in-heaven, what is wrong with her? I feel so useless just sitting here. There must be something I can do to help her."

In his mind's eye, he saw her face from the night before, pleading with him to let *her* help *him*. He'd been unable, unwilling, to accept the compassion in her dark eyes after his repulsive treatment of her.

Shame descended on him once more, flogging him with well-deserved ridicule. He had no right to be here at her side. He should have sailed away this afternoon when he'd had the chance. She would be better off without him. He had nothing of worth to offer her, not even himself. She deserved better. She deserved more.

He gazed upon her face, grateful to see that the frown had vanished. Somewhere in her darkness she had found peace. In the minimum light of the candle, he noticed a soft serenity that seemed to almost glow from her smooth skin.

The face of an angel.

The still, small voice in his head made him smile. Perhaps she was just that, he mused, not really accepting the childish belief in celestial beings. And yet . . . What sort of *real* person could have such a kind and generous heart? What sort of walking, breathing human being could reach out to someone like him as she had done? He envied her. To be able to reach out to another person. To be vulnerable. To be exposed. To be hurt, yet respond in love. She brought out a protectiveness in him he had not known existed until now. He wanted to guard her goodness, shelter it from the darkness in this world.

His throat tight with emotions he didn't understand, he warned softly, "If you don't watch out, Mrs. Edwards, you just might make me fall in love with you."

"No . . ." came her quiet reply, though her eyes were still closed. Had she heard his confession or was she dreaming again?

"Cara?" He touched the blanket on her shoulder. Her head lolled to one side. He lowered his face close to hers. "I am here."

Floating in a warm pool of oblivion, Cara heard the sound of two voices—one male, one female—speaking in unison, *I am here.*

Aunt Gaby? Blake? Together? How could it be? She struggled to open her eyes. Her vision cleared. Deep-blue eyes peered at her, first with concern, then relief.

"Blake?" she managed, barely making a sound.

He nodded, his dark eyes suddenly bright with moisture.
His hand cupped her head. As his lips brushed hers, she
felt something pass between them. A nebulous infusion of
radiant heat flowed through her body.

"Welcome back," he said, his voice as raspy as her own.
The faintest smile settled into the tiny creases at the outer
corner of his eyes. The pad of his thumb stroked her temple,
soothing her.

She attempted to smile. "Where have you been?"

"Not far." His gaze roved over her face as if reassuring
himself of her presence. Then he said with more conviction,
"*Never* far."

"I thought you might have left without me."

"For the briefest moment, I actually considered it . . . for
your own sake."

"Mine?" She licked her dry lips. "Why?"

"To save you from me."

Her chest tightened with the sadness she felt for him.

"Please don't say such things . . ." The last few words
got tangled around her cotton-coated tongue. He brought a
cup of water to her mouth and lifted her to take a drink.
After several sips, he lowered her back to the bed.

"I will be better tomorrow," she whispered.

"We shall see." He appeared skeptical, then looked
away as he placed the cup back upon the table.

"I *will* be on my feet, Blake." With such a weak voice
and body, her attempt to convince him was futile. "I must
look for Andrew."

"I asked about your son," he offered, turning back
to her. "There was a boy here who fit his description
but—"

"He's gone," she said at the same time as he did.

His eyebrows shot up. "You know he ran away?"

"No, he was kidnapped."

"But the priest said—"

"He doesn't know the truth," she whispered. "Andrew
was taken to a different ship by some other men."

"How can you be so sure? You have been sick with
fever all day. Perhaps you were dreaming."

A knock at the door interrupted them. Blake straightened in the chair, calling out in Spanish for the person to enter. Behind him, Cara saw a stoop-shouldered, white-haired woman come inside carrying a covered platter.

Her heart pounding, she lifted her head. "Aunt Gaby?"

"No," answered the woman, walking up to the bed. *"Me llamo Guadelupe . . . Lupe."*

Cara watched her hand the tray to Blake, then remove the cloth. Steam rose from the plate centered on the wooden board, filling the tiny room with an aroma of fresh-baked bread and other tantalizing smells.

"¿Dondé está Gabriella?"

In Spanish, Lupe answered solemnly, "She is gone."

"But she said she would stay with me."

"Why do you ask such a question?" She leaned over and felt Cara's forehead. "You must still be sick with fever."

"No . . . I saw her. She was here."

The woman pulled back, made a quick sign of the cross over her breast, then pressed her palms together. "You have been visited by someone other than me? A woman. Old as I?"

"Yes. My aunt. Aunt Gabriella."

Blake interrupted, "What are you two talking about?"

Lupe glanced nervously at him, then at Cara. "Gabriella, she was one of us. But she died last year."

"But you said—"

"I said she is gone. But I have heard of others who say they have seen her just as you claim."

"Nonsense," muttered Blake.

Cara ignored his disbelief. She had seen the same reaction many times before in her life when someone found out about her own psychic abilities. It didn't surprise or disappoint her to see it again. "Then what I experienced . . . ?"

"I-I don't know." Lupe looked down at her hands. "She has been called the angel of mercy."

Silence fell upon the little room. An erratic flickering of candlelight danced across the white adobe walls. As the tiny flame spit and sputtered, Cara glanced over at the last of the tallow being burned away.

"I will go and get another candle," offered the old woman, hurrying out the door and leaving it ajar. A sea breeze slipped through, bringing a chill into the room and extinguishing the dying flame.

"Blake?" asked Cara in the sudden darkness. She heard a slight movement beside the bed and assumed that he had placed the tray on the floor.

"I'm here." His hand settled on the blanket over her arm. She withdrew her hand and reached for him. After an awkward bump of fingers and knuckles, he clasped her hand in his. "Is that how you know about Andrew?"

"Yes." She lightly squeezed his fingers. "Trust me, Blake. I don't know what else to tell you right now. But I know that boy was kidnapped."

"*That* boy?"

Now she'd gone and blown it. So tired and weak, she couldn't keep up with all the lies and half-truths. Cara held her breath, waiting for the inevitable question.

"You meant to say 'your' boy, right?"

"Y-yes, of course." She sighed heavily, perhaps more than was necessary. But she wanted to make sure he heard a sadness in her voice. "Forgive me, Blake. I'm not myself. I will be better tomorrow."

"So you said."

"Yes." *And I promise I will tell you everything then.*

"I will let you get some sleep." His voice had taken on an edginess, not quite sharp, yet not the same gentleness as before.

"Yes, you should find a table to eat your dinner."

"I intend to."

The dark room kept her from seeing his face, his expression. But in her own intuitive mind, she saw his features without the need for light. His wary eyes. His fixed chin. His tight jaw. She sensed his drifting away again.

"Are you coming back later?"

A long pause followed, then he finally answered in a weary voice. "I will see you in the morning."

Holding his hand a little longer, she wanted desperately to break through the barrier he had restored in the blink of an eye. She tried to read his thoughts. Only stoic silence met her, but she felt his hurt and a twinge of anger.

"In the morning, then." She tried to keep her spirits up. "I'll be ready to sail with you."

"We shall see."

Though they were the same words he'd said earlier, this time he did not sound worried for her health. Instead, he sounded as if the question of leaving *with him* was the issue. Dear Lord, she hoped not. She had to go with Blake. Somehow she knew he was the only one who could help her find Andrew.

A glimmer of light moved into the room, preceding the old woman as she entered with a new candleholder in her hand. After she set it on the table, Blake lifted the tray from the floor, draped the cloth over it, and stood to leave.

"Goodnight, Cara." He turned, nodded at Guadelupe, *"Buenas noches, señora."*

The woman glanced between them, then frowned. "No kiss from a husband to his wife?" she asked in Spanish, hooking her hands on her hips. "If you two have quarreled, she will not sleep restfully. That is no good, Captain. You make amends. I come back soon. Very soon."

Lupe left. He hesitated, then placed the tray on the seat of the chair and leaned over the bed. "Sweet dreams, my dear and precious wife."

Cara saw a spark in his eyes as he lowered his mouth to hers, uncertain if it was anger or humor. The flu-like symptoms she'd battled all day seemed to be wreaking havoc on her mental radar.

Expecting a gentle kiss, she was surprised by the sensual press of his mouth. Despite her exhaustion, her blood pressure shot up. An uncontrollable moan of pleasure murmured deep in her throat. She reached up and cupped the back of his neck with her hand. He slowly pulled away, revealing eyes dark with carnal desire.

His gaze drifted over her mouth, her chin, her neck. A sardonic smile tilted one corner of his mouth. She looked

down and saw that the blanket had slipped downward, un-
covering most of her chest, exposing the upper curve of
darkly pigmented circles.

Without touching her, he gingerly grasped the edge of
the blanket where it tented across the shallow valley between her small breasts.

Her breathing grew shallow. Her fever returned. With a
deliberate and calculated move of his hand, his gaze steady
and direct, he dragged the covers up, one millimeter at a
time, allowing the coarse wool fibers to rub across her nipples. She felt them grow taut, sending a tingling, gnawing
need to the pit of her belly.

She knew he was well aware of what he was doing to
her. It was torture, sweet torture.

And she was putty in his hands.

No matter how sick she had been earlier, no matter how
exhausted she was now, she could not stop the escalating
arousal from this erotic stimulation of her nipples.

She was ready for more, ready for him to continue his
seduction, to finish what he had begun. This time it would
end differently than in his cabin. This time he would slip
under the blanket with her and hold her tenderly. He would
enter her and move inside her with the caress of a gentle
lover.

"I need you, Blake," she whispered desperately, her
arms reaching out to him.

Wordlessly, he dropped his lips to hers, claiming her
with a rough and hungry kiss. She groaned, her fingers
groping for the buttons of his shirt.

Abruptly, he tore his mouth away with a gasp. "No! Not
here. Not now."

She wanted to scream, *Yes—dammit! Take me! Here!
Now!* God, she was ready to burst apart at the seams. She
didn't care if the old woman was waiting outside, ready to
walk in at any moment. Right now, she didn't care if it
was high noon in the center of a dusty pueblo . . .

The image of gawkers standing over them stopped her
wild speculation.

I'm losing my mind.

She rolled to her side, turning her back to Blake, feeling aroused, frustrated, rejected, incredibly sad and not knowing why. She felt a cool chill run down her spine and realized the blanket had pulled away from the mattress and was now draped over her hips. She wasn't about to feel around back there to cover herself for his sake. Let him look. Let him see what he's missing.

"Good night, Blake."

"Good night . . . Mrs. Edwards."

At sunrise the following morning, Blake lay in his borrowed bed, his hands behind his head, his ankles crossed, staring at a spider creeping across the ceiling of a room similar to the one Cara occupied. A rooster crowed. Somewhere outside his window, dogs yipped playfully.

Had he slept at all? The entire night had seemed like one long, torturous endurance test of his iron will. How many times had he paced the floor instead of rushing back to her room? How many? A hundred?

When he'd tried to sleep, his dreams had been filled with visions of her—waking, sleeping, laughing, loving. He'd felt connected to her, an eerie, frightening, frustrating connection. His mind had filled with vivid images of sliding into bed with her and simply holding her body next to his. He saw her beneath him as he made love to her slowly, tenderly.

"I need you, Blake," she had whispered in his dream, just as she had done in her room last night. This same scene played over and over in his sleep throughout the night. He would kiss her, losing all thought of control. She would reach for his shirt. He would tell her "no."

But then the dream would take an abrupt turn from the reality of the previous night.

He would hear her cry out, "Yes—dammit! Take me! Here! Now! I don't care if the old woman is waiting outside, ready to walk in at any moment. Right now, I don't care if it is high noon in the center of a dusty pueblo . . ."

His dream included a very public display of intimacy that

drew a perverse gathering. In the midst of their lovemaking, she would moan, "I'm losing my mind."

Inevitably, the dream would end there. Each and every time, without fail, Blake was left with nothing but frustration and need.

The rooster crowed again. He shoved himself off the bed, relinquishing any notion of gaining another moment or two of rest. No, he would not get another full night's sleep until he was rid of one Cara Edwards.

Or bedded her.

Chapter 9

BENEATH DARK CLOUDS in the early-morning hours, Blake found little serenity for his restless soul as he passed by the *companario*—the bell-wall—and walked among the ruins of the great stone church. All that remained from an earthquake in 1812 was a section of wall and a single dome, one of seven. As he stood in the quiet hours of dawn, he thought of the forty Indians who had lost their lives on the very ground beneath his feet. He considered for a moment the strange twist of fate that had placed the victims in a house of worship, in a sanctuary of holiness, when their end came. What sort of divine reasoning was that?

For as long as he could remember, he had pondered the many unanswered questions about fate and faith. Here at the mission, he found himself asking again if there was a greater plan in life, in *his* life . . . or was everything merely a maelstrom of haphazard events, with each person fighting to make sense of it all?

A songbird caught his attention with a light whistling tune. Another answered. The melodious cheerfulness should have lifted his pensive mood. Instead, it merely nudged him to move on to other parts of the mission grounds.

Waiting for an appropriate time to check on Cara, he wandered about, picking up a stone now and then and tossing it a good distance. As often as not, he missed the object he had been aiming at. He wasn't surprised. He wasn't his usual self this morning. Tired, irritable, and wound up tighter than a watch spring, he did not deal well with idle time on his hands. He wanted to be on his way back to the ship. Even more, he wanted to be on deck under full sail in a fair wind.

You are lying to yourself, whispered a taunting voice.

If truth be told, he wanted only to see Cara, preferably awake and well. Nothing else seemed as important. Yes, he was still upset with her missteps and falsehoods. But his distrust was as ineffective against his carnal desire for her as an anchor that went down foul, failing to bring up a mooring ship with too much headway.

He distracted his mind with a casual inspection of the soap vats and brick kilns, tanning tanks and presses—most of which had sat idle since the Franciscans had been stripped of their authority over the Indians by the Mexican governor. The few Indians left at the mission stayed by choice.

Even after death?

Apparently so. That is, of course, if he were to believe Lupe's story about the angel of mercy. Obviously Cara believed it.

Cara, again.

Every avenue of thought led back to her. Drawn like an ancient mariner to the siren song, he felt the ever-present tug to return to her.

He raked his fingers through his hair, then kneaded the tight muscles in the back of his stiff neck. With a glance heavenward, he scanned the gray clouds, hoping the weather would hold until he could take her safely back to the *Valiant*. Then what? Did he abandon her in San Diego before sailing for Boston? He should. Whether he *would* remained to be seen.

Shaking off the mental dilemma, he headed back, retracing his steps past the monastery, through long open-air corridors and past cloister arches. A sad loneliness echoed with his footfall, drifting out of every corner and crevice, twin-

ing around him with the scent of moist earth and wild rose
and salt air. The melancholy call of a mourning dove accompanied his solitary walk.

When he was a few yards from Cara's door, Lupe came
out of the room, her face turned away from him. But when
she looked back and gave him a polite nod, he saw she was
another old woman of similar stature and dress. Perhaps
that was why she seemed familiar. With a gentle smile, she
hurried off, her short legs remarkably quick for her age.
Rounding a corner, she disappeared as he knocked on the
door.

"Come in," Cara called. Opening the door, he found her
lying in bed, propped up on one elbow, the blanket clutched
to her chest. She had a sparkle in her brown eyes and
healthy color in her cheeks. Her recovery had indeed been
quick, as she had promised. "Good morning, Blake."

"You look well." His thoughts fell back to the previous
night and the kiss that had prompted a long night of erotic
dreams. He forced his mind away from the memory, determined not to venture into those deep waters again.

Searching for safer territory, he inquired about the
woman who had just left. "Is she helping Lupe?"

"That *was* Lupe. She just left to get breakfast for me.
There'll probably be plenty to share—"

"The woman I saw outside your door was *not* Lupe."

"Of course it was. You knocked not two seconds after
she went out. You couldn't have missed her. If it wasn't
Lupe, who else . . . ?"

Gabriella.

Blake knew her thought without hearing it. Her expression left no doubt of her speculation.

Cara cautiously asked, "Would you say she looks a little
bit like . . . me? In the eyes, maybe?"

Mildly curious, he went to her bedside, sat down on the
chair, and leaned forward. With a gentle grasp of her chin,
he turned her head slightly from one side to the other and
back. Taking into consideration the vast difference in age,
he realized there was a striking resemblance in color and
shape. This revelation unnerved him.

She is one of us.

His gaze locked with hers. Remembering the words Lupe had spoken yesterday, he stared at Cara for a long moment before he found his voice.

"Who *are* you? Who was that other woman? Tell me why it is you look like her, like these people?"

Cara slowly drew back, then slid down under the covers until her shoulders were completely covered, much to his relief.

"I am one of them, Blake. My ancestors are of these tribes. My great-grandmother was a Gabrielino who married a Mexican soldier. My mixed blood is also Luiseño and Italian. I'm quite a duke's mixture, actually."

"What about the Indian woman with your eyes?"

"Aunt Gaby?"

"Gabriella?"

She nodded.

"Cara, I am willing to accept the possibility that you have a relative here at the mission. But I cannot believe the woman I saw was a ghost. She was as real as you and me."

With a frustrated sigh, she brought her hands up over her eyes. "I can't explain it in any way that will make sense to you. I wouldn't even know where to begin."

"No, I don't suppose it would be easy to explain how it is that you have seen someone who has been dead over a year. Or how it is that *I* have seen her, too."

Lowering her hands, she entwined her fingers and rested them on her chest. Staring at the ceiling above her, she stated calmly, "There are things I know. Things I see. Things I hear. Things no one else knows or sees or hears. Things that tell me how to help others, how to help myself."

"Are you saying you hear people who are not there?"

"I don't consider them people, not in the flesh-and-blood sense. Though I have to admit, Aunt Gaby sure showed up pretty solid, didn't she?"

Her head rolled to one side as her soft lips curved into the smile of a delighted child. Unfortunately, his body responded to her quite differently. Still, his mind could not comprehend her claims of peculiar knowledge or of knowing spirits. The very idea disturbed him greatly.

He leaned back in the chair, folding his arms. "Either you are having a joke at my expense or you are still delusional from fever."

"Do I look delusional?"

He eyed the soft light in her eyes and the glow of her skin. His gaze traveled over the woolen blanket molded around her feminine curves. She looked inviting, tempting, anything but delusional. "Then you are teasing me." *In more ways than one.*

"Gabriella was here, Blake. You saw her with your own eyes. I know it sounds incredible. There's no easy way to convince a first-timer that they're not crazy, that it did really happen, and that there's no normal explanation."

Unable to sit still any longer, he rose from his chair and walked to the window. "I don't believe you, Cara. I'm sorry."

He truly felt sorry. For her. For himself. He had known all along there was something not quite right with her situation. Now he realized she was mad. Quietly so, thankfully. Had she been a raving lunatic, he would not have been so quick to offer his help in locating her son. In all likelihood, her mind had snapped from the death of a child, sending her on a blind search for the boy. But she was insane all the same. Yet he could not help being attracted to her beauty and her compassion.

What did he do now? Walk away? Leave her here to be cared for by Lupe?

And Gabriella.

He gave a derisive snort at the preposterous notion of guardian angels, then recalled Lupe's reaction. Even the Indian woman believed in the rumors of the angel of mercy. Superstition. All of it. And Cara Edwards—if that was really her name—was weak-minded enough to be susceptible to the suggestions. He had seen it before. A young boy in Keoni's village on Kaua'i was a simpleminded child who would do and say anything he was told, mimicking his caretakers.

Yet as he went back over the events of the preceding days, he knew Cara had not behaved like a simpleton.

"Tell me about Andrew," he said, deciding that her response might lead him to some answers of his own.

"Andrew?"

He turned at the strange croak in her voice. "Your son?"

"I-I know." Clearly she was uncomfortable.

"Is there something wrong?"

"No, but I . . . that is, I'm a little surprised you suddenly changed the subject."

"Not really."

Her dark eyes narrowed slightly, eyeing him with wariness. He could almost feel her defensiveness.

"Andrew . . . is not my son."

Ah, now we are seeing progress. Leaning against the adobe wall, he propped his elbow on the deep ledge of the window opening. "Go on."

"His name is Andrew Charles. He's from . . . well, let's just say he disappeared from his home and I'm trying to find him."

"Why?"

"Why," she repeated with contemplation. Or was she stalling in an effort to fabricate another lie? "The boy's father had many people looking for him, but he seemed to think I was the only one who could actually get the job done. Luckily, I did pick up his trail."

"A man hired you to find his son."

"Yes, that's right."

"A man hired a *woman* to find his son."

"You don't have to make it sound so offensive." She rolled her eyes. "I suppose you think it's perfectly all right to hire a woman for her body but not for her mind?"

"I suppose that depends upon the lady's *state* of mind." Which, for her, was questionable at this point. He ignored her exasperated groan. "So you have tracked Andrew to this mission. Now he's run away."

"Kidnapped," she reminded him.

"Oh—yes, I do remember you clarifying that detail. And

how was it you came by this information? No, let me guess—Gabriella told you.''

She glared at him, her lips a tight line.

''Am I right?'' He had been joking with her, but he should have known better. Her silent stare made him grow increasingly uncomfortable. ''By God, I *am* right.''

''Does it really matter, Blake? No matter what I say, you'll still think I'm crazy. Am I right?'' she mocked, cocking her head to mimic his surprise. ''By God, I *am* right.''

''Can you honestly blame me for feeling this way?''

His question took the wind out of her sails. ''No, I can't,'' she answered in defeat. ''Nearly everyone reacts the same as you have. Some more so than others. Believe it or not, there are times when even I question my own sanity. Especially now.''

She wanted to say more. He saw it in the shape of her mouth, her lips parted as if she were about to speak but decided against doing so. Her frown deepened.

From where he stood at the window, he sensed a certain hopelessness, a certain despair. He wanted to go to her side but held back, reluctant to fall into the trap again. Keoni had warned him about dancing to her tune. Her sadness played upon his weakness for her. Damned if he didn't feel a knife in his gut, cutting him clear through.

She broke the silence between them, her voice soft and low. ''After everything you have done for me, Blake, I have no right to ask another favor of you . . .''

''What is it?''

''Please, don't leave me behind here at the mission.''

''Do you think I would?'' A twinge of guilt poked at his conscience. She could not have possibly known he had been contemplating those very same thoughts. ''Why do you suppose I have been waiting around since yesterday?''

''Things have changed now. But I swear to you, I'm not crazy. And I won't cause any trouble. Honest. Just promise me you'll take me to San Diego, Blake. Promise me?''

Her pleading tore at him. He had to get out of the room before he found himself comforting her. For he knew if he allowed himself within two feet of her, he would be unable

to resist reaching out and touching her. And if their past
was any evidence, he would not stop there. He would want
to hold her and kiss her.

And make love to her.

"I must find Lupe," he said abruptly, heading for the
door. "She should be on her way back with your breakfast."

"Blake, wait."

He paused, looking back over his shoulder. "I *will* return, Cara."

Late in the gloomy morning, Cara bathed and dressed in
her clean clothes Lupe had brought back to her. Although
the distance to the beach was only a mile on the high, flat
tableland, Blake wanted her to be ready to leave after the
midday meal in order for them to have ample time to de-
scend the cliff trail. He was concerned about her lack of
strength and planned to make her take as many rests as
necessary.

Despite her quick recovery from the twenty-four-hour
bug, she knew it would take her a while to feel completely
restored to normal again. But she intended to make it all
the way back to the ship without a single complaint. She
didn't dare do anything that would risk losing her trans-
portation to San Diego. Even though her sixth sense had
not been very keen over the last day or so, she had picked
up something from Blake about his reluctance to continue
helping her. Right now, she had no other ally to aid her
search for Andrew. Until someone else came along with
the means to get her from port to port, she had to make the
best of things.

After eating a hearty lunch that included more medicinal
broth, Cara accepted a leather pouch of the herbs from
Lupe, who told her how to prepare it. As she said good-
bye to the old woman, Blake walked up to the two of them.

"*¿Cuánto le debo?*" he asked Lupe, reaching into his
jacket for money.

She shook her head. "I am only a handmaiden of my

Lord,'' she told them in Spanish. "He sent you to me so I may be of help. No money is expected."

Extending his gratitude, Blake held out a handful of *reals*. Again, she waved it off with a shake of her hand. He glanced at Cara. "You speak their language better than I do. Tell her if she will not accept for herself, at least take it as a gift to the church."

After Cara spoke reassuringly to Lupe, the old woman nodded, accepting the charity on behalf of the mission. Their farewell was interrupted by a small boy approaching with two horses that had been saddled and bridled, both having lassos coiled around the large pommels.

When Blake asked for her assistance with the language once more, Cara learned from the barefoot child that the animals were sent by the *mayordomo* of the mission for the short journey to the cliffs.

She stroked the white blaze on the chestnut mare, who nuzzled her palm. "She's beautiful. Bet she runs like the wind."

"You know how to ride astride?"

"Oh, sure."

"I suppose I should not be surprised."

According to the boy, the *mayordomo* expected the extravagant sum of sixteen *reals*, the normal cost of a full day's use. This amount of two dollars was actually for the saddles, not the horses, which were more or less thrown in for free.

Blake considered the deal, then turned to Cara. "Perhaps if you were a bit stronger you could handle her. These horses know only two speeds—a slow walk and a fast run. Nothing in between. It would be best if you rode with me."

She didn't welcome the idea of the two of them on the back of one horse, with her arms wrapped around his middle, her breasts pressed against his back. Nope. Huh-uh. This was not a good thing. She was already having a tough enough time keeping her hands to herself, continually reminding the little horny devil inside her body that ladies in the nineteenth century didn't go around groping handsome and virile men.

Ladies don't do ANY of the things you've been doing since you got here.

A valid point, she told that impish voice. Still, she somehow managed to resist the temptation to let her libido run amok.

"I think I'd rather walk," she said, hoping to convince Blake that she didn't need the horse. "It's only a mile. I could use the exercise."

"Nonsense."

He paid eight *reals* for one mount to the wide-eyed boy, who ran off to deliver the money to his superior. Blake led the chestnut mare to a low stone wall so Cara could easily climb up behind him.

Well, at least she'd given it a shot. Now it looked like she was going to be snuggled up to Blake whether she liked it or not. That was the trouble . . . she knew darn well she'd like it. Too much.

As they rode toward the mission entrance, the *padre* and his two helpers stood at the gates, their faces without smiles. Cara sensed their suspicion and fear. When the horse passed, the neophytes took a step back, crossing themselves. The Reverend Father remained rooted in his spot, his chin high as if in defiance.

Though she and Blake bid *"Muchas gracias"* and *"Adiós,"* the slender man barely acknowledged their words, giving an almost imperceptible nod.

Cara maintained her smile, murmuring, "What's gotten into them?"

Leaving the mission behind, Blake turned his head slightly to speak over his shoulder to Cara. "Perhaps Lupe told them about your . . . vision."

"If so, I doubt they would've behaved so oddly. Seeing the angel of mercy would be a blessing. But they acted like we've been cursed."

A cold chill prickled her arms with goose bumps.

"I would bet it is *you* who frightens them," he said.

"Me?!"

"Didn't you notice that the father never once came to your room?"

"Actually, I was sort of out of it yesterday."

"Out of it?"

She clarified, "I didn't notice much of anything." *Except Gabriella.*

And you.

"When I carried you in there unconscious, he thought you were a boy in those clothes, with that shorn hair. He was quite taken aback to learn you were a woman. I wouldn't be surprised if someone told him about Lupe's claim that you were one of them."

Unable to keep the sarcasm from her tone, Cara itemized, "So I am a woman, which immediately puts me on a lower rung of intelligent life. And I dress like a man with short hair, which marks me for suspicion. I'm part Indian, which means less than zero. Ah—! Let's not forget I had the audacity to survive my illness."

"Not only survive, Cara. To them, your turnaround probably seemed miraculous. You beat the devil."

"Or else they think I *am* the devil." Another involuntary shiver rippled through her body.

"Cold?"

"A little," she fudged, though it was partly true that the cool, stiff breeze was a bit uncomfortable.

"Try not to dwell on it," he suggested. "Think of something warm."

"I am." *Your body.*

The rest of the ride proved to be just as difficult as her mind had predicted. By the time they arrived at the trailhead at the top of the cliffs, her muscles were sore from the tense position she'd maintained the entire time, trying to keep from relaxing too much, leaning too close, holding on too tight.

She slid down from behind Blake, landing with a jolt that nearly buckled her weak knees. He followed, but with more finesse than she'd displayed. Then again, he hadn't been sick in bed yesterday either, she reminded herself.

"What do we do about the horse?" she asked, giving an appreciative pat to its cheek.

"She knows her way back to the water." He headed toward the trail with his leather bag in hand.

The animal turned its face to her. She smiled into the dark equine eyes, silently thanking the mare. "Yes, I suppose you do."

"Are you talking to that horse?"

"Don't you talk to your dog?"

"That's different."

"It is?"

"Of course. Bud is . . ."

"One of God's creatures, just like this sweet mare." The chestnut dropped her head, allowing Cara to give her a quick kiss on the bony ridge of her nose. "Be a good girl now and show me how you can find your way home."

Impatient with her, Blake groused, "Oh-for-the-love-of—"

His muttering was silenced as the horse turned back toward the mission. Cara made a big production of dusting off her hands, then casually marched right past the slack-jawed captain, left staring at the departure of one very perceptive and obedient horse.

Her smug victory in one-upmanship was short-lived, however. Stopping at the edge of the cliff, she looked down four hundred feet to the surf below. Getting there was going to be far more difficult than the climb had been two days ago. And that was before the fever and chills had knocked her for a loop, draining her of half her energy.

On the way up, she'd been extra careful to follow a few yards behind Blake, noting every placement of his step so she could duplicate it. As agile as spider monkeys, they'd jumped over breaks and scrambled up steep faces. Always keeping her eyes focused upward, she'd seen only the gray skies beyond Blake.

Now, she had an entirely different view of the near-vertical drop. Looking down, she saw the craggy shoreline white with foam from the crashing waves. Any other day she might not have balked at this adventurous test of her physical and mental outdoor skills. She and Mark would have considered it a Sunday stroll in the park. But today she wasn't up to snuff. Not by a long shot.

Leading the way again, Blake stayed close, almost too

close. Though grateful for his constant handholds to steady her, she had to concentrate all the harder when a zing of electricity would zap through her body at the slightest touch of his flesh.

Calling directions up to her, he told her how far to inch her foot to the left or right for the safest toehold. She practically jumped out of her skin the first time his fingers gently wrapped around her ankle, guiding her shoe down to an imperceptible lip in the rock. Twice, he was positioned below her as if on the lower rung of a ladder, coaching her downward movement until she was sandwiched between the slick granite and his hard body. His labored breathing in her ear was more disconcerting than the dizzying height.

The second time it happened, she briefly squeezed her eyes shut, trying to regain some equilibrium.

"How are you feeling?" he asked, his breath warming her neck.

"Shaky." *Thanks to you.*

"Then we'll rest here for a few minutes." He slightly shifted his stance to stabilize his weight on the ledge.

"Here?" she squeaked, acutely aware of his pelvis against her bottom.

"I don't want you to become overly tired."

What about overly stimulated? she wanted to ask but decided against letting him know she was getting turned on while perched on a twelve-inch precipice one hundred feet above the jagged rocks.

By the time they reached the stony beach below, her nerves were beyond frazzled, though not only from their exhaustive descent.

Her entire time-traveling experience had become one big, scary high-wire act strung between two centuries. Struggling to keep her wits about her with Blake, she had leaned too far one way with the lies about Andrew. Before she lost her footing completely, she had tried the truth and went too far the other direction. Up until now, she had tried both deceit and honesty, only to find that neither one had worked well with Blake.

Doubts and fears rolled over her, threatening to upset her precarious balance even further. Once again, she began to wonder how in the world she was ever going to find Andrew, let alone get home.

Chapter 10

Not long after Blake and Cara reached the base of the cliffs, the Kānaka from the *Valiant* brought the longboat to shore. He helped her to board, settling her in the stern sheets near him, then gave the order to shove off. Facing aft, his men stretched out well at their oars, pulling them through the rough swells while Blake took the place of the steersman.

The skies grew darker with each passing minute. A sense of impending danger settled in his bones. With luck, they would reach the ship before the gale, slip anchor, and escape the clutches of another southeaster. Masking his concern, he glanced at Cara, surprised to see her watching him.

Her eyes searched his face.

She knew.

Damnation. He wanted to reach out and pat her hand reassuringly. But guiding the boat took precedence, for which he was grateful. Better to have his hands occupied with his duties than to display gentle emotions in front of his men. As a commanding officer, he had the sterling reputation of being a fair-minded disciplinarian, *not* a tender-hearted fool.

The boat dropped heavily into a deep trough, jarring his teeth. The next swell rose in a high arc, then collapsed over the bow. Two of the Sandwich Islanders were drenched, yet they whooped in laughter, joined by the other two.

Whether they enjoyed the exhilaration or loved defying death, he did not know. Perhaps a little of both.

From the greenish look of Cara, she didn't share the same exuberance for the wild ride. Lord, how much more could she take? No woman should suffer as much as she had. Still, she gave him a weak smile and clung to the boat.

He urged the men on. The Kānaka complied. They could not have given any more of their strength or spirit. Several more waves dumped water into the hull before they reached the *Valiant*, where Bud barked excitedly. No sooner had they climbed aboard than the rain descended upon them.

"Lay aloft and loose those topsails!" bellowed Blake as the anchor chain surged and snapped and surged again. Crewmen sang out at the sheets as they hauled them home. The storm bore down as the sails filled and the ship pitched. He told the mate to leave the longboat tied off at the buoy. They would return for it later when they retrieved the anchor. With no time to think, he relied on instinct.

Grabbing Cara's hand, he tugged her toward the hatch. Bud followed close behind. In the midst of the madness, Keoni suddenly appeared, raindrops splattering off his wide shoulders. The wind roared. Squinting up at his huge friend, Blake hauled Cara in between them.

"Get her below," he commanded, grabbing her a bit too roughly by the back of her shoulders and pressing her toward Keoni.

Cara shouted over the noise, "I can make it on my own."

"No, goddamn it!" he shouted back, mad as hell at her spunkiness and scared as hell of losing her. He glanced up at the Kanaka. "*Get her out of here!* And make *damn* sure she's safe. Sit on her if you have to!"

He knew he'd catch the devil from her later, but right now all that mattered was saving this ship. And he couldn't be clearheaded if he worried whether she'd been washed overboard on her way to his cabin.

As Keoni started to escort her away, Blake headed toward the helm, shouting over the wind to his first mate, "All ready forward?"

"Aye, aye, sir, all ready," responded Mr. Bellows.

"Let go!"

The chain rattled through the hawsehole. "All gone, sir."

"Let go aft!"

A startled cry spun Blake around. He saw Cara's eyes widen in fright, then look upward as if scanning the rigging for something or someone. He saw nothing but McGinty working his way down to the fore topmast. Having no idea what she was doing and no time to ask, he motioned angrily at Keoni.

The cook caught her around the waist with his right arm, lifting her off the deck and bracing her against his side, her back to him. She grasped his bicep, squirming in his hold without any luck.

"Blake, I need to tell you . . ." Her words faded away as Keoni carried her off, Bud following them. He thought he heard the words "fore topmast" and "yardarm," though he had no idea what she meant. And no time to consider the question. The mast looked perfectly fine to him.

Two hours later Blake went down the companionway, stripped off his wet tarpaulin, and headed toward his cabin to check on Cara. His wide gait did little to accommodate the erratic motion of the storm-tossed ship. In the meager light of a lantern swaying from a hook, he knocked twice on the door of his cabin, paused, then rapped once. The floor beneath his feet tilted violently, pitching him against the bulkhead. If he had not been so tired and miserably wet, he would not have been so easily buffeted.

The door was opened by his steward, who stood stiff and nervous in the presence of his captain, while Bud rounded the boy's legs and came out to greet Blake.

Without looking down at his dog, he tossed the tarpaulin against the opposite bulkhead and patted him on the head but kept his attention on Jimmy. "Where's Keoni?"

"Sir, he left me in charge, sir," a lilt of Irish clinging to his words.

Bracing his hand on the door frame to maintain his balance, Blake almost laughed at the absurd idea of this young man trying to keep Cara in line. They were equal in height and weight. Having seen the fine tone of her arms, he would bet money that she was just as strong, if not stronger, though her recent illness might have given her a disadvantage.

"How is . . . Mrs. Edwards?" he inquired.

"I'm fine," came her weary voice from behind the door.

She appeared beside the teenager, clearly unobservant of the young man's smitten expression. *Must she arouse every male in her presence?* he wondered, as if it were her fault. Which it wasn't. He was being petty, he knew. Perhaps it was his exhaustion, he told himself, refusing to accept the possibility that he might actually be jealous of a sixteen-year-old who was still wet behind the ears. If Jimmy had the chance, he would not know the first thing about pleasing a woman like Cara.

Shucking off his damp jacket, then scooping up the dripping tarpaulin, Blake held them both out to the young man. "I need dry clothes . . . again. See to it they're in my temporary quarters as soon as possible."

"Aye, aye, sir." The lad took the woolen garment, then turned to Cara, his nervousness bringing out the brogue. " 'Twas a pleasure to sit wit' you, ma'am. If you be a'needin' anythin', I'll be happy t' get it. Anythin' a'tall. I'll come back—"

"Thank you, Jimmy," she answered, smiling at him as she clung to the door for balance. He swallowed hard, his Adam's apple bobbing up and down.

As he slipped out of the cabin, her attention was drawn to Bud, trotting past her legs and flopping down in his favorite corner. With an amused expression, she turned back to Blake and invited him to enter.

Behind her, another lantern swung from the ceiling above the dining table. The dancing candlelight cast a shimmering halo about her head and shoulders. Her short dark hair framed the beauty of her luminous eyes. A man could drown in the depths of passion that he saw in those eyes.

He could hardly blame Jimmy for his behavior, feeling his own response to her sensual presence.

As he walked through the portal, he glanced about his quarters, noticing that Jimmy had stowed every loose item for the duration of the storm. His enamored steward was quite the reliable boy.

He went to a drawer and withdrew a small towel to dry his hair, then turned around and leaned against the bureau, his feet planted wide to counter the turbulent motion. He noticed Cara had taken a similar position with her back against the closed door, her hands by her narrow hips, her palms pressed against the wood. She wore an entirely different set of clothing, with a pair of trousers that fit quite well. And she was barefoot again.

"Different clothing, I see." *Still the same fascinating toes,* he silently added, then scrubbed his scalp vigorously with the towel.

She glanced down at the white duck trousers. "Jimmy found a storage locker of old clothes."

Blake did not tell her that the locker had been removed to make room for the uncured cattle hides they had been collecting from the ranchero owners. Along with all the other excess cargo, the chest had been left in San Diego for the duration of their stay on the California coast.

Either the lad had bartered with one of the crew for her present set of clothes or he had "borrowed" them. Then Blake realized that the fit was as close as her own garments, perhaps better. The clothes were Jimmy's, he realized. No doubt about it. He stifled a smile.

Cara asked, "Why are you smiling like that?"

Flattening his palm on his chest, he softly mimicked the Irish lilt. "Ah—Cara, m'darlin', you've won another heart."

"Jimmy?"

"Yes, indeed." He dropped the accent. "And Keoni and whoever else happens within a hundred yards of you."

"Not the *padre*," she reminded him, leaning far to her left to compensate for the ship's list.

"He is *supposed* to be immune."

Slowly making her way across the unsteady cabin floor, she headed toward the bed, her arms extended for balance like a tightrope walker. He would have offered to help but decided it was best to stay as far away as he could from his berth and her body.

After she reached her destination, she plopped down on her fanny, looking as exhausted as he felt. Her legs dangled over the wooden rail that she gripped with her hands. Her bare feet enthralled him.

"Did you come here with a reason?" she asked, her torso shifting with the motion of the storm. "Or is this just a social call."

Damn, how she can distract a man from his purpose each and every time.

"No . . . yes. That is—" He stopped drying his hair and gripped the towel in his hands. "I wanted to know about the message you wanted to give me before Keoni brought you down here."

"About the mast? Did you keep an eye on it as I asked?"

"We lost it. Snapped like a twig in the wind." He let out a tired sigh. "McGinty was up there."

"Oh—no!" Her hand cupped her open mouth, then dropped away. "Is he all right?"

"Yes. Though I doubt he would be if I hadn't been hearing your voice echoing inside my head about that damn mast." He paused, staring down at the rough cloth in his hands. "How did you know the mast was going to go?"

"I . . ."

Her hesitation brought his eyes up. An unsettling feeling began to grow inside him. He cocked his head, studying her for a long moment, then repeated, more insistent this time, "How did you know to tell me, Cara?"

She dropped her gaze to the floor at his feet and took a deep breath. The long exhale bore the weight of the world.

"Okay, here it is—" She looked back up at him. "I saw it happen while I was up there on deck. That is, I saw it in my head—the broken mast, the ripped sails, the tangled rigging."

"When I heard you gasp—"

She nodded, her shoulders hunched. "But I didn't see the sailor. I didn't know about him. Usually, I pick up *something* if a person is in danger."

The southeaster gale keened and moaned. Waves dashed against the windows. The *Valiant* pitched and rolled. And Cara seemed to be taking the blame for it all, as though she had somehow let him down by not knowing of the accident with the seaman.

A part of him didn't believe her story. More accurately, could not begin to fathom it. She was a madwoman, he reminded himself, his gut twisting from a deep-seated fear that he could not quite name. Was he afraid of her? Yes. No. Perhaps.

Staring at her slumped figure at the edge of the bed, he didn't see a wild-eyed sorceress or a frightful witch. He saw only a woman he had grown to care about in a very short time. Maybe he had fallen under her spell. Yes, definitely so. Whether it was natural or mystical he couldn't say. Yet no argument in his head seemed to be able to stop him from going to her side and sitting down next to her.

"It doesn't matter now. Your warning kept me alert. If it hadn't been for you, I doubt McGinty would be alive. Everyone was too busy handling their own work to notice he was in trouble. I'm the one who spotted him because I kept looking up there, thanks to you."

"Do you actually believe me?"

"That you have a gift of sight?" *No! It's impossible. It's merely a coincidence. I can't possibly accept . . .* His mind screamed all the reasons to denounce her as a deranged female. Instead, he answered with a lie. "I suppose I haven't much of a choice in the matter now, have I? Not when you throw something like that at me."

"I didn't *throw* anything at you."

The ship pitched, flinging her to one side. Blake's hip slammed against hers, nearly collapsing him atop her. Though he would rather have pursued his baser instincts, he righted himself, then offered his hand to pull her back up to a sitting position.

"Perhaps I should blame Mother Nature for doing the tossing and throwing."

Another wave rocked the vessel in the opposite direction. Cara practically flopped into his lap like a rag doll. His hands gripped her shoulders, bringing her back to center.

"Why don't you lie down?"

When her eyes widened, he almost forgot his manners and kissed her right then. Instead, he vowed to behave as a gentleman. He knew he should. He felt guilty enough for saying he believed her stories so she would feel better. He certainly didn't need to add to his guilt by taking advantage of her.

"I'm fine sitting here." The muscles in her arms tightened as she held on to the rail during another shift of the ship.

"You're wasting what little strength you have left in trying to battle the inevitable. This storm is going to last all night, perhaps longer. Best to get in bed."

"*Staying* in bed—now there's the problem."

"Rolling out, are you?"

She nodded. "Rope would solve it. You could tie me dow . . . uh, scratch that last suggestion, would you? Just forget I said it."

"Consider it forgotten." But try as he might, he could not quite erase the fascinating image created by her slip of the tongue.

"These rails aren't much help, either," she added, tapping the polished wood with a fingernail. He smiled at her nervous chatter. "They're more like speed bumps. All I get are bruises from flying over them."

"Speed bumps?" he asked, a curious frown creasing his forehead. "What the devil are speed bumps?"

"Uh . . . my mistake. Never mind."

If it were possible for a hellacious southeaster to gain any more momentum, this one did, jerking them and jostling them. Waves battered the windows. Cara's head snapped around.

"Is that glass strong enough to hold out?" Her body fell against him. Instinctively, his arms went around her.

"Don't worry."

To hell with the blasted windows, Blake thought, feeling his body respond to her soft, womanly curves. The question he pondered was which would give way first—that glass or his own chivalry.

She felt good against him, her head tucked under his chin. His hand lightly rubbed her back.

"That's . . . nice," she murmured into his chest.

He had sworn to himself that he would not become romantically involved with this woman. Only this afternoon he'd realized she was probably insane. Now this evening, she demonstrated an uncanny ability to see into the future like a fortune-telling gypsy. Though he still preferred to dismiss the event as a coincidence. After all, she did not predict McGinty's involvement. And any storm as severe as this one could snap a mast in two. So her expression of fears was not so far-fetched. She would have to perform something far more extraordinary to make a believer out of him.

Oddly, the more he learned about her, the more mysterious she seemed.

Yet his body still craved her.

Now more than ever.

His hand seemed to rise on its own accord, stroking the back of her head. She sighed, a soft feminine sound. God help him, he knew he should stop, but he couldn't seem to manage.

Amid the noise and turmoil of the storm, he gently pressed her backward onto the bedcovers. She looked up at him with smoky eyes, her gaze flitting to his mouth. The tip of her tongue ran along the seam of her mouth, licking her lips.

"An invitation, perhaps?"

"Perhaps." The word sounded like a feline purr.

He moved up onto the mattress, lying next to her, his arm draped over her waist. With another roll of the ship, he tightened his hold, keeping her from slipping out of the bed.

"Still want the rope?"

"This works much better."

He lowered his mouth to the curve of her slender neck. "I shouldn't be doing this," he murmured, kissing her soft skin.

She whispered, "Don't you need to be on deck with your men?"

"I *need* to be down here with you." His hand cupped her cheek, turning her head toward him. "Mr. Bellows knows his duties. He is the most reliable mate in foul weather."

"Then what is your job?"

"Right now?" He gave a sly smile. "*This* is my job . . ."

He dropped his mouth to hers, gently seducing her to open to him. When her lips parted, he resisted the urge to take her too quickly. As the tempest raged outside, he intended to soothe their souls with the most tender of touches, making love to her with a slow, deliberate rhythm that would rock her to her very core.

With an inner smile, Cara read his thoughts through a dreamy haze of sexual arousal. Somewhere in the back of her mind she was relieved to learn that her psychic ability was beginning to emerge again. While there was never any complete predictability about her gift, it could be stronger at some times than at others.

And right now she relished the passionate imagery that Blake was unintentionally sending to her. The things he wanted to do to her! Lord, he possessed a vivid inventiveness for pleasuring her.

The kiss was no longer enough to satisfy her. His erotic thoughts had already stimulated her body to the point of readiness.

With a soft mew of need, she let him know her thoughts, her desire to be touched. He responded, skimming his hand over the outside of her clothes. He pressed his palm against the apex of her thighs. She arched against his hand, feeling the sensation through the rough cloth. The barrier added a forbidden element, escalating the hunger for the touch of his skin.

Quelling the urge to unbutton his damp shirt or unbuckle

his belt, she held back, recalling his violent response to her aggression. Instead, she allowed him to lead at his own pace. But, Lord, it was costing her. Her restraint knotted every muscle. If Blake didn't make love to her very soon, she was going to go crazy.

Crazy... mad... insane...

The words ricocheted off the inside of her skull. She realized the thoughts were not her own but his. His words echoed like a taunting chant. As he began to undress her, she read his mind, feeling his emotions battling one another. His disbelief in her stories waged war against his burning desire to claim her body.

Pressing her hands against his chest, she pulled away from his kiss and gazed up at him. His heavy lids lifted. His blue eyes expressed his bewilderment.

"I'm *not* crazy, Blake," she said, unable to hide the hurt in her voice. "I'm not mad or insane."

"Did I say those words?" Uncertainty flickered across his face as his hand stilled. She knew he was wondering if he had, indeed, spoken his feelings aloud.

"That's what you think of me, though. Isn't it?"

"Cara, I—"

Her fingertips touched his lips. "I'm not angry with you, Blake. A little hurt, maybe. But I should've known better by now."

The sexually charged current of electricity continued to hum so loud in her ears that she could barely hear the sound of the wind and rain. Physically, she still wanted him to make love to her. But at what emotional cost to herself? Knowing he doubted her "stories," knowing he doubted her *sanity*, she couldn't allow herself to go any further.

Slipping out from under his arm, she levered herself up to sit on the edge of the berth. The motion of the ship rocked her. She glanced back at the wave-washed windows.

"I *must* be crazy," she muttered, turning her back to the glass. And to Blake. "Hopping into bed with you in the middle of this killer storm *is* insane. What was I thinking?"

"The same thing as I." His husky voice wrapped around her like a warm blanket as his fingers trailed down her spine. Her eyes drifted shut. Her heightened sense of awareness received more of the erotic images in his mind.

"Don't do that, Blake."

His hand paused. "Do what? This?" His fingertips continued downward to the small of her back.

"No—" *Oh . . . but it feels sooooo good.* "I meant . . . I know what you're thinking . . ."

He tugged her shirttail free. Then his hand slipped beneath the material and traveled upward again. Back rubs had always been one of her greatest weaknesses, turning her into a puddle of mush.

"What *am* I thinking?"

Relaxing more and more, she smiled to herself as his naughty thoughts poured into her head. His palm smoothed over her shoulders, swirling back and forth in a lazy-eight.

She began to describe his fantasy. "There is a quiet, secluded cove beneath the cliffs on the northern coast of Kaua'i." The movement of his hand slowed. "I'm stretched out on a grass mat while you give me a back rub." His hand stopped. "And we're both naked—"

"That's enough," he commanded, yanking his hand from under her shirt. He pushed himself off the mattress, his boots landing with a loud thud. Bud jumped to his feet, alerted to his master's mood.

"Was I right?" she asked, knowing she was. "Or am I crazy?"

"Goddammit, woman, you are making *me* crazy!"

"I know."

She told herself that she should have felt guilty for scaring the bejeezus out of him. Instead she felt smug. Vindicated. He couldn't deny it this time. He wanted proof that she had a gift. He got it. Right in his face. There was no way he could write this off as a coincidence.

He headed toward the door without calling Bud, expecting the dog to follow. When he didn't, Blake whistled for him. Still no response. "Bud, get over here," he ordered.

Cara spoke to the dog. "It's okay, Bud. He won't bite."

The black Lab thumped his tail, his tongue hanging half out of his mouth in a happy pant. His big head swung back and forth, sizing up the two argumentative humans. Finally, he loped over to the wide berth, leaped up on the mattress, turned around, and flopped down, exhaling a whoosh of air from his canine lungs. Ready to call it a night, he rested his chin on his front paws.

"Traitor," groused Blake, swinging the door open.

"Bodyguard," corrected Cara in a syrupy-sweet tone. The dog didn't budge, but his eyes rolled up to look at her with a soulful expression of adoration. His tail thumped again. She turned back to Blake and shrugged. His eyes rolled upward too. But his expression was one of resignation.

"Good night, Mrs. Edwards. I'll send Jimmy with some rope, if you need it."

"I might, at that."

Chapter 11

THE SOUTHEASTER RAGED for three days. By the time it expended the last of its fury, it had blown the crippled *Valiant* more than one hundred miles off course. On Wednesday, the twentieth of March, the sun rose on a blue sky as crystal-clear as the water beneath the bow. All hands had already been called at daybreak and were fast at work with their daily chore of swabbing the deck, supervised by chief mate Mr. Bellows.

While his barefoot men toiled from stem to stern, Blake went forward with his first mug of hot coffee in his hands. Standing on the forecastle, he stared ahead at the tranquil ocean. He heard footsteps behind him.

"*Kaikaina*, you plenty quiet dis mornin', eh?" teased Keoni, holding his own full mug of coffee as he stopped beside Blake. "Maybe you think of da lady sleepin' in your bed instead of you. Or instead of *with* you. Maybe?"

"I am 'plenty quiet' because I have not slept well since the first night of the storm."

"Naw, you not sleep well since the first night of the *wahine*."

In a peculiar Kānaka sort of way, the words almost made sense to Blake. "Is it so obvious?"

"Only to me," answered Keoni with a broad smile, his speech pattern shifting away from the Islander dialect.

"I've known you a long time. And I've never seen you this way."

"It is not affecting my duties as the captain of this vessel."

"Did I say it was? And I would have, if it had been necessary."

"You are honest to a fault, *kaikua'ana*." Blake glanced over his shoulder at McGinty and another man scrubbing the deck. "There is no damn privacy when I want it."

"Your cabin . . ."

"*She* is there," he groused. "And you know full well she is."

"Aye, sir," he mocked.

Christ, it was hard to have a friend as a subordinate on a vessel, thought Blake, though he was always happier for the companionship than regretful of the decision to sail with Keoni.

He turned and headed aft with his friend beside him, hoping to find some distance from listening ears.

"I'm at my wit's end with her," he admitted reluctantly, finding it difficult to share his feelings even with his close friend.

"Dancing to her tune, are you?"

After a sip of coffee, Blake slowly lowered the mug. Part of him wanted to wipe the smug smile off Keoni's face. Another part of him wanted to admit the truth and ask for some Kanaka insight into the situation.

"She is . . . different."

"Yes, her appearance and her speech—"

"She knows my thoughts."

"Women do those things." Keoni glanced over the rim of his mug that didn't hide his grin. "They also like to tell you what you are thinking even if you are not thinking it," he quipped, then took a drink.

"Not Cara. She knew *exactly* what I was thinking."

"Were you kissing her at the time?"

"As a matter of fact . . ."

"Then I imagine your two minds *would* be on the same path."

"No, it was more than that." Blake looked directly at his friend. "She described things in my head that she had no possible way of knowing. She has the gift of second sight."

The big Kanaka fell silent. He was clearly as disturbed as Blake by this unsettling information. The two of them stood side by side, drinking their coffee, gazing at the horizon.

Several minutes later Keoni finally spoke, his voice low so as not to be heard. "The broken mast—is that what she was jabbering about when I took her below?"

"Yes, she knew it was going to go."

"Is that how you spotted McGinty?"

Blake nodded.

"I assumed she was ranting because of her fear of going down in another shipwreck."

"At the time, I thought so too." He gazed at the bottom of his empty cup. "There is something else—the boy I promised to help her find is not her son, as she first said. She claims to have been hired by someone to search for the child."

"Do you believe her?"

"No, and I am not even sure there is a child." His thoughts drifted back to a comment made by Lupe. "However, there is a possibility she is *with* child."

"Yours?"

With an adamant shake of his head, he speculated, "Perhaps her husband's. Perhaps not."

"Has she mentioned it?"

"No." Blake felt a little guilty for insinuating that Cara would have a baby out of wedlock. Somehow he did not expect it of her, though he couldn't say why, considering the element of mystery surrounding her. "The woman at the mission suggested the notion of a child, based upon Cara's fainting spell and exhaustion."

Keoni took the empty mug from Blake's hands. "Now I understand why you have been so quiet, *kaikaina*. You have much to think about."

Blake leaned on the low rail, his narrowed gaze focused

on a whale breaching windward. "I'm leaving her in San Diego."

"Alone?"

He nodded. His insides clenched.

"She might be pregnant."

"She might not be."

He heard Keoni let out a long breath. "It's your decision, *Captain*."

Blake briefly turned his head to the side to give his friend a quelling look, then turned back to the peaceful seascape of the migrating whales.

"I cannot take her with me," he muttered.

"No, I don't suppose it would sit well with the ship's owners or the crew."

He pivoted about, leaning against the rail, his arms folded across his chest. "She would be an unpaid female passenger using my quarters during the entire trip around the Horn. Not wise. Not wise at all."

"I believe we've already established that, *aikane*."

Blake looked up and blinked a few times. "Are you still here?"

"Last that I checked."

"Don't you have some duties? Such as breakfast to cook?"

Keoni appeared unoffended by the short-tempered order. "Aye, aye, sir," he answered in full voice. But before he turned to leave, he said quietly, "You will do what you must. No matter what happens, it will all work out for the best."

Blake watched the dark-skinned Kanaka saunter off toward the galley, his arms swinging casually at his sides with a mug dangling from each hand.

"I hope to God you are right, *kaikua'ana*," Blake murmured, turning back to view the big grays in the distance. He'd made his decision. He would not take Cara with him. Yet the thought of saying good-bye to her made his chest feel as though it had suddenly been bound with anchor chain.

Inhaling deeply of the salt air, he vowed to clear his head

of any thoughts of Cara for the rest of the day.

Much to his discontent, he thought of nothing else throughout the entire morning and afternoon and long after the sun had set.

The loss of the fore topmast and the retrieval of the ship's anchor off San Juan delayed the *Valiant* a full five days before she reached the wooded point of land protecting the bay of San Diego on March 25. Only a short distance from their destination, the wind had died, leaving the brig sitting in the water like a bobbing duck at sunset with nowhere to go.

Gazing out the starboard windows of the captain's quarters, Cara sat on the berth with her legs drawn up to her chest, her arms wrapped around her knees. Bud was curled up at her feet, snoring.

Even without the travelogue chats with Jimmy, Cara would have recognized the high ridge of land rising up north of the bay, having seen it many times from the deck of a small Capri 25 owned by a friend a long time ago. Or actually a long time ahead. She stared at the spot where the little white lighthouse would be built in about twenty years, remembering the visits with Mark.

Thinking of her dead husband brought a familiar wave of sadness, though not as strong as during those first months after losing him. She supposed there would always be a part of her that would hold him close to her heart, even if she found someone else to love as much as she had loved Mark.

Someone else . . . such as Blake.

She dropped her head back with a silent groan, wishing these thoughts would quit popping into her head. She couldn't keep going back to this . . . fantasizing about him, dwelling on the feelings he'd stirred in her. If only he would have shown up in her life in the twentieth century.

Refusing to dwell on regretful if-onlys, Cara concentrated on the "what now?" By tomorrow, weather permitting, she could proceed with her much-interrupted search for Andrew. It was now the third week in March. He'd been missing since December 22. Three months on his own. She wondered how he was dealing with the confusion and nightmares of time-travel and abduction.

And where was he now? Could he be here in San Diego or was he halfway around the world? Unfortunately, she couldn't just pick up a phone and call the port authorities to look out for a blond-headed, ten-year-old kid who looked entirely out of his element.

A knock at the door came as a welcome reprieve from her worrisome thoughts. "Come in, Jimmy."

Instead of the young steward, the Kanaka cook walked into the cabin with her dinner. *"Aloha ahiahi, e Cara. Pehea 'oe?"*

"Aloha nō," answered Cara, her spirits lifting. Among the few bright moments the past few days had been learning a little Hawaiian from Keoni during his brief visits. So far she had learned a few easy phrases, including tonight's question of "How are you?"

Attempting to respond with, "I'm fine, thank you," she said to him, *"Maika nō au, mahalo."*

"The word is *maika'i*, not *maika*," corrected the cook, erupting into a roar of laughter.

This woke up Bud, who jumped down off the bed, allowing Cara to do the same. She padded over to the table and "accidentally" elbowed Keoni in the ribs as she lifted the cover from her supper.

"Ow—!"

"Then quit laughing at me. It couldn't have been *that* funny."

Through chuckles, he described to her the word she had used. Apparently, she had called herself an ancient Hawaiian term for a round stone used in some sort of game. She could hardly hold back her own giggle. Instead of "I'm fine," she'd said, "I'm a shot put!"

Falling back on her tried-and-true English, she invited the Kanaka to stay for a while, then realized he probably needed to return to his duties in the galley.

"I can sit a few minutes." When the dog bumped his huge black head under the cook's hand, Keoni glanced down. "But not too long, eh, Bud, you hungry boy."

As she ate, the cook taught her a few more words, and she practiced pronouncing yet another strange string of vowels. She was determined to learn the language, if for no other reason than her own enjoyment. God only knew when or where she would ever use it. Then again, if she didn't make it out of the nineteenth century, she could always relocate to Kaua'i, her favorite place on earth in the future days of Aloha Airlines and condos on the beach.

Slipping a chunk of beef to Bud, she glanced at Keoni apologetically. "Sorry, force of habit. I can't stand to see a dog drool in my presence."

"He likes you."

"No kidding." Her quip brought a perplexed look from him.

"Bud is a good judge of character."

"Thanks. Would you mind telling that to Captain Masters?" Cara hadn't seen the man once since the first night of the storm. During the short periods of time she'd been allowed on deck in fair weather, she noticed his conspicuous absence. "He's avoiding me like the plague."

"I've noticed."

"I asked you before about him, but you refused to talk. Won't you at least tell me about how you met?"

He studied her for a moment, then nodded. "He was a cabin boy on a merchant ship much like this one. The captain was one mean son of a—uh, that is . . . He was *'a 'ole maika'i.*"

"No good?" translated Cara.

Keoni gave her an encouraging nod, then went back to his story. "Blake ran off, stowing away on a whaler bound for the Islands. But he was discovered the second day out."

"Did that captain hurt him, too?"

"No, thank God. Blake never wanted to set foot on a ship again, so he was brought to my father. We've been brothers, ever since."

"What made him go back to the sea?"

Keoni shrugged his massive shoulders. "Time heals . . ."

Cara understood the old saying. She also understood her vision of Blake. The abuse he'd suffered had been unspeakable.

"Time hasn't healed Blake," she said solemnly. "The wounds are still there."

"So you saw the scars on his back."

"Yes, but I'm talking about something deeper—a hurt that kills the soul. I think I can help him, but he won't let me."

"You should concentrate on finding Andrew." Averting his gaze, he looked toward Bud. As he stroked the dog's shiny black coat, she sensed something was wrong.

"Blake is going to leave me in San Diego, isn't he?"

The Kanaka's head came up slowly, a silent apology in his black eyes. "Yes, he is."

Her appetite suddenly vanished. She pushed the plate away. "I was counting on his help to find Andrew, and I blew it! I scared him off. Damn!"

Out of the corner of her eye she saw the Hawaiian's surprise. "My turn to apologize," she said. "I shouldn't swear."

He grinned. "It seems to come quite easily to you."

"Perhaps too easily. I need to watch myself more carefully." She pivoted in her chair and put her hand on the man's thick forearm. As before, he guarded his thoughts well. Still, she sensed certain things. "I am aware of how . . . different I seem to you and everyone else. Keoni, I need your help."

"I will not betray *ko'u kaikaina*." *My younger brother.*

"I'm not asking you to." She felt a kinship of her own with the Hawaiian. "In your world, you have beliefs that a *haole* cannot understand, let alone accept as real. Some of the stories told as myths and legends are based on fact. Am I right?"

He agreed.

"Keoni . . ." She hesitated, praying that he would listen and accept what she was about to say. "I know Blake has told you about my second sight."

"Yes, we have talked. But then, it would be easy for you to guess that we have discussed you."

"If he hasn't been here in this cabin in days, how would I know he is concerned about my condition?"

"You were terribly ill in San Juan—"

"Not with morning sickness, as he is wondering."

"You overheard us talking when we were on deck," he said, pointing upward. "Or you heard the woman at the mission."

He had a ready explanation for everything she tried to use to make a case for herself.

"I'd like a chance to prove myself. May I hold your hand?"

He balked, then reluctantly complied. Though it wasn't necessary to close her eyes, she did it to aid her concentration.

"Think of something I would know nothing about."

Pictures and images popped into her head. She smiled at the vision of the large half-moon bay of calm blue water on the north shore of Kaua'i.

"Ah, that's easy—Hanalei." She heard his sudden intake of breath. Considering that the island was his home, she wasn't surprised to pick up his memory of it. Actually, it was almost too simple. She wanted more of a challenge. "Think of a special day in your past . . . There you go . . . Good . . . I see some of your people around you."

Cara gave a precise description of each person, naming his mother and father and siblings. And bride. It was his wedding day. As he quietly acknowledged her observation, she suddenly received a torrent of images as if a floodgate had been opened. He had lost his young bride in a hurricane during his first long voyage, later learning about their twin babies with her.

"Oh, Keoni . . ." Sympathy swelled her heart. She reached up and tenderly cupped his cheek. "I'm so sorry. Here I have been talking about Blake and his painful past when you, too, have scars that have not completely healed."

His fingers wrapped around her wrist, holding her tight

yet not hurting her. She sensed that this man would never harm her.

"How can you know these things?" he asked, awe in his voice.

"A gift from the gods."

This was the moment of truth. She had to tell him the truth. With luck, he would believe her. Then maybe, just maybe, she would have an ally on board the *Valiant*, someone who could reason with Blake. "Keoni, I am not from this time. I have come here from the future. Far in the future. The end of the next century."

His grip slackened. His eyes grew wide. His jaw dropped. Any second now, she expected him to hightail it out of there faster than a speeding bullet.

Then he said, "I believe you."

The following morning a fair breeze picked up again, allowing the *Valiant* to round the high point. Entering the narrow outlet of a small river, the crew fired the bow guns in salute, which was returned from the shore. With barely enough clearance for their single ship, the crew brought her through this snaking waterway that followed the inside face of the point and curved inland around a finger of land where the bay opened to a spacious anchorage.

To the north, a chain of hills ran inland from the point. To the east and south, the landscape was low and green from spring rains, yet sported only a scattering of trees, none of which were taller than six or eight feet. On the beach, four long wooden hide houses were lined up end to end, the only signs of civilization. The presidio and its village were three miles eastward; another three miles further was the mission.

Mooring within a cable's length of the sandy shore of San Diego, the *Valiant* joined two other vessels at anchor. One was the brig *Pilgrim* from Boston, another the *Ayacucho*, a long, sharp brig bearing the British colors, each standing off the beach in front of a hide house that was under their use while on the coast.

Blake had sent his steward to fetch Cara, unwilling to set foot in that cabin and risk being alone with her. After his last visit, he had vowed to stay away from her, though it had been almost impossible to keep from going to her. Yet, if he'd gone to her one more time, he would have made love to her. He was certain of it. Then he would never be able to leave her alone in this uncivilized territory with its volatile political coups and rough men.

She had asked his help to bring her to this port. He owed her nothing more than that. His decision had been made. He would sail for Boston within the week without Cara. And nothing would change his mind. Nothing.

When Cara appeared on deck, every man in the crew became aware of her presence, glancing her way. Even with her male clothing and cropped hair, she was unmistakably female with her large, expressive eyes and full lips. In the bright sunlight, her Indian and Spanish blood was much more evident in her light coppery skin. His own blood warmed at the sight of her, stirring up thoughts he had no right to be thinking.

Angered by his powerful urges, he barked at Mr. Bellows to get his men back on task.

Allowing Jimmy to assist Cara into the boat, Blake stood back until the last, then called Bud, who looked forward to these land excursions after confinement on the small ship.

No words were spoken during the short trip to shore with the Kānaka oarsmen, including Keoni. Halfway, Bud began barking at the pack of dogs living around the hide houses. They responded with their own raucous yips and howls. Before the longboat landed, Bud leaped off the bow, splashing into the foot-deep water, where he was greeted by a tall, agile canine that outweighed him by several pounds.

"Welly!" cried all the Kānaka in unison, greeting the jowled namesake of the Duke of Wellington that was a strange mix of broad-faced mastiff and long-legged grey-hound.

"What *is* it?" Cara asked Keoni, rather than Blake, who was closer to her. Her friendship with the cook had rapidly grown into a bond that sorely chafed Blake. After noticing the numerous ''language lessons'' over the last several days, he did not like the way her smiling eyes gazed at his jovial brother instead of him.

While Keoni told her about the leader of the pack, Blake ground his back teeth to keep from interjecting himself into the benign conversation.

As soon as the boat was pulled up on dry land, he leaped out and turned to offer his gentlemanly assistance to Cara, only to see her being lifted off her feet by Keoni, whose wide hands spanned her small waist. When she was set down, those hands remained on her waist far longer than Blake thought was necessary.

Tipping her head back, she looked up at Keoni and thanked him, saying, *''Mahalo nui loa.''*

''No'u ka hau'oli.'' The pleasure is mine, he said in his native tongue, then offered to take her to speak with the Kānaka about the boy she was searching for. A number of them lived inside an enormous baking oven, built and abandoned by a Russian crew and large enough to sleep nearly a dozen men. All the Islanders gathered together to smoke, drink, and have a fair time while in port at this ''Kānaka Hotel'' or ''Oahu Coffeehouse.''

As she paused with a concentrated effort to translate his words, Blake stepped forward to put an end to their lesson.

''She does not need your services, big brother,'' he said to Keoni in the Island language. ''You ask questions about the boy here at the beach and the oven.'' Then turning to Cara, he grasped her upper arm. ''In the meantime, *I* will take you to the village to ask if anyone there knows about him.''

She wrested her arm away from him, clearly perturbed with him for taking the decision out of her hands. ''I'll go on my own, thank you.''

''You'll do nothing of the kind. This is not a safe place for you alone.'' He gestured toward men bringing off uncured hides from the ships and piling them outside the houses. Others worked at pickling, drying, and cleaning the cattle skins for the five-month storage in the hull of the vessels bound for home.

Would he need to explain to her that this male-only community offered few opportunities for the men to see a lady, let alone socialize with one? Couldn't she see the reason for his concern?

"You win," she agreed halfheartedly, though she didn't offer her arm to him. "Let's get going. No horses, though. I've been cooped up too long without any exercise. A three-mile walk will do me good."

Leaving a smiling Keoni behind, Blake motioned in the direction of the small village. "This way . . ."

"What about Bud?"

"He'll romp with his friends for hours."

As if the dog wished to make a fool of his master, Bud raced up to them and fell into step next to Cara. She chuckled. "I guess he still feels he needs to protect me."

Blake grunted in reluctant agreement, then fell silent. They had not walked far when Cara glanced over her shoulder, paused, then turned to gaze down at the bay. Sunlight glinted off the calm water. The four long wooden hide houses stretched out on the beach below them. Her attention was drawn to the south end of the last building, where three sailors worked out of sight of the other men on the beach.

A dark Indian approached them, cautiously looking around. At his side was a woman in a dress that was nothing more than an earth-brown sack.

"He is her husband," explained Blake as the Indian appeared to be speaking to one of the hide workers while the other two listened, also glancing around nervously. As the husband nodded, his wife was circled by the three men and led around the corner of the hide house. The Indian then turned, walked several paces, and sat down on the ground.

"Omigod," breathed Cara in horror. "We've got to *do* something to save that poor woman."

Before she started down the hill toward the building, he grabbed her hand. "Wait, Cara."

"I can't stand here while those men rape her!"

"As appalling as it may sound, she agreed to that arrangement. No one forced her. She went of her own accord."

Cara stared at the Indian. "He's just sitting there? Letting his wife—"

"Indian wives are often brought here by their husbands to make money for their families. They cannot sneak down here at night without alarming the dogs. When they are really desperate, they come here during the day. If she is caught by the *alcaldes*, she will be whipped."

"Just her? Not the men? Not her husband for bringing her?"

"Only the women are punished for illicit behavior. But the authorities have been known to look the other way if the woman is merely an Indian who is not worthy of having her virtue protected."

"Willing or not," she said sadly, her voice barely audible, her eyes shimmering with unshed tears, "it's still rape."

Blake suddenly imagined Cara in a similar situation, forced to earn her living by selling herself to these men. The very idea angered him. She could not be left to fend for herself. Before the week was out, he would find a safe home for her. He would also leave behind enough money for her to live modestly, if not well. But for how long? Until she found this boy named Andrew? That is, if the ten-year-old boy actually existed.

"Andrew *does* exist, Blake."

Breaking free of his hand, Cara spun away from the view of the hide house, her pained expression etched upon her face. She marched up the hill, leaving him speechless.

Regaining his composure, he said to her retreating backside. "Dammit, you did it again, didn't you?"

"Yes," she hollered over her shoulder. Bud traipsed along between them, then pulled up short when Cara turned around. Planting her feet wide, she hooked her hands on her hips. "And I will manage without you or your money, thank you very much. I assure you that I have no intention of selling this body to anyone.''

"Good," Blake barked. Bud barked, too. "Shut up, Bud."

"Don't take your anger out on him. He's only reacting to you."

"He's my dog. I'll say or do whatever I please with him."

"Well, you may own him, but you don't own *me*. So I would prefer you keep your thoughts to yourself."

"I *did* keep them to myself. You are the one who took them without my permission," he argued, silencing her.

The absolute absurdity of his statement hung in the air. The corner of her mouth twitched as she fought to keep from smiling. The smallest chuckle slipped out. His dog yipped in playful excitement, then dashed toward her.

Blake lunged forward. "No, Bud!"

With startled laughter, she caught the huge front paws with her hands as Blake grabbed the boisterous canine from behind. Stumbling on a rock, he joined the momentum of the leaping dog. The three of them went down. Twisting his body during the fall, he managed to keep his full weight, and Bud's, from crushing Cara.

In the midst of trying to get his dog out of the way, which was impossible, he grunted, "Are . . . you . . . hurt?"

"No, but—" She sputtered. "He won't quit licking me. No, Bud. No more kisses."

Damn dog, he groused silently. *Damn LUCKY dog.*

Blake was not yet ready to let go of his anger and frustration with Cara. Or with Bud. Finally freeing the arm that had been pinned under his dog, he knelt on his knees and tugged Bud to his feet, scolding him soundly and sending him off to explore the bushes.

Breathless from laughter, she lay on her back, her arms flung out at her side. Her giggles completely melted his annoyance. Her rich, coffee-colored eyes danced with mirth. Dusty and mussed, she still looked enchantingly beautiful. He gazed at her smiling lips, wanting to kiss her, knowing he shouldn't.

Reaching out, he brushed his knuckles across the hollow of her cheek. She stilled.

"What am I thinking now?" he asked, his mind filled with thoughts of wanting her.

"That I frighten you."

Chapter 12

BLAKE PULLED BACK. "You are wrong."

"I know you want to make love to me. It's obvious we *both* want it." Cara's gaze was direct, unwavering. "But underneath all that lust, I scare the hell out of you."

He shot to his feet. For an instant, his gentlemanly manners prompted him to offer his hand to help her up. Then he walked several feet from her, putting some much-needed distance between them.

He heard her approach, then felt her hands come around his waist. She pressed her cheek to the middle of his back. When he realized she was probably peeking into his mind, he tried to empty his head of all thoughts. But the harder he worked at it, the harder it got.

"Let go, Blake."

"Let go? *You* are the one holding *me*."

"I meant for you to stop holding on to the demons from your past."

"You are mistaken, Cara. I have told you before that I have already let go of my past, so much so that I have forgotten it entirely."

"But I have the key that will open that door. I *am* the key. I know things about you—"

"Through Keoni."

"No, through touching you. I saw something terrible happen to you as a boy. And, through me, you can learn about your past. You must go back before you can move forward.''

She said nothing more but remained standing behind him, holding him in a gentle embrace. Radiant heat from her body seeped into every fiber of his being, infusing him with her warmth and compassion. He closed his eyes and took a shaky breath, giving himself time to think of what she had said, what she had meant. While he had no basis of knowledge to comprehend the concept of this ''letting go'' of which she spoke, he somehow knew inside himself that Cara's statements had a ring of truth.

In these few brief moments of contemplation, he'd had no intention of reviewing his past, remembered or forgotten. Yet he found himself mentally exploring a cove on the island of Kaua'i with his new friend and adopted brother.

''You and Keoni, that's good,'' encouraged Cara's soft voice. ''Is this right after you came to the islands?''

''Yes, I was fourteen.'' He saw the officer who had brought him to live with the Pahinui family. He saw his new parents and sisters and brothers. Then he remembered their tears when they saw the scars across his back.

''How did you get the scars? Think back . . .''

''Captain Myers.'' Blake's body tensed at the memory of the man who possessed the face of Satan himself. The heinous leer bore down on him, growing larger and larger. ''No!''

''It's all right,'' soothed Cara. ''You're safe. Stand up to him. He can't hurt you now.''

Blake broke away from her. ''I can't do this. Come, let's go to the village to look for Andrew.'' He started off again, leaving her to decide whether to stand there or go with him.

With a heavy sigh of resignation, she followed him. ''Do you believe he exists or are you just pacifying me?''

''I don't know what to believe anymore,'' he murmured as Bud came up beside him and nudged his hand for a pat.

The village consisted of a few dozen squat adobe huts and some larger whitewashed houses, all of which were clustered at the base of a hill on which the old fort stood in a state of near ruin, though still occupied by a ragtag group of Mexican soldiers.

As they approached the small community, Cara had a feeling that she would learn nothing about Andrew from the people here. After talking with women, particularly mothers, without any luck, they walked up to the fort. They learned nothing more when they met the pompous commandant and his family, who did not know and did not care about a lost little boy.

They left the presidio with Bud loping ahead of them, flushing a flock of small brown birds from the bush. He took off after them with no hope of catching a single one.

"I need to go to the mission," she said, watching the black Lab.

"It lies another three miles east of here in a valley. Are you sure you want to walk?"

"I may regret it tomorrow, but right now it feels good to stretch my legs."

"But the *padre* will probably tell you no more than the villagers, that they know of no yellow-haired child."

She had a feeling Blake was right. Still, she knew in her gut she must go, even though it might be a wasted and tiring trip.

The hike turned out to be more than invigorating for Cara. The smell of spring was in the air with a rich scent of the earth mingling with the sun-warmed tall grass and green bushes. The lack of abundant trees didn't seem to matter. There was a perfection in the untouched, untainted landscape that only someone from the urban sprawl of the future could appreciate. It all seemed so wide open and spread out.

Following a worn trail over low hills and uneven terrain to a lush valley, she spotted in the distance a tiered bell tower with five bells and a cross on top. After what seemed like half an hour or more, they crossed a small stream and entered Mission San Diego de Alcalá. The perimeter was marked by a row of tall white buildings on one side, smaller structures on another side, the large church taking up the whole of the third side, then a long wall that finished the enclosure of the square. The place appeared as deserted as the one at San Juan Capistrano. Occasionally, a half-dressed Kumeyaay Indian walked from one doorway to the next, not acknowledging their presence.

While Blake looked around, Bud followed Cara to the church, where a large fountain spouted four columns of fresh water into its base. As the dog sat at her side, she cupped her hands to catch some water and bring it to her mouth. Free of chlorine and other purifying chemicals, the water tasted so refreshingly clean it could almost be sweet. When a paw brushed her leg, she glanced down at Bud.

"You had plenty to drink at the stream," she reminded the dog, then chuckled at his woeful expression. "Oh, all right." She scooped more water, knelt down, and offered it to him as Blake approached, but most of it dribbled onto the ground.

Somewhere behind them, a man emerged from a building and called out an exuberant greeting in Spanish. He was dressed in the more civilized apparel of the region—a wide hat, short jacket, open-neck shirt, red sash, knee-length pants, white stockings, and deerskin shoes ornamented with Indian beads. He also had a set of keys dangling from a neck chain, which indicated his stewardship of the mission. As the *mayordomo*, he offered them food and wine and a bone for the dog, but no information about a blond ten-year-old.

After their meal, Blake compensated the man with a few *reals* in much the same way that he had handled payment for services to Lupe in San Juan.

When Blake suggested visiting the Indian huts to talk with the people, Cara agreed, despite her certainty that they would not be any help either. Still, there was some reason she'd been compelled to visit this mission. Why? What was this niggling feeling just out of reach in the back of her mind?

The *mayordomo* accompanied them, to interpret the Kumeyaays' native language. Beyond the mission walls was a tiny community of crude twig domes with naked little children running about. The men could be seen in the distance, tending cattle and a large plot of land with numerous vegetables and abundant fruit trees.

The women wore sack dresses similar to the one on the woman who had sneaked off with the three sailors on the beach. She wondered if any of these women were also forced to visit the hide houses, though she couldn't imagine the need to do so when she saw the garden. Still, her full stomach gave her a guilty conscience for consuming a huge lunch while others were suffering from lack of food.

Bringing her concentration back to the search for Andrew, Cara followed the *mayordomo* around the small village, learning nothing as he asked questions about the missing boy. As he spoke to a feeble, shriveled-up little man who could easily have been more than a hundred years old, she noticed an old woman hurry away and disappear through the huge gates of the mission. Cara's internal radar perked up.

"Blake, would you stick around and ask the questions for a little bit while I go back inside the mission?"

"Why? What's in there that you need?"

"I'll just be a few minutes," she said, purposely being vague. If she told him about her hunch and it turned out to be wrong, he wouldn't let her forget it. "I'll be back before you know it."

"Very well. But stay inside the walls. Don't wander away."

"Aye, aye, captain," she answered obediently, then turned to leave, only to stop and tell Bud not to follow her. The black Lab's ears drooped as he plopped down in the dirt.

Walking away, she overheard Blake grumble, "That's the first time someone's had to make my own dog stay with me."

Leaving him with the *mayordomo*, she passed through the entrance and glanced around the square. The door of the church was closing. Instinct prodded her to follow.

The interior of the enormous adobe church was cool and dark in contrast to the warm spring sunshine outside. Cara paused to let her eyes adjust to the low light, then looked around. The sanctuary was empty.

"Hello?" She spoke quietly, yet her voice seemed to bounce off the walls in the silent house of worship. She heard the skittering of a small animal, then saw a field mouse running along the base of the rough white wall a few feet away.

Walking toward the altar at the front of the church, she again called out, and again received no answer. She stopped alongside one of the first few benches, absorbing the feeling of reverence and sanctity. Moving over to the wooden seat, she kept her eyes forward, staring at the crucifix. She slowly sat down. And waited.

Even though her parents had all but abandoned their affiliation with the Catholic Church when Cara was young, there was something about the traditional church setting that prompted her to fold her hands and bow her head. A compulsion to pray for Andrew prompted a spontaneous yet awkward one-sided conversation with her creator.

"Please watch over him," she murmured. "And show me how to find him. I'm having a hard time accepting that I came all this way without catching up with him. So what do you say? Can you throw me a few clues?"

A sudden tap on her shoulder made her leap to her feet as if a needle had pricked her backside. "Blake—" she scolded in hushed anger as she spun around. She stopped, stunned by the sight in front of her. It couldn't be. Not again. This was too strange . . . even for her.

"A-Aunt G-Gaby?"

The woman smiled sweetly and gave a slight nod. *"Estoy aquí, mi Cara."*

"Uh-uh. No way. This can't be possible." She turned and walked a few paces, then pivoted. "Okay, I've got this figured out now. You've had a week or more to travel down here from Capistrano by donkey."

"No," Gabriella answered in Spanish. "I am here, Cara. Simply accept this. Don't try to understand how."

"I may be psychic. But I'm just not used to these real-life visitations. It's downright spooky."

Her aunt kept on smiling that familiar, lovable smile, then gestured toward the bench. "Come and sit."

"I'm more comfortable standing, thank you."

"Easier to run away if you get too scared?"

"You're reading my mind."

The woman chuckled silently. "I came to you during your fever, Cara, but I want you to understand that you can 'see' me whenever you wish. Or you can simply hear my voice."

"So, you're a figment of my imagination."

"Not entirely. But if that is how you wish to believe, so it shall be."

"It's not like you to patronize me, Aunt Gaby. I *want* to comprehend what's happening here."

"Do you 'comprehend' your time-travel experience?"

"I—" Unable to describe the complex confusion of acceptance and bewilderment, Cara backed up to a bench on the opposite side of the aisle from her aunt and sat down. She looked down at her hands, turning them over and studying her palms. "I know I am here in the flesh. I feel the sea breeze and taste the water. I see the ships and hear the birds. I experience the passage of days and nights. So to answer your question—I cannot grasp *how* it is I am here in this time, but I do accept I am here now."

"Then why is it so hard to accept that *I* am here with you now?" Gabriella came over and joined her on the bench. "You have stepped beyond the portal of Time. Now step beyond the portal of Mind."

Her aunt reached out, taking Cara's hand. The warmth of Gabriella's skin defied logic. But wasn't that the point? Here and now, there was no logic of twentieth-century science. Her own psychic abilities defied scientific logic. Yet she lived with it every day of her life. Funny, how easy it was for her to accept one thing and not another, especially when the average man on the street would refuse to accept any of it and consider anyone who did just plain crazy.

As Blake did.

"Okay, I don't have a fever, so you're not the Angel of

Mercy that Lupe talked about. And you're definitely not a ghost.''

"Don't be so sure."

Cara glanced up, then saw the teasing in Gabriella's eyes. "That's meant to be a joke? Ha, ha.''

"Is it so important to define who I am or what I am? No, it's more important to find Andrew.''

"That's why you came to me again, isn't it?"

"Yes."

"Then why all the hocus-pocus?'' She launched herself to her feet, squelching the urge to fire off a few curse words inside the church. Pacing in the aisle, she said, "If you know where he is, tell me and I'll go get him. Better yet, why aren't *you* the one bringing him back to his parents?'' She halted in midstride and spun around. "Wait a *second! You* talked me into taking this case in the first place! *You* knew damn well what I was getting into!''

"Now, now, watch your tongue. You're in a church, Cara.''

Cara glowered. "What the hell—excuse me, *heck*—is going on, Aunt Gaby? I think I have a right to know.''

"This journey is as much your destiny as it is Andrew's. For now, that is all you need to know.''

"No, I *need* to know where to find him so I can take him back. He's been gone more than three months. I've been gone nearly two weeks. The authorities are probably dragging Dana Point Harbor looking for my body and Andrew's.''

"He is on a ship called the *Ballade*, bound for Boston.''

"Is he being treated decently? No abuse? Please tell me he's not being harmed.''

"Life is hard for him, but he's strong, a survivor.''

"But what about—?''

"His treatment has been harsh but not cruel. He hasn't suffered the way Captain Masters suffered when he was a cabin boy.''

"You know about Blake?'' Her eyes searched her aunt's face, hoping to learn more about his traumatic past and how to help him. She threw her hands up. "Why on earth am I asking you such a dumb question? *Of course* you know about him. You know everything else about Andrew and me. Why wouldn't you know about Blake?''

''Whether you realize it or not, you are healing him, Cara. You must make him remember his past.''

''Getting him to do anything is tough enough. *Making* him do something he doesn't want to do is impossible.''

''Just as it is impossible for me to be sitting here talking to you? As impossible as traveling through time?''

''Okay, okay. I get your point.''

''I must leave now.'' Her voice dropped to a whisper as she rose from the bench. ''Blake is coming for you.''

''Will I see you again?''

Silently, Gabriella cocked her eyebrow as if to say, ''Need you ask?''

At that moment, Bud yipped from the open doorway as he saw Cara in the aisle at the front of the church.

''Quiet, Bud. Stay!'' ordered Blake, standing beside his dog.

Cara walked up to the two of them. Resisting the urge to reach up and touch Blake, she gave her attention to Bud, petting him affectionately and scratching behind his ears.

''Did she know anything about Andrew?'' he asked.

''Who?''

''That woman who walked out the side door just now.''

In a way, she was relieved to know he'd actually seen someone. Yet she was also surprised, considering the way her aunt left in such a hurry, as if she hadn't wanted Blake to spot her. Then again, why hadn't Gabriella simply vanished into thin air, since that seemed to be her modus operandi. ''You saw an old woman? With me?''

''A glimpse.''

''Well, Blake,'' she sighed, ''you wouldn't believe me if I told you, anyway.''

''You are absolutely right,'' he remarked a bit too adamantly. ''I do *not* want to know.''

''Fine by me.'' She headed toward the entrance gates, with Bud brushing alongside her leg.

Blake caught up with her, then fell into step. "I want to know."

His reversal amused her, but she kept walking without uttering a word. She knew it wasn't his curiosity he wanted appeased. In her gut, she was certain he had his own hunch, just as she'd had one when she'd seen the old woman leave the Indian village. But Blake didn't want to admit it. Instead, he wanted her to say who was with her in the church. Then he could spout off about the absurdity of it . . . just as she'd done. And he would refuse to believe it . . . just as she'd done. Okay, so she wasn't exactly open to every bizarre twist the universe could throw at her. But at least she'd gotten over it quickly enough. Blake wouldn't.

They walked in silence out of the mission and crossed the small stream. On the opposite bank, he gently grasped her arm and pulled her to a stop.

"Was it that blasted angel again? Or your aunt? Or whatever she calls herself."

She gave him her most mischievous grin. Without saying a word, she turned back to the well-worn path and started again toward the presidio.

"Ca-ra," he called after her. The touch of warning in his voice sounded more playful than threatening.

"If I tell you now, you'll only get upset and ruin a perfectly beautiful afternoon walk back to the beach."

"*You* are not returning to the beach with me. Or the ship."

She abruptly pulled up, remembering Keoni's disclosure that Blake was going to leave her here in San Diego. "Is that so?" she asked, pretending not to know she was about to be dumped. "Did you have somewhere else in mind?"

"There is bound to be a family in one of the big houses who will take you in."

"But Andrew isn't here. Why would I stay if he's not here?"

"I can't take you with me, Cara."

She stared at him for a long moment, seeing no apology in his determined gaze. "Can't or won't?"

"I don't want to argue. As you said a moment ago, it is too nice of an afternoon—"

"Forget that. I'm telling you now, I must find a way to get to Boston. You're headed there. So why can't I go with you?"

"How is it you suddenly have a need to sail to Boston when you have never mentioned it before today?"

"Andrew is on the *Ballade*, bound for Boston."

Blake narrowed his eyes, studying her. "Did Gabriella tell you this in the church?"

She scuffed the dirt with her shoe, then scratched an itch by her eye. Finally, she decided to face the music. Looking straight at him, she tried to be as casual as she could. "Sure, yeah, of course." *So much for casual.*

"I'm sorry, Cara."

"You won't take me?"

"No. I will find someone to rent a room to you, which will be at my expense. You needn't worry about money."

As the afternoon sun shone on his tan face, she realized that too soon he would be gone from her life, leaving her alone in the past, in a weird time warp that she'd never asked for. He was her stabilizer, her security. The realization stung the back of her eyes and closed her throat.

"You need me, dammit." Her shaky voice betrayed her emotions. "You need me as much as I need you."

"Don't make this hard . . ."

"But it *is* hard, Blake. I have to find Andrew. And I don't want anyone else to take me to Boston because I'm scared to death I might end up with a perverted, sadistic bastard of a captain who might do to me what was done to you."

"What do you mean 'what was done to me'? A woman would never be flogged."

"I'm not talking about being whipped."

"Then what *are* you talking about?"

She stared at him, regretting her outburst. He had not reached the point of remembering. Or else he'd refused to remember. Either way, he honestly didn't understand her meaning. How could she explain the atrocities committed against him? She couldn't. Not only would he be horrified, he would call her a liar. There had to be a better way to get herself on that ship before the week was out. This way was not it.

"I'll go to the village," she acquiesced, hoping that somehow she would find a way to convince him to change his mind in the next few days.

They walked along for quite a while, up hills and down, following the general direction of the stream, which could occasionally be heard in the distance. Both of them were lost in their own thoughts, neither of them in much of a mood to talk. Bud seemed to sense that the two dreary humans were not about to throw a stick for him, so he trotted ahead of them, content to carry one with him in case they changed their minds.

About midway to the presidio, Cara looked around for a tall thicket to serve as a privacy screen for a sudden need.

With a little embarrassment, she asked Blake, "Would you mind if I walked over there a little way so I can . . . uh, use a bush?"

Understanding her situation, he nodded. "Keep a keen eye out for snakes. They are quite abundant this time of year."

"I will."

Bud followed her twenty or thirty feet through low shrubs and around large rocks before she shooed him off and took care of business as best she could in the primitive surroundings. Afterward, she was headed back to the trail, winding past a cluster of small boulders, when she saw the dog racing toward her.

"Not again," she laughed, dashing off toward Blake to avoid being pounced on. Bud was in hot pursuit when she heard the distinctive hiss and rattle just ahead of her.

Trying to stop, she skidded in the dirt. In a blur of motion, the diamondback struck out at her right foot, barely missing the toe of her shoe. With lightning speed, it retreated into a coil at the base of a rock, well within striking distance of her ankle. The black Lab charged past her leg, growling.

"No, Bud!"

Ignoring her, he lunged for the snake.

"NO! Oh, dear God . . . Blake!"

Dust flew. Snarls. Snapping jaws. A pained yelp. It was over as fast as it had begun. Bud shook the dead rattler in his mouth vigorously as Blake ran up.

"Drop it, Bud."

The dog obeyed, releasing the thick, four-foot reptile from his mouth. It flopped lifeless onto the sandy soil next to the rocks. Blake tossed it a great distance, then knelt to praise his dog for saving Cara. Bud immediately settled down from the excitement, then began to whimper.

Blake glanced up, agony in his eyes. "He's been bitten."

Chapter 13

DROPPING TO HER knees in front of Bud, Cara ran her hands over his head and down his shoulders to his front legs. His pitiful whine grew louder as he took his weight off his right paw.

"The swelling has already started," she noted, searching for the injury.

"Oh, Christ . . ." Blake's groan was a tortured whisper of vulnerability, yet his face hardened into a determined mask. Cara was aware of how much this dog meant to him. Beneath his stoic facade, he was already grieving the inevitable loss of his companion. She couldn't blame him. She felt much the same way.

"We have to work fast." Cara yanked her belt from her pants, intending to use it for a makeshift tourniquet. Without the antivenom serum of modern medicine, she had no other choice but to try an outmoded technique, praying it would work as well on a canine as on a human, and praying she didn't have any open wounds in her mouth for the poison to seep into. She had to chance it though. For Bud, for Blake and for herself.

"What are you going to do?"

"Save his life, I hope. Get out your knife, then hold him so he can't move," she directed, wrapping the belt around the dog's upper leg. Blake quickly supplied the weapon, which had been hidden beneath the leg of his trousers. He then used gentle force to lay Bud down and held him there while she cinched the belt tight. Bud struggled, crying loudly.

Cara searched for the puncture wounds beneath the black fur, soothing the Lab with her voice. "Hang on, sweetheart. This might not feel too good, but it'll be over quick, I promise."

Turning to give instructions to Blake, she saw her own fear reflected in his eyes. "Pin him down—he's going to fight like hell when I cut him."

"Are you bleeding him?"

"Not exactly." Looking down at Bud, she saw a strange calm come over him. Though she sensed it was as much from dizziness and the drop in his blood pressure as anything else, she saw that his black canine eyes gazed back at her with complete trust. She hoped it was still there after she got finished with him.

With more conviction than she felt, she vowed, "You're going to live, fella."

Blake straddled his dog's body. "I hope to God you're right." He took Bud's muzzle in a firm grip to keep him from instinctively biting at the infliction of pain.

"If he starts to vomit, let go so he won't choke on it."

"Aye."

Relying on gut instinct and a little luck, she cut a small incision, dropped her mouth to it and sucked.

"No, Cara! I won't let you die for him!" Horror in his voice, he demanded that she stop. After she spat out the poison, she glanced up at him.

"Don't shout at me! Now be quiet and let me do what I've got to do." She lowered her head again and sucked on the wound.

Spit, don't swallow. Spit, don't swallow.

The chant stayed in her head while she worked over the suddenly frightened and squirming dog, its cries muffled. Blake fought hard to keep Bud from breaking free. Soon Cara sensed that she had done all she could, and she sat back on her heels. Blake released his hold on the dog's muzzle, and Bud lay exhausted on his side, panting heavily.

"Stay here with him. And don't try to stop the bleeding until I get back." Clutching the top of her pants with one hand, Cara dashed to the stream, fell down on all fours, and washed out her mouth.

Nausea crept up into her throat as the shock of the attack began to wear off. What if she'd accidentally swallowed some venom? The best thing to do was to get rid of any possible poison that might have gotten into her system. With her stomach already churning, she put her fingers to the back of her mouth to initiate a gagging reflex.

"Cara?" came Blake's concerned voice from behind her. Leaning over the stream, she impatiently waved him away. This unpleasant task wasn't something she wanted to do, especially in front of Blake, but it had to be done. When it was all over, she hung her head between her shoulders for a moment, feeling like a wrung-out wet rag. She felt his hand rest on her back, then slide to the nape of her neck.

"Cara?" he repeated with worry. His tender touch conveyed his unspoken anguish that she had deliberately poisoned herself in order to save Bud.

Despite her fatigue, she reassured him, "I'll be okay."

After rinsing her mouth again, she asked Blake to go back to Bud, check the wound, wrap it if necessary, and bring him to the stream. "He's going to be thirsty so we need to have him near water."

Several minutes later, Cara looked up to see Blake, his torn shirttail flapping in the breeze. With her belt dangling from one hand, he carried the bandaged dog down to the sandy bank and lowered him to the ground next to Cara. She cupped her hands and scooped up some water, offering it to Bud. As some dribbled through her fingers, he took a few halfhearted laps. She repeated the procedure several times before he brought most of it back up again.

"It was bound to happen," she explained sadly to Blake. "That's why we've got to keep him hydrated . . . that is, give him plenty of water."

Blake sat down on the other side of his dog, petting him

in slow, methodical strokes. "Do you really believe he will live?"

Mustering a weak smile of encouragement, she said honestly, "I can't be sure I got enough of the poison out of him."

"How could you risk your life that way?" His deep-blue eyes were filled with awe.

"I couldn't let him die."

"But what about you? What if the poison—"

"Don't say it." She looked down at the dog. "I did what I had to do. And I don't regret it."

"How long until we know if he will live?"

"I'm not sure. But I don't think we should move him any farther until morning." Intuition told her to keep his heart rate down so the remaining poison would not circulate as quickly in his bloodstream. "We need to keep him as still as possible."

"If we stay here, we will have coyotes to deal with come nightfall. We'll need shelter and a fire."

Cara considered the uneven terrain they'd covered during the day, recalling nothing that could provide shelter.

Blake offered to scout around the immediate area for a safer place to wait out the night. "I'll gather some firewood as well."

She was more than willing to let him, preferring to lie down with Bud and rest a while.

"Don't go too far," she said, the warmth of the late-afternoon sun adding to her lethargy. "And watch out for rattlesnakes."

A hundred yards down the dry wash, Blake came across a shallow cave high on a steep embankment near a bend in the stream. Crouching low, he brought out his knife and cautiously entered through the opening between two large boulders. The interior dimensions were sparse but sufficient for protection from predators. The low ceiling would allow for sitting up, with enough headroom to be comfortable rather than feeling claustrophobic.

Noting the stony ground, he gathered a few pebbles into

his hand and bounced them in his palm, taking into account that his injured dog would have to lie on the rocks all night. Tossing the pea-size pebbles like a pair of dice, he turned and left the cave. After several trips back with armloads of long green shoots of grass, he managed to cover the floor of the small cave with a thick, sweet-smelling bed.

For Bud, he told himself. Yet he knew very well that he had gone to a great deal of effort to soften the hard, rocky ground for Cara as much as for his dog. It was the least he could do after she had risked her life to draw the venom out with her own mouth. Looking back at the tense moments when she'd worked over Bud, he was truly amazed by her presence of mind to act so quickly and efficiently.

Hardly the presence of mind of a crazed woman.

And where had she learned such a technique?

True, he could not deny his growing admiration of her, even though it did conflict with his determination to leave her behind.

Returning to the site where he'd left Cara with Bud, he found them both sleeping on the bank of the stream. Cara had stretched out behind Bud, her right arm tucked under her head as a pillow and her left draped over the dog. As he drew nearer, his boot heel landed upon a dry twig. Her eyes flew open.

"Oh, it's only you." She relaxed with a long exhale.

"I didn't mean to awaken you."

"I was only catnapping." Rising up on her elbow, she gazed down at the sleeping canine, her palm resting on his chest. "His heart's racing."

"Is that bad or good?"

"It's one of the symptoms. I don't like it, but if that's all he does, we'll be lucky." She didn't want to tell him about the possibility of convulsions.

Blake stroked Bud's head. "I found a place for the night."

"Near the stream?"

"Close enough."

Blake and Cara lifted the limp dog. Supporting Bud's head, Cara walked alongside him until the gully narrowed and she was forced to walk behind. Walls of dirt and rock grew higher, nearly ten feet in some places.

When they reached the curve in the stream, the sides of the wash opened wide again into tall, sloped banks. Blake nodded toward the mouth of the cave about four feet up the embankment. Nearby sat a pile of dried and broken branches that he'd collected to make a fire. He watched her eyes gauging the distance to the water and noting the awkward climb to the entrance.

To set her mind at ease, he explained, "I'll bring his water up in my boot."

After struggling up the incline with the dog, Blake placed Bud on the grass-covered floor just inside the opening, leaving enough room for Cara to get around him. She sat down behind the dog, studying the canine for signs of decline or improvement. With a solemn shake of her head and a heavy sigh, she didn't give Blake much hope.

As he sat down at the lip of the cave to remove his boot, Cara stopped him. "Take *my* shoe. Then you won't have to climb across those stones with bare feet."

"My boot would hold more water."

"Then take both of mine," she insisted, handing them over to him across the prone body of his dog. "I'm not going anywhere."

"Very well, then."

He came back with the two shoes filled. Together, they dribbled some of the water down Bud's throat. The process was tediously slow, making it necessary to allow only short periods of rest between the sessions. Fortunately, Bud seemed to have a few lucid moments when he could lap the water if they held his head up.

As the afternoon wore into evening, Blake saw no change in his dog's condition. He shouldn't have gotten so attached to a dumb animal, he told himself, despite his sure knowledge of the intelligence that this canine possessed.

The agonizing wait drove him to distraction. He was in no mood to talk, so he wasn't good company for Cara. After whittling down five twigs into a pile of curled shavings, he sheathed the knife. "I am going to go for a walk."

"Watch out for snakes."

"Are you going to say that every time?"

"The rest of my life, no doubt." She offered him a sad smile.

"If you do have this gift, as you claim, why did you not know about the danger?"

"It doesn't work that way, Blake. Sometimes I learn things ahead of time. Sometimes I don't."

"Yet you *knew* I carried a weapon."

"I don't need a sixth sense to know you wouldn't walk around this godforsaken country without something to protect you. You even pointed out the dangers when we were on the beach."

"Dangers to *you*."

"You could just as easily be robbed and killed," she said before her stomach rumbled loudly enough for both of them to hear in the small cave. "Sorry."

"I should have gone to the village for food."

"I'm not really hungry."

"Tell that to your belly."

"I will." As she rubbed her stomach, he found himself wishing his own hand was stroking her in much the same way, but not for the same reasons. Mentally chiding himself for his wayward thoughts, he turned and went out into the twilight of early evening.

The temperature had dropped with the setting sun. His invigorating walk in the cool, damp air did not alleviate his worries over Bud as he'd hoped. Instead, he grew more concerned that the dog might take a turn for the worse and he wouldn't be there. On his way back to their little camp, he passed the spot where the attack had occurred. His mind relived it, compounding his guilt at not having been able to intervene.

Arriving at the cave, he first checked with Cara about Bud's condition, then collected the wood shavings to start the fire at the base of the embankment. Once it was burning nicely, he hunkered down on the slope, his back to the cave. Using his knife, he shaved a long stick into a pointed skewer.

In the distance a coyote yipped. Another answered. Closer still, an owl hooted. The nocturnal sounds seemed to signal the start of a very long night.

Cara looked up when Blake entered the cave, blocking the minimal amount of firelight from below. It looked as if he had something in his hand, possibly a stick. But she couldn't be sure. Then a delicious smell reached her.

"I brought something for you to eat. And for Bud, if he can manage it."

"We can try to feed him. I don't know if he'll keep it down."

"Here," he offered, thrusting a warm piece of meat into her mouth. Her muffled protest prompted his quick apology. "My eyes haven't adjusted to the darkness."

"You're lucky it tastes good."

"And if it hadn't?"

"You'd be wearing it."

"I guess I am lucky, at that. Have another." This time he was more careful, giving it to her gingerly. Her lips closed around the meat, brushing the tips of his fingers, distracting her terribly.

"Thank you." Her voice sounded too breathless, too husky.

Bud stirred beside her. His panting started again.

"Should we give him some of this?" asked Blake.

"Maybe it's not such a good idea yet." She reached for her shoe. Realizing the last of the water had seeped out, she asked Blake if he would fetch more. He took the shoe and started to leave. "And more of that— What kind of meat *is* it?"

Just before he slipped out, he answered, "Rattlesnake."

"What?"

Her raised voice brought Bud's wobbly head up. When she touched him reassuringly, he lay back down. She swore under her breath, ready to strangle Blake as soon as he crawled back inside the cave. Of all the dirty, rotten, low-down tricks to play on somebody! If she hadn't been so distracted by his finger feeding, she might have realized exactly what he'd been serving her. And she certainly wouldn't have enjoyed it as much as she had.

She recalled a wilderness adventure in the Mojave desert when Mark had tried to coax her into trying snake meat. He'd warned her there might come a day when she would be forced to rely on whatever the land could provide, be it insects or worms or, if she was lucky enough, rattlesnakes. A shudder of disgust rippled through her. Lucky! Ha!

Tastes like chicken, he'd told her. *Everything* tasted like chicken to him, including the fried frog's legs he'd ordered in a restaurant. As far as she was concerned, amphibians and reptiles simply were not in the food chain for human consumption. Not like chickens, anyway.

But then again . . . If she had to admit it—which she would never do—the roasted meat wasn't half bad. And since she'd lost her lunch over that damn rattlesnake, it almost seemed like poetic justice to have it served up for dinner. Almost.

In the dim flicker of indirect light, she stroked Bud's black coat. A moment later, Blake came back into the cave with the water. Putting aside her remaining pique over his mean trick, she helped him urge the dog to drink.

"He should be moved farther inside for the night," Blake suggested. "That way I will be near the opening in the event we should have any unwelcome visitors."

Cara agreed and helped Blake lift the weakened Lab, placing him on his side with his legs toward the back wall. By the time Bud went back to sleep, the small fire had died down considerably, leaving them in darkness.

"I hope he makes it," he said with tender sadness. His hand accidentally bumped hers as they both petted the panting dog. Through his touch, she felt the depth of his emotions.

"I know how hard it is to watch someone in pain, whether it's a person or an animal." Her remark was met with his silence. "He'll pull through, Blake. I believe it."

"But do you *know* it?"

"Right now, I can't say for sure, one way or the other. Which is why I have to rely on faith that Bud will live.

Sometimes believing is the only thing you have.''

"For you, perhaps. Not for me," he said bitterly. "I do not assume that everything will work out well if only I believe it will. That's rubbish.''

"You have every right to feel the way you do. Especially after what happened to you—''

"Don't bring up my forgotten past again, Cara. At least not tonight.''

"I understand.''

The awkwardness between them was palpable. She needed an excuse to put some distance between them. Groping in the dark for her soggy shoes, she found one and put it on.

"What are you doing?''

"Trying to get my shoes so I can go outside one last time before calling it a night.''

"But they're wet.''

"No kidding," she deadpanned, feeling around for her second shoe. Her hand ran into his leg.

"That's not your shoe.''

"Two for two. I'm impressed," she groused, the heat of her body climbing ten degrees. "How about helping me find the other one?''

"Here it is.''

"Where? I can't see a thing. It's pitch-black in here now.''

"No kidding," mimicked Blake, his hand making contact with her upper arm, then sliding down to her hand and putting her shoe in it.

"The blind leading the blind.''

"I'm going with you.''

"No, that's okay. I prefer the privacy.''

"And you shall have it when you need it. Until then, you will have me with you.''

"Fine. Play Sir Galahad, if it suits you.''

Several minutes later, when they came back to the cave, Blake insisted on adding more branches to the glowing embers so he could have a makeshift torch to check inside the cave for extra guests, such as a relative to their dinner.

Realizing that another snake might be spending the night with her, Cara was more than glad to wait until the coast was clear.

After Blake came out and gave a nod of all-clear, Cara climbed the four-foot slope and crawled in behind the dog, near the back. Slipping off her shoes, she handed them over one last time for the night so Blake could fill them for Bud.

When they finished the routine, he bid Cara good night, saying he wanted to sit by the fire a little longer. In a way she was relieved by his decision. The tiny cave was going to make sleeping arrangements more than cozy. At least if he stayed outside for a while, she might be able to doze off before he stretched out next to her. If she was lucky, maybe she wouldn't even notice his return.

Fat chance.

Cara didn't know how long she might have dozed off or if in fact she'd fallen asleep at all. But she knew the moment Blake came to bed down for the night. Her entire body went on alert at the sound of him making his way up the embankment. He squeezed into the narrow space between her and the two boulders at the entrance of the cave. She had stretched out alongside the dog, her arm slung over him, using herself as a human heater to keep him warm in the cool coastal air.

With muffled grunts, Blake attempted to settle onto his back. When his elbow dug into her waist, she bit down on her lower lip to keep from making any noise that would let him know she was awake. He ended up shifting to his side, spooning his body with hers. The warmth of his breath caressed her neck. Her entire back, bottom, and legs tingled, sending messages to her brain that she tried to ignore.

As his arm slid over her, she kept her breathing steady, wondering where his hand was leading. But then he reached over and petted his dog. At first she wanted to laugh at herself for the mistaken assumption that Blake had been making a move on her when he'd actually been trying to get to his dog. But the humor quickly dissipated as she realized the poignancy of his need to connect with the critically ill animal.

Unable to hold her silence any longer, she quietly offered, "We can switch places so you can sleep next to him."

"No, I prefer to stay here. That is, if you don't mind my reaching over you every so often to check on Bud."

"I don't mind at all." She wanted her body to stop reacting to this man. This was not the time to be thinking about sex. Blake was in a miserable place right now, grieving for his beloved pet. In her mind, she felt his emotional pain. Yet her body was feeling entirely different things that were not at all appropriate, given the circumstances. Refusing to act on her impulses, she closed her eyes and inwardly sighed. "Good night, Blake."

"Good night, Cara."

Blake had not slept at all during the entire night. Several times, he'd gotten up to tend the fire while the coyotes barked and howled from a good distance. Each time he'd returned to the cave, he had managed to fit into the tight space next to Cara, though with great difficulty. Once he woke her to ask if they should give Bud more water, which they did, then settled back down for the rest of the night.

Now as he lay on his side, with Cara fitted against the front of him, he noticed the soft light of dawn beginning to dispel the darkness of the cave. He wanted to get up and stretch his sore muscles, which had been cramped into the same position most of the night. But he was reluctant to leave the warmth of Cara's body. He liked having her tucked under his protective arm. His hand was no longer resting on Bud. Instead, it was precariously close to her breast.

Cara stirred, murmuring something incomprehensible as if she were having a dream. Her back arched slightly, enough to bring her small breast against the knuckles of his curled fingers. She responded in her sleep with a soft sound of pleasure. Her bottom pressed into his groin. A slow heat began to stiffen him.

Damn. The last thing he wanted was for her to wake up right now. He attempted to pull back so she couldn't feel his full arousal, but there was no room behind him.

"Blake?" she whispered. "Are you awake?"

There was no point in pretending he wasn't. Sooner or later he needed to do something about his predicament, which was not going to solve itself by feigning sleep.

"Yes," he said in a raspy voice, managing to sound somewhat groggy.

"It's morning."

He smiled at her astute observation. "No kidding." After his teasing remark, he waited for a jab of her elbow in his ribs to chastise him for mocking her. It never came. Instead, she reached out and placed her hand on Bud's ribs.

"He's breathing comfortably now. His heartbeat isn't racing anymore, either."

"Do you think the worst is over?"

She turned her head to look up at him in the pale light. The corners of her lips curved up slowly in a drowsy sort of smile. "He made it through the night. I think it's safe to say he'll more than likely pull through."

He kissed her in gratitude, then said, "Thank you."

She seemed to be half asleep, still languishing in the dream that had affected both of them. Her dark eyes stared at him for a long moment. "You're welcome."

Unable to resist the taste of her lips, he lowered his mouth to hers once more. She made a sweet noise again, a low, kittenish purr, as the backs of his fingers brushed across her breast. He unbuttoned her shirt and slipped his hand inside. Her skin was flushed with heat. He caressed one nipple between his thumb and finger with gentle tugs.

When Cara shifted onto her back, her hip rubbed against his swollen flesh, causing him to moan with the ache of wanting her. Her lips parted further. The tip of her tongue touched his, teasing him, inviting him.

As the kiss deepened into a slow, seductive dance, he freed the remaining buttons of her shirt, then opened it. Her back arched, pressing her breast into the palm of his hand. He brought his head downward, taking her other nipple into his mouth. The gentle suckling caused her breathing to grow shallow. His own body tightened, throbbing low in his belly.

Vowing to himself that he would take her slowly, not brutally as he'd nearly done before, he reached for her buckle.

Her hand dropped to his wrist, stopping him.

He glanced up.

Silently, she brought his hand back to her breast, then began to unfasten her own belt. He gave her a slow smile and a slight nod of understanding, returning his attention to her firm, rounded breasts and the delectable feel of the pert nipple against his tongue. She shifted and moved beneath him, removing the last of her clothing as he pleasured her with his lips.

Slow . . . go slow . . . take her slowly.

His hand slid down along her flat belly, over the soft curls at the apex of her thighs. As he dipped his fingers into her moist feminine folds, he felt the slick wetness of her womanhood. Her readiness prompted a need in him so great that he had to fight for control.

His heart pounded in his ears. His entire body throbbed. Yet he somehow managed to maintain the slow, deliberate seduction. Freeing himself from the restraints of his trousers, he shifted his body over her and positioned himself between her thighs. Her hands slid down to his buttocks, grasping them and pulling him into her. He held back, resisting his desire to take her fast and hard. The tip of his manhood entered her, then pulled out again. She gasped and writhed. He was torturing her, he knew. He was torturing himself as well.

Little by little, he entered her farther, then withdrew completely, each time stroking the outer folds of her flesh as well as her inner core. Her fingers dug into him, but he refused to hasten his pace. And it was killing him. His mouth suckled her neck, harder and harder as he held back his release. Her teeth bore down on his shoulder, biting him as her breath quickened. Her body stiffened beneath him, then gave way to its own quivering spasms of ecstasy. Her gasps came loud and hot in his ear.

Overpowered by his own body's need, he slid his hands under her and wrapped his arms around her. Then he drove deep inside her, filling her completely, pressing against the hot barrier of her womb.

That one feeling, that one sensation surrounded him, stilling his movement. Nothing else existed at that moment except the feeling of warmth and pleasure. He felt as if his entire being had left behind his physical body and nested within the deepest reaches of this mysterious woman.

Somewhere in the nether regions of his mind, he heard her soft voice. "Let go, Blake. Let go . . . Take me with you."

Pictures and images raced past his mind's eye. Things he'd never seen before. Boats with bright, fanciful sails. People in odd clothing, nearly as bare as the Kānaka. Yet they were not Sandwich Islanders.

Panic swept up his throat. God, what was happening to him? He was making love to Cara, wasn't he? Why was he seeing—

"Let go, Blake. Let go . . ."

"NO!" His yell was muffled as he buried his face in her neck. He bucked against her, pounding the images from his mind, bringing back only the unsatiated male need. Desire mounted with each thrust. Then came the huge burst of excruciating pleasure, followed by wave after wave of shuddering release.

Collapsing on top of her, he refused to kiss her or thank her or say anything at all to this sorceress. The mere touch of her flesh did things to him unlike anything he had ever before experienced, reaching deep inside him, making him remember the past. But now . . . what were the strange pictures he'd seen? How could his mind be filled with such vivid imagery, as if he were transported to another time and place?

Cara felt her heart still pounding wildly from their lovemaking as her mind filled with his silent curses. Holding him in her arms, she bit her lower lip, trying not to cry yet unable to keep from hearing his fearful accusations. He damned her for manipulating him into this sexual liaison so he would take her with him. Then he wondered if she drove other men from her bed stark raving mad.

He had every right to blame her, she thought, remembering the surreal pictures of fireworks and the Fourth of July that had darted through her head during the heat of passion. Only after Blake had cried out did she realize he'd also seen the alarming glimpse of her modern world. In his mind he accused her of casting a spell on him, destroying his sanity.

"I'm sorry, Blake," she whispered between gulps of air, her breathing still erratic.

"As am I," he said on a long exhale, then lifted himself off of her.

Chapter 14

AFTER BLAKE LEFT the cave, Cara curled up on her side, too stunned to do anything as sensible as gather her clothes together and get dressed. Their lovemaking had started out so beautifully but ended so badly. Never had she experienced the level of completion, yet afterward . . . something had happened that she couldn't begin to understand.

She had always believed the union of a man and a woman was more than the sexual joining of two bodies, that for a brief moment it was the transcendence of separate existences. Intertwined as one, they shared the same thoughts, same breath, same beat of their hearts. With Blake, she had felt all of that and more. Much, much more.

Then everything had abruptly changed with the strange vision of a holiday unlike any memory of her own. She had no recollection of the people or the place. But it had been enough to scare the hell out of Blake.

Now as she lay on the sweet-smelling bed of grass, she wiped away a tear trailing down her cheek. She didn't want to believe he thought he'd been coerced into doing this against his will. But it was quite obvious that *he* believed it.

He believed she was using him, that her feelings were detached, that she would use any means to see that he took her with him when he sailed.

Confused and disillusioned, she swallowed the sob lodged in her throat. A shudder of cold shook her, and she groped blindly for her clothes. Finding her panties inside her trousers, she had started to put them on when Blake reappeared at the opening of the cave. His smoldering gaze settled on her erect nipples, taut from the sudden chill. She made no move to cover herself. Instead, she surreptitiously slipped the tiny scrap of cotton underwear into the pocket of the pants.

She sniffed, tilting her chin up. "I'm getting dressed."

"So I see." He came inside anyway, shuttering his initial reaction to her naked body. "Here."

She looked down at his extended hand, holding out a wadded wet cloth. She took it but said nothing.

"I thought you might want to wash," he explained, a tough edge to his voice. "It's the best I could do. I'll bring more water."

As he turned to leave, she saw that he had cut off the rest of his shirttail for her. Why? How could he hate her so much in one instant and treat her with kindness in the next? Was she afraid she'd put a hex on him if he didn't?

She slipped into her shirt, buttoning it just before he came back with both her shoes filled with water.

"I'll give one to Bud while you clean up and get dressed."

She nodded mutely, then watched him minister to his dog, his back to her, allowing her a modicum of privacy.

A short time later, they headed back to the path leading to the small town. Bud was awake but too weak to walk so Blake carried his sick dog the entire way. When they reached the village, Cara expected to be dropped off on someone's doorstep. Instead, Blake led her to a stable, where he hired two horses to ride the final three miles to the hide houses. She didn't dare question his actions. While his mind was preoccupied with getting his dog back to the *Valiant*, she wasn't about to remind him of his promise to leave her.

As their mounts descended the hill overlooking the

beach, Keoni and the other Kānaka ran up to meet them. Blake handed his injured dog to his friend, saying only the word "rattlesnake," then dismounted and helped lower Bud to the ground. One of the men was sent for water as the dog tried to raise his head to look around. Keoni asked another man to go back to the oven for some of the herb the Kānaka kept for snakebite.

Getting down off her horse, Cara picked up the reins of Blake's horse and stood with both mounts, watching and waiting for Blake to realize finally that he'd forgotten to dump her on a family back in the village.

Then again, he could be planning to send her back alone to return the two horses. No, she told herself, he would not send her off after the way he'd acted yesterday about her safety. And unless he bodily dragged her back to the village, she wasn't going anywhere but back to the ship.

She listened as Blake explained the events of the last twenty-four hours to Keoni, discreetly leaving out the love-making at dawn, she noted. Then he took her completely by surprise—given his surly attitude—by mentioning her daring risk to save his dog from the snakebite. She found herself feeling a little flattered that he actually gave her credit for saving the animal's life.

Kneeling across from his captain, Keoni looked straight at her, his broad face creased in a smile. "*Wahine* do good, eh?"

Cara forced a grin, but noticed that the Hawaiian was well aware that something was wrong. He frowned, glancing from her to Blake and back again. His eyebrows arrowed upward, then a sly smile crept across his face. He turned back to Blake.

"Maybe *wahine* do good med'cine for Bud, she good med'cine for all-a us, eh *kaikaina*?"

"No, not for *all* of us," corrected Blake with a sharp tongue. "I only brought her back to care for Bud until he's completely recovered. After that, she goes. Either way, we sail within the week. Without her."

Cara's spine stiffened. His words hurt, especially after the intimacy they had shared. But she would be damned if he'd leave her behind. She had to find Andrew.

One of the men carried a small wooden bucket of water up the hill. When the bucket was set down, Bud struggled to stand but required support. Cara watched the thirsty dog briefly lap the water before he collapsed. Her heart went out to him as she watched him battle his weakness. With a determined spirit, he propped his chin on the edge of the bucket between his two front legs. After a moment's rest, he stretched his neck and drank until he had to pause again.

"Lazy man's way," laughed Keoni, breaking the tension in the air. A dark-skinned Sandwich Islander ran up and handed Keoni a little leather pouch, which Cara assumed contained the herbs he'd requested.

Blake lifted the dog into his arms. "Let's get him to the ship so you can give him some of your Kānaka medicine."

"What about the horses?" asked Cara, holding up the reins in her hands.

Blake had already started down the hill toward the bay. He turned and looked at her as if to say, "I don't give a damn what you do with them."

Keoni said something in Hawaiian to the Kānaka who'd brought the pouch. The other man eagerly took the horses, happy to have free use of them until the owner sent someone to get them.

On the way down to the water, Keoni spoke to Cara loud enough for Blake to hear. "I heard talk at the oven last night of a yellow-haired boy on a ship bound for Boston."

"That *must* be Andrew," cried Cara. "Blake, did you hear him?"

Blake had not only heard, he'd stopped dead in his tracks until Keoni paused alongside him. Then he asked the cook, "The name of the ship?"

"The *Ballade.*"

With a whoop of joy, Cara threw her arms around Keoni and started to kiss him on the cheek. But his head turned at the last second, and he took her kiss full on his mouth. Embarrassed, she pulled back, but he leaned forward, prolonging the unintentional intimacy before he chose to break it off. Her gaze flitted to Blake, who stared at her with narrowed eyes.

She stared right back at him, daring him to make more out of an innocent kiss of a friend. Besides, he obviously didn't want anything to do with her anymore, so he couldn't possibly care whom she kissed.

Oh, but his indifference hurt.

Was he upset because Keoni had just proved her right about Andrew? Of course! That had to be it. And now he was full of piss and vinegar because once again he had proof that her mysterious way of knowing things was not the behavior of a crazy person. She was as sane as he was. And he was going to have to accept it.

With her own information corroborated by a reliable friend, Cara had to convince Blake to take her back to Boston with him. There was no other option. She *had* to sail on the *Valiant*.

"Marry her, *kaikaina*."

"Are you mad?" Blake nearly choked on a sip of rum.

They stood at the rail adjacent to the ship's galley, staring out across the calm waters of the moonlit bay. It was after eight bells. The watch had been set. The rest of the crew had gone below into the forecastle for the evening. Bud was resting comfortably in the cabin, recuperating slowly but steadily. This was the time of evening when Blake could enjoy a bit of the spirits, of which he was in much need, especially after the mess he'd made of things with Cara. Three days had passed since the incident in the cave. In three more, the *Valiant* would set sail.

He still couldn't get past the feeling that he'd been used. That she'd wanted him bound to her so she would be assured passage on his ship.

"You can't leave her here alone. And she has no money to pay for fare on another ship. Even if she sails as your wife, the men may still do a good bit of grumbling about the bad luck of a woman on board. The owners of the *Valiant* may not be too pleased either. But at least she will not have traveled as an unpaid female guest of the captain, which could cost you dearly.''

"Then *you* marry her.''

After a long pause, he answered, "All right.''

"What?!''

"If she will have me, I will marry her. Tomorrow.''

"You *are* mad! What sort of spell has she cast upon *you*?''

"None.'' He turned to leave, clearly angry, which was a rare sight.

"Wait, Keoni . . .'' Blake couldn't believe his friend would go through with this. "You can't be serious, *kaikua'ana*. She will never agree to live four or five months in your small cabin.''

"If it is the only way to reach Andrew, she will.''

"This marriage would be in name only,'' stated Blake firmly, expecting his friend to agree.

"Have you seen the size of my berth?'' The Kanaka cocked one eyebrow. "After five months together in my cabin, what do *you* think?''

Blake was momentarily stunned by the insinuation, then angered by the image of his Kanaka brother lying with Cara in his arms. "I think you are both insane and deserve one another. Congratulations and best wishes for a long and fruitful marriage.''

He downed the last of the small amount of liquor, shoved the cup into the cook's hand, and stormed off, bellowing for Jimmy to prepare his things so he could go ashore.

"Wait, *kaikaina*.''

Blake looked down at the hand on his shoulder, then glared at his friend. "Get the hell out of my way.''

"Where are you going to go at this hour?''

"Why, to celebrate, of course. I intend to go to the *pulpería* and toast your future with . . . her.'' He jerked his head toward the aft cabin. "I might even find a young *señorita* to keep me company for the night.''

"Don't be a fool.''

"We will see who is the bigger fool tomorrow.''

*   *   *

Blake woke up to a terrible pounding pain in his head. With his eyes still closed, he rubbed his temples to soothe the tremendous ache, but to no avail. The insides of his eyelids felt like gritty sand scratching at his eyes. Disoriented and in agony, he could not recall where he was or what he had done since leaving the *Valiant*. As his fuzzy mind cleared, he realized he was in the dark and narrow berth of his temporary quarters. How he came to be here was a mystery to him.

The sudden knock at his door sounded like a cannon fired next to his ear.

"Go away!" he growled, then groaned at the intense throbbing in his head caused by his own voice.

"Aye, aye, sir."

"Jimmy? Augh . . ."

"Aye, sir. Are you all right?"

"Yes. No. Ah, hell. Just open the goddamn door."

The boy obeyed, letting in the tiny amount of lantern light. "May I get you anything, sir?"

"Bring me something for my headache. No, wait. Send Keoni down with it. I want to speak with him."

"He left with Mrs. Edwards, sir. About four hours ago."

"What?" He sat up and immediately regretted it. Holding his head for a spell, he remained still, muttering at his feet. "Did he say where they were going?"

"To the mission, I believe, sir. To see the priest."

"God-damn-sonovabitch!" roared Blake, launching to his feet. "Get the gig ready. I'm going ashore."

"Again, sir? You just—"

"That's an order!"

Trembling in his boots, Jimmy responded, "Aye, aye, sir," then dashed off.

Blake scratched the stubby growth of whiskers on his cheek, then looked down at his rumpled clothing. He looked more like a ruffian than a respectable captain of a merchantman. But he had no time to dawdle with cleanliness.

Four hours. My God, the deed could already be done.

He stumbled up on deck, wincing at the bright sunlight.

Leaving Mr. Bellows in charge, he got himself down into the boat, anxious to get to the mission and put a stop to the wedding. Battling the lingering effects of over-indulgence, Blake was a powder keg ready to explode. He kept a close watch on his temper, though, reminding himself that Jimmy should not be made to suffer for anger and resentment that needed to be directed at the proper parties.

At the *Valiant's* hide house, he borrowed the roan stallion tethered outside the door and tore off at breakneck speed. The six-mile run cleared his head but did little to sweeten his sour disposition. Entering the gates of the mission, he raced his mount to the steps of the church, swung down from the saddle, and marched up to the doors, throwing them wide.

"Keoni! Cara!" He strode down the center aisle, glancing around the empty sanctuary.

"*¡Silencio, por favor, señor!*"

Blake turned to see the *mayordomo* standing in the back corner. "Where are they?" he demanded in Spanish.

"*¿Quién?*" Who?

Struggling with his poor translation, Blake managed to ask about the woman who had accompanied him earlier in the week and a tall Kanaka. Although his words seemed to have been understood, he received only the response of a shrug and shake of the head. To his relief, the two had not yet arrived or visited the priest. Then where were they?

Thanking the *mayordomo*, he stormed out of the church, stopping at the fountain to cup his hands under the flowing water. He would go to the village next, he decided, bringing the water to his lips. There was nowhere else they could have gone.

Sweat trickled down his back. His temples pounded. Bending at the waist, he dunked his entire head into the cool water, then lifted it out. Gripping the rim of the circular trough, he let the water sluice over his face while his thoughts went back to Cara and Keoni. The idea of the two of them sharing a marriage bed disturbed him more than he cared to face right now. He was out to save his Kanaka brother from making a misguided mistake, not Cara. She was *not* the one he was trying to protect.

Oh, no? questioned a little voice inside him.

I want nothing to do with her.

You are wrong, Blake. Dead wrong.

She is a witch, a sorceress—

A mystic.

The word echoed through his mind. He didn't quite understand it or deny it. Yet the idea of Cara being a mystic seemed oddly appropriate somehow in the jumble of confusion surrounding her.

Lifting his head, he ran his hands through his hair, slicking it back as he straightened and walked back to the exhausted roan at the wooden trough for the animals. He thought of all the times Cara had proved her mystical gift of insight. He remembered her descriptions of visitations by an angel named Gabriella. Even if she were indeed touched by the divine, he still did not know what to make of the strange images he'd seen in the cave.

Out of the corner of his eye, he saw a blur of motion near the gate. He turned to see one horse and two riders coming into the square. His dark-skinned friend rode in the saddle, grinning broadly and waving. Cara peered around the man's broad shoulders, her smile as broad as the Kanaka's. What had they been up to all these hours alone? he wondered, then banished the thought, preferring not to know.

He remained rooted, waiting for them to approach. Their horse stopped in front of him. Keoni murmured something to Cara that Blake could not hear, then helped her slide down from the horse. He swung his leg over and landed lightly on his feet next to her.

Placing a protective arm around her shoulders, he faced Blake. "Are you here to witness the ceremony?"

"There will be no ceremony." Blake kept an even tone, controlling the urge to let his fists fly and knock some sense into his foolish friend.

"You are my captain, not my keeper."

"I am your brother."

"Then you will not stand in our way."

Blake looked at Cara. "Did you agree to this?"

She nodded, her dark eyes bringing back the memory of her sleepy gaze.

"Then marry him, if you must." He watched her face register surprise. "But it will not gain you passage on my vessel. Keoni will stay here with you. I will find another cook."

"You can't mean that," she said in disbelief, stepping toward him.

"I do." Damning himself for feeling hurt by a betrayal he had unwittingly instigated, he couldn't bear the thought of them together intimately. He had to stop this impulsive wedding.

"You bastard!" she seethed in a low, contemptuous tone, then slapped him. His head jerked to one side. But he showed no emotion, which appeared to infuriate her all the more. Keoni came forward, gently grabbing her by the shoulders and pulling her back against him.

"I'm staying with her, *kaikaina*. I will collect my things in the morning."

Masking his disappointment as well as despair, Blake stared at his Kanaka brother, the one man he would lay down his life for. Over the years they had talked about the day that would come when they might part company, leaving one to settle down with a family while the other continued to sail the seas. He had always expected a woman would come between them. He just never thought that woman would be someone he wanted as well. A mystical woman neither of them should have.

"Is this how you want it to be?" he asked Cara, noticing unshed tears shimmering in her eyes.

Her lower lip trembled. From anger, he suspected. He *was* a bastard. She was right. Again. Only this time, she didn't need second sight because it was plain as day, even for him.

"Blake . . ." she pleaded.

His gut twisted, waiting for her to admit she had been using Keoni to get herself aboard the ship. Now that she no longer had her passage secured, would she confess her deceitful trap and release the Kanaka from his commitment to her?

"Is it him you want?" *Or me?*

"I—" She faltered, then glanced over her shoulder at the Kanaka. "I can't do this to you, Keoni. I won't be responsible for having you kicked off your ship."

Then she turned back to Blake and moved closer. For a moment, he thought she might slap him again. But she raised her hand to his cheek where a reddened imprint was certain to be outlined on the skin. Tenderly, she cupped the side of his face. "I want *you,* Blake. God help me, but I need you—"

"I know. For passage to Boston."

She slowly shook her head. "There's more to it than that. You have to feel it, too. The night we spent together . . ."

He glanced uncomfortably toward his friend, then grabbed her arm above the elbow and led her a short distance away. He kept his voice low. "You planned for that to happen—"

"Planned?" she echoed quietly, her expression filled with sadness. "How could you even think I would intentionally stage an attack by a rattlesnake that nearly cost your dog his life?"

"Very well, then—I say you used the unfortunate circumstances to your advantage, allowing me to claim your body so I would feel bound to you, unable to leave you. I heard your words as you were toying with my mind. If you think my lust for you will assure a place in my berth until we reach Boston, then you are no better than a vulgar whore who takes money for her services."

Cara reeled back, stunned by his accusation. What she had considered an exquisite moment between them, he had diminished to a manipulative prostitution of her body. Damn him! She wished she could slap him again, but she'd already done it once. And it not only hadn't done a bit of good, it horrified her to think she had stooped to physical violence, something she'd never done in her life.

"You sound as if your mind is made up." She let out a

long and defeated breath. "No matter what I say now, I'll never be able to convince you that I had no ulterior motives the other morning. I wanted you to make love to me. That's all. Nothing more. I didn't think about the ramifications, which now, I realize, was my second mistake."

"And your first?"

"I made the mistake of *believing* in you." Her throat tightened. She rapidly blinked back the damn tears that seemed to be the only constant in her life lately. "I honestly believed you wanted to help. Not me, but Andrew. *You* know what that kid is going through right now, Blake!" She stared at him in challenge, her heart and throat aching with emotion.

"Keoni told me how much you missed your parents those first few years with his family. You kept wishing they would come looking for you. Now you're putting Andrew through that same hell because you can't put aside your feelings about me, about us! You are condemning that little ten-year-old to a life exactly like your own—lost and alone."

Taking a much-needed breath, Cara swiped away the tears running down her cheek, her voice growing louder. She didn't care if Keoni overheard. Let him hear!

"You don't have to do this to him, Blake. He *has* parents who love him and want him back. And I am the only one who has made it this far, the only one who knows where he is. If you don't take me on that ship, he hasn't got a snowball's chance in hell of getting back to his father and mother."

She stepped up to him, raising her finger to his face. "And one last thing—I am *not* a frigging whore. But if that's what you want, and that's what it takes to rescue Andrew, then you got it. No phony wedding required. I'll *work* my way to Boston. In your bed. On my back."

"That's enough, Cara," growled Blake.

"It *better* be enough," she shot back, adding a different meaning to his warning. Her finger poked him in the chest to make her point. "Because all I've *got* for barter is my body."

Leaving him slack-jawed over her crass proposition, she started to drop her hand and storm off, but his fingers caught her wrist.

Her heightened agitation shortened her breathing. She glanced down at his viselike grip, then up at his stony face. If he chose, he could snap her delicate bones in the blink of an eye. She knew he wouldn't, but his steely-eyed gaze and flared nostrils told of his battle for self-control. Brutality was more than familiar to him and to most mariners of the early 1800s. Violence bred violence. For Blake, his horrid past could have easily turned him into a monster, but it hadn't.

Their silent face-to-face standoff lasted through several of her rapid breaths. He released her. His gaze drifted downward to the rise and fall of her breasts beneath her shirt. She didn't need to be clairvoyant to know he was mentally undressing her. Good. Maybe he would actually let his primal urges sway his thinking.

He finally spoke, his anger still evident. "No marriage?"

"No marriage. Just sex."

Eyes narrowing, he shook his head. "No sex, either."

Unable to hide her surprise, she asked with a sudden croak in her voice, "None?"

"None," he repeated. "I have no intention of touching you ever again."

Three days later, on the morning of April 1, Blake stood on the deck of the *Valiant*, only a few hours away from hauling anchor and setting sail for Boston. The air was calm. The sun warm. The bay as smooth as glass.

"Is she ready?" he asked Keoni, who was standing next to him.

"I doubt it."

Blake's head snapped around. "What are you saying, *kaikua'ana*?"

"Women are never ready on time," answered the Kanaka with a mischievous wink. "And especially on their wedding day. Keeps the groom on his toes."

"*This* groom is not going to be kept waiting," muttered

Blake, stepping around his best man. If he had to throw her over his shoulder and haul her up the companionway, he would do so.

This impromptu ceremony had not been his idea in the first place. If not for the first mate's message of grievance from the crew, Blake would have abided by his agreement with Cara. Instead, he was made to realize that a disgruntled, superstitious lot of seamen in the forecastle could make for a mutinous journey around the Horn. Rather than take such a risk, he was willing to stand before the captain of the *Pilgrim*, speak a few meaningless words, and be done with it. That is, if the bride deemed to honor them with her presence.

Then he saw her. A jolt went through him so strong that, had he not known better, he might have thought an anchor was pulling him down into the depths of the ocean.

She was wearing the new clothes he had purchased for the occasion, requesting that she don something other than her standard male attire for the wedding. In truth, he could hardly stand before his crew and pledge his troth to a person who looked more like a man than a woman. At a distance, anyway. He would be the butt of jokes for the entire voyage.

Earlier, when he'd given her the wrapped package, he'd felt compelled to apologize for the humble peasant clothes, knowing that most women would have preferred a bridal gown of satin and lace. Though whatever possessed him to feel guilty, he did not know. She'd thanked him anyway, regretting she had nothing to give him for a wedding gift. He'd dismissed her comment, citing no need to reciprocate his practical gesture.

Now she stood before him on the deck of his ship, dressed in a soft, creamy-white blouse with a drawstring neckline that curved across her delicate shoulder bones. The blouse was tucked into the waistband of a gathered calico skirt, accenting her small waist. The toes of her new black slippers peeked out from beneath the hem.

He had never seen any woman so beautiful as Cara with her large brown eyes as deep and dark as twenty fathoms.

Chapter 15

CARA SPENT THE rest of her wedding day alone in the captain's quarters while Blake stayed topside with the crew, getting his ship under way. He did not even bother to join her for the sumptuous meal Keoni provided for them. Instead, the Kanaka sat with her, talking about his island home and his adolescent brotherhood with Blake.

Neither of them dared to speak of their successful bluff three days earlier regarding their own intentions to marry. They had purposely dawdled half the day away, expecting Blake to come after them in a jealous rage, as Keoni had predicted. Still, she had been willing to go through with a marriage to the Hawaiian, if necessary. He had become a good friend and confidant. With his own staunch beliefs in the island myths and legends, he accepted her stories about psychic powers and her other life in another time. Without doubts or questions, he had offered his unconditional respect and devotion. The feeling was mutual. But it wasn't love. Not that love was required for marriage, she realized reluctantly. Her current situation being a prime example.

Even though she prolonged her meal to keep Keoni around, he finally had to excuse himself and get back to his duties. "Not look good if da new bride spends more time alone with da cook than with da groom," he told her with a wink.

She answered halfheartedly, "Not good if da new bride

spends her wedding night without da groom.''

Keoni reached out and took her hand. "You made a deal with the devil, *kaikuahine*.''

Smiling at the Hawaiian word for "sister," she answered, "I'm afraid Blake may think he's the one who made the deal with the devil.''

"You will change his mind soon enough.'' He winked. "Pretty *wahine* like you won't be alone in that bed for long. I know I would not be able to resist you.''

"You're not Blake. Oh, forgive me, Keoni. That didn't come out the way I meant it. Any woman would love to have you—uh, that is . . .''

"Say no more. I bruise easily.'' The Kanaka laughed, gave her hand an affectionate squeeze and released it. "Now I go and talk some sense into that husband of yours. Not wise to let the men see their captain wandering the deck on his wedding night. Might think something is wrong already.''

"Yeah, I know—*Ho'omanamana*. Superstitious. So go out there and drag my dear, devoted husband home to me, sweet Keoni. I will be here with waiting arms," she quipped sarcastically.

"He will not be able to hold out too long, *kaikuahine*. Trust me," he said, grinning wide as he took her empty dishes and left the cabin.

For a few hours she passed her time reading one of the precious few books that Keoni had borrowed from a scholarly old salt in the forecastle. While she sat at the table using a candle for added light, Bud slept on her bare feet, literally. His warm body served as a toasty comforter. The Lab was doing pretty well, all things considered. He probably wouldn't be very good company for a while yet, but she was certain he'd come around eventually.

Unlike his master.

She turned the page of the book while muffled noises filtered down through the ceiling. The men sang out, hauling lines to the tune of some sea chantey, as much a sound of the sea as the wind and waves. The ringing of the bell told her it was nine o'clock, or twenty-one hundred hours in ship time.

When she could not stifle the third big yawn, she gave up her attempt to stay awake for Blake's return. Obviously, he wasn't planning to spend the night in the honeymoon suite.

She scooted back the chair, slipped her feet out from under Bud, and walked over to the drawer that had been cleared out for her meager collection of belongings. With money from Blake, she had been able to go ashore with Jimmy to purchase a few necessities, such as a nightgown and a hairbrush. Speaking with the proprietor's wife, she had also acquired strips of muslin for her menstrual cycle, which would begin soon, though she had only a vague idea of how to handle the daunting chore of laundering the cloth in the confines of a small cabin on a ship full of men.

Standing at the open bureau, she unfastened her skirt and let it drop to the floor. After doing the same with her drawers, she pulled her blouse off over her head and reached for the clean, new gown.

Suddenly the door opened behind her. Fumbling with the folded material, she looked over her shoulder.

"Blake!" She gasped as he closed the door. She kept her back to him while she struggled to get the nightgown over her head. "Turn around! Can't you see I'm naked?"

"No kidding," he deadpanned. She was getting really tired of this running gibe between them, especially when it was at her expense. The billowy nightdress whispered over her bare skin, draping into soft folds until it touched the floor.

"Wh-what are you doing here?" She searched for the armholes and slipped her hands through. "Why didn't you knock?"

"It's my cabin," came his answer to her first question. "And you should have locked the door."

"How were you supposed to get in if I was asleep and didn't hear you knock?"

Closing the drawer, she noticed her nipples outlined beneath the white cotton cloth. She folded her arms over her chest and pivoted about to see him standing in the same place, watching her with a predatory gaze. She felt her pulse race.

"The point is—" Slurring his words, he removed his jacket and walked toward her. "You are *not* asleep, now, are you, Mrs. Edwards?"

She didn't bother correcting him. "You're drunk."

"Ah, now, that I am. It seems my men felt a need to give me a condolence—that is, a *wedding*—gift of some fine brandy."

"Condolence" was probably the right word, considering what Keoni had told her about the superstitions the crew had regarding a woman on board.

"Well, as you can see, I was about to go to bed." She leaned over to scoop up her clothes from the floor. His footsteps came closer until his boots stopped in front of her. When she straightened with the skirt, underdrawers and blouse clutched against her breasts, he stared at her lips until she had an uncontrollable urge to wet them with her tongue.

His blue eyes darkened. A flutter started in her stomach and traveled lower. She silently cursed her body's instantaneous reaction to him. She wasn't about to have sex with him when he was soused. With her luck, he would no doubt blame her for his intoxication!

"Yer in m' way," he muttered. Certainly not the words she'd expected to hear. "Unless y' want to fe-fetch me a bottle out of the cabinet over there."

"I'd probably choose the wrong one." She stepped around him, draped her clothing over the top of a chair and climbed into bed. "Good night."

"*I'm* stayin' up a while."

"I didn't *ask* you to come to bed."

"And I'm not offering to join you. Remember—no sex."

"I don't need to be reminded."

He swore an oath under his breath as he pulled out a bottle, uncorked it, and poured a full glass. Unwilling to watch him drink himself into a stupor, Cara rolled over and faced the inside of the berth, pulling the covers over her shoulders. Maybe he would pass out at the table, saving her the discomfort of his warm body pressed against her back.

Her thoughts drifted back to the night in the tiny cave when the limited space forced them to curl up together. There had been some good parts about that night. And that following morning. If only it hadn't all ended so disastrously, she thought wistfully.

Blake was stone-cold sober, but he'd be damned if he would let on to Cara. Oh, he'd had a small drink or two topside with Keoni but not enough to lose control.

After walking in on her a few minutes ago, he was glad to have kept his wits about him. The view of her firm, round bottom had immediately aroused him. For the briefest instant, he'd been tempted to come up behind her and claim her swiftly and effortlessly. She would have let him, too. The invitation had been all too obvious by the coquettish manner in which she'd pretended to struggle with her gown. She was quite the actress, he'd give her that. She had wanted to display her nudity, showing him what he had turned down. Yet he'd refused her seduction, even when the tip of her pink tongue had moistened those luscious lips, inviting him to kiss her, enticing him to lose control again.

But, by damn, he hadn't given in.

He sat down at the table, sipped the liquor, and stared across the small cabin at the woman lying in his bed.

My wife.

He could not even begin to address her as such. It still seemed too strange to his own ears. And the arrangement itself could not have been more peculiar either. What could he have been thinking? Ah, that was the crux. He had *not* been thinking properly when he'd permitted her to live in his cabin or when he had agreed to matrimony. Though both had been decisions for her own well-being, his vow to abstain had been a decision for *his* own safety. Or, more appropriately, his sanity.

He remained in the chair for at least an hour. Bud got

up and scratched at the door, prompting Blake to take a brief circle of the deck with his dog. When he came back, he was relieved to see Cara had been perfectly safe behind the unlocked door in his absence. Perhaps he did worry too much about her well-being. Struck by the notion that he could still worry over her, he was not comfortable with the idea that she had worked her way under his skin despite all his efforts to be rid of her.

As Bud settled down for the night in his favorite corner of the cabin, Blake poured another glass of liquor. He wasn't ready to bed down next to his wife. Not yet. Perhaps not ever. The floor was beginning to look like the best option. He took a drink, then stared at the amber liquid as he felt the numbing effects drift to all parts of his body. All parts, that is, except one.

He gulped down the last drop, and started to pour another, then stopped, not wanting to be drunk in her presence, awake or asleep. As it was, he felt a nice warm glow, nothing more.

Returning the bottle to the cabinet, he heard an uncomfortable moan coming from his berth. He glanced over to see Cara gasp and sit up, staring at something beyond the end of the mattress, her eyes wild.

"Bl-ake!" she screamed.

Every protective instinct he possessed reared up. He was across the room before he even gave it a second thought, and grabbed her by the shoulders.

She blinked, finally seeing him, then buried her head in his chest, murmuring repeatedly, "Oh-God, oh-God, oh-God."

"Shush, now. It was just a dream." His palm on her back felt her pounding heartbeat. Oh, how good it felt to hold her in his arms again.

"No . . ."

"Yes, it was. Look at me, Cara." He pulled back and cupped her face in his hands. She was a strong woman, maybe too strong at times. To see her so vulnerable touched something inside him. "I'm here. I'm real. Nothing bad is happening."

She shook her head tentatively. "Nothing is what it seems, Blake. It's all an illusion."

"You're talking nonsense," he soothed, taking her in his arms again. Her whole body trembled like a leaf. As much as he wanted to convince himself that she was staging the entire act, he knew in his gut that she was deathly frightened. And, God help him, he wanted to protect her, to save her from the monster in her dreams.

"I couldn't stop them from hurting you, Blake."

"Who?"

"Three men—Captain Myers and two others he called Landers and Barney," she answered, describing them with detailed accuracy.

Blake felt his palms go clammy. Nausea roiled in his stomach. He knew Myers was a name she'd heard him say before. But she could not have known the moniker of the bulky seaman Landers who had been the mate aboard the *Emery*, the ship from which he'd escaped. The second man was Barnsdall, or Barney. Blake had not remembered their names until she spoke of them. And yet now, everything about those men and that voyage—the horror, the sickness, the depravity—came rushing back to him as if it were only yesterday when he'd been a twelve-year-old cabin boy.

He couldn't seem to stop himself as images and words pounded through his mind like caged beasts desperate to be set free. For the first time in sixteen years, he spoke of those days of enslavement . . . enslavement to a sadistic, perverted captain. His own deep voice sounded distant and unfamiliar, the story wrenched from him without will.

"I was beaten and whipped within an inch of my life many times," he said quietly, the clamminess becoming a cold sweat. "The first few times, I prayed to live. After that, I prayed I would die and be done with the pain and the . . ."

He could not bring himself to say the rest, mortified by the sudden, vivid, ugly remembrance of the things that had been done to him. Cara's hands reached for his, holding him, becoming his anchor.

"For many months I endured their abuse. I lost all faith

in anyone or anything that would save me from the hellish
service to those vile bastards. When I was too weak or too
battered, they took other boys from foreign ports of call,
leaving them behind when we sailed again. But never me.
They never left me behind no matter how much I prayed.
I was their favorite . . .''

Gulping great gasps of air, Blake broke away from Cara
and shoved himself off the bed. He staggered to the table
and braced his hands on each side, curling his fingers
around the edge. The memories of his violation slammed
into him with renewed pain and torture. Deep, wrenching
sobs broke through as a vivid scene unfolded in his mind.

"There was a boy . . . He was younger than me . . . I
saw—'' He squeezed his eyes shut. His hands gripped the
table. ''I saw Landers and Barnsdall *murder* that boy,
smothering him in the midst of—'' Crying in anguish, he
hung his head in shame, feeling responsible for not being
able to stop the violence. ''Th-that child died because he
hadn't *pleased* the captain.''

A roar of outrage erupted from his lungs. Lifting a chair
and heaving it to one side, he screamed, ''THOSE GOD-
DAMN BASTARDS!''

Blindly, he bellowed and swore and lashed out, slamming his fist into the bulkhead, then smashing another chair
against the door. Wood splintered and flew. His tirade es-
calated as he ranted at his abusers. He saw nothing but
black fury. Someone burst through the door and grabbed at
him. He swung and felt the satisfaction of his knuckles
smacking into flesh and bone with a crack.

A punch caught him square in the stomach, doubling him
over and knocking the wind out of him. He gasped for air,
then came back with another animal roar, ramming his head
into his assailant like a bull with horns. He punched wildly,
both arms pumping blows into the belly of the beast.

A fist clipped his temple. His head whipped to the side.
His knees started to buckle. Hands grabbed his shoulders
from behind.

''Not again!'' He cursed, fighting against two now, instead of only the one. ''*Never* again!''

His arm swung back to ward off the person in back of him. As his elbow struck hard, he heard a woman scream, distracting him for a mere second. Long enough to take a hit under the jaw. He reeled backward and went down.

Through a red haze of dissipating anger, he saw Cara and Keoni kneeling on each side of him, leaning over him. The Kanaka cupped his hand over one eye, swearing at Blake in his native tongue.

Cara was wide-eyed with a dazed yet concerned expression. Grasping his left hand, she brushed her fingertips across his forehead. Her gentle touch cleared the ugly, debilitating mist of his past. When she grazed his temple, he winced. More from humiliation than from any physical pain.

"I warned you," he growled at her. Misery and degradation suffocated him. "I didn't want to remember. . . . Now I understand why."

"It's better to have had it come up now." Her voice was achingly gentle, filled with an emotion that sounded a lot like love. She attempted a weak smile of reassurance. "At least you took it all out on your furniture . . . and a friend who won't hunt you down and kill you for a few fists in the face."

Blake pushed himself up to a sitting position, then looked up at his friend. "I'm sorry you had to walk in at the wrong time."

"Better me than her."

"I never would have hurt Cara."

"Oh, no? Who do you think screamed?"

Blake's gaze jerked to her and he spied a reddening mark on her cheekbone. "Tell me I didn't—"

"It's nothing. Just a bump." Her dark eyes were unable to lie.

He reached out to her face, recalling that his elbow hit something when he'd swung it around. Now he realized she'd taken the blow. "Please forgive me," he whispered. "You must think I'm a monster."

"No . . . never."

Keoni rose to his full height. "I betta get somethin' for

my eye, eh? We talk tomorrow. Maybe you explain. Maybe not. Make no difference. I go. Leave you two.''

Cara smiled up at him. *''Mahalo nui loa, kaikunāne,''* she said, thanking her new big brother. Blake echoed her sentiments, offering his hand.

Keoni leaned down, grabbed the hand, and hauled Blake up for a big Kanaka embrace. In his Island language, he spoke a private message, much of it in words unfamiliar to Cara. ''You my brother for life. Nothing change that. Fighting don't change that. Women don't change that. But you have something very special in her, more special than you know. Don't lose her from your pigheadedness. It is time to make her your wife.''

''She is already my wife.''

''Not in your heart. You make love. You let her in. She is your destiny, little brother.''

Without words to speak his emotions, Blake could only nod. Then he embraced his friend and bid him good night. Keoni turned to Cara, who had stood up, and kissed her on the cheek. ''One helluva welcome into our little family, eh, little sister?''

As she smiled a sad smile, he went out the door laughing at his sense of humor. After he'd closed the door, the room fell silent for a few minutes.

She asked, ''Do you want to talk?''

''No.'' The pain of the memory was too new, too raw and too mortifying. To recall his past had been bad enough, but to do so aloud for another to know of the violation compounded his shame. ''Don't hover, Cara. I am through breaking furniture.''

She reached out to him. He stepped back, closing his eyes against the hurt he saw in her eyes. Hating himself for putting her through more anguish, he couldn't help the way he felt right now.

''Blake,'' she begged.

''Please don't touch me. It is when you touch me that I remember. I don't understand it, but I have to believe it because I experienced it. And it hurts too much. I cannot take any more memories. Not tonight.''

Turning his back on her, he fought to make sense of a past so dark that he'd buried it for years. He needed to do so alone.

As she walked over to the bed, his heart followed her. He thought of what Keoni had just said to him. His Kanaka brother possessed a deeper knowledge of spirits and such, of which Blake knew only through his limited education from the Island elders. Perhaps Keoni knew more about Cara, understood more about the mystical woman. When told of Cara's gift of insight, he'd seemed almost indifferent, accepting the stories as if there was no question of their credibility. Despite his friend's example of embracing the unknown, Blake remained leery, unable to drop his guard, unwilling to let anyone in.

And now he knew why. Or, at the very least, he might have stumbled upon the beginning of some answers. But for the time being, the memory of his horrid past was not something he wanted to think about. Tomorrow, maybe.

Bud moved in the corner, drawing Blake's attention to his dog's bewildered expression. He went over and gave the Lab a comforting pat on the head, yearning for someone to give him similar reassurance.

You have Cara.

No, he told himself. She was more the cause of this turmoil than the cure. His life had been content until she had arrived and pushed him to remember his past.

Refusing to believe that she was anything but trouble for him, Blake sat down in one of the remaining chairs and removed his shoes and stockings. Methodically undressing, as in his regular nightly ritual, he failed to remember that he could not crawl under the blankets in his usual state of undress. Not while she was there. He pulled his long shirt over his head, sufficiently covering himself.

After extinguishing the lantern, he walked through the dark to the berth. Hesitating, he considered sleeping on the floor, then thought of the unforgiving hardness of the wood. Unwilling to waken to stiff joints and sore muscles in the morning, he mildly chided himself for the irrational notion of suffering another sleepless night when there was a mat-

tress large enough for two to share. Quietly, he slipped
beneath the covers, trying not to touch his wife.

Cara felt Blake pull away, though the warmth of his body
still caressed her back. She held back a sigh, wanting to do
something to ease his torment. But she was the last person
in the world he would trust right now. Nothing she could
say or do would allay his fear of her. And she couldn't
blame him.

She'd been through this before. She should be used to
it. But every time it happened, her heart ached from the
pain of being rejected for something she couldn't change
any more than she could change the color of her eyes or
the pigment of her skin. She was different. She was psychic. It was not a disease of the mind that was somehow
contagious. Yet she was a pariah to those who didn't understand or could not accept the evidence of a supernatural
world around them.

None of the previous hurts had affected her as much as
this one from Blake. His rejection was the hardest of all.
But it wasn't his fault. Sometimes even she didn't know
how to handle the psychic phenomena that could crop up.
After the strange vision in the cave, he'd looked at her as
if she were a two-headed monster. God, how it hurt to see
that distrust in his eyes. She balled her fist and pressed it
to her mouth, holding back the sadness.

Love him, Cara. Give him your heart. The voice was not
her own, but held the soft, Spanish cadence of her great-
aunt Gabriella.

But I can't, she silently argued. He won't let me even
touch him, Aunt Gaby.

*Do not judge him by what you see or hear. He needs
you.*

He doesn't want me! He said so! Do you know how
much it hurts to hear him say that?

*Look beyond the fear in his mind and search for the love
in his heart. It is there, Cara. So deep, so hidden, that Blake
cannot find it.*

I'm not the one to help him, Aunt Gaby. I thought I was, but I'm not. I was wrong.

Touch him, Cara. Heal him.

No, I can't.

Trying to block out the disembodied voice of Gabriella, Cara covered her eyes with the palms of her hands. She refused to go through with the request that had been made of her. She couldn't risk putting herself out there on a limb only to have Blake shove her away. He had made it perfectly clear—he didn't want her.

A small twinge of pain came from her belly. It was the same feeling she always got when she didn't want to do something she'd been prompted to do.

No, she couldn't listen to her gut this time, preferring the pain of a little stomach acid over another, deeper kind of pain. She couldn't afford to create more complications by consummating their phony marriage. If she managed to reach past the barrier around his heart, then went back to her own time with Andrew, where would that leave Blake? Where would it leave her? Both of them would be worse off than if she'd left well enough alone.

She shifted to her back, but the discomfort in her abdomen only increased. She rolled to her other side, facing Blake's back. Her stomach clenched tighter.

You're not playing fair, Aunt Gaby.

Love him, Cara, repeated the gentle voice.

I want to love him, but . . . what if he won't love me back? What if he can't?

Cara tentatively reached out to Blake. Her hand paused over his shoulder blade, not quite touching him.

With a silent prayer for guidance, she splayed her fingers across the soft cotton yoke of his shirt.

"Don't." The threatening tone gave her a start, but she kept her hand in place.

"I'm not going to hurt you," she whispered.

"Leave me alone." He rolled his shoulder forward, shrugging off her touch. His rebuff stung, yet somehow she found the strength to continue. She slid her hand to his waist, drawing her body up close to his.

"I'm not sorry I made you remember everything. Now that you've faced the horrible truth about your past, I want to help you put it to rest."

"Go to sleep, Cara."

Her hand moved up his chest.

"No sex," he reminded her adamantly.

"This isn't about sex, Blake. I want to make love to you."

"Sex. Love. What's the difference?" he murmured as her cheek rested against his back. "Whatever you want, I can't give it."

"I'm not asking for anything from you. Nothing at all. Just let me love you."

Her palm slowly skimmed down the front of his shirt to his waist, then curved around his pelvic bone and over his hip without touching him intimately. Her intention was to allow the rest of his body to feel the tenderness in her caress. Her short fingernails lightly grazed the length of his leg to his ankle, then came back up the inside of his other leg, stopping at the edge of his shirt.

He said not a word. But she felt his muscles relax and sensed his resistance weakening. Inch by inch, she kneaded the muscles in his right leg, then his left. Shifting her body, she moved her hands to his back, stroking the heel of her palm up his spine, then circling down to his buttocks and to his shoulders again.

Expect nothing in return, Cara. Give of yourself.

Silently, she massaged his upper arm, his lower arm, his hand, his fingers. With a gentle tug, she coaxed him to lie on his back, which he did without comment or hesitation. She reached for his other arm. As she kneaded the muscles of his biceps, she sensed his pleasure and wanted to give him more.

You have the power to heal him.

Her hand traveled to the ends of his fingers, caressing them one at a time between her thumb and forefinger. Leaning over his chest, she brought his hand to her lips and kissed the back of his knuckles.

His other hand slowly moved from his side, reaching up

in the darkness and touching her cheek. She felt her heart
catch. He guided her head down to his. She held her breath.
His lips brushed hers, a tentative touch at first. A question
without words.

His bewildered thoughts came through to her—Should
we do this? Should he risk his lucid mind?

Her lips parted, inviting him, giving entrance to him. His
tongue skimmed her teeth, then delved deeper as her mind
filled with the sound of his inner voice.

Dear God, I want her. I need her.

His mouth moved over hers as she slipped her hand beneath the hem of his shirt and brought it to his waist. In a
slow yet fluid movement, she slid her leg over his hips and
lowered herself down onto his rigid shaft, sheathing him in
the hot core of her body.

He inhaled sharply. She tightened her feminine muscles
around him, eliciting his moan of pleasure.

*Take me, Blake. Take all I have. All the love. All the joy.
All the happiness.*

Oh, Cara . . .

She rose up and came down in a gentle rhythm that he
met with his own hips.

*Let go of your pain, Blake. Give it to me. Let me take
away all the hurt that's been locked up inside you.*

As their pace quickened, she felt his sadness well up
inside her, filling her with a poignant grief that arrowed
into her heart. The loss of his parents, the loss of his childhood, the loss of his innocence. His mournful sorrow burrowed down into the depths of her soul.

With an anguished cry, he reached out for her, drawing
her to him, clutching her body to his. He buried his face
in the curve of her neck at the moment of his climax, yet
she could still hear the soft sounds of his quiet weeping.

She kissed his temple and tasted the salt of his tears.

"I love you, Blake. I think I have loved you from the
first moment I saw you on that ship."

"No, Cara." His raspy voice was barely audible. "You
don't need to say these things to me."

He tried to lift her off of him, but she tightened her knees at his hips, unwilling to let him get away so easily. He tensed, still sheathed inside her. Her feminine muscles flexed around his manhood, then released.

"What are you doing to me?"

"Keeping you interested until I finish what I have to say."

"You've said enough already. And I know you hoped I would be able to repeat the same words to you, but I can't."

"I didn't *ask* you to. I don't *expect* you to." She kissed his mouth, his cheek, his chin. "But I'm going to keep loving you, even if you can't love me back. And I'm going to keep showing you."

Her secret sensual squeezes continued until she felt his arousal growing, hardening, fitting snug against the feminine walls of her womanhood.

"I thought we had an agreement," he reminded her half-heartedly. "No sex."

Wordlessly, she sat back, reveling in the thickness of him filling her, pressing the entrance of her womb. Lifting the edge of her nightgown, she peeled it over her head and let it drop to the floor. Then she unbuttoned his shirt, leaving it open so she could explore the muscles of his chest. As his hands cupped her breasts, she leaned into his palms.

"No sex," she agreed, her breathing escalating as her own passion grew. "Just pure, unadulterated love."

Chapter 16

THE FOLLOWING MORNING before dawn, Cara awoke to a kiss on her bare shoulder. She smiled and stretched like a contented kitten, purring with pleasure as Blake nuzzled the soft spot behind her ear. He had changed during their long night of passion, despite a few moments of fitful sleep from dreams of his past. Everything had changed between them. The tiny ache between her thighs reminded her of the daunting stamina of the man she had married.

His light kisses drifted over her breast to her belly. As his head moved lower, he spoke lovingly in the language of the Islands. Softly, she asked him to teach her to say the words for fantastic lovemaking.

"*Ho'okela o ka ho'oipoipo.*" His intimate kiss sent a spiral of tingling heat to her nerve endings. "And you are an *ipo ahi*—an ardent lover."

"*Ipo . . . ahi.*" She moaned, relishing the personal tutoring technique of his amazing tongue as her body trembled under his touch.

A half hour later, the warm sun angled into the larboard windows of the cabin as the two of them lay together on their sides, legs and arms entwined.

Blake slowly stroked his thumbnail down her spine, marveling at a strange new feeling of peace. "I must get dressed, *laua'e*," calling her "beloved" in the language of the islands.

"Never."

"You want more?" He kissed the top of her head, smiling to himself. "If we keep this pace, I will fill your belly with many babies."

Recalling the concern of the woman at San Juan, he wondered once more if she were already carrying another man's child.

"Blake . . ." Her serious tone braced his mind for the worst. "I am not pregnant."

Thank God. "Then you soon will be," he vowed, imagining their little brown *keiki* toddling about the beach of Hanalei. "Perhaps after last night—"

"No," she said softly, tilting her face up to gaze at him with apology in her eyes. "I am unable to bear children, Blake. I'm sorry. It never occurred to me to tell you until now."

"But how can you be so certain?"

"I've had tests. They all came back negative."

"Tests? There are tests for these things?"

"Yes, where I come from." She touched her fingers to the downturned corners of his mouth. "Babies mean a great deal to you, don't they?"

"No." He lied to spare her his disappointment. Though he'd always thought someday he would return to Kaua'i to raise sons and daughters with the woman he loved.

"You deserve to have those children." Her dark eyes reflected his thoughts. "When the time comes for me to return home with Andrew, we will have our marriage annulled so you will be free to find a fertile wife."

"I don't want that," he snapped. "I want you. If we cannot have our own children, we can find others who need a home."

Her eyes became moist, glistening with emotion, but she said not a word. She lifted up and kissed him. He murmured his enjoyment, wrapping his arms around her.

When a knock came at the door, he answered impatiently,

"Yes?"

"Sir," answered Jimmy, "I've come to ask if you'd be wantin' yer breakfast or should I just be bringin' the noon meal, sir?"

"Breakfast."

"Aye, aye, sir."

The retreating footsteps prompted Cara to snuggle her face into Blake's chest. "Where were we?" came her muffled voice before she nipped lightly on his nipple.

"As much as I would like to indulge us one more time, I mustn't."

He brought her face up to his, kissing her soundly. With a moan of frustration, he broke away and dropped his legs over the edge of the berth. As he leaned over to snatch his shirt from the floor, her fingertips traced the narrow tattooed ribbon of designs along his left thigh, similar to the band around his arm.

"What are the symbols?" she asked.

"'*Aumakua*—family deity." Glancing down, he touched the tattoos with reverence. "When Keoni's parents adopted me, I earned the right to wear the mark of their '*aumakua*— their ancestors who come back in different form than human. Since I had no knowledge of my own ancestry, my adoptive father took me to a *nīnau kupapa'u*, who gave me my own '*aumakua*."

"A *nīnau kupapa'u?*"

"A person who consults the dead or familiar spirits." He smiled at the irony. "When I was young I didn't believe in such things, mind you. It was the tradition of my new family, and I wanted to belong, be a part of their lives. But it was impossible to accept that there was anything godlike that would protect me, especially after what I had gone through. I understand so much now."

"Do the Kānaka have people like me?"

He nodded. "*Mea punihei i nā āiwaiwa*—a mystic. Literally, it means a person entranced in the mysterious ways."

Cara slowly repeated his pronunciation, tracing the indigo lines imprinted on his flesh. Suddenly an eerie realization dawned on her, sending a chill down her arms. "That was the name of the ship that went down in San Pedro, Blake. The *Mystic*."

"I had forgotten until now, but it seems rather appropriate. Everything considered, I mean. There you were on that ill-fated brig, one of only a few survivors. All of the twists and turns of fate *could* be described as mystical."

"Yeah . . . mystical." She thought of her trip through time, as well. How could she begin to explain something so far beyond his realm of comprehension? It was hard enough convincing him of her own psychic abilities, which he hadn't accepted until he'd seen proof for himself. How could she claim to be from the future without something to substantiate her story?

"If I had not witnessed all the mysterious events, I doubt I would believe any of it," he said, confirming her worries. "But it would make a fascinating piece of fiction, don't you agree? The telling of a great adventure on the uncivilized coast of California?"

"Someone *will* tell it, Blake. A young Harvard man named Richard Dana will write a book. Not about *our* experiences but about his own journey. He'll expose the injustices of a sailor's life and title it *Two Years Before the Mast*."

He shifted sideways on the edge of the bed and stared at her for a long moment. His expression told her that his skepticism was creeping back in. Her warning bells went off. She had to take this slower, to let him adjust to her clairvoyance before dropping another bomb in his lap.

"How *do* you know such things?" The corner of his mouth quirked into a teasing grin of disbelief. "Did Gabriella pay you another visit?"

"No, her recent assistance is new to me." Sidestepping his question about the book, she avoided any mention of time travel. "As for how I know things . . . I've been called a freak of nature because of my sixth sense. But I'm not a freak. To me, my gift is as normal as breathing. I just breathe deeper than most people."

His black brows pinched together in a frown of confusion. "I don't understand."

"My intuition is stronger than most people's," she amended with a weak smile. Still, he continued to look perplexed. "Haven't you ever had a gut feeling about something?"

"Yes, of course."

"And do you pay attention to it?"

"Usually."

"Well, I do, too. But my gut feelings also come to me in different ways. Sometimes it's in my stomach. Sometimes I have thoughts show up as if I've just read them or heard them a moment earlier."

"Are you saying you hear voices?"

"Not always." She grinned sympathetically at his obvious bewilderment. "Let's say, for the sake of explanation, that I get the sudden thought 'Jimmy's leg hurts.' I don't hear someone tell me. The thought is just there, in my head, in the same way that a memory is there in your head. The only difference is the memory is a recollection of a previous event, such as actually witnessing Jimmy hurt his leg and remembering it afterward. Well, I get the word or thought *before* it is happening in the physical sense. For lack of a better term, I dubbed it my 'Reverse Memory.' "

Blake gazed down at her in awe, seeing the love and compassion in the depths of her dark eyes. She *was* a mystic, and a most beautiful one. "You amaze me."

Clearly uncomfortable with his reverence, she averted her eyes as an endearing blush crept into her cheeks. He watched her expression change into uncertainty.

"What's wrong, *laua'e?*"

"Are you sorry I came here? That I have caused you so much pain?"

"If I said no, you would read my thoughts and call me a liar. In the beginning, I *was* sorry, but now I see things differently. If anyone should be apologizing, I should—for my behavior, my distrust."

"You reacted naturally. I never meant to hurt you." Her velvet touch drew him back into her arms.

"I know that now."

"Touching me doesn't bring back any more bad memories?"

"No longer. Touching you has made new memories for me. Good memories. Mystic memories. Whatever you may be, you have me completely enchanted. I am at your mercy."

"No, it is you who have weakened me with all of this lovemaking. Correction, *wonderful* lovemaking—*Ho'okela o ka ho'oipoipo.*"

Unfamiliar feelings deep in his heart bewildered him, feelings that he was not quite ready to examine, not quite ready to name. His hips nestled snug against the juncture of her firm, slender thighs as his mouth came down upon hers, hungering for her as though he had not tasted her in days and weeks and months. He could never imagine having his fill of her.

The sound of scratching at the door told him Bud was wanting to go out. At the same time, someone rapped twice.

"It is no use," Blake sighed, levering himself off her sweet, enticing body. "My other duties will not allow me to dawdle the day away, my dear. Be forewarned, however. I may very well come down here at any given time to lift your skirts and have my way with you."

"What skirts? I intend to sleep until you return." She yawned and stretched again, arching her back with a satisfied smile. The sunlight spilled across her coppery skin, causing him more anguish at the idea of donning his clothes and leaving her here without him.

The knocking persisted.

"All right, all right," he called out, then quickly dressed as Cara covered herself and burrowed deep beneath the bedclothes.

Though he expected it to be Jimmy on the other side of the door, he was not surprised to see Keoni had been the annoying one. As Bud slipped out, Blake glanced down at the tray of food. The delicious aroma suddenly triggered his delayed hunger.

"It's about time," he scolded in jest.

The Kanaka glanced toward the bed. "Yes, it *was* about time, *kaikaina*. But I think you already got plenty good stuff for a starving man, eh?"

After two weeks of fair winds and fast sail, then nearly a week of slow passage through the doldrums, the *Valiant* crossed the equator on April 23. Alone on the open seas, she was now more than two thousand miles off the northwestern coast of South America.

In the captain's quarters, Cara stood next to Blake at the table, looking down at a map rolled out and anchored at the curled corners.

He shook his head adamantly. "The *Ballade* would not be in Callao, Cara. Peru is too far out of the way for a merchantman to stop on his way back to Boston. You can see for yourself how far off the coast the trade winds have taken our own ship."

"But Andrew might be there," she insisted.

"Are you sure? What about Juan Fernández?" He pointed to a small island about three hundred miles west of Valparaíso, Chile. "If there had been a need to make land for supplies, which I doubt, then it would more likely have been here."

She slowly shook her head as she stared at the map. "I just don't see him on an island."

"How can you be so certain?"

Throwing her hands up in the air, she spun away from the table. "I am *not* certain. That's the problem. I told you before, this psychic ability is not one hundred percent accurate. I'm lucky if it's seventy or eighty percent. I'm just telling you what I'm picking up."

Since their wedding night, when Blake had regained his memory, Cara knew he shared her desperate need to reach the boy and was praying he had not fallen victim to a sadistic captain as had Blake. While his nightmares had lessened, he still suffered from long silent spells of painful anguish. Sometimes he would allow Cara to soothe the hurt. Other times, nothing could be done to alleviate his melancholy. She knew he needed more time to heal, perhaps months or years.

But time was something Andrew didn't have. During the hours Blake had spent on deck with his crew, Cara had been left with little to do but fret about the boy's fate. She'd searched her mind. She'd meditated. She'd even called upon Gabriella for help in locating Andrew.

Not until this morning had she finally felt like she was onto something. She'd been staring at the map for the hundredth time with the same unsettled feeling in the pit of her stomach. Her gut instinct had told her the *Ballade* was not as far out ahead of them as they'd assumed. While she wished the *Valiant* could stop at every port between California and Boston, she knew Blake would not be able to account for such a delay to the shipowner. Studying the yellowed paper, she had been drawn repeatedly to Peru. Callao, in particular. Acting on a hunch, she'd broached the idea to Blake. But he would not be easily swayed into changing his course.

He came up behind her and slid her arms around her waist. She rested her hands on his, dropping her head back against his shoulder.

"We will find him, *laua'e*," he promised. Though he often used her pet name, he never said he loved her in either English or Hawaiian. She, on the other hand, told him at least twice a day. Each time, though, she felt a twinge of remorse, knowing she would have to leave him after she found Andrew. The thought of losing Blake always tore at her heart, and it did so now.

She turned in the circle of his arms and looked up into his blue eyes. "I need to tell you something . . ."

How could she find the words to explain about her journey through time? He had barely managed to comprehend her clairvoyance and other supernatural occurrences, like Gabriella's appearances at the two missions. Without proof of her claim to be from another time, she knew he'd never believe her.

He smiled his sweet, sexy smile, melting away her determination to come clean with the truth. ''I know what you are thinking.''

''You do?'' Taken aback, she couldn't hide her surprise or nervousness.

In recent days, he'd started to show little signs of his own sixth sense, finishing her sentences, handing her something before she'd asked for it. He'd dismissed it as a silent language between lovers. But she suspected he might be clairaudient—able to hear her inner thoughts—and highly receptive.

''You are thinking of Andrew. And wondering how you will talk me into going along with your idea,'' he said, relieving her mind of concern. Obviously his radar wasn't zeroing in on her dilemma over telling him about traveling through time.

''Are you saying there is a possibility you *can* be coerced into sailing to Callao?''

''With you, it seems anything is possible. Whether it is *probable* is another matter altogether.'' He lowered his head and kissed her. His amorous thoughts never seemed to venture too far off the same track.

Bracing her hands on his arms, she gently pushed back a few inches from him to look at him. ''Don't try to distract me. We were having a discussion, as I recall.''

''Uh-hmmm.'' He squeezed her bottom, pulling her tight against his hips. She broke away, turning to the map on the table. She leaned over to get a closer look and calculate the miles to Peru. He leaned over behind her and kissed the nape of her neck, sending erotic messages to every nerve ending.

''The way I see it, if you reconfigure the navigational course . . .'' Her words trailed off despite her attempt to return his attention to the topic at hand. But his own hands were busy hiking up the back of her skirt. ''We can head straight to Callao . . . ohhhh, Blake!''

Three weeks later, in the middle of May, Blake stood on the deck of the *Valiant* as the ship headed toward yet another port, the third since crossing the equator. Callao had been the first. And damned if Cara had not been right about the *Ballade*, though they had missed the ship by only a week. From what he'd been able to learn, the merchantman had been becalmed for an inordinate amount of time in the doldrums. He'd also discovered allegations of illegal trade, which explained the visits to shore.

After Callao, Blake had strongly suspected the *Ballade* would have similar business on Juan Fernández. Despite Cara's insistence otherwise, they had set out for the island, yet found no satisfaction there. Vexed by his own mistake of ignoring Cara's instincts, Blake had been more malleable when she wanted to look for the elusive ship in Valparaíso.

Now, during morning watch, a man aloft hollered down, "Land ho!" All eyes turned toward the Chilean port in the distance.

Blake expected Cara to appear at his side any moment now, certain that she'd heard the cry. As usual, she did not disappoint him. Bud, who had fully recuperated now, was with her.

"Good morning, Mrs. Masters," he greeted formally, aware of his crew working around them.

"Good morning, sir."

He suppressed a grin at her strained effort to maintain proper decorum in front of his men. They had all softened somewhat toward the idea of a woman on board, or at least to having Cara in their midst. He suspected the misfortune of her bruised and swollen cheek from the wedding night brawl had garnered the sympathy of every sailor in the forecastle. With or without their silent censure, he would always feel like a bastard for the accident. Yet she had healed quickly and without complaint—and had found begrudging respect among the men.

"I still say the *Ballade* is halfway up the Atlantic by now," he speculated, reaching down to pat Bud on the head so as to occupy his hands with something other than touching Cara.

"I hope it isn't," she answered over her shoulder, heading forward. He watched his dog trot after her, wishing he could do the same.

"The bow will get there no sooner than the stern," he called after her. She glanced back at him, a merry twinkle dancing in her dark eyes.

" 'Tis still a better view, my husband," she answered in a saucy tone unlike her own. Her steady gait aboard the moving brig made her bottom sway seductively beneath the soft drape of her skirt.

A better view? Hardly. He enjoyed a far more pleasant view from the stern, he thought to himself, eyeing his wife. He wished he could call her back and draw her into his arms, but he held himself in check.

As she passed McGinty on his knees scrubbing the deck, she smiled apologetically and stepped gingerly around the water. He sat back with a foolish grin, watching her go by.

"Back to work," ordered Mr. Bellows.

When Blake saw Keoni step out of the galley and join Cara at the rail, he knew his wife was in safe company as he went back to his duties.

A few hours later, they sailed into the bay with the traditional gun salute. Using his glass, he made out a little hermaphrodite brig flying American colors from her mizzen peak. Fairly certain it was the *Ballade*, he muttered to himself, "Well, I'll be . . ."

He looked around for Cara, expecting to lock his gaze on her smug expression of triumph. But she was nowhere to be seen. Neither was Bud. Calling for his steward, he asked if Jimmy had seen Mrs. Masters.

"Aye, sir. She asked me to fetch a set of clothes to match the rest of the crew. I just now delivered them to your quarters, sir."

"Ready the gig. I shall be paying a visit to the *Ballade*. That will be all for now."

As the boy left, Blake headed below to inform Cara of the other ship, though it would hardly be news to her.

In his cabin, he found her sitting in a chair, bent at the waist, tying the laces on a worn pair of work shoes. Bud rested in the corner, head on his paws, looking a bit worried.

"I must insist you stay here, Cara. Let me handle this—captain to captain."

"I've come too far to sit back and wait," she argued, reaching up and shoving aside a lock of dark brown hair that was falling across her eyes.

In the two months since he'd found her aboard the *Mystic*, her hair had grown longer, softening her feminine features all the more. Although he had initially been fooled by her disguise, she could not possibly expect to pass herself off as a young man any longer.

"Then we will pay a cordial visit as husband and wife," he informed her, fingering the soft, dark wisps at the nape of her neck.

"But—"

"Listen to me, *laua'e*." He gently grasped her arm and brought her to her feet. "I do not wish to do anything that will cause suspicion before we can find out if Andrew is on that ship. Few, if any, would mistake you for a boy, especially when there is no storm to distract them from seeing those beautiful big brown eyes."

Her lips parted as if she were about to give a rebuttal, but he silenced her with a deep kiss. In spite of her muffled protest and the resistant press of her hands on his chest, he persisted, knowing her weakness for him, knowing his own weakness for her. When she melted into him, he could not contain the grin that ruined a perfectly wonderful kiss.

With a ragged breath, she whispered against his lips, "Damn you, Blake Masters. You never play fair."

He gently swatted her fanny with his palm. "Get changed back into that skirt, wife. I will return for you when we are ready to leave for the *Ballade*."

Several minutes later, Cara sat up straight and stiff in the chair as Keoni stood behind her, snipping at her hair with a pair of scissors.

"You must tell him the truth, *kaikuhine*."

"I will. Soon." *But not yet.* She needed more courage to tell Blake about her past in 1998. He had accepted her as a mystic. But her current role as a time-traveler would take a much bigger leap of faith.

"If you don't sit still, I might cut off your ear. You want that?"

Her hands gripped the arms of the chair as she made a conscious effort to stop fidgeting. "Did you think of me as a mystic, Keoni? Blake said I was a *mea punihei i nā āiwaiwa.*"

The scissoring paused, then began again. "I think of you as a special friend. A sister. And yes, a mystic, as well."

"But I don't *feel* like one."

Keoni chuckled. "And how is one supposed to feel?"

"Not like me, that's for sure." Cara smiled to herself, envisioning a Chinese monk speaking slowly and eloquently, poised in a peaceful, centered calm. "When I was growing up, I was taunted for being strange and scary. So I worked hard to be as normal as possible. I'm not the type to sit on a mountaintop, waiting for lost souls to seek me for divine guidance."

Keoni laughed. "You are a contented little *keiki* who would rather sleep than wake up to the early-morning sunlight, *kaikuhine.* It is time to open your eyes and enjoy the dawn."

His kind words silenced her as she weighed their meaning in her mind. She thought of her life before she'd stepped through the portal. Looking back at her grief-stricken loss of Mark six years earlier, she could see how his death had pushed her forward, strengthening her clairvoyance in her effort to find his murderer. With her life-path irrevocably altered, she had gone into private investigation. And yet, she still hid her psychic abilities from most people, though not as much as when she was a child. Her fears had almost turned away Mr. Charles, had it not been for Aunt Gaby. Now here she was, living day to day on little else but her supernatural instincts.

"I still find it hard to accept myself as a mystic. Maybe that's why my stomach is giving me fits."

"See? Even your *'ōpū* says you cannot avoid your true calling any longer. And maybe it's also trying to tell you that your husband has a right to know everything about you, especially about your journey from the future time.''

"And he *will* find out.''

"After you have gone?''

The knot twisted in her stomach. "Keoni, please . . . just get back to cutting my hair. I'll deal with one problem at a time. For right now, I must focus all my energy on Andrew.''

She heard the shears behind her left ear as Keoni asked, "Do you still sense the boy on that ship?''

"Yes, more than ever. But—'' She hesitated. "I have a really bad feeling that I can't quite figure out.''

"Someone getting hurt, maybe?''

"I'm not sure. It's like there's a black veil obscuring the picture in my head.''

"You betta be careful.''

"I will.''

He patted her shoulder. "*Pau.* Finished.''

"*Mahalo,* Keoni. I owe you one.''

"You pay me back by telling Blake the truth.''

"Soon,'' she repeated. "I promise.''

Chapter 17

OVER AN HOUR later, Blake needed a few more minutes to give final instructions to Mr. Bellows, in case a hasty departure became necessary. Concerned about his minor delay, he sent his steward to bring Cara up from the cabin. Jimmy reappeared shortly, with a nervous look in his youthful eyes.

Blake scanned the deck for his wife. "Where is Mrs. Masters?"

"Sir, she wasn't in your quarters, sir."

"What?"

"Sir, I said—"

"I heard you, dammit. Where the hell is she?"

"I'm right here, Blake."

He spun around. Cara had been standing with her back to him, not ten feet astern. Dressed in white duck trousers, red neckerchief, and checked shirt, she was hardly recognizable.

"You cut your hair." He strode toward her. "How? Who—?"

"Keoni proved to be quite helpful with a pair of scissors," she explained with a sheepish grin. "If he ever gives up cooking, he could become a barber."

He still did not know how she could bluff anyone with her disguise, but then his opinion *was* a little bit biased.

The cook walked up and stood beside him. "She make a good sailor, eh, *kaikaina*?"

"Sometimes I wonder whose side you are on, big brother—hers or mine?"

The Kanaka laughed. "Both, of course."

Blake eyed her neatly clipped layers, hardly two inches at the crown and shorter at the nape of her neck. He addressed his question to Keoni. "Is this your revenge for that black eye?"

"Naw, I forgive and forget."

"Ha!" Though he feigned anger with his friend, he felt a crooked grin tug at the corner of his mouth. "You have turned my wife into a man, for devil's sake."

Cara spoke up. "Could you stop talking about me like I'm your pet poodle after a hack job at the groomers?"

"What?" they asked in unison.

"Oh, never mind," she said with a resigned sigh. "Let's go, Blake."

Keoni stepped forward. "I want to go along with you, in case there is trouble."

Blake looked at Cara, wondering if her psychic insight sensed the need for the brawny Kanaka's support. Her glance darted between him and Keoni, then she nodded solemnly.

"Very well, he goes, but—" He held up his finger. "Keep your eyes downcast and do *not* smile. Your pearl-white teeth will surely draw unwanted attention to your face. No matter what I say, go along with it."

She nodded, and he knew how much it cost her.

After Keoni went down into the boat where Jimmy waited as steersman, Cara climbed down like a regular sailor, took her place next to the Kanaka and manned an oar.

"I'm a little rusty at this," she warned Keoni while Blake settled in the stern sheets. "Just don't put too much muscle into it or we'll be going in circles."

The cook grinned. "Aye, aye, Lady Captain."

The gig was shoved off, and they began to row toward the *Ballade*. Within a few strokes, Cara managed to give the appearance of knowing what she was doing. Once again, she was grateful for the crash course on seamanship she'd taken in preparation for the reenactment role in the twentieth century. Little did she realize at the time that she would be actually living the part.

Her stomach fluttered with nervous anticipation. She recognized the good sign, knowing a bellyache would've meant she was on the wrong track. Instead, she sensed that the end of her search was getting closer and closer with each stroke of the oars.

Her back to the bow, she looked across at Blake, facing her. "If I can make a suggestion . . ." She pulled the oar with all her strength, able to speak only during the reach. "When you go with the captain to his cabin . . . I'll go with Keoni to visit with the crew."

"I don't want you out of my sight."

"Too risky to take me along . . . only your steward would go with you . . . but not me, not a regular sailor."

"Then I will provide an excuse for you to accompany me."

Keoni spoke up without the need to hesitate between each stroke. "She has a point, Captain. We three have a better chance of finding him belowdecks, especially if one of us has an opportunity to slip away."

Blake glared at his Island brother, then at Cara. "Very well, but if anyone is going to snoop around, let Jimmy do it. *You* stay with Keoni." He turned to his steward. "Those are my orders, James. Do *not* let my wife undermine them or there'll be hell to pay."

The wide-eyed adolescent nodded vigorously. "Aye, aye, sir."

Keoni echoed the affirmative response, prompting Cara to do the same.

With a few more strokes, they came alongside the *Ballade*. Blake gave his name to the mate in the gangway, who called out to his commander, "Captain Blake Masters of the *Valiant* coming aboard, sir!"

While the four of them climbed onto the deck, Cara felt an eerie tingling throughout her body. A sense of evil seemed to emanate from every plank, stem to stern, throbbing like a pounding heartbeat. The sickening sound pulsed inside her head. With a difficult swallow, she forced down a wave of nausea.

Glancing toward Blake, she saw his eyes narrow at her unspoken alarm. Then, just as quickly, his cool composure returned.

A bellowing voice came up from the companionway. "Bring Captain Masters down to the cabin."

"Follow me, sir," invited the first mate, a dark-haired man of average height with thick and hairy forearms.

As Blake departed for the aft cabin, Keoni headed forward, prompting Cara and Jimmy to step lively to catch up with the Kanaka's long strides. Acting as if he would be welcome anywhere—and well he would be on most ships—he put his head down into the forecastle and received a stiff yet polite invitation to join the shipmates of the *Ballade*.

The partial crew of seven seemed cordial enough, sitting around and smoking pipes while the other half stood watch topside. Cara, however, sensed an undercurrent of tension that lay just a hair's breadth beneath the surface of their friendly smiles and light banter. Keoni introduced himself and Jimmy, dismissing Cara as a new boy who had come on the *Valiant* in San Diego from a whaler heading back to Lahaina.

"Edward appears to have a disease of the mind," he added, cleverly using her former surname. "Doesn't talk. Doesn't look at you. Wanders off, making more work for the rest of us."

"What's your cap'n want with a 'soger' aboard?" asked one young man. To a sailor, there was nothing more insulting than to be referred to as a no-account soldier, or "soger."

An old salt winked at her. "There be reason enough, eh, dandy-boy?"

Comprehending the deviant implication, Cara dropped her gaze, shuffling back into the shadows.

Keoni responded in a none-too-pleasant tone, "Captain

Masters has a new bride in his quarters. Edward here assists Jimmy.''

''He's right,'' piped up the steward, getting his ire up. ''A fine an' fair gentleman, the cap'n is.''

Keeping her eyes downcast, she listened to the exchange, hoping it wouldn't get out of hand. The one thing she didn't need right now was a brawl, at least not before she could have a chance to snoop around. Although Blake had given those particular orders to Jimmy, it was quite obvious that the steward was in the thick of the conversation and would be missed if he were to sneak off. On the other hand, Keoni had set up a perfect scenario for her. If she were caught, the crew already knew she had a feeble mind and a reputation for roving.

The tension soon passed, much to her relief, and the men settled into amicable banter. She stared at her feet, trying to appear bored and distracted while her nerves were taut as a bowline. Anxious to get going, she finally slunk far enough into the shadows for an easy exit.

With some time remaining before the next watch, all hands would be either topside or in the forecastle, giving her the opportunity to venture farther below. Unlike the *Valiant*, the lower hold of this ship was not filled to the beams with cattle hides, but with all sizes of crates and barrels, stowed and lashed, leaving little, if any, space to hide a child.

Her frustration mounted. She could almost hear a clock ticking off the seconds. Her hands balled into tight fists as she looked around, feeling the ever-present pulse of fear in the ship's belly.

Come on, Aunt Gaby. Show up and tell me where to find him.

You have the answers within you, Cara, came the voice of Gabriella.

No. I need your help.

Trust yourself.

You picked a fine time to leave me in the lurch!

I am here for you, Cara. But I can only tell you how to do it. I cannot do it for you. In the silence, you will know.

She squeezed her eyes shut, emptying her mind of the fears and the questions. As the black veil behind her lids blossomed into a violet light, she felt the tension ease from her body, replaced by a sense of calm knowingness. There were no words, no pictures, no voices. Yet she instinctively knew the direction to take.

In a matter of moments, she came upon the captain's quarters, where men's voices could be heard in a muffled conversation. Adjacent to the cabin was another door with a slide bolt mounted on the outside, above the knob. Moving quietly, she reached up to slide the bolt. Touching the metal sent a sudden jolt of fear up her arm as if she'd stuck her finger in an electrical socket.

He's here!

With a silent prayer, she twisted the knob and opened the door. On a berth inside the closet-size cabin lay a small figure curled up on his side, his back to her. His blond hair was long and matted, but it looked to be the right color.

She took a soft step inside, closing the door behind her, then whispered, "Andrew?" When no answer came, she leaned over his head. "Andrew Charles?" She lightly touched his arm.

The boy yelped like a scared pup. She clamped her hand over his mouth. He squirmed, rolling onto his back. His blue eyes widened in terror.

"Shhh, Andrew. It's okay. I've come to take you away from here. I've come to take you home."

The boy fought her a little longer until her words seemed to finally sink in. He went still, staring up at her.

She smiled reassuringly, slowly lowering her hand to his chest. "Your father hired me to find you. It's going to be tricky to get off this ship, but you have to be brave. Okay?"

He remained mute, unable or unwilling to acknowledge her instructions.

"Andrew? Do you understand me?"

His haunted eyes studied her. For weeks, Cara had wondered and worried about his safety, never thinking about how she would deal with his state of mind when she found him. Now that she needed his cooperation to escape, she realized he was too traumatized. He was incapable of conscious communication.

Running out of time, she took his hand. He yanked it away, then scooted backward, pressing his body against the bulkhead.

"I'm not going to hurt you, sweetheart. I'm here to help."

Again she tried to reach out to him, slowly, cautiously, reassuringly. She touched his cheek. He froze. In her mind, she felt his fear. He thought she was a sailor coming to take her away like the one who had abducted him at the mission.

"I'm not a real sailor. And I'm not kidnapping you." Her ability to read his thoughts startled him. "I'm a woman *dressed* as a man so I can rescue you."

From what she could pick up, he was as confused as ever. But she couldn't wait around for him to decide whether she was telling the truth.

"Come on, sugar. We've got to get out of here."

Though reluctant at first, he finally let her take his hand and lead him out the door.

Cara had no way to signal Blake or Keoni that she'd found Andrew. Without their help, she could only head for the gig and hope to get as close as possible before they were inevitably caught. It wasn't a matter of if they would be spotted, only when.

She brought Andrew up the companionway and nearly made it to the rail before the mate called out from the quarterdeck. "Where the hell you goin' with that boy?"

Whirling around, she pulled the ten-year-old behind her with a hasty order under his breath. "Get over the side and into the boat. No one will hurt you down there. Now go!"

Andrew darted away from her side as she braced herself, ready for an attack from fore and aft. The chief mate bore down on her. Out of the corner of her eye, she saw another man coming from the opposite direction and lunging for the boy. She heard a high-pitched scream.

Cara spun about as the sound of a splash came up from the water. *"Andrew!"*

She frantically tried to assure herself that he would know how to swim, recalling the sailboat docked behind his home in Huntington Harbour. But she couldn't take a chance of being wrong. She swung one leg over the rail and paused to locate the bubbles so she wouldn't jump on top of him.

Suddenly a hand grabbed her by the scruff of the neck and yanked her backward. A knee slammed into her right kidney, then a blow struck her shoulder as the mate cussed a blue streak behind her. Crumbling to the deck at his feet, blocking the pain from her mind, she thought only of the boy in the water. She had to get to him. Bracing her palms, she pushed herself up onto her hands and knees. The kick to her ribs tumbled her onto her side with an anguished cry.

Her eyes slammed shut from pain. She battled the black oblivion that sucked her into a downward spiral. She *had* to fight back. She'd come too far to lose Andrew now. As she struggled to get up, she heard a thunderous echo through the wood beneath her head like a herd of horses galloping through the hold of the ship.

Blake's voice roared, "You bloody sonuvabitch—"

She opened her eyes but saw only feet and legs in a scuffle. More thundering noises. More shouts. An all-out melee erupted, with the sound of grunts and fists smacking flesh. In the midst of the madness, gentle hands gripped her shoulders and hurriedly helped her to her feet.

"Gotta . . . get . . . Andrew," she gasped, barely acknowledging Jimmy's help as she stumbled to the rail.

Looking down, she saw the boy treading water, his wide eyes focused on something ahead of him.

Dear God, don't let it be a shark, she pleaded. With her heart pounding in her throat, she followed his gaze. Paddling toward him was the huge black Labrador retriever, followed by another boat from the *Valiant*.

"Way to go, Bud," she cried, thrusting both fists into the air. Pain stabbed her right side. She sucked in a sharp breath, nearly doubling over. The men in the second launch waved back, indicating they had everything under control.

"Good," she murmured to herself. "Now I can pass out."

Turning, Cara slumped to the deck and watched helplessly as Blake grappled with the captain, both of them gripping knives in their hands. Keoni fought with his brawny fists, first one man, then another. Two unconscious sailors were sprawled on the wooden planks. Yet, strangely, the rest of the crew stood aside like a cluster of curious spectators.

A moment later Blake held his startled opponent at blade point. "Tell your men to back down, Captain Pritcher."

The frightened officer croaked, "Ease off, men."

"Aye, aye, sir," answered the hands, who had already stopped fighting with Keoni when they'd seen the knife at their captain's throat. Cara let out a pent-up breath, then winced at the additional pain caused by the sigh of relief.

"I *was* negotiating to offer a sum for the boy, but all this fuss has put me in a foul mood. I am taking him off your hands, with or without your permission, Pritcher."

"Take him. He's yours."

Blake kept the sharp tip at the man's throat. "Where is he?"

Cara spoke up, her voice weak from the beating she'd endured. "He jumped overboard before you got—" She gasped on another stabbing pain.

"Keoni, take the captain until we're safely off this brig." The Kanaka quickly switched places, then Blake barked at his steward, "Help me get my wife down into the boat."

"Your *wife*?" The astonishment of the *Ballade*'s captain received no response.

Blake strode over to Cara, sitting on the deck with Jimmy's support. She watched her husband kneel in front of her, worry darkening his blue eyes.

"How bad is it?"

She attempted a smile but gave up. "I can make it down into the boat on my own." *I hope.*

He carefully lifted her to her feet. Swaying with dizziness, she gripped the front of his torn and dirtied shirt to steady herself.

He cupped her jaw, the pad of his thumb stroking her

cheek. "This is turning out to be one rough-and-tumble honeymoon."

She chuckled, then winced. "I think I've got a couple of cracked ribs." In a low voice meant for only his ears, she added, "We might have to postpone the wild nights for a while."

"No kidding."

By sunset, the *Valiant* had fled the Chilean coast, leaving behind a captain cursing the theft of his property and vowing to seek revenge. Blake doubted that the threat would be carried out, not as long as there were more profitable ventures along the coast than chasing after a mere child.

His concern focused on Cara as she slept in their bed, her ribs tightly bandaged as per her instructions. It seemed she understood the care of injured ribs as well as rattlesnake bites, he thought to himself, staring down at her peaceful face.

As for Andrew, he had yet to speak to anyone. Resisting all attempts to be taken below, he now sat on deck, huddled in a little ball. Bud seemed to be the only one allowed to join him in his silent misery.

Mr. Bellows had given his account of the surprising bravery of the dog. Apparently, the crew had been anxiously watching the *Ballade* when they saw the boy jump overboard. Before anyone could respond, Bud had leaped into the water. The first mate had quickly dispatched two men to fetch the dog and the child, who were dragged into the boat and hauled back to the *Valiant*.

Shortly thereafter Blake had returned with the others, ordering the first mate to sail immediately. In the organized chaos, and because of his worry about Cara, he had barely taken the time to acknowledge the presence of the boy.

Now Blake sat on the edge of the mattress, gazing down at his battered and bruised wife. Renewed fury raged within him, recalling the sight of her fallen body at the feet of that bastard aboard the *Ballade*. Chastising himself for his belated arrival on deck, he slipped his fingers beneath her hand and stroked the back of her scraped knuckles. He should have been there for her.

"Quit blaming yourself." Her soft voice drew his head up.

"How are you feeling?"

"I've had better moments in this bed." Her meager attempt to laugh at her own humor only caused her more pain. "I didn't think I had so many body parts that could hurt so much."

"I should have killed him."

"I'm glad you didn't." She raised his hand to her lips and kissed the back of it. "I'm also glad you didn't get yourself killed, by him or the captain. I was afraid if I closed my eyes, I would wake up and find out I'd lost you."

"Never."

Her smile faltered. "I wish I could believe that."

"What is there not to believe? You are here with me now. After my obligations are fulfilled in Boston, we will set sail for the Islands and live out the rest of our lives there."

"You're forgetting about Andrew," she reminded him with a sad smile. "Is he still on deck with Bud?"

"Aye, he is. And a sorrier sight I've never seen before."

"Probably a lot like you when Keoni's family took you in."

Blake acknowledged her perceptiveness. "I suppose I am the only one aboard who truly understands his fear and isolation."

"Talk to him. I think you can bring him out of his shell."

"I will give it my best, but I doubt I have the touch you do." Releasing her hand, he skimmed a fingertip along the contour of her cheek. "Mystical and motherly—a healing combination."

"Do you think you could coax him to come down to see me?"

"If I fail, Bud will surely lead him to you."

"It would probably work. That dog is his hero."

"I can make a bed for Andrew here on the floor so we can keep an eye on him. When he realizes Bud sleeps here, he may be willing to stay as well."

"You don't mind sharing the cabin with him?"

"He needs to feel safe, *laua'e*. As long as he remains frightened and withdrawn, he should be here with us."

"What if he can't pull himself out of this state of withdrawal?"

Blake shook his head sadly. "I don't know, Cara. We can only do our best with him until we take him back to his parents."

"*We?*" She jerked upright, then groaned and fell back onto the mattress. "This was *my* responsibility, Blake. You can't go back with me."

"I can and I will," he stated adamantly, brushing a short lock of hair off her forehead. "You once said Andrew was your son, then recanted the story. Yet you never clarified where he was from."

"California," she said weakly, staring out the aft windows. "I have to go back right away."

Her words slammed into his stomach like a fist. "You can't! Even if you were not hurt, you could not risk traveling alone with the boy. Besides, Captain Pritcher will be sailing these waters, keeping an eye out for Andrew at every port. You must come to Boston with me. As soon as I dispatch my duties to the shipowner, I will be free to go with you. Better still, I will captain another ship around the Horn, one that will take Andrew to California, then take you and me to Lahaina. From there, we will go to Kaua'i."

A single tear slipped from the corner of her eye. "You make it all sound so easy, so perfect." Her face turned toward him. Her gaze penetrated deep into his soul. "I wish we could be together forever, Blake."

The finality of her words made him wonder if her injuries might be far worse than she had initially claimed. "And I wish you would not talk as though you were dying, *laua'e*."

"I'm not going to die," she reassured him. "But it feels like it whenever I think of saying good-bye to you."

Fear coiled around his heart, squeezing tight. "I cannot lose you . . ."

"It's not up to me." She paused, struggling to go on. "There's a possibility I may not be able to find my way back to his parents. I only have a vague idea how to reach them. But I have to try, for their sake and for Andrew. If I fail, I'll stay and raise Andrew as my own son."

"What if you succeed?"

"If I succeed . . . I won't ever see you again."

"Then you *must* fail," he demanded, shoving himself up from the bed. He walked a few paces, then turned back to face her. "Forget taking him back. Stay with me. We will raise Andrew together."

"Is that what you want for him? To deny him the chance to see his parents again because of our own selfishness? What if Keoni's parents had kept you from being reunited with your real parents?"

After a moment of thought, he reluctantly acknowledged the validity in her compassionate words. "I would be angry and resentful. For years I had dreamed that my mother and father were still out there, somewhere, looking for me."

"Andrew is only ten. He has so much time left to spend with his own family. I must try to take him home."

"Then let me help you," he repeated, his frustration mounting.

Shaking her head, she beckoned him with an outstretched hand. The sadness in her eyes drew him to her. "I need to tell you something . . . This is so hard . . ."

"Say it."

"Blake, I'm not from here. Neither is Andrew. We are both from a distant time. The future, Blake. One hundred and sixty-five years in the future, to be exact. The day I left in search of Andrew was March thirteenth . . . *1998.*"

"That is impossible."

Chapter 18

"I KNEW YOU wouldn't believe me." Cara sighed with tremendous disappointment. "But I *am* telling the absolute truth, I swear to you."

She read the myriad emotions dashing through his mind—shock, doubt, astonishment, suspicion, wonder. He could not begin to sort them all out, she knew.

"I have wanted to tell you. Keoni has been on my case for weeks to—"

"Keoni? He *knows* about this? You told *him*, yet you didn't see fit to tell me? Why?"

"If you could hear yourself right now, you wouldn't have to ask why. Keoni believes in the supernatural. He accepts it more readily than even I do. After all your years as brothers, you should know this."

"I do, but it hurts nonetheless that you went to him rather than me."

"He is my friend. My big brother. He understood me when I needed someone to listen without prejudice, without judgment of my sanity. There's no reason to be jealous. He hasn't stolen me from you."

"I am not jealous! I am angry that you have been lying to me."

"I didn't lie. I just didn't reveal the entire truth."

"Our marriage . . ."

"You know as well as I do the wedding was never meant

to be real. We were *both* fabricating the marriage to appease Mr. Bellows and the rest of the crew. You said yourself there would be no consummation.''

"But there *was*.''

"And everything changed between us. I didn't plan it, Blake. It just happened. Just like everything else. As much as I desperately wanted to make love with you, I died a little inside every time I thought of leaving you to take Andrew back to my own time.''

As he stared silently at her, she saw the turmoil in his soul turn into despair. His eyes misted. "My God . . . you *are* telling the truth, aren't you?''

"Yes.'' Her own eyes suddenly burned. "I wish I weren't. I wish I could wave a magic wand and make my past disappear.''

"And Andrew?''

"I know . . .'' She might want to wish away her previous life, but she couldn't wish away Andrew. She was his only hope for his safe return to his parents.

Her heart went out to him as she recalled the tough little guy jumping into the water. When she had returned from the *Ballade,* she had tried to hug him, but he wouldn't have any part of it. Not quite a young man and yet no longer a little kid, Andrew was torn between his grown-up determination to be strong and his youthful need to let someone else slay his dragons.

"Please go and get him, Blake. Bring him to me.''

"Of course.''

A few minutes later the door opened and Bud trotted in, heading straight toward the berth. Putting his front paws on the mattress, he nudged his wet nose into the palm of her hand, checking on her in his canine way. She smiled, then looked past him to the bedraggled boy in damp clothes and woolen blanket. Eyes downcast, he shuffled into the cabin with Blake's hand cupped around his small shoulder.

"Hello, Andrew,'' she greeted him, pleased to see that the simple touch had been allowed. He did not speak, but let his gaze go to the dog. Seeking a mutual connection, she directed her attention to Bud, petting him affectionately.

"We need to get you a big bone as a special thank-you for saving Andrew. That was so brave of you—just like when you saved me from that rattlesnake."

Catching the look of surprise on Andrew's face, she glanced up at Blake to see if he had seen the response. He nodded and stepped around the boy to pull a chair over to the berth.

"Maybe I should check his leg where the snake bit him." When he sat down, Bud dropped his paws to the floor and put his chin on Blake's knee. "No, not your face. I want your leg."

The dog lifted his head, cocked it to one side, then propped his left paw on Blake's lap. It was a gesture Cara had seen a dozen times whenever Bud wanted his ear scratched, but now it looked so real, as if the dog knew his role.

"No, not your *left* leg," Blake mildly chastised, putting the paw down. "Your *right* leg."

A quiet giggle came from Andrew. Cara watched as Blake turned to the child. "Can you help me out, Andrew? You see, Bud was hurt a few weeks ago. He almost died, but Cara saved his life. Perhaps *you* can coax Bud into showing off his scar."

During a long moment of consideration, Andrew studied the three of them separately, as if putting together the pieces of a puzzle and coming up with a portrait of trust he was able to accept. Slowly and silently, he moved over to Blake's side.

As if on cue, Bud repeated the signal for an ear scratch, once again placing his left paw on Blake's knee.

"Wrong one," sighed Blake, then dipped his head close to Andrew. "Tell him the *right* leg."

Uncertain, the boy slid a sideways look at Blake, who nodded encouragingly. Instead of speaking, Andrew leaned over and gently took Bud's left paw and lowered it to the floor, then reached for the other one. As he brought it up to Blake's knee, he came nose to nose with the Labrador and promptly received a huge lick from a very large pink tongue. A grin spread across his face. The child's giggles delighted Bud, inviting an onslaught of more canine kisses.

In that one single moment, Cara knew the healing had begun. With the help of Bud, Andrew was going to start to pull himself out of the worst of his nightmare. Like Blake, it would take more than a day or two. She watched them, realizing she'd worried for nothing. It hadn't been her job to fix things for Andrew. It had been Blake's. She could see now that the man and boy needed to be together, at least for a while. They would heal each other.

Gazing at Andrew and Blake inspecting the scar on Bud's leg, Cara made her decision. She and the boy would continue on to Boston. From there, they would return to California with Blake. Hopefully, the shipwrecked *Mystic* would still be beached at San Pedro. And, with some divine guidance, she would find the doorway leading back to 1998.

Later that night, when it was time for bed, Andrew became quiet and withdrawn again as he crawled onto the bedding Blake had laid out for him on the floor. With his back pressed to the wall, he wrapped his arms tight around a bunched-up blanket that he was using for a pillow.

Cara drew back the covers and started to go to Andrew, but Blake stopped her. "You shouldn't get up yet."

"I'll be careful. And you can help me."

"Very well. But I won't allow you to stay up too long."

She smiled at him as he climbed out of the bed to assist her. With him standing behind her, she sat down on the floor in front of Andrew and took his hand.

His little-boy voice filled with a quiet sadness. "My mom used to . . ."

Sing to me. He did not need to finish his thought for her heart to break from the feelings coming through to her. Her connection to him brought visual images of his mother, a beautiful blond woman with kind eyes and a soft smile.

"I miss my family, too." She smoothed a strand of his disheveled hair from his forehead, catching a glimpse of unshed tears.

He squeezed his eyes shut and pulled his hand out of her

grasp, then turned his face into the bedding so she couldn't see him cry. His yearning for home and all things familiar was a physical pain that tortured his small body. She felt it in her own. How she longed to take on his suffering for him. But despite the fact that she could feel what he felt, she couldn't alleviate his despair.

"Andrew?"

He refused to answer. She touched his shoulder. He pulled it away. How could she help him? What do you say to a frightened ten-year-old caught in the middle of a living nightmare?

Speak the truth. Speak from your heart. Touch his spirit with your own.

"I'm staying right here," she vowed, again reaching out to him. This time he did not shrug her off. Her fingers curled around his thin arm and gently squeezed with reassurance. "I'm not going to leave you. We're stuck together like glue."

Cara sensed his unspoken plea: *I don't want you. I want my mom and my dad. Why didn't THEY come to get me?*

Closing her eyes, she tilted her head back and took a long, deep breath for strength. Speak the truth? Speak from her heart? How? How was it possible to explain the unexplainable? She didn't know the whys or hows of this strange and mysterious universe, let alone dimensions in time and space that were not their own.

"I know you don't want me here. I know you wish your mother was sitting here instead." Her accuracy as to his thoughts startled him. His sudden tension radiated into the palm of her hand. "Your parents are worried sick about you. Believe me, they would be here themselves if they could. But it didn't happen that way. I'm here with you. I'm going to take care of you. And I'm going to try to get us back home where we belong."

His small voice murmured one word: "How?"

"I'm not sure, exactly. I'm going to take it one day at a time. Right now, we're going to Boston with Blake. After that, we'll be heading back to California to find the *Mystic*."

"No!" His face turned toward her. His eyes were wide with terror. "I won't go back. I won't! *I won't!"*

Cara held out her hands, trying to bring him back to her. He frantically shook his head. She was losing him. She could see it in his ashen face. It was all unfolding just as it had with Blake.

Please, don't let it be the same.

She felt Blake's hand on her shoulder. Then he dropped to his knees next to her. His eyes filled with anguish for the boy.

He whispered helplessly, "I can't bear to see this, Cara. We must do something."

As he started to reach out to Andrew, Cara grabbed his arm. "No," she quietly insisted. "He doesn't see you. He'll think you are attacking him. Remember how you reacted to Keoni?"

"Then let him fight me and win. I'm willing to let him use me to fight his demons."

"He's not as big as you, Blake. You'll frighten him all the more. Let me try to help him."

The boy's gaze was fixated on something beyond the present moment, on a monster from the past. Her fingers touched his sleeve. He jerked his arm away with a scream. Tucking his frail body into a tight ball, he shielded his head with his arms.

"Shh," soothed Cara, trying to bring him back, to save him from the dark abyss of his memories. She slipped her arm around him to draw him close. He sat up and leaned into her. "You're safe, Andrew."

Her mind's eye saw the nightmare he was reliving. She could see the beating by Captain Johnson in his slovenly quarters aboard the *Mystic*.

"Oh-dear-God . . ." She held him tight as his sobs emerged from deep inside him. Andrew was only a kid, not a full-grown man who could have fought back. Yet she did not see anything in the vision of further abuse as Blake had experienced. Andrew had been spared the ultimate violation. For that, she was grateful. Seething with anger against Johnson, Cara thanked the deadly southeaster that had dispensed the maximum punishment against the vile captain.

Blake's arms came around her and Andrew, encircling the three of them together in a small huddle of pain and comfort.

After several minutes, the boy's crying subsided into whimpering hiccups that brought Bud over to the little group. The dog nudged his wet nose into the tight circle as if he wanted to find the source of the strange noises.

"Oh, Bud . . ." whined Andrew in a tone that was not as impatient with the dog as it might have been intended. There was something about Bud that was magic for Andrew. A four-legged therapist to the rescue.

"I don't want my hair cut!"

Scissors in hand, Keoni stood back from the chair where Andrew sat, arms crossed, with a glower that was meant to intimidate the huge Kanaka.

Blake propped his hands on his hips, watching the two square off. The three of them had left Cara resting in the cabin, giving her peace and quiet, while they had come to another battle of wills in the between decks where the carpenter and sailmaker worked at their benches.

"Well?" Blake raised a questioning brow at Keoni.

"Well, what? I'm not about to have my shins kicked by this *keiki kāne* like the last time we attempted this."

"You're bigger than him."

"He's faster. Make him sit still. You are *ho'omakua kāne,* for now at least."

Performing the role of a father, however temporarily, was not easy. Yet the challenge to his patience did not change the yearning to raise Andrew as his own son. Over the past few days since the rescue, he had grown fond of the lad. He understood and admired the stubborn streak that had kept him alive and strong against all odds. Through Cara's insight, Blake had been relieved to learn that the boy had not suffered the extent of mistreatment that Blake himself had endured. Andrew had been beaten physically but not broken in spirit. Thankfully, the bastards who had imprisoned him had not been monsters of the worst kind.

Blake hunkered down in front of the boy. "Andrew, you insist upon sleeping with the dog every night. And I have allowed it. But we cannot even drag a comb through that rat's nest. It must be cut."

"Keoni has long hair."

"Keoni keeps it neat and clean and tied back. Otherwise he would have to cut it too." Blake tried the opposite tack. "There is nothing wrong with short hair, per se. Even Bud has short hair. Cara, too."

He wasn't quite sure if it was the mention of the dog or of Cara or both. Whatever it was, it seemed to do the trick. Andrew acquiesced, though not without sitting with a protruding lower lip in protest.

"That's my boy." Blake stepped back, keeping the smile to himself until he was behind Andrew and couldn't be seen with the foolish grin on his face. "Keoni, you may begin."

After the barbering session was finished, the Kanaka was obviously well pleased with his work. "So *here* is the young man that was said to be on board our fine ship."

With a crooked grin, Andrew rolled his eyes heavenward. "Can I go now, Blake?"

"I believe you have something to say to Keoni before you leave?"

"Yes, sir." Swiveling in his seat, the boy tilted his head far back to look up at the tall Kanaka. "Mall-hall-oh."

"Mahalo," corrected Keoni with a big smile, adding *"'A'ole pilikia*—You are welcome."

The boy mimicked the words sufficiently for a ten-year-old, then looked to Blake for permission to be dismissed.

"Stay with Jimmy at all times," he ordered, though he knew it was unnecessary to say so. The young steward had taken Andrew under his wing in much the same manner as Keoni had befriended Blake many years earlier. It seemed there was no shortage of companionship for the bright— and, at times, mischievous—young child aboard the *Valiant*.

"Yes, sir," answered Andrew, darting toward the companionway.

Blake watched him leave. "It appears as though you now have two language students, *kaikua'ana.*"

"He is a smart one, that boy. He is doing well."

"Except at night. The darkness has a way of bringing back the demons . . . for both of us."

"You, too, *kaikaina?*"

"It is a wonder Cara gets any sleep at all. But she never complains."

"She makes a good mother," said Keoni.

"She makes a good wife," added Blake.

"You are no longer angry with her?"

He shook his head. "Nor you, my big brother. I have had much to think about, much to learn, much to accept. It is overwhelming, at times. But I have come to understand as best I can. If I am not able to spend the rest of my life with Cara, I will not waste precious moments in hurt or anger."

"Your heart is wise."

"My heart is already in mourning. I don't want to lose her, Keoni. I can't . . ."

"Perhaps you won't."

"I wish I could believe you."

The days grew shorter and the nights longer as the *Valiant* sailed south toward Cape Horn. By May 27, the sun barely rose in the sky, riding the horizon before it slipped out of sight for another sixteen hours of blackness that brought with it freezing-cold temperatures. Though ice floes had made passage precarious, the heavy seas and foul weather had yet to strike.

In her modern-day life, Cara had never been much of a seamstress, but she spent hour upon hour learning from Jimmy how to sew. With his help, along with Blake's, she managed to put together enough heavy clothing for both her and Andrew to last the duration of their winter voyage through the Southern Hemisphere.

Andrew was, at times, as willful and impish as a five-year-old. Then there were moments when he seemed old beyond his ten years, mature and articulate. Trying to deal with his vacillating moods was a challenge, even without the trauma of his time-travel experience.

Lately, he was sleeping more peacefully. Whenever a nightmare did return, she curled up with him on his bedding on the floor, sandwiching him between her body and Bud. To comfort him, she softly hummed a familiar old song, usually a Lennon-McCartney ballad, which drew Blake's interest.

With a young boy under their care, Cara and Blake settled into a domestic family life aboard ship, with stolen moments of intimacy being few and far between. Occasionally, Andrew was invited to spend the early-evening hours learning Hawaiian from Keoni, who made the offer as much for the benefit of the newlyweds as for the boy. Aware of this, Cara was a little embarrassed but also grateful.

During their Saturday night dinner on June 2, Blake seemed to be anticipating another secret rendezvous. He gazed at Cara across the table with a predatory look that set her heart racing. If not for Andrew sitting next to him, she was certain he would have swept her out of the chair and into their bed, leaving the rest of their meal until after he'd had his fill of her.

Thankfully, Andrew was oblivious to the covert glances that had charged the air in the small cabin. The boy chattered about some drawings he'd done for Keoni in the cook's own personal journal. Blake seemed to be working hard to follow the animated conversation. Cara managed a little better, but not much. She was deeply fond of Andrew and wouldn't hurt him for anything in the world, but her present longing for Blake was driving her to distraction. It was all she could do to keep from fidgeting at the table.

After Blake cleaned his plate, he raised his napkin and carefully blotted each corner of his mouth. She stared at his slightly parted lips, sensing his unspoken suggestion. Her pulse sped up as a warm flush spread heat to every inch of her body. Perspiration beaded between her breasts. She gave him a pleading look to stop his silent seduction.

He answered a question for Andrew, then reached for his

wine. All the while, his cocky grin played havoc with her nerves. After taking a sip, he held the stemmed glass in one hand and slowly circled the rim with his index finger.

Cara couldn't keep from thinking of those hands touching her, thrilling her. She knew he was enjoying his silent torture of her. "When . . . uh, that is, how much longer will it take to get around the Horn, do you think?"

"I would like to say a week, but there is never any guarantee." He acted so cool, so calm. Yet he had to know what his game was doing to her. "We should see the Atlantic no later than the tenth of the month, I hope."

Andrew piped up in a worried tone, "I heard some of the guys talkin' about how dangerous it is to go 'round the Horn. Is it really bad, Blake?"

"I won't lie to you, son." He set down the glass and gave the boy his full attention. "From here on out, we will have some rough seas. But I have the best crew a captain could want. And the *Valiant* is built as strong as they come. No matter how bad it gets, you just remember that."

The boy dropped his gaze, clearly disturbed by this bit of news. "Okay, sir."

"I want you to listen to me," said Blake with paternal tenderness as he lifted the child's chin with the crook of his finger. Andrew reluctantly looked at Blake. "You have been very strong, despite everything that has happened to you these past months. Nothing that lies ahead for us will ever be as bad as those days were for you. We have each other now. Do you understand?"

Andrew gave a tentative smile and his shoulders relaxed. "Yes, sir."

"Very well, then. If you are finished with your supper, you may join Keoni for the rest of the evening. He mentioned playing a game of cards with Jimmy and thought you might join them."

"Cool! I'm done eating. Can I go right now?"

Blake eyed the half-eaten plate of food, then glanced at Cara for her approval. She cocked one brow dubiously. As much as she wanted to be alone with her husband, she knew that every morsel of food was precious. There were no snacks waiting in a convenient refrigerator for a growing kid who would get hungry in a few hours if he didn't finish his dinner.

"Better clean your plate," advised Blake under his breath to Andrew. "Cara might have my hide if I let you get away without finishing up."

"Aw, gee, Cara," grumbled the ten-year-old, picking up his fork and spearing a slice of potato. Within a few minutes, he'd polished off the meat and vegetables, stuffing his cheeks until he had to be admonished for his table manners. Blake snatched the remaining chunk of bread from the plate, winning a smile of gratitude from Andrew. "Now?"

"Go. Have fun. I will come and get you when it is time for bed."

"Okay."

The child whirled out of the cabin like a small tornado, leaving his guardians shaking their heads in amazement. Dropping the bread onto his own plate, Blake rose from the table, latched the door, and turned to Cara, holding out his hands as if he were a magician who had just executed a great illusion.

Sitting in her chair, she applauded lightly. "A magnificent performance, Captain. Do you just make children disappear, or do you have other tricks up your sleeve?"

"Madame, I have only *begun* to amaze you." He took her hand and led her to their bed, where he spent the next two hours dazzling her with a repertoire of his talents.

Afterward, Cara curled up next to Blake as he lay on his back, staring up at the ceiling with a sated smile. She propped herself up on her elbow and gazed down at his rugged face, memorizing every plane and angle. She never wanted to forget anything about him.

"I love you so much," she whispered, her voice husky from the raw emotion stuck in her throat.

His hand slid to the back of her neck and pulled her down to him for a brief kiss that could convey the feelings he was unable to express in words. She lowered her head to his chest, content to listen to the reassuring, steady thump of his heart while his fingers combed through her short hair.

"Cara?"

"Hmm?"

"What is the name of that song you hummed to Andrew last night? The one I liked so much?"

She hummed a few bars for him.

"Yes, that's the one."

"It's 'Yesterday,' by the Beatles . . . or *will* be someday," she explained, as she had done about other future inventions. When he became understandably confused about the name of the band, she gave him some brief background on the music of John Lennon and Paul McCartney.

"Do you know the words?"

"I'm not a good singer."

"It doesn't matter," he reassured her, kissing the crown of her head. "Please sing it to me."

She tried an a cappella rendition of the song, but when she reached the middle verse, the poignancy of the lost lover caused her voice to falter. "I-I can't, Blake. I'm sorry."

He hummed the rest of the song to her. "It's beautiful," he said wistfully.

"You must have a natural ear for music if you could finish a song after hearing it only once."

"Not really. There is just something about the melody that strikes a chord in me."

As he went on to hum the tune a second time, Cara smiled at the vibration of the sound in her ear resting against his chest. There was almost a cozy, buzzy quality to it. Her eyes closed. Her mind drifted. She saw sanguine images of a summer afternoon in the late twentieth century.

"You are doing it again, *laua'e*."

Cara smiled at his telepathy. "What do you see?"

"Boats. All sizes of them, with smooth white hulls. Some with sails, some without—how odd."

"Those are powerboats. They have engines inside them."

"Hmm—interesting," commented Blake. "It appears they are on a waterway in a sheltered harbor that I believe might be in Connecticut."

The images vanished. She jerked her head up. "How do you know?"

"Having sailed the eastern seaboard, I know I have been at this place."

"I haven't. How could I have projected something from my mind that *I* never saw before? But *you* have!"

He shrugged. "You are the mystic with the answers, not me. I haven't the vaguest idea where this scene came from. Perhaps you saw a book—"

"No, Blake. I think maybe it could be *you* who is sending the image to me."

"Impossible. I know nothing about the strange power-boats. I merely recognized the deep river port of the Mystic River."

"Mystic?" She sat up, her warning bells going crazy. "Are you joking?" She glanced at his serious expression. "No, I guess you wouldn't be. Wow, this is giving me the biggest set of goose bumps! Don't you see the correlation? The shipwrecked *Mystic* and the seaport of the same name? Oh, man, there's got to be something going on here!"

"Cara, I do hate to dampen your enthusiasm, but there is a simple explanation. The Mystic River has a number of shipbuilding companies and is growing every year. I do not doubt there are at least half a dozen new vessels launched every year. Perhaps more. To have one of those ships christened with the place of her birth is not entirely unusual."

"Oh . . . well, I guess maybe my imagination *did* go a little overboard. But I still think it's weird you knew the location."

"My lady, there is no lack for inexplicable happenstance where you are involved. I am learning to become somewhat blasé about it all."

"You? Hardly."

"Six months ago I would have agreed with you." He reached out and stroked her bare leg. "But you have changed me."

Her heart melted at the husky tone of his voice. She went back into his arms, stealing a few more minutes before Blake had to bring Andrew back to the cabin.

Chapter 19

THROUGHOUT THE NEXT twenty days, the *Valiant* fought wind, rain, snow, and sleet, battling her way to the Horn, only to fall back twice. Blake received reports from his first mate that some of the men believed Cara to be the bane of ill luck. However, he never held a moment of fear for her personal safety, as had been his initial concern upon her arrival in San Pedro. She had won too many friends during the voyage to be threatened. Yet when a sailor's fate is in doubt, superstition can play a heavy hand.

Blake waited until Andrew was occupied elsewhere before voicing the worries of his crew over the fear of losing the ship, and their lives, in the arctic climate. Thankfully, her second sight did not perceive any grave mishaps. In her mind's eye, she saw the *Valiant* sailing through the tropics, all hands in shirtsleeves again, which pleased him.

With confidence in her intuitive knowledge, Blake decided to push for one last try upon the Horn rather than turn back toward the Cape of Good Hope. During the most difficult days that followed, he often spoke with his crew, reassuring them of a safe deliverance from the master of the deep.

In the third and final attempt, they met with success on Wednesday, June 21. At daybreak of the summer solstice, the ship entered the waters of the Atlantic. Setting a northeast course around the Falkland Islands, Blake was greatly

relieved to leave the Horn astern. As were the men. Their
chanteys reflected the new and buoyant mood of the entire
lot of them.

Two weeks later, the crew had cause to be in fine spirits
again. Spending the Fourth of July under a clear sky and a
warm sun, they realized that this particular Independence
Day took on a special meaning after the harrowing weeks
on the ice-shrouded brig. The *Valiant* stood nine hundred
miles east of Rio de Janeiro, sailing a swift six knots with
ease. As Cara had predicted, the men returned to their
checked shirts and white duck trousers. Their Cape Horn
rigs had been cleaned and stowed in their lockers for the
remainder of the voyage.

Despite the festive mood, this was still a working
Wednesday, not a leisure Sunday. There was much to be
done to ready the ship for arrival in Boston Harbor so she
would look good in the eyes of the shipowner and other
observers as she came into port. In the days ahead, the ship
would be scraped and cleaned and painted and varnished,
inside and outside, from stem to stern, and from skysail
truck to waterline. All the ironwork would be freed of rust
and blackened with coal tar. Sails would be taken down
and got up.

Holiday or no, Mr. Bellows expected a full day from the
hands, encouraging them with the words "We're home-
ward bound," which always seemed to lighten their burden
of work. As Jimmy polished the brass capstan, Andrew
took a cloth to the ship's bell. Cara found a quiet corner of
the quarterdeck to "soak up the sun," as she had called it
in her own peculiar way of saying things. Nearby, Bud
dozed in the shade.

When Blake wandered into the galley to escape the heat
of the day, Keoni welcomed the opportunity for a brief
respite from his own duties. After he set up a pot of tea to
brew, he brought out his journal, opened it to the middle,
and handed it to Blake. "I want you to see this."

A large number of pages were filled with drawings.
Blake glanced up. "Andrew's?"

The Kanaka nodded. "He is quite an artist."

"So it seems."

Keoni pointed out the words printed beneath each rendering. "Since I teach him my language of Kaua'i, he is teaching me his language of the future. That is a tel-uh-viz-in." He enunciated carefully, indicating a square box with a picture drawn inside it. "And tel-uh-fone. And com-pu-tur."

"And an airplane," said Blake casually.

"Did he draw one for you, too?"

"No." Grinning, he gave a light shrug. "I must be learning a little of Cara's tricks."

"What about this one?"

"A powerboat," answered Blake, remembering the visions with Cara. "And that one is a steam train . . . a race car . . . a rocket."

Keoni grasped his arm. Blake stopped and looked at his friend. "Yes?"

"You are not reading the words, *kaikaina*."

"Of course I am."

"No . . . Andrew wrote 'engine,' not steam train. And only a 'car,' not *race* car. A 'space shuttle,' not a rocket."

An odd chill came over Blake, then a strange dizziness. As he studied the drawings, his heartbeat grew louder in his ears. Sights and sounds came rushing back to him. A different life. A different time. He remembered building plastic models of sailing ships. He recalled going to Mystic Seaport on several visits. With his parents! For the first time in years, he could see the face of his mother looking back at him from the front seat of the car.

"Great-God-in-heaven, Keoni . . ." Swallowing a sob of relief and joy, he looked at his Island brother. "I remember! My childhood . . . I remember everything! I was there. In the future!"

"*You* were lost in time like Andrew?"

"Yes!" He laughed and cried at the same time, grabbing Keoni and giving him a hearty slap on the back. "I'll explain more later. Right now, I need to show this to Cara."

"Of course. Go."

Leaving Keoni in the galley, Blake went quickly to the

quarterdeck. As he approached Cara, she slowly looked up
from a book that lay open in her lap. She gave him a sweet,
contented smile that warmed him more than the heat of the
midday sun. Pausing in front of her, barely able to contain
his enthusiasm, he thrust the journal toward her.

"What is it?" she asked, taking it from him.

"The pictures that Andrew has mentioned during our
dinner conversations." As she scanned several pages, he
moved to her side and dropped to one knee to view the
sketches with her.

"He's definitely talented," she remarked.

"Cara, I *know* these things."

She turned and stared at him as if he'd grown another
nose. "What do you mean?"

"I am saying"—he reached out and flipped pages ran-
domly, pointing to one sketch after another—"*that* is a
bicycle . . . a camera . . . a lightbulb. And I am not reading
the words, Cara. I recognize these inventions."

He shot to his feet and paced nervously. His hand trembled as he raked it through his hair. "It all makes sense to
me now. The haunting melodies of those songs. How it was
that I knew about the Mystic River when you didn't." He
whirled around and pinned her with his gaze. "Do you
remember that morning in the cave?"

"It's not something I could easily forget."

"Remember the images of a picnic? Fireworks? Fourth
of July?" He glanced around, came closer and lowered his
voice. "That was the Bicentennial celebration in 1976. I
was nine years old that summer. Those were *my* memories,
Cara. Mine!"

He grabbed her hands and pulled her out of the chair,
spilling the books to the deck.

"Do you know what this means?" He cupped her face
between his hands, then kissed her quickly. Excitement
raced through him. "You unlocked my past. I remember
how I ended up on that ship when I was twelve years old.
I—"

Blake caught himself before he made the mistake of saying too much in front of his crew. He took Cara's hand and led her back to their cabin.

Alone together, he hauled her into his arms and kissed her once more, this time with deep gratitude and deeper passion. When he pulled back, she was as out of breath as he. Her cheeks were flushed pink. Her breath came hard and fast. He didn't know which he wanted more—to tell her everything he remembered of his past or to make love to her in the heat of the moment.

He laughed at his giddiness and indecision. In a mad rush of words, he told her about his childhood home in Connecticut and his obsession with the old ships at Mystic Seaport. His last memory of that time period was during one of his many visits.

"Something happened aboard an old square-rigger," he explained hastily. "And I found myself in 1815 aboard a ship with Captain Myers, sailing out of Boston."

Cara gazed at him, tenderly touching his cheek. "And after what happened during that voyage, there isn't any wonder your mind repressed all memory of the past. It was all too much for a young boy to deal with. In order to keep from going crazy, you *had* to forget everything."

"But all of that has changed because of you. I owe you so much . . ." His mouth claimed hers as his hands roamed over her hips to her buttocks.

She leaned against the closed door and unfastened his belt. Their lips parted briefly. She beckoned him, "Share your memories with me, Blake."

Kissing her deeply, he gathered her skirt to her waist while she freed him from the confines of his trousers. She stroked him fully. He touched her intimately. Then he entered her, pinning her against the wood with his body. Her arms wrapped around his neck. He lifted her legs, bringing them up around his hips, and impaled her with an urgency unlike any he'd ever known. His mind was devoid of all thought, save for the sensation of their flesh joined together as one.

In his final moment of surrender, he felt a love like no other in the world. Cara was his entire life. His breath. His reason for being. With a guttural moan of ultimate pleasure, he felt a burst of rockets and saw a glorious display of fireworks.

Exhausted and panting, he kissed her neck and murmured, "I love you, Cara. I never want to lose you." He lifted his head and gazed into her dark eyes. "Take me back with you."

"Oh, Blake, I want that more than anything in the world," she said breathlessly, lowering her feet to the floor. "I'm just not sure if you *can* go back."

"What do you mean? I'll simply follow you."

She shook her head sadly. "It would seem that simple. But it might not be. I came through a portal that apparently Andrew had found aboard the *Mystic*. But I don't know how it appeared in the first place, or if it'll still be there when we get back to the wrecked ship in California. And even if we can get back to the *Mystic*, we can't recreate the fault-test explosions that *might* trigger the right electromagnetic disruption to correspond with the winter solstice."

"You are speaking gibberish. I don't understand."

She kissed the corner of his frown, then dropped her head to his chest and hugged him to her, trying to explain the surveys for earthquake faults on the West Coast.

"It may very well be gibberish," she added with a heavy sigh. "That's the problem, Blake. All I can do is take it one step at a time. My gut instinct tells me the *Mystic* is the key. Outside of that, I have nothing else to go on."

Blake could not help but wonder if her theory was incorrect. "What if there are hundreds of ways for the anomaly of time and space to be distorted? My own experience took place on the eastern seaboard, where such tests were not used, at least not to my knowledge."

"My point exactly." She moved out of the embrace and began straightening her clothing, prompting him to do the same. "The chances are slim to none that you can take the same path as Andrew and I. It is entirely possible that your only way back to the future may be through the same portal that brought you to the nineteenth century."

"But I have no idea where that ship is now, or if it still exists." His euphoria vanished as he realized he was no better off now than when he hadn't known about his past. Whether he stayed or tried to return to the future, he would lose the woman he loved more than life itself. Putting aside his own feelings, he knew he must act in the best interests of Cara and the boy. "Our plans remain the same. After I am released from my duties, I will take you and Andrew back to San Pedro."

Throughout the final six weeks of their voyage, Cara struggled with the uncertainty of their future, together or apart. Aware of Blake's own dilemma, she knew what it cost him to stand by his offer to take them back to California. If only she could fulfill her commitment to Andrew's safe return and still be able to come back to Blake. Better still—if only she could use her psychic abilities to find the passage to the future for Blake. But then, there was no guarantee where they each might end up or whether they could find one another if they were separated.

As Boston grew nearer with each passing day, the atmosphere of the ship became filled with quiet anticipation. Yet Cara was no closer to any answers to her questions. On the eve of their arrival in port, she asked Blake to take Andrew on deck for a little while so she could have some time to herself in the cabin.

During a quiet meditation, she closed her eyes and stilled her mind of all the chatter and worries and concerns. She let go of her own need to control the outcome of her life, of all their lives. Somehow, somewhere, deep inside herself, there was a knowingness that would guide her. Whether or not it was Gabriella didn't matter anymore. She had been brought this far by a force that was greater than herself, and it would take her the rest of the way.

Ask, Cara. And it will be shown to you.

"How do I help Blake?" she said aloud, then waited.

Mystic . . . memories . . . Mystic . . . memories.

The two words cycled through her mind repeatedly. She tried to figure out if there was a message in them, yet there were so many meanings to choose from. The ship. The seaport. The Hawaiian term, *Mea punihei i nā āiwaiwa*. Her recollections even brought back the night he spoke of making their own mystic memories. So where did these words lead her now? What did they mean?

Mystic . . . memories . . . Mystic . . . memories.

As the words became a chant, the scene of the Mystic River came into her mind; she almost dismissed it as the previous memory that Blake had given to her. Then she realized the modern boats were missing from this vision. Instead, she saw large wooden ships on the water, as well as half-built hulls sitting in cradles on the shore of the river. She paid attention to the details of the houses and buildings. A face of an older woman appeared, looking worn and sad. As quickly as the vision came, it disappeared. But she'd seen enough to convince her that they had to go to Mystic.

Dropping her hands to her lap, she drew a deep breath and slowly let it out, then got up from the chair to search for Blake.

Finding him on the forecastle with Andrew and Bud, she came up beside him and slipped her arm around his waist, smiling up at him.

"Did you find the answers you were looking for?" he asked, bringing his own arm up behind her back.

"Yes, I did." Reluctant to speak in front of Andrew, she asked him to take the dog to the cabin with him. "We'll be down in a little bit to make sure you are in bed."

"Aw, gee, Cara."

She smiled at his standard reply. "Enough whining, young man. Now, scoot."

As he trotted off, Blake gently squeezed her arm. "I could not have done it better myself."

"You? Ha! You are as bad as him with bedtime. If you had your way, you would let him stay up all night gazing at the stars with you."

"Not if we had separate cabins. I will be sure to remedy this situation when I get my next ship, which will be very soon, I hope."

"I need to talk to you about that, Blake. Over the last

several months, I've been getting the word 'mystic.' I'd thought it was about the ship. But tonight I got a vivid picture of the river."

"Is this the same sort of message you received regarding Valparaíso?"

"Sort of."

"Then it is settled. We shall go to Mystic as soon as I am released from my duties to the owners of the *Valiant*."

"Just like that? No questions? No arguments?"

"None." He turned her into his arms, then pressed his lips to her forehead. "I will take you wherever you wish to go, *laua'e*. And I will stay with you as long as is humanly possible. When the time comes for you to leave me, I will go with you in spirit."

She hugged him tightly to her breast. "I don't want to lose you, Blake."

"Please don't cry, Cara. I couldn't bear it."

She sensed his tenuous hold on his own emotions and realized how hard it was for him to be strong for her sake. Fighting back her tears, she whispered, "I love you."

Stroking her hair, he said softly, "I love you, too."

The following morning, as the final salutes sounded from the bow guns, Cara watched in awe as the *Valiant* sailed slowly past the low sand hills of Cape Cod and into the Massachusetts Bay of 1833. There were all sizes of boats and ships on the water, which seemed strange after so many months at sea without a single vessel in sight. Stranger still was the feeling of participating in a Spielberg movie of epic proportion, as if all the extras had been called up for an early shot.

As they went past the lower lighthouse, Blake joined her to explain that they would spend the night anchored in the harbor and take the ship into dock the next day.

On Saturday afternoon of August 17, the crew manned the capstan for the last time, pulling the ship into the wharf with a loud chorus. The entire deck was swarming with all sorts of people, from customs agents to friends.

Jimmy came over to say good-bye to Cara and Andrew,

who showed his disappointment in losing his new friend.

"Where will you go now?" she asked the sixteen-year-old.

"I'll be off t' visit my da for a bit, then . . ." The young man shrugged. "I dunno. Maybe I'll find myself back wit' the cap'n again. Captain Masters is as good as they come, ma'am. I've heard frightful yarns about how bad a sailor's lot can truly be on board most ships. It made me glad I was on the *Valiant*. So I'd be more than happy to sign on under the cap'n."

"Then perhaps we will see you soon."

"Maybe, ma'am." He petted Bud one last time, shook Cara's hand, then Andrew's, and left the ship with his canvas bag over his shoulder.

While Bud sat next to her, Cara kept Andrew at her side, unwilling to let him out of her sight and risk losing him in the crowd. Boardinghouse runners pestered her, insisting upon taking her luggage on the carts they'd brought to the docks. She refused their offers, sometimes having to be almost rude with them.

In a very short while, each crew member departed with two years' wages. Everyone else soon followed, leaving only Keoni and Blake, who was officially turning over the *Valiant* to the shipkeeper from the countinghouse.

As the Kanaka knelt down to give attention to the dog, he looked up at Cara. "Our chests have been sent ahead to a house where we stay whenever we are here in Boston. You should find it to be comfortable accommodations until we leave for Mystic in a few days. And as for Andrew here—" He turned to the boy. "You will actually have your own room with a real bed."

Andrew asked, "Do I still get to sleep with Bud?"

"Certainly not in the bed with you," answered Cara, but she saw a wink from Keoni which made her wonder if they were conspiring to bend the rules a little bit.

Blake walked up to the three of them. "Time for us to go."

"What have you done with the papers from the *Mystic*?"

asked Cara, aware of his intention to deliver the news of the wreck to the ship's owners.

"They are with my belongings. I will pay a visit to the company Monday morning, after I have had an opportunity to bathe and make myself a bit more presentable."

Though Cara was eager to be on their way to Connecticut, she accepted the necessity for Blake to wrap up any and all obligations first.

"The *Mystic* is headed home."

Blake had walked into the parlor Monday afternoon, interrupting the tea and conversation between the proprietress of the house and several ladies, including Cara. Dressed in a plain white blouse and dark skirt that must have been borrowed, Cara set the cup in the saucer, clattering the china as she put it down on a low table in front of her.

"Pardon my ill manners, Mrs. Barnes, but this is rather important news to us." Aware of half a dozen pairs of female eyes perusing him, he strode to the center of the well-appointed room and extended his hand to Cara. "But will you please excuse my bride?"

"Certainly, Captain." The attractive redheaded woman smiled demurely as a couple of the ladies tittered nervously at the audacity of a male invading their cozy parlor.

Blake nodded to the women, bidding good day as he escorted his wife to their private chambers.

"How? When?" asked Cara, after he closed the door. She practically pounced upon him. He kissed her first, then gave her the full account of the information.

"The owners told me that another of their merchantmen had been loaded with hides and prepared to leave San Diego when the *Mystic* was blown ashore. Apparently they sailed back to San Pedro to inspect her damage, determined that she could be refitted, and put their first mate as captain of her. They believe she could arrive as early as next month."

The rescue of the brig did not surprise him in the least. It was a common practice, even for captains of vessels belonging to other companies. A man could earn a tidy reward if a disabled ship could be refitted, hauled back into the water, and brought around the Horn with a ragtag crew. So, it seemed, was the case for the *Mystic*.

Cara gazed at him with a worried expression. "Can a ship with that much damage make it through the bad weather we experienced?"

"There are no guarantees that *any* vessel will survive those conditions."

"If only we could have gotten back there before she was repaired . . ."

He wrapped his arms around her for comfort. "There is nothing for us to do now but wait, *laua'e*."

"But if she goes down, my chances of returning Andrew go down with her."

"So it seems," he said, wondering if it would be the best outcome for all of them. Without that ship, she would give up her quest to find her way home. And he would have no reason to find his own passage to the future to follow her.

"What about Andrew?" asked Cara, sharing his thoughts.

"I remember how hard it was to lose my parents. But I also remember the kindness of Keoni's family. If we are unable to take Andrew back, you and I can provide a loving home for him."

She remained quiet for a few minutes, content to let him hold her. Then she looked up at him. "I still get the feeling we need to go to Mystic. Something is drawing me there."

"Then we shall go, find out whatever it is you need to learn and return here to wait for the ship."

The mouth of the Mystic River was a long, deep, protected harbor that was a safe haven for ships and an excellent location for the shipbuilding trade that had sprung up along the banks. Following her gut instincts, Cara had told Blake that she wanted to visit each company. One of them held the answers. She just wasn't sure which one.

After finding an inn for their brief stay, Blake and Cara rented a carriage, leaving Keoni in charge of Andrew and

Bud. They went to four different shipbuilding sites without any luck. But as they approached the fifth one, Cara felt the familiar butterflies in her stomach.

"This is it, Blake. I can feel it."

He helped her down to the wet ground. A midday shower had passed through the valley during their last stop, drenching the ground before they had emerged from the building. At first Cara fretted about soiling the new skirt and shoes Blake had purchased for her shortly before leaving Boston. But there was nothing she could do about it, and she was impatient to get inside to ask questions.

As she entered the office on Blake's arm, she recognized the solemn woman who greeted them as the person from her vision. Cara tightened her fingers around his sleeve. He glanced sideways at her, silently bidding her to loosen her grip.

"We are seeking information," Blake stated after introducing himself and Cara. "Might the owner be available to talk with us?"

"My husband died three weeks ago," said the woman, her weary face pinched.

He offered their condolences, which she did not acknowledge. "Perhaps you might be able to answer our quest—"

"I don't know a thing about this business. Fact is, I'm only here to see a gentleman about an offer to buy the company, land and all. Thought maybe you were him."

"No, ma'am, I am not. If you will excuse us, we will be on our way."

Cara abruptly spoke up. "I was on a ship called the *Mystic* that wrecked on the coast of California. Would you happen to recognize the name? Could it have been one of your husband's ships?"

The old woman's face lost all color. "Wrecked, you say? How many died this— Uh . . . that is, did anyone die?"

"All but two of the crew." Cara released Blake's arm and stepped forward, placing her hand on the woman's bony shoulder. "Please tell us what you know."

Even though Cara could see images and read thoughts

from the frightened woman, she wanted to hear the whole story in her words. Suddenly the widow broke down, revealing her husband's deathbed confession about a cursed ship that had been salvaged to repair war-ravaged vessels.

"It was more than eighteen years ago. In the spring," she clarified. "He had secretly arranged to have that old shipwreck dismantled and brought here. Later, stories came back about sailors vanishing from those ships that my husband had fixed with boards and such from the wreck. He had only himself to blame, he'd said. Started drinking heavy then, too."

She excused herself to get something she thought they might want to see. Returning to the room a few minutes later, she handed over a document listing the names of all the ships that had some piece of the wrecked vessel on board.

Deciphering the elaborate cursive handwriting, Cara realized that any of these ships on the list could be floating time-passages by way of a small scrap of lumber or hardware.

Blake pointed to one name. "That was the one I was—" He stopped, then chose his words more carefully. "I went back on the *Emery*. That's Captain Myers's ship."

Cara stared at the name on the page, stunned. Regaining her composure, she thanked the widow and hurried Blake out of the building. When he helped her up into the carriage, he gazed at her with a puzzled expression, but said nothing until he was seated next to her and they were on their way.

"Would you care to explain?"

"Early in my investigation on Andrew's disappearance, I researched the ship and learned that it'd had a number of names. The *Emery* showed up in the record around 1810, then a second time in the 1970s."

Blake interjected, "It was the summer of 1979 when I went to Mystic Seaport with my parents for the last time."

"Ten years later that same ship was sold to a new owner, who renamed it the *Mystic* again and took it to California, where it's used as a floating classroom of maritime history for kids like Andrew. He came back to this time period last December when the ship was in western waters. And I followed in March. This means . . ."

"I was on that very same brig when I stepped through the bulkhead into the captain's quarters. We all went through the same time portal."

She reached over and gave him a quick hug around the neck. "It all fits exactly with Andrew's and my experiences. We're going back, Blake. All three of us are going back *together*!"

$\mathscr{C}hapter$ 20

A MONTH LATER, on September 19, Cara woke up early from a dream, instinctively knowing the message it had conveyed—the *Mystic* would be docking in two days. Saturday, September 21, would also mark the first day of autumn, she realized, wondering whether the equinox was a significant factor or a mere coincidence.

With a sense of excitement and anticipation, she couldn't wait for Blake to open his eyes so she could tell him the news. She gazed down on his sleeping face, feeling more love for him with every passing moment. Smoothing his black hair off his tan forehead, she pressed her lips to his temple. He slowly blinked, then gave her a lazy smile.

"Good morning, *laua'e*."

The love in his deep-blue eyes stirred the familiar yearning deep inside her body. "Hi, sleepyhead. It's half past the crack of dawn and you still haven't made love to me yet today."

"I believe I can remedy that mistake." He took her hand beneath the covers to show her that his own desires had already been awakened. Pressing her onto her back, he moved over her, into her, and throughout her entire being.

After he had given himself to her, he remained in her arms, his hips still nestled against the inside of her thighs. "Yes, we will."

Her hand stroked his bare back. "Will what?"

"You are thinking we will need to get ready for the arrival of the *Mystic*." He lifted his head and gazed down at her with a little grin. "Am I right?"

She fingered the black curls at the nape of his neck. "It is a good thing you're the only one who can read my mind."

"Only when I am with you like this." As he withdrew from her, she felt his reluctance to separate from her body for even a moment, let alone an entire day.

"Tonight," she promised, "neither one of us will go to sleep until we have had our fill of each other."

During the rest of the day, Cara brought out her costume from the reenactment ship and mended several rips and tears. She'd already acquired a new watch cap and replaced the jacket that she'd lost her first night. Andrew's clothing was in fairly good shape, despite the rough treatment he'd been given. At least he hadn't been caught in a shipwreck and washed ashore as she had.

Recalling the photos and visions of Andrew prior to her travels, she instructed Keoni in cutting the boy's hair to the shorter length. Overriding Andrew's protests, she sensed an importance in returning him "shipshape and Bristol fashion." She also sat for a trim.

By that evening, news of the *Mystic*'s appearance in the outer bay had reached them.

The following afternoon, the four of them stood on the wharf, silently watching the last of the people leave the brig. Bud had positioned himself at Blake's feet, looking dejected, as though he knew his ownership had been passed to the Kanaka.

Blake dropped his gaze to the big black dog who had been his loyal companion. He had once teased Cara for talking to the horse at the cliffs in San Juan, yet now he found his own feelings toward an animal had transcended mere affection for a pet. Leaving Bud was as difficult as leaving Keoni, perhaps more so. At least his Island brother understood the circumstances and wished him well.

"I think everyone is gone now," said Cara, drawing

Blake away from his thoughts of leaving Bud behind.

He looked at Keoni. "Don't let Bud wander off looking for us."

"I won't." According to their plan, the cook intended to distract the shipkeeper by feigning interest in serving on the next voyage. After Keoni persuaded the man to show him the galley, Blake would sneak Cara and Andrew into the main cabin. "I only hope dis Kanaka don't fall through another time-hole while I'm on her."

The Islander's joking dialect received a slight smile from Cara. "Me, too."

"Very well, then," sighed Blake. "This is *aloha, kaikua'ana.*"

"*Aloha, kaikaina. E mālama pono.*" *Take care.* Wrapping his arms around Blake, Keoni held him in a long and heartfelt embrace, conveying the sorrow of departure and the joy of their brotherhood that could not be spoken aloud between them.

After a few moments, Keoni hugged Cara, then Andrew, wishing them much luck and happiness. Cara thanked the Kanaka with tears streaming down her cheeks. As he turned to leave, he called Bud, but the dog refused to budge.

Blake's heart lodged in his throat as the three of them stroked and petted Bud for the last time. When Blake could stand it no longer, he straightened, gesturing with his hand. "Go now, Bud. Go with Keoni."

The dog's eyes held a doleful expression as he slunk away, glanced back once, then turned and followed the Kanaka onto the ship. Sniffling, Andrew spun into Cara's arms, hiding his eyes from the wrenching sight of his departing friends. Blake, too, had to look away as hot tears stung the back of his eyes.

Several minutes later, he found the strength to push his sadness to the back of his mind. "I will go aboard first," he said in a strained voice. He cleared his throat. "When I know it is safe, I will wave for you to come ahead. Walk softly on the deck."

Cara nodded. "Be careful."

Soon, he gave the signal and led them silently down into

the captain's quarters. As Blake quietly closed the door, Cara walked to the forward bulkhead and studied the dark varnished panels. Finally she nodded.

Looking over her shoulder at Andrew and him, she whispered, "I think this is it."

He read the slight apprehension on her face. They had often talked about this moment. So much was at stake. He knew how much she wanted to be right about the existence of a time portal, yet even if she were, it could be a doorway leading to an entirely different place than they wanted to go.

With the boy standing in front of him, he mouthed the silent words, "I love you," which seemed to give her the reassurance she needed from him.

Blake watched as she tentatively reached toward the bulkhead. When her hand slipped through the solid panel, he blinked twice, staring at the incredible illusion.

Terrified, Andrew backed up into him, whimpering quietly. "I don't want to go anymore. I wanna stay here with Keoni and Bud."

Pulling her hand back, Cara turned around, guilt written on her face as if she were to blame for scaring the child. She came back to Andrew. "I understand you're afraid," she said, keeping her voice as low as possible. "But you won't be hurt, I promise. Remember when you came through before?" He nodded. "It just feels a little funny, like a tickle. That's all. Remember?"

Again he nodded, but again he refused to step through the portal.

Blake hunkered down in front of Andrew. "This is the only way for you to return to your mother and father."

"I . . . know," answered the frightened boy, his lower lip trembling.

"Will it make you feel better if you see me go first?" he asked. The ten-year-old looked at him for a long moment, and finally glanced at Cara and slowly nodded.

"Very well, then." Blake straightened and caught Cara gazing at him. How he wanted to draw her into his arms and kiss her deeply one more time. Yet he did not dare.

This was only supposed to be a brief separation until the three of them were united again on the other side. Reluctantly, he settled with the lightest touch of their lips. "See you soon."

He walked boldly toward the bulkhead, paused long enough to verify the illusion for himself by placing his palm against the paneling. When it sank into nothingness, he looked back with a foolish grin, then stepped into the unknown.

Cara exhaled a pent-up breath, praying that Blake was now safely transported to the future. With a deep breath, she turned to Andrew. "Let's go home."

When he hesitated again, she felt a small amount of panic. Blake had already gone. She couldn't stay without him. But she couldn't leave without Andrew.

"I promise I'll be right behind you. Besides, Blake is over there waiting for us." *I hope.*

She took his hand and led him all the way up to the paneled wall. After demonstrating the ease in which her own hand went through the seemingly solid wood, she coaxed him to try. Aware of the minutes ticking by, she became nervous, fearing someone might walk in. What if Keoni had assumed it was safe to let the shipkeeper go back to his duties?

Trying not to force Andrew, she gently guided his hand into the wood until he felt the mild tingle. "It *does* tickle," he marveled.

"See? I told you. Ready to go now?"

"Yeah, I guess so." Andrew slowly walked forward and vanished into the woodwork.

Sending up a fervent prayer, she took a deep breath and stepped through the portal.

Darkness surrounded her.

Refusing to panic, Cara waited for her eyes to adjust to the lack of light. Just because she could not see Blake or Andrew didn't mean they weren't there with her in the dark.

"Blake?" she whispered.

Silence.

"Andrew?" Her voice grew louder.

When the floor beneath her feet gently tilted, she knew she was on a ship. *But what ship?*

Should she go back? But what if they weren't there?

Blindly reaching out, she swept her arms in a slow arc until her left hand touched a wall. A strong, solid wall. In her mind's eye, she saw herself in the small mate's quarters. To her right would be the berth. She checked. She was right.

"Blake!" she called out as a slender thread of terror wound around her throat.

Still no answer.

"Andrew!"

The door flew open and a shaft of light illuminated the tiny cubicle. A flashlight, Cara realized, then looked around her.

She was alone.

Several voices came through the darkness at her. "What's going on here?"

"What's wrong with her?"

"Did she see a ghost?"

"Are you all right?" asked the last one.

NO! she wanted to scream. *Where are they? What happened to them?*

Another voice came through the open doorway. "Move aside. Let me through. Everyone go back to bed. I'm handling this."

When she saw the short blue jacket and white trousers, she cried out, "Blake! Oh, thank Go—"

But it wasn't him.

She recognized the man who had been portraying the captain of the *Mystic* on the night she'd gone back in time. He held up a small battery-operated lantern that cast a glow throughout the little room. He had brown hair, not black. He had green eyes, not deep ocean blue.

"What happened?" he asked in a gentle voice, not quite loud enough for those outside the door to hear.

"I-I'm not sure . . . exactly." Disoriented, she dropped

down onto the berth, a strange numbness coming over her.

"Are you ill, Ms. Edwards? Should I take you ashore?"

"You remember my name?"

"Yes, of course. Why wouldn't I?"

Because I've been gone six months.

But had she? This man, whose own name she couldn't recall, acted as though she'd never been gone. If she had disappeared like Andrew, someone on board would have discovered it the next day. They would have had another news story on their hands. With her reappearance, the captain would have at least been surprised. But he wasn't.

"What . . . is the date?"

"The *date*? March thirteenth."

Cara stared at him as his words gradually sank in. With a shake of her head and a bitter smile, she almost laughed at the ironic twist of fate that had brought her back to the exact night she'd left.

"*Friday* the thirteenth," she murmured in disbelief. Though she was certain her vivid memories of 1833 were real, she put on a slight grin of embarrassment. "I guess my superstitious mind got caught up in a nightmare."

"This old ship has a way of doing that to some people," he said casually. "Do you want to come up on deck for some air?"

"S-sure," she said, her voice still shaky.

Leading her out of the cabin, he addressed the small gathering of adults. "Sorry he is, mates. Just a bad dream is all. Didn't mean t'wake any of you."

She followed the captain up the companionway to the main deck. The lights of Dana Point twinkled from buildings and boats around the harbor. She turned and stared at the cliffs, remembering the arduous climb to the top with Blake. Her heart lurched. Catching the sob before it broke loose, she reached for the rail and held on tight as if it were her only link to the past, to the man she loved.

Next to her, the captain maintained character, talking like an old salt to the children standing watch in the chill night as if they were McGinty or Jimmy or Mr. Bellows.

"Feeling any better, Mr. Edwards?" asked the captain, referring to her male character.

"Not really, sir." In spite of her confusion regarding the whereabouts of Blake and Andrew, Cara couldn't blow her cover to the captain, who was unaware of her true reason for being on board. She knew in her gut that Blake and Andrew were not on the ship. What her instincts didn't tell her was *where* they were now. "It's not the dream that's bothering me. I believe I may be coming down with the flu."

The captain nodded compassionately. "I'll take you ashore."

"Can you spare me?"

"Yes. Now, why don't you get your gear together while I tell Doc and the first mate that we'll be leaving."

"Thank you, sir," she said. His words brought back more memories as she went below to retrieve her sleeping bag.

By saying the doctor, or Doc, he had meant the cook, which was the typical handle on board most ships. Except on the *Valiant*. Keoni was, and always would be, Keoni or Kanaka. Some of the crew called him Doctor, but she had never heard Blake call him anything else, unless it was *kaikua'ana*, big brother.

Ah, damn . . . Her eyes flooded with tears for Keoni and Bud. And for Andrew. But especially for Blake.

Swiping at her wet cheeks, she considered going back into the portal again. But she knew Andrew would not have gone back without someone coaxing him as she had done. Her primary purpose all along had been to locate the boy and bring him back to his parents. Now she'd lost him. Her next step was to find out what happened to him.

Cara tied her sleeping bag into a loose bundle, giving it a larger shape to appear as though her missing bag might be wrapped inside. After a final glance at the mysterious bulkhead, she turned her back and left the cabin.

It was one o'clock in the morning when Cara thanked the captain and walked toward her locked car. Without her backpack, which she'd lost in the southeaster off San Pedro, she had no money, no driver's license, and no car keys. If the alarm hadn't been set, she might have found a way to jimmy the lock and drive home. Instead, she went to a pay phone near the parking lot of the marina.

She listened to the computerized voice operator. "Will you accept a collect call from . . . Cara Edwards?"

"Yes," answered Gabriella, with surprising alertness for the middle of the night. It was as though she had been waiting for the phone to ring.

Cara clenched the receiver. "Aunt Gaby?"

"I'm here, Cara."

The familiar words sounded so wonderful to her ears that she chuckled despite her misery. "Why is it you were there for me in the past, but now I have to call collect?"

"That was your choice, dear. And this is *my* nickel, so tell me what you need."

I need Blake!

"Car keys," she said instead. "I should have called Lucy to bring my spare set from the house but—"

"That is what you *want*, Cara. And yes, you should probably call your sister to bring them down to you. I don't drive the freeways like I used to, especially alone at night."

No, you just flit throughout the centuries.

"Now tell me what it is you *need*," her great-aunt repeated.

She released a long and trembling sigh. "Blake . . . Do you know where he is, Aunt Gaby? And Andrew?"

"Andrew is home with his parents."

"Oh, thank God."

"There is something else, Cara. Andrew was never reported missing."

"He came back to the same date he left here, didn't he?"

"Apparently so."

"If I came back last night . . . and Andrew came back in December—" She paused, closing her eyes, hoping she was wrong. "Then Blake went back to the day he disappeared in 1979."

"It would seem probable."

"Don't you know for sure?"

"Cara . . . we are not always allowed to know."

"We? Or just *me*?"

After a long pause, Gabriella switched the topic. "Call your sister. Tell her to stop by your house and look inside your mailbox on the curb. Your extra set of keys will be inside."

"When did you—? How did you know—? Oh, never mind." Realizing the futility of such questions after six months of traveling through time, Cara accepted the unacceptable. "Thanks, Aunt Gaby."

"Go home, Cara. Get some sleep. We will talk more later."

"I'll call you tomorrow."

Two hours later, Cara greeted her bewildered kid sister with a tearful hug, unable to hold back the emotional damburst. Aside from Aunt Gaby, Lucy was the only person who might be capable of believing everything that had just happened to her.

When her sister insisted on pouring some coffee into Cara before either of them drove home to Long Beach, they parked their cars at a twenty-four-hour coffee shop nearby and went inside. The reintroduction to modern society after six months in the 1830s was a strange experience in itself. In a way, she was relieved to have Lucy with her instead of having to face the rest of the dark night alone with her thoughts.

And without Blake.

After sharing her bizarre journey through time, including their great-aunt's participation, Cara knew she had to let her sister go back home to her own family, who were probably concerned about the emergency that had dragged Lucy out of bed.

It was six o'clock in the morning by the time they said good-bye in the parking lot.

Cara decided to drive home along the Pacific Coast Highway rather than take the freeway where higher speeds and traffic would be too much for her to handle. She felt like a crystal vase that had been shattered and glued back together again. Her body was here and whole, but her life was in pieces of confusion and shock and grief. There was a part of her that wanted desperately to turn the car around and go back to the ship. But another part of her resisted, knowing that Blake would not be in 1833 anymore.

She passed through the beach cities, stopping at traffic lights, staring at the early-morning joggers or watching surfers in wet suits on the water. As Highway 1 wound along the coastline through Sunset Beach, she realized she was going to pass by the entrance to the Huntington Harbour community.

"Andrew," she whispered to herself. She had to stop at three pay phones before she found a phone book and the address she needed. Turning off PCH onto Admiralty Way, she found the house and parked in front, intending to wait until eight o'clock before disturbing the family. With luck, Andrew might open the door.

Within a few minutes, however, Mr. Charles came out to get his Saturday morning *L.A. Times*. Obviously an early riser, he appeared to be dressed for a day on his sailboat. Cara left her car and approached him as he started back to the front door.

"Mr. Charles?"

He turned around with a pleasant smile, which quickly faded into a puzzled glance at her rumpled costume. "May I help you?"

She could see he didn't recognize her. "Is Andrew home?"

Mr. Charles's eyes narrowed with suspicion. "No. He . . . spent the night with a friend. Why would you want to see my son?"

"I just wanted to know how he's doing."

"He is perfectly fine." He looked over her shoulder as if searching for someone or something. "What is this about? Who are you?"

"My name is Cara Mas- uh, Cara Edwards, sir. I've been investigating a disappearance of a child from a ship in Dana Point called the *Mystic*."

"Yes, my son went on it with his class last December."

"If you don't mind, I'd like to speak to Andrew regarding my case."

He shook his head. "I don't recall any news about a missing child lately. Something like that would be all over the papers and television."

"The police are trying to keep it quiet," she lied, sensing his suspicions escalating. "Please, Mr. Charles. I need to see Andrew."

"No, I won't allow it. As far as I know, you could be some kook trying to get at me through my son. If some kid was lost or fell off that ship recently, you wouldn't need to be coming here after all this time to talk to Andrew."

"But I must—"

"Get the hell out of here." He started toward her, but she stood her ground. When he grabbed her arm and started to escort her to the curb, she felt his fear. Through his touch, she saw a vision of Andrew with dark circles under his dull, lifeless eyes.

Pulling her arm from his grasp, she turned to face him, knowing she had nothing to lose by telling him the truth. She hastily explained his desperation to find his son a few weeks earlier, how he'd come to her for help, and how she had brought the boy back last night. And yet Andrew had ended up returning to the actual night he'd disappeared.

"The boy with the hollow eyes is not the same child who went onto that ship on December twenty-second, Mr. Charles. He needs help. He needs someone to talk to, someone who will believe his story. Andrew will keep slipping away unless you reach out to him."

She knew her emotional barrage had stunned the man into silence. But now that she was finished talking, she saw his shocked expression turn into fury.

"You are a disturbed, delusional nutcase, lady." He pointed his finger an inch from her nose. "If you come anywhere near my son, I swear to God I'll have you committed to a mental institution for life."

With his political and financial clout, he could probably do it, too.

"I'm leaving, Mr. Charles," she assured him. "And I

promise to stay away from Andrew. But I want you to know I would never do anything to hurt your son, even though you might not believe me. Good-bye, sir.''

Without saying another word to her, he stormed into the house, slamming the door behind him as she walked toward the curb.

Cara drove the rest of the way home feeling like a shell-shocked war victim. As she maneuvered her car on the streets of Long Beach, a wave of sadness washed over her, bringing tears so heavy she could hardly see the blurry road ahead of her.

Where did her life go from here? How could she possibly pick up where she left off yesterday? Or was it six months ago? She knew she couldn't simply go into her house, take a shower, and get a good night's sleep, expecting to feel fine in the morning.

By the time she parked on her shady street, she had drifted back into the numbness. Her body was functioning on autopilot, walking along the flagstone path past her land-lady's house on the front of the property. She let herself into her little bungalow, dropped the keys next to the phone, and automatically hit the playback button on the answering machine out of habit.

Half listening while she headed toward the bedroom, she heard a message from Lucy, calling from a cellular phone in her car, wanting to make sure Cara had gotten home okay. Another message was from a friend who wanted to go sailing next weekend.

Been there, done that, she mused with a tired smile of irony.

After calling her sister, Cara turned down the volume on her answering machine and went to bed. By noon she gave up trying to sleep and took a shower. Dressed in a blue chambray shirt and jeans, she paced her living room floor in spite of her exhaustion, ignoring the ringing telephone, unwilling to deal with solicitors or anyone else at the moment. Her mind went over and over the speculation that had been gnawing at her all morning. Blake must have gone back to 1979, and yet she sensed a strong, tangible connection to him, as if he were somewhere near.

Somewhere . . . but where?

She sank down onto her rattan rocker and went through the steps to quiet her thoughts so she could pick up any information about him. Instead, she saw a vision of Andrew talking to his father. Cara knew in her heart that Andrew would be okay.

But what about Blake?

Nothing came to her.

She tried to block any outside thoughts, but her mind kept going back to the memories of Blake holding her and loving her. When the pain became too great for her to bear, she shot to her feet. "Why?" she cried out in anguish, shaking her fists at the ceiling.

She demanded an answer. She *deserved* an answer.

A sudden impulse drove her to grab her keys and run out the door.

Chapter 21

WITHIN TEN MINUTES, Cara arrived at her aunt's doorstep.

"I knew you would come," said Gabriella, holding out her arms for a hug. Cara went to her and felt the comfort and love she so desperately needed right now.

"Please help me, Aunt Gaby. I've got to try and make some sense of all this or I'll go mad."

Gabriella took her hand and led her into the living room, where both of them sat down together on the sofa.

Cara looked at her aunt. "I don't know what reality is anymore," she said, chilled by the idea that she might very well be losing her mind. "I feel like I'm coming apart at the seams."

"You have been through so much, I know. But there are reasons for everything. You have to believe . . ."

"Believe in what?" Her despair turned to anger. "I'm supposed to believe in some god, some universal force that goes around messing with people's lives, then leaves them in a state of shock, wondering if they are insane? Why! Tell me why this had to happen, especially to Andrew and Blake. They were just kids!"

"Children disappear all the time throughout the world. Hundreds. Thousands," explained Gabriella with the gentleness of an old soul passing along her wisdom of the ages. "They slip through to another time more easily than adults because they have not yet built a wall in their minds of superstitions and beliefs about what is really real and what is not. Their minds are fertile, craving to learn more, willing to accept the impossible. They go and never come back. Or rarely ever come back.''

''Then why did I interfere? Why did you talk me into searching for Andrew?''

''It was as much your own destiny as Andrew's and Blake's. You have the gift of believing in the things that most people refuse to admit are possible—seeing and hearing and knowing beyond the scope of defined reality in this present-day culture.''

''But why the children? And why the abuse?''

''Not every child who goes to another time is hurt and abused. Most of them find loving homes. Think of it, Cara. A child travels on a train, then goes back in time and grows up to become an inventor who *knows* that trains are possible because he has already experienced it.

''Such knowledge for a child can move technology forward unlike anything an adult time-traveler could ever do. The adults are often crippled by their fears and their determination to make sense of their supernatural journey through time. They put all their energy into trying to get back. A child adapts sooner. A child can arrive less conspicuously and be taken in by a loving family who cares for him until he is of age. A child who has lived in another time never questions the advances in technology but is at the forefront of advances, leading the way.

''Think about the leaders in science, in religion, in social reform. They are often called freethinkers, and 'ahead of their time.' How many of them might have been children who had come through from another time?''

Cara asked, ''But what about Andrew and the other children who return from their travels?''

''Usually they convince themselves their time-traveling was all a fantastic dream.''

''Or a nightmare,'' muttered Cara. A shudder went through her as she recalled the horrible visions she'd seen of both Andrew and Blake. ''But they can't even talk about their traumatic experience because it would sound crazy to people of today. A kid could be convinced that it was all a bad dream. But an adult? What about Blake?''

Gabriella patted Cara's hand reassuringly. ''When you live in a society of limited beliefs, you tend to unconsciously mold yourself to the accepted reality. And so, as an adult with certain fears and a certain shutting down of reality, Blake might very well have also relegated his previous experience in another time to merely a dream.''

A finality in her aunt's tone of voice prompted Cara to persist in seeking her answers. ''But where does all this leave me? Where is Blake? How do I find him?''

''What does your heart tell you?''

''I don't need riddles, Aunt Gaby. Please tell me.''

''No, it is not up to me to tell you what to do. I have given you the information. Now it is up to you to choose the path you will take. And you already know what it is. Look inside, Cara.''

Unable to deny the strong pull toward the *Mystic*, Cara searched her aunt's eyes, drawing strength and wisdom from her. She realized she had only one choice.

''I'm going back.''

The warm spring day had drawn a heavy crowd to the beach by midday, causing congested traffic on the freeways by late afternoon. Still dressed in her chambray shirt and jeans, Cara cursed the extra time she had taken to retrieve the period clothing that she'd left at her house. As her car crept along at a snail's pace, she glanced over at the costume lying on the passenger seat. She was scared as hell, but the flutter in her stomach told her she was doing the right thing.

It was twilight by the time she reached Dana Point. The institute was closed and the longboats locked away for the night. She had no alternative but to ''borrow'' a small inflatable lifeboat from the marina.

Under the cloak of darkness, she rowed along the curve of the shoreline rather than taking the more direct route from the west basin, which might have aroused suspicion.

Instead, she came around near the institute so as to appear to be someone going out to check the ship.

Her heart raced with a rush of adrenaline during her final strokes of the oars. She grabbed the small bundle of clothes she'd tied with the belt and climbed aboard the brig.

The smell of tarred timbers and salt air intensified her memories of Blake, bringing her closer to him. The earlier feeling of a strong connection intensified, as if he were all around her.

She had slipped down into the mate's cabin and started to change her clothes when her hand paused on the zipper of her jeans. A sense of dread crept up from her toes. Slowly, she reached out toward the bulkhead. Her fingertips touched the wood. She leaned forward, pressing harder.

No! It can't be!

Frantic, she placed both hands on the rough panel, sliding them this way and that way, trying to find the void. Nothing happened. The wood was as solid as the floor beneath her feet.

She spun around and headed toward the captain's quarters, groping her way through the shadowy interior of the ship, stumbling again and again.

Inside the large cabin, she rushed to the wall and searched for the portal from the past. But not even her sixth sense perceived that anything was there, or ever had been there.

Unable to hold back the overwhelming sense of pain and loss, she pounded her fists against the wood panel, crying and cursing at her fate. How could she have finally found love again only to have it snatched away? She didn't even get to say good-bye.

"Why was I given this psychic gift to help others and not myself?" Sinking to her knees, she buried her hands in her face. "Why can't I see him just one last time?"

"I'm here, Cara."

Her head jerked up. She turned to see a man descending the steps into the captain's quarters. Blinking back tears, her gaze traveled up the tan slacks to a white cotton Henley that set off a dark tan. His wavy black hair had a touch of silver at the temples. Deep-blue eyes gazed expectantly at her.

In an instant, her heart knew.

"Blake!" She vaulted to her feet and rushed into his arms. In her crazy euphoria, she kissed his lips, his chin, his nose, his eyes until he reached up and captured her face between his two hands. She stilled, staring at him in disbelief.

His cheeks were streaked with tears as he spoke to her in a husky rasp. "God, how I've missed you."

He lowered his mouth to hers and kissed her, parting her lips with his tongue. He probed and caressed and promised more, leaving her yearning to take him into her completely.

As he dropped his face into her neck and pulled her tight against him, she arched her body into him. "I thought I'd lost you."

"So did I," he murmured.

She tried to talk despite her tears of happiness. "How did you get here?"

Blake straightened and looked down into her eyes with a cocky smile. "I own the *Mystic.* Or more accurately, my corporation is the legal owner."

"You what?" Her jaw dropped.

Ignoring her question, he kissed her quickly, then gently demanded, "Where have you been? I waited for you this morning on the dock. When you didn't disembark with the rest of them, I panicked, thinking you might not have returned from the past. I nearly went after you, until I learned from the captain that you'd left the ship in the middle of the night. I called your house nearly a dozen times today. I even drove to your house early this afternoon, but you weren't there. About an hour ago, I felt an overwhelming need to come back to the ship."

He kissed her again, then led her over to the berth.

"I must have been drawn here by you. It seems that a little of your psychic abilities have rubbed off on me." The corner of his mouth tilted up in a boyish grin.

Though she couldn't help but return the smile, she still eyed him with curiosity. "Were you the corporate exec who gave permission for me to work undercover as one of the crew?''

He nodded smugly.

"Do you mean to tell me you have been here all along?"

Again, he nodded, sitting down on the edge of the mattress. "If I had approached you in February and told you about our life together in 1833, I know you wouldn't have believed me. In this day and age, you'd have thought I was a crazy man stalking you."

Cara remembered the reaction by Mr. Charles when she'd tried to convince him of his son's adventures in the past with her. She knew she'd sounded like a wacko. She couldn't blame the father for telling her to get lost.

"You're right." Sitting down next to him, she touched his cheek. "I wish I could be mad at you, but I understand why you had to do it."

"If you had known about me before you'd traveled back in time, it might very well have changed the outcome."

She could see his point. Searching his eyes, she asked, "But what happened after you stepped through the bulkhead? Where were you? Where did you go?"

Telling her of his own experience, he confirmed her speculation that he had wound up in Mystic back in 1979. But he was not the twelve-year-old boy who had gone on the ship's tour. He had spent eighteen years on the sea. As a grown man of thirty, it had been impossible to go home to tell his parents that he was alive and well. So he'd left New England, fully aware of his past in the early nineteenth century and yet not quite sure about the actual reality of it.

Haunted by those mystic memories, he had become obsessed with making his meeting with Cara come true. Unable to share his dream with anyone, he had set in motion all the right conditions for her to travel back in time, including the purchase and renovation of the brig that he'd renamed the *Mystic*. Had it not been this need to bring the ship to California, he might not have been led to make such high-risk investments in advanced technology, which had paid off so handsomely.

Retelling the story to Cara, Blake admitted to a great deal

of trepidation as 1997 had drawn to a close, realizing that he had worked nearly twenty years toward a series of events that might have been only a figment of his imagination. More than once he had feared he might have been delusional about the time-travel.

"My only regret is that Andrew has been a helpless victim in all of this."

"Andrew will be all right," she assured him, sharing the vision she'd seen earlier. "Aunt Gaby said it was as much Andrew's destiny as it was yours and mine."

"Gabriella, huh? Is she a ghost or an angel or what?"

"She is as real as you and me."

He gently guided her to her feet and brought her in front of him, positioning her between his thighs. He gazed at her with a bewildered smile. "That is no answer at all."

"Reality is what you believe it to be." She unbuttoned her shirt and peeled it off, then unfastened the front of her lace bra and let it drop to the floor.

His eyes darkened as he dipped his head to the hollow between her breasts. She closed her eyes and let her head fall back. Her fingers combed through the silver-streaked hair at his temples.

"Make love to me, Blake. Share your memories with me."

In the solitude of the darkened cabin of the ship, he undressed her with a reverence that touched her heart and soul. With soft caresses and whispers of eternal love, he cherished her body with his own. Throughout the night, he loved her thoroughly.

As the morning light filtered into the cabin, Cara awoke to find Blake leaning over her, watching her sleep.

"Marry me, *laua'e*."

She smiled happily. "We're already married, as I recall."

"Over a century ago. I want it made legal in *this* century, with a big celebration. Besides, every bride should be given the opportunity to walk down a church aisle wearing an exquisite gown of satin and lace."

"I don't need all that, Blake."

"But you deserve it. We both deserve it. I want to make everything special for us, including a huge wedding and a *very* long honeymoon."

"You have already made everything special for me," she said, another tear slipping out of the corner of her eye. "But I'll concede to a modest wedding. And a *life*long honeymoon creating all new memories."

"Mystic memories, my love."

Epilogue

ON THE FIRST floor of Bancroft Booksellers, a growing line of people waited for an autograph by the bestselling author Hilary Tucker, a local resident of the beach city. Flanked by her publicist and agent, she signed another copy of her latest book and handed it back across the table.

A woman in a business suit clutched the newly autographed novel to her chest, as well as dog-eared copies of four other previous titles that she'd brought with her for autographs. "I can't wait to read it, Ms. Tucker. I wish I could have brought in all of your books to get them signed."

"Maybe next time," offered Hilary, smiling up at the avid reader. "I'm glad you enjoy my writing. I hope you'll feel the same about this one."

"Oh, I know I will."

As the woman departed, Hilary looked up at the next person in line, a well-dressed gentleman in his thirties with a deep tan and dark-blond hair. He held out a copy of her current release, *Mystic Memories*.

Accepting it from him, she glanced at the book and frowned. "You must've accidentally picked up a damaged copy from the shelf. Let me get one in better condition—"

"That's my personal copy," he informed her with only the slightest smile.

"But it was just released today." She glanced at her publicist, then her agent, then the store clerk standing nearby. They all shrugged as if they didn't know how the man had obtained an early copy. "How did you get this?"

With a noncommittal shrug, he managed a half smile. "You might say I have the tenacity of a bulldog. When I want something enough, I am a difficult one to turn down."

"I'm flattered you went to that much trouble for *my* book, Mister . . . ?" She had flipped to the title page and poised the pen, waiting to inscribe his name.

"Charles," answered the gentleman. "Andrew Charles."

"Ah—*that's* what piqued your interest. You share the same name as the boy in my story. No doubt the character of Andrew reminds you of yourself at that age?" His silence prompted her to look up into blue eyes staring intently at her.

"It *is* me. I came here to ask you how I might reach Cara Masters. Or Cara Edwards. I'm not quite sure which name she would be using."

Hilary glanced over her shoulder and past the publicist to an aisle of the romance section several feet away. Cara smiled sheepishly at her friend's questioning gaze, then tapped her husband on the shoulder to draw his attention from a book in his hand.

Blake followed her gaze to the man at the autograph table. "Is it him?"

With a nod, she slipped her hand into his and walked with him toward the crowded table. The incredible revelation from Andrew had spread down the line like a gale-force wind, leaving the entire gathering of fans gaping in awe.

As they approached, Cara could still see the young boy in those sky-blue eyes of the mature adult watching them with curiosity. For a moment, she wondered if he would recognize them out of their nineteenth-century clothing and with a few extra character lines on their faces. Blake still cut a handsome figure with his silver hair and broad shoulders. She still could feel her pulse quicken whenever he was near. He felt the same way, frequently reminding her with little tokens of his love.

"You look wonderful, Andrew," said Cara, her eyes misting. "All grown up and everything."

In those few brief seconds, he looked ten years old again, blushing and awkward with his emotions. But when she slipped her arms around him for a quick embrace, he relaxed and kissed her cheek. As she stepped out of the way, he greeted Blake with a handshake that led to a brief hug.

"All these years," Andrew explained in awe, "I never knew what happened to you. I thought I was the only one who came back. After a while I stopped believing that any of it had really happened."

Cara glanced at the bewildered Hilary. "It was a bit devious of me to suggest our story as the plot of a fictional novel but"—she turned back to Andrew—"I knew it was the only way to open a door for you to contact us."

"Until this week I might have left that door closed."

"I know," she said.

Blake slipped his arm around her waist. "Cara hasn't been able to get you off her mind for quite some time. She had a gut feeling that you were headed into troubled waters."

"I need your help." Visibly shaken, Andrew paused to gain his composure. After taking a deep breath, he sighed heavily. "My boy is missing."

Dear Readers,

Mystic Memories had a strange and unusual beginning long before I ever thought of writing this story . . .

In January 1987, I was the scout leader for a troop of third-grade girls, who participated in an overnight adventure aboard the brig *Pilgrim II*, a replica of the original ship that Richard Henry Dana Jr. had sailed around the Horn to California in 1834. The following morning, I recalled a vivid dream in which I had gone back in time. Nearly ten years passed before I took the thread of a dream and wove it into the story you see today.

Another event occurred during the early stages of this book—a tall ship sailing off the coast of California lost a sailor overboard in rough seas. Despite attempts to save her, the woman vanished without a trace. Believe me, it was an odd feeling to be writing about a fictional character disappearing from a ship, only to have a similar incident happen in real life.

Several months later, synchronicity offered another opportunity to witness a historical reenactment—a mock sea battle between four ships under full sail, including realistic cannon fire! As luck would have it, I ended up on the *Hawaiian Chieftain*, a small coastal vessel that could have been the model for the fictitious *Mystic*. To my amazement, Captain Ian McIntyre was strikingly similar to my fictional hero, Blake Masters—right down to the black hair and blue eyes!

The *Hawaiian Chieftain* also had the only ship's dog— an unflappable black Labrador with the rather common name of ''Bud,'' which is also the name of the most recent canine addition to our family. When I asked Captain Ian if dogs were common aboard early-nineteenth-century ships, he said the Hawaiians usually kept them for food! Having Keoni as the cook presented a perfect opportunity to bring Bud on board as a fictional character. Even though research revealed that Labradors were not officially introduced to the Americas until the middle of the century, I chose to believe that a ship's captain might have acquired the breed during his voyages. With Bud now firmly ensconced in the story, I made an interesting discovery at the Mission San Juan Capistrano. In the soldiers' quarters stands a full-size painting of two Spanish conquistadors of the 1700s with a black Labrador retriever lying at their feet. Coincidence, I'm sure. Still, it goes to show that truth is sometimes stranger than fiction.

To those of you who fell in love with that adorable black Labrador, you can learn more about him and the *Hawaiian Chieftain* through the Internet at:

http://www.hawaiianchieftain.com

I would love to hear from you. Please feel free to write to me at P.O. Box 15053, Long Beach, CA 90815-0053.

Sincerely,

Susan Leslie Liepitz